WHAT IF...

Anne Perreault

Edited by Lisa DeBartolomao
Cover design by Natasha Perreault
Images by Pixaby.com, Unsplash.com,, Graphicstock.com

Printed in the United States of America by Create Space

ISBN-978-1724980298
ISBN 10- 1724980297

Lyrics by Horatio Spawford

Scripture verses taken from the King James Version of the Bible

Facebook: Into the Light Fiction
Webpage: intothelightfiction.weebly.com

Thank you so much for support.

God bless

To Hans and Annelore Klemp, my parents. Thanks for the adventure. This one was one of my favorites. Especially the looong train ride.

Glossary of words

Aasalam-o-Alaikum – Hello, Peace be with you, Greeting.

Nana- Grandfather

Nawasa- Grandson

Nani- Grandmother

Shukriya- Thank you

Shabb bakhair- Good evening

Sub bakhair- Good morning

Kuday hafez- Goodbye

Moi je suis- I am

Bonjour- Good day, hello

Merci beaucoup- Thank you very much

numero- number

Joyeux Noël- Merry Christmas

Part I

We are troubled on every side, yet not distressed;
we are perplexed, but not in despair;
persecuted, but not forsaken;
cast down, but not destroyed.

2 Cor 4:8,9

1

The sheer mass of people sharing the platform with her sent shivers down her back. Sweat soaked her T-shirt, making it cling to her like a second skin. Emily was swept away in a dark, foreign, exotic wave. It seemed utterly futile to struggle against it. The weight of the heat and humidity settled on her like a wet, suffocating blanket as she was jostled and bumped this way and that.

She almost broke down in tears of relief when she spotted the sign to the Shalimar Express. She fought her way to get there, her duffel bag clenched tightly to her chest. The sound of the wheels of the suitcase she was dragging behind was swallowed up by the noise all around her. She tripped over someone's feet and almost went down, had it not been for another passenger, dark and mysterious, holding her up.

"Thank you," she stammered.

The man just nodded and was swept away in the sea of humanity. She shuddered as something jammed against her knees, almost making her lose her balance again. A dark-skinned, skinny kid – no older than perhaps seven – brushed past her and hurried on without even looking back.

Her heart jumped into her throat as she checked her pockets for the ticket for her next leg of the journey. No ticket meant no ride on the train. She exhaled slowly when she felt it crinkling and pushed her way forward. Going against the natural flow of the bone-crushing sea was difficult and exhausting.

When she finally reached the conductor, a man dressed in a smart, spotless uniform, Emily allowed herself to take another breath.

She was almost on board.

"Welcome to the Shalimar Express, ma'am. I hope you have a pleasant journey," he said in heavily accented English, flashing her a bright smile.

Waving for a porter to take her suitcase, he stepped aside to allow her access up the steep stairs.

Why did she feel as if she had been given the key to the kingdom? Emily nodded her thanks and climbed up. With her ticket in hand, she looked around, determining which way to her seat. The inside of each coach gave her a sense of stepping backward in time, to a period in history when women with fancy hats and elaborate dresses were escorted by their male companions, also dressed in a fashion long forgotten. She pictured white-clad attendants rushing about to fetch their tea, anything they could do to make their long journey across this country more pleasant.

It's like being on the Orient Express.

Emily grinned and continued to clutch her bag to her chest. It took her some time to find the right compartment, with the right seat. With a long, drawn-out sigh she dropped into the soft, worn, red velvet and pressed her forehead against what she hoped would be a cool, tinted window.

No such luck! Heat from the outside saturated the glass and it gave her no relief from the oppressive humidity.

Oh, I hope they have air conditioning!

Wiping the back of her hand across her soaked forehead, Emily turned to stare out onto the platform she had just left. Outside, masses still moved past her view. It seemed to be organized chaos for the lack of a better definition.

A dark-haired boy, about three years old, clasped his father's hand with all his might. His large, brown eyes were open with anticipation. As his father stretched to pick him up, his dark face lit up and he clutched his little hands around his father's neck and clung to him.

The last day or so had been... interesting.

Emily had never imagined herself in a country where she couldn't understand the native language, surrounded by people foreign and exotic. A tingle in the pit of her stomach spread through her as she shifted in her seat.

Emily had just arrived in Karachi, Pakistan, the previous day. This morning she had ventured outside of her hotel, only to be gobbled up by the masses who flowed through the city. It was as though she was a leaf in a steady flowing brook. She had to fight to get out of the current, as going against the multitude was nearly impossible.

She continued to observe the goings on outside as she waited for the train to leave, more sweat dripping down her face and back. The porters were still loading up luggage and people. Another train was getting ready to leave the station from the track next to them.

Now I've seen it all!

Passengers sat on the roof of this locomotive or clung to its side. The compartments looked as though they would burst with the sheer number of people crammed into them. If they added one more person to the mix, they surely would! The windows were barred with metal – no glass.

Her own compartment was nearly empty. In the section across the aisle, she noticed an older man, intent on his reading. Next to him sat a much younger woman, dressed in the traditional Sari. Emily figured she was either his wife or his daughter. She looked more like his wife. Emily's mind began to wander and she pondered the questions popping into her brain.

What kind of life did this woman have to have married someone so much older than her? Was this an arranged marriage and if so, did her husband love her? Did she love him?

Shaking her head, Emily leaned back into the seat. The eighteen hours on this train would be incredibly long and lonely. In anticipation, she had stocked up with a few novels as well as her favorite snacks, stashed in the bag on the seat next to her in easy reach.

Why couldn't you just get on another plane and fly from Karachi to Lahore? Would it have been so difficult?

Emily, her head resting against the warm window, contemplated this question over and over again. The heat from the outside seeped through the glass and soon the compartment would be sweltering with the humidity that always turned her dark blonde hair into a frizzy mess.

This is your chance to see the country, remember? It's what you wanted.

What she wanted...

A sarcastic snort escaped her lips. This trip was supposed to cure her of that once and for all.

The compartment door opened, admitting more heat and humidity as well as another fellow traveler. This passenger – a westerner – entered and glanced around, then his gaze rested on her for just a fraction of a second.

Just her luck, because he took his seat across from her, and stuffed his ticket back into the pocket of his light tan suit coat after checking his seat number. For a second, Emily caught herself watching him out of the corners of her eyes.

Emily Martins! Get a grip!

She swallowed a laugh.

The compartment was virtually empty, allowing him to sit anywhere.

Why did this guy have to sit near me? I don't want to talk to anyone! Least of all a...

What if...

Emily forced her attention back to the mayhem outside the train. With the compartment still close to empty, would they be waiting until it filled like all the rest of the trains? If so, she would get out at the next station – six hours away – and rent a car!

She allowed herself to get lost in the chaos outside her window, watching a group of children – no parents in sight – push through the crowd. Nobody seemed to bother with them. Their attire looked dirty and worn, their faces grubby.

Emily had heard about the plight of children in this country. When her pastor had spoken about the number of abandoned babies that sometimes ended up as slaves, her heart had been touched. At first, it was just a slight, tender prodding. When a speaker from India had come in to talk to their congregation about the orphan problem in his country, she had felt that nudge intensely and – in a typical Emily fashion – had started to do her research that afternoon.

Four days later she had made contact with a representative and two months later she was on a train traveling to a remote village in the Himalayan foothills in Pakistan.

I hope I didn't make a mistake.

It took another ten minutes until finally, the train pulled slowly away from the station. The platform, and with it the masses, receded into the distance and Emily settled herself in her seat, her forehead pressed against the window, the vibration tingling through her.

Once the train left the station, she became thoroughly aware that she certainly was no longer in her comfortable, wealthy town in Connecticut. They passed mountains of rubbish. Her heart contracted in sympathy when she spotted a small hut made of what could be gathered from the heap of garbage. A wrinkled old man sat on his haunches surrounded by trash, staring at the passing train. Slowly, as if he barely had enough strength, he lifted his hand in a greeting.

An almost inaudible moan escaped her mouth as Emily felt drawn into his sad, tired expression, and she fought the tears that burned in her eyes. The man's eyes were filled with sorrow and loss. She felt it so deep in her soul that she nearly burst into a sob. When he finally disappeared from her view, Emily felt the weight that had slowly been pressing down hard on her chest lift, and she was able to breathe easier again.

What must it feel like to live without hope?

The train picked up speed as it left the city limits. Soon the countryside became a monotonous continuation of dirt and sparse shrubbery. Here and there, Emily spotted cows and donkeys just wandering freely and nibbling on the dry vegetation. The further they traveled from the city, the fewer houses she saw. Most of them would not be fit to live in according to the strict guidelines of the housing codes in the States. Here, there seemed to be no standards.

People built anything for shelter. Many of the houses she saw were more like huts. They either had corrugated, rusty metal roofs or their roofs were thatched. For the next hour, Emily stared out the window, her nose pressed hard against the glass to feel the vibration, her mind wandering.

"First time in Pakistan?"

Emily pulled herself back to reality and was tempted to ignore the question. Because answering it would force her to enter into a conversation with this guy she worked so hard to ignore thus far.

This trip was supposed to cure her of that desire.

But as her gaze reluctantly came to rest on her fellow traveler, she became aware that it would be so much more difficult than she had planned.

I do NOT appreciate Your sense of irony. This isn't fair!

What if...

The gentleman in the seat across from her was roughly her age.

Thank You. No, really. Thank You!

Back home he would have been considered eye candy and that alone should have warned her off. But fool that she was, she had to do the opposite.

His gaze settled on her and she found herself sucked in. Sapphire blue eyes, deep and burning with intensity, locked onto hers. Emily tried to avoid eye contact as if once she did look at him she'd become blind – like someone staring into the sun for too long without glasses. Alas, she struggled in vain.

It's the accent. Why does this always have to happen to me?

With a mental groan, she turned to her traveling companion.

"Does it show that much?" she asked. *Shut your trap, Emily! Just pretend you're a deaf-mute.*

"It's just that people don't take this train much unless they are either loaded or they're tourists with a lot of time on their hands. I take it you're one of the latter."

She was about to laugh when she thought better of it. This conversation had to end – now!

"I'm neither. I'm here on business," she said sharply.

"Is that so?"

The gentleman had been working on entering data onto a laptop, which he now closed. His gaze roamed her face and his eyes narrowed. He pursed his lips and folded his hands, resting them on top of his device.

"What's your business?"

Emily's heart threatened to bounce out of her chest at his inspection. His dark blue eyes had close to a magnetic pull on her, throwing her into an uncomfortable loop-de-loop. One that had her scrambling to make a hasty retreat and hide behind the pages of the novel she had stashed somewhere in her bag. She drew the duffel bag into her lap, holding it like a shield.

"Er..." She fingered the zipper. *The book. Just think.... book.*

The guy across from her noticed her discomfort because he gave her an incredibly disarming smile, one that didn't help her at all.

"I'm sorry," he said, his voice vibrating with a deep drawl. "I do that all the time! My mother always complains that I just jump right into a conversation without any manners. Jack Russel. From Texas."

Emily trained her features. She had, after all, a lot of experience keeping her thoughts to herself. But she just couldn't help herself this time.

"Jack Russel?" She cocked her head. "As in..." She gave a very soft *woof* and swallowed the laugh in her throat.

Her traveling companion gave her a blank stare until his face contorted as if he had consumed a lemon. "Yeah... like I've never heard that one before! I'll tell you a secret, though." He moved in closer and his outdoorsy cologne tickled her nose, making it difficult to focus. "My bite is worse than my bark!"

Emily swallowed and clutched her duffel tightly to her chest.

Would it be poor manners if I didn't introduce myself?

Putting the bag down, she found herself caught in his mind-zapping gaze. Everything became a haze and her thoughts flew right out the window. Now, *that* was unexpected.

Why is he staring at me? Oh, yeah. Introduce yourself already.

She opened her mouth and hurried to give her response. "I'm Emily Handsome."

The muscles in her jaw went slack and she closed her mouth with a soft *pop.* Heat rushed to her face immediately and she would have preferred to have pounded her forehead with her thick book until she was unconscious, to forget this whole conversation ever took place.

"I... I... Emily Martins. From Connecticut," she corrected breathlessly.

Jack Russel stared at her for what seemed like forever, then the corners of his mouth twitched slightly. He extended his hand as if nothing had happened.

Oh, just take me away from here!

She accepted the good, firm handshake. Her father always told her she could judge what a person was made of by the way they shook hands.

If only she heeded his sage advice more often.

He nodded with a soft grunt. "A pleasure to meet you, Miss *Martins,*" he replied with a twinkle in his eyes.

Thankfully Jack took his gaze off her and studied the interior of the compartment. With his focus somewhere else, her world was once again a more orderly place. When he redirected his attention to her, a feeling of utter chaos rushed through her from head to toe.

"I'm a computer software designer."

He pointed to the laptop.

"Ah, interesting," she managed to croak, her face still burning.

Her gaze slipped to her bag. It was time to crawl into a make-believe world right now before she could make another embarrassing blunder. This eighteen-hour ride on the train was supposed to be the balm to keep her sane.

"So?" He drew the word out, leaving no doubt in her mind that he expected her to answer.

Emily sighed inwardly. Her novel was calling to her, beckoning her to ignore the prompted question. It was drawing her into its own fantasy world where everything turned out just right in the end.

"Uh." She inhaled deeply to allow her mind a chance to come up with a reasonable explanation of why she had traveled to the opposite side of her world. "I'll be working at a missionary orphanage."

She hoped that would keep him from asking more questions. Her traveling companion seemed to be impressed by that. He nodded his head slowly.

"I see. I hope you won't be offended, but you do have tourist written all over you."

She didn't know if that was an insult or a compliment.

"How long are you going to be working here?"

Emily stared longingly out the window. *Shut up already! None of your business!*

Irritation began to replace that excited flutter her heart was doing when she thought about getting to her destination.

"I'd rather not talk about it. I don't know you at all and... Well. I'm traveling on my own and all."

He gave a disarming laugh, catching her off guard, causing her world to tilt. "Fair enough. I can appreciate that. You have nothing to fear from me. I truly am one of the good guys." He spread his hands out in front of him as if that was some sort of demonstration of his purity.

I just bet you are! I know your type.

2

As she opened her book, the spine cracked – the way it usually did the first time it was read. She made it past the title page, but her thoughts were not on the reading material in front of her.

"Do you travel a lot in your line of business?" she heard herself ask after attempting to read for about an hour and not getting anywhere.

It's official. You're a fool! You need to heed your own advice and yet... here you are! Whatever happens next, this one's on you.

Jack Russel placed a stack of papers on the empty seat next to him and lifted his face. A grin made the corners of his eyes crinkle.

"I've been here three months. My service area is Pakistan, Western India, and Sri Lanka, with an occasional hop into Afghanistan. Pakistanis are colorful people, so I enjoy it here. The food isn't too bad if you like chicken and curry. The history here is amazing. I'm somewhat of a history buff."

"I'm not." Emily chewed the inside of her cheeks. Was she this bored already to have a conversation with a total stranger?

Why can't I just stick to myself? "I'm more interested in the people."

Jack settled back into his seat. "Well, then. We have that in common. See? We're getting to know each other." He beamed a smile at her that made her spiral completely out of control and usually make a fool of herself.

"Yeah..." Emily replied weakly, ignoring the heat traveling up her neck, and turned to the window, hoping he'd get the hint.

To her surprise he did.

Emily lost herself in the monotonous landscape, her thoughts turning back to her troubled heart and her unsettled life.

This was why she had come.

To escape her perfect life at home in the States.

Why, when she had everything a girl could want!

Her family loved her and supported everything she did, even this crazy sidetrack she insisted on undertaking. They usually understood her. So what was wrong with her?

She didn't want to inquire of the Lord to find that out because she dreaded the answer.

But she dreaded the silence even more.

She leaned her forehead against the window again. It was something she had always done ever since she was a child, feeling the vibration of the car when they traveled anywhere long distance. Now she felt the movement of the train. It began to lure her to sleep.

Before she was deep in dreamland, she startled partially awake because the train jerked. Her mind went right back to thoughts of home.

Did her parents miss her already?

Emily knew the answer before the question had formulated in her mind. Her mother would be counting the days until their youngest daughter returned, praying for safety. Her father would be more practical, telling her mother that this was a great opportunity for their daughter.

Her sister, who lived in Pennsylvania with her husband and baby, would tell her that she was out of her mind and would advise her to seek help.

Her sister was a psychologist.

Emily breathed a laugh and forced herself to pick up the novel again. Hours and hours of boring, monotonous travel time lay ahead and she had picked up a cheap spy romance at one of the airports she had passed through.

She loved any good romance! And that was her biggest problem.

Nope! Let's just read the book, shall we?

After all, she had eighteen hours followed by six months to contemplate the lack of her miserable, nonexistent love-life.

There you go again! You're complaining and whining.

"Would you like some water?"

Emily's head snapped up and found herself mesmerized by those scrutinizing, sapphire-colored eyes. Once again, her world tilted and she feared that if she held his gaze too long she'd spill every secret of her life.

Whoa!

With a shake of her head, she opened her bag. "I've got my own, thanks."

With it, she conveniently pulled out a chocolate bar.

Fine! I'll be social.

"Would you like a piece? I picked up another bar on my way through Germany and I just about ate the whole thing in one sitting, it was so good." No lie there. There had been two pieces left, which she had consumed with great pleasure for breakfast this morning.

Jack grinned and held up his hand. "Thank you, but I'm not much of a chocolate guy. Give me a piece of fruit any time."

"Ah, health conscious? That's good." Emily snapped off a section of her chocolate bar and bit off a piece, suppressing a groan. Heaven.

"Let's just say that it's one thing I can control when it comes to my welfare. That and exercise."

"Yes," she answered as the sweet taste of chocolate swirled around her mouth. "Your doctor must love you."

He took a swig of his water. "Not particularly."

"So, it sounds like you travel a lot, Mr. Russel." What was wrong with her? Hadn't she just basically told the guy to back off? And here she was...

The truth was, the pesky thoughts in her head were bugging her and a conversation with a handsome stranger never hurt anyone.

"I do, Miss Martins. That's why I do this job." He pulled out an apple and cleaned its already shiny red skin thoroughly. "How about you?"

Feeling like a total country bumpkin, she swallowed her chocolate.

"Would you believe if I told you that this is the first time I ever left the Continental United States?"

The juice of the apple squished out between his teeth. Jack quickly wiped at it with a paper towel from his backpack, turning his entire attention to her.

Everything inside her was being rearranged by his gaze.

"And you came here? Most people would rather travel to Europe for their first time. It's a lot safer there. Aren't you afraid?"

Emily stared out the window again. More dirt, shrubs and broken down huts. Oh, she even spotted a beaten up car, rusting along the road!

"I haven't thought about it. I can get hurt on my way to work too, you know. Coming here seemed the right thing at the time. Why are *you* on this train? I mean, wouldn't it be easier for you to fly?"

He laughed and pointed at his computer. "I have a better chance of getting work done than I do when I'm flying. And there are no distractions, usually."

"Well, I'll leave you to your work then," she smiled and opened up her book, exhaling a relieved breath.

He pointed to her novel. "You like spy stuff?" he asked as he pulled his laptop back onto the small table in front of him.

Emily closed her book for a second. "Who doesn't? There is nothing more exciting than getting lost in a good intrigue of international espionage."

Jack's eyes crinkled as he shook his head. "I wonder if it actually is like they describe in those books."

"Does it really matter?" she asked.

"For someone like me, it would. I like the facts."

Emily nodded. "I do, too. But sometimes it's just fun to think that the world is just like it would be in a spy novel."

If only!

In the end, the handsome spy always gets the girl.

The train ate up the miles through the terrain. Between staring out the window and reading her novel, Emily was beginning to have an outstanding time by herself. Occasionally she would answer a random question directed at her. Mostly Jack was busy entering in figures from the stack of paperwork he had sitting next to him.

Once in a while, her gaze would wander to him.

Of course, she would have to run into someone like him. God certainly had it in for her. He was just her type: dark hair, athletic – something one wouldn't associate with a computer guy. Jack Russel oozed intensity with every breath he exhaled.

Realizing that she was staring, Emily forced her attention back to her novel, remembering her vow before she left Connecticut.

She was done with guys, period.

Her last relationship had ended a month before she decided to go on this crazy missionary trip. She had been dating a guy from church for close to a year. On Valentine's day, instead of proposing as Emily had hoped, he had told her that she was too clingy. He wasn't looking for a lasting relationship, just some fun.

That had stung!

Her parents had taught her that a relationship ought to be considered serious. The problem with her was that for as long as she remembered, she wanted to have a family. She wanted the whole deal – the house, the white picket fence, the dog and cat, the two point five children and yes, dare she say it? The minivan!

Therefore, she pursued her dream.

When she was an undergrad, she had come as close to marriage as she possibly could. But the demands of a challenging program had caused them to eventually part ways before they could get there. Emily had run into him at a conference a year ago. Doug was now married to a nurse he had met during his residency. It seemed that the guys she dated had no intention of building a lasting relationship, at least not with her.

With a sigh, she turned back to her book.

Emily was at an exciting part, where the spy and the girl were being chased through the streets of Manhattan by the arch nemesis. Bullets were flying around their heads. She grabbed at her chocolate with her hand without taking her eyes off the page, coming up with air.

She frowned and lowered her book. Immediately blue eyes bored into hers, sending her into a frightening, out of control spiral. To break the hold on her, she wrenched her eyes to where her chocolate had been, finding only an empty wrapper.

Ya did it again!

Emily bit her bottom lip in embarrassment. She had lost herself not only in the story but also in her sweet obsession. A whole bar later, she would have to do a lot of running to counter the sugar she had consumed.

Jack bit back a laugh, when her hand came back empty this time and she came up with air.

"Good book, huh?" he asked and closed his computer. He rubbed his tired eyes.

"So far," she mumbled. "Done with work?" She pointed at the computer.

"For now," he replied.

The scenery outside was changing as they were nearing a town. She could see broken down buildings along streets. Cars, pedestrians, bicycles and others forms of transportation mingled into one messed up traffic situation. It amazed her that nobody seemed to be fazed by this. Everyone seemed to know just what they were expected to do, so the human mass flowed by easily without rhyme, reason or order.

People milled about without much concern at the station. Again, the sheer amount of people in the area made her cringe. She couldn't imagine trying to get through that mass of people.

"Do you want to eat something more substantial than chocolate?" Jack asked and pointed to a street vendor advertising his ware loudly.

The thought of eating food that had been sitting in the hot sun all day was not attractive to her. Emily's stomach turned.

"I think I'll pass. I brought a sandwich and some chips."

"But you're missing out on a whole new level of culinary experience." His lips twitched into an evil grin.

"You know," Emily mused and steepled her fingers together. "I think I'd rather not catch whatever they are selling. I like to keep my lunch in my stomach, where it belongs."

Jack snickered. She had a sense of humor.

Nice!

3

Weariness settled in as soon as they got back on their way again. They had been going for six hours and still had twelve hours left! It was cold on the train, the air conditioning in the compartment working much too well. Emily rifled through her bag and, finding a thin jacket, she slipped her arms into it. Who would have figured she'd need a jacket riding on the train?

"Would you like a sweater?" Jack asked. He was just finishing off the last of his salad.

"I think this will do the trick." She shivered slightly.

"It's no problem. I came prepared. This isn't the first time I've made this trip. I'm a seasoned traveler. They crank the air to make us all believe we've gone on an arctic expedition." He handed her a thick, navy sweater. She held up her hand.

"Thank you, but I think this is good enough."

"Well, if you find that it isn't," Jack put it on the seat next to him, "it's there if I happen to fall asleep. Which I highly doubt." He stretched and yawned. "I'm gonna stretch my legs."

He walked up and down the compartment, swaying with the motion of the train with an athletic balance. Not being used to sitting around, Emily rose and stretched.

The train lurched to the side and sent her sprawling all over the sleeping man a few seats from her. Extracting herself, apologizing continually, as his body odor assaulted her senses. The man nudged his head from side to side.

"It is not a problem," he said over and over again.

Of course, it wasn't a problem! For him!

After walking up and down ten times, clinging to the back of the seats for dear life, she realized that the jacket was not going to keep her warm for the next twelve hours. But she shouldn't accept a sweater from a perfect stranger. No matter what he looked like! Emily rubbed her hands up and down her arms, trying to instill some warmth.

The door of the compartment opened and an official with a blue hat and uniform walked toward her. He smiled at her, dipping his head briskly.

"Ma'am, would you take your seat, please. I need to see your ticket."

"Oh," she answered. For hours nobody had come to check on them. Now they wanted to see her ticket.

She stumbled along to her seat and handed it to him. He punched a small hole into it and moved on to ask her companions for theirs. Jack handed him his.

"Do you know if the train is going to be on time?" he asked as the man nodded to him and returned the ticket.

"It should be, sir. We made up the delay in Karachi, so we are expecting to arrive well within the reasonable range," the conductor answered in accented, yet crisp English.

"Is it possible to turn down the air in here? It's like a freezer in here and all I have is this jacket." Emily shivered involuntarily.

The conductor bowed his head. "I will see what I can do, ma'am. We generally can't turn it down much. I'm so sorry. We do have a dining car where you can purchase tea or coffee to warm you."

"Thank you." She folded her arms around herself.

Jack pointed to the sweater. Shaking her head, she rose.

"I'm going to get a warm drink."

Even though there were less than a handful of passengers, she had read in the informational material she had received before she left, that she should not leave her bags unattended. But the thought of lugging her belongings into the dining cart didn't appeal to her.

"I'll watch over your stuff," Jack volunteered as he watched her stand hesitantly in the aisle.

"I don't want to impose on you."

"Go on." He inclined his chin in the direction of the door. "I can't get off this train right now, can I? Your stuff is safe with me."

If she ended up with a cold, she'd not be able to do the job she had come for. With a nod, Emily started toward the dining cart.

"Thank you. I'll get you something. What would you like?"

Jack shook his head. "Thank you. I have all I need right here."

Emily sat at the white linen-covered table. Traveling on this train was similar to how she would have imagined traveling on the Orient Express. It was quaint, even though it was slightly outdated. The cup of tea warmed her immediately and she headed back to her compartment, nearly passing by her seat. Jack hadn't moved much, his gaze on his computer. He nodded upon her return, handing her the sweater.

"Seriously, take it," he said. "And I had to fight off a ton of people to defend your secret stash of chocolate."

His eyes crinkled when he said this. Emily frowned, nibbling on the inside of her cheek.

"I see. Thank you." She reluctantly took the sweater and slipped it over her T-shirt, swallowing a relieved sigh when she felt warm again. "And they say chivalry is dead."

Jack laughed and turned his attention back to his work.

After searching her bag for another secret stash of the German chocolate bar, she returned her attention back to her book. The hero, the poor, confused fool, had just professed his undying love for the girl. She had turned around and shot him, leaving him bleeding on the streets of Manhattan.

Perhaps therein lay her problem. Emily lacked the *chutzpah* this woman in her book displayed. If she were a character in a novel, she'd be the no-name character on page three that had no part in the plot.

Emily made sure that she followed the rules, the expectations. She had graduated in the top ten percent of her class because she felt her parents would be disappointed if she didn't. She drove a sensible foreign sedan, nothing flashy or extravagant. She had even talked her parents into installing solar panels onto the roof of both her garage apartment and their house. She gave at church, both of her time and money.

She even voted every time!

Emily gazed out the window, staring at her reflection on the glass.

Nothing special there.

The guys she dated mentioned that it was her personality that intrigued them, certainly not her looks.

Her sister, on the other hand, must have received her share of looks on top of everything, because she was drop-dead gorgeous. Guys fell over themselves to gain her attention, with her corn-colored hair, her baby blues, and high cheekbones. But then again, she was living Emily's dream with her amazing husband and adorable baby.

Groaning inside, Emily rested her head against the vibrating glass. This was getting her nowhere.

"Would you care to join me in a card game?"

Startled out of her daze, Emily turned to her fellow passenger – the only one who kept on insisting on engaging her in conversation. Continuing to stare out the window and ponder the bleakness of her life was unappealing.

"Why not. Deal me in."

Jack spread out the cards between them.

"What made you come to Pakistan? Isn't it slightly out of the way?"

Emily glanced at her cards. "I needed a change of scenery."

She was unwilling to admit that it was another broken relationship, a deep disappointment with God, a need to escape from reality that had driven her from her comfortable apartment and cushy job.

"Must be an incredibly uncomfortable scenery at home to send you all the way over here. So, what made you decide to come to Pakistan to work in an orphanage?" Jack took a slow sip of his now lukewarm water and rubbed his tired eyes.

He's like a bloodhound! What gives?

Emily settled back into her seat and took a bite of her chocolate bar.

"Just exactly that. I needed a fresh perspective on life, perhaps."

"In a foreign country where some people aren't all that keen on Americans?"

"I know how to take care of myself. I'm a grownup," she said indignantly.

Jack chuckled softly to himself and focused on the cards in his hands instead of his traveling companion.

"I would just be careful, Miss Martins. This is not your basic suburbia."

Emily huffed and rifled through her cards. "Thank you, Mr. Russel. I didn't know that." She rolled her eyes. "For your information, I've been around for a while. And I have watched the news. I know what's going on in this country. I also know we are a hop, skip, and a jump to the Afghanistan border. I'm well aware of the dangers of traveling here."

"Good. Just keep your eyes open. How long are you staying in Lahore?"

What's with the twenty questions? "I'm staying just the night. Tomorrow I'm traveling on by bus to the orphanage ."

Jack frowned. "I hope you aren't planning on taking any public transportation, are you?"

"Why wouldn't I want to travel by bus? I'm using the train, aren't I?"

Jack smiled, but this time his eyes didn't crinkle. "Miss Martins. This is *not* a public train. This is the Shalimar Express, the crown jewel of locomotives. Remember, you're traveling in style here. I'm sure you saw the other train that left the station in Karachi. The buses look just like that. Except, did you say you are traveling into the mountains? I'd hire a car and a driver for safety, if I were you."

Emily glared into the night. Who did he think she was? She may look like a tourist without a clue, but she was highly educated! And she was giving of her time to be a missionary. It wasn't like she had come here on a whim.

An uncomfortable twinge passed through her.

Besides, she had carefully read the information packet the missionary society had sent her and was fully aware that the public transport held certain – perils – and advised her to seek out private transportation. Emily shook off the irritation she felt about the whole conversation.

"Thank you, Mr. Russel," she said somewhat coldly.

She was gnawing on the inside of her cheek to keep from letting him have it. After all, he was just trying to be helpful.

"When you get to your hotel, go to the concierge and ask them to hire you a private car and driver. Are you going a long way out of Lahore?" he continued.

Boy, he was bursting with helpful information and questions.

"Yes, the orphanage is in the foothills."

"Just make sure you hire someone," Jack's face was filled with concern as he focused on her. "We wouldn't want you to go missing, would we?"

"Missing?" she snorted in disbelief before a tremor vibrated through her. Waiting for it to pass, she examined the packaging of her chocolate bar with great interest. "Have a lot of people gone missing in this area?"

Jack leaned forward to study her with those probing eyes as if he was trying to read her heart and mind. Then he frowned.

"Like I said, this is not the American suburbia. Be careful, Miss Martins. Might I suggest you carry a weapon?"

Emily gasped in disgust. "I don't do guns. I don't even know how to handle one. They hurt people. I... don't."

Jack snorted. "That's the politically correct thing to say. Where you are going, people carry weapons. Even the boys carry some sort of weapon. When you step into those mountains, you are stepping into a whole new world, where a woman is of no consequence if she goes missing, and usually fetches a high price on the black market. Especially one with long blonde hair and a milky complexion."

Emily swallowed, her heart beating as if she had spent all day on a treadmill. Was he just trying to scare her, or was he telling the truth? Going to the mountains had seemed so harmless. Now she wasn't so sure about going by herself.

It couldn't be as bad as he was making out!

"Have you ever traveled... alone into the mountains?" she asked.

Jack gave a haughty laugh. "Yeah. All the time."

She allowed her chin to lift slightly and chose to hold his gaze, even though it made her feel like she was in an uncontrolled free-fall. "You haven't gone missing yet, have you?"

Jack forced his attention on the cards in his hands.

"How long will *you* be staying in Lahore?" It was fun to turn the table on him, see him squirm slightly.

He did exactly that – twist uncomfortably in his seat.

"It depends on the job." He put down his cards with a grin.

Emily rolled her eyes and scrunched up her face.

"Do you like it?" Emily asked. Talking to him certainly chased away the boredom.

Jack nodded. "I guess I do. I never know what I'm gonna get. I don't get bored. And there is the perk of traveling. I'm usually gone fifty weeks out of the year."

Emily stared at him. That had to be a lonely existence. "What does your family say to your traveling? Don't you miss them?" *Oh, Emily! You didn't just go there?!*

Now it was Jack's turn to stare at her and swallow the grin that threatened to spread from ear to ear.

"My mom lives an hour from me. She and her husband live in a comfortable community. My sister lives down the street from me. We get together as often as we can when I'm home. My father passed away. That's it. There is no one else. What about your family?" He shouldn't enjoy conversing with this intriguing woman. "Aren't they concerned about your safety?"

Emily took another bite of her chocolate bar.

"My parents weren't too thrilled about me traveling by myself all the way across the world, but they couldn't stop me."

Jack's lips twitched in the corners. "No husband, no kids? No significant other?" *Way to go, dude!* But what did it matter anyway? In a few hours, they would go their separate ways and he'd never see her again.

Emily closed her eyes for a moment, savoring the sweetness in her mouth. "None of the above. Kind of makes it easier to travel, doesn't it?"

"It does indeed." He studied her through his lowered lids. "But why an orphanage in Pakistan? Aren't there plenty of others closer to home?"

"You ask a lot of questions, don't you?" she scowled.

Jack's eyebrows danced in amusement. "I'm a curious kind of guy. So...?"

"I don't know. It seemed like a good thing at the time. I went for it. They needed someone and I was available."

"And your job at home? I assume you had one."

His questions were becoming too personal. He was still a stranger, and she was still traveling alone. Emily wasn't born yesterday.

"It will be there when I return."

"Ah, that's convenient. Not a lot of bosses would keep the job open. It's nice you have that luxury."

It was time to end this conversation. Once they had finished their card game, she nodded her head.

“Thank you. That was more fun than sitting here without much to do.”

She reached into her bag and pulled out her book again.

“So, I'm gonna...” She opened it slowly.

“By all means. I should get back to work.”

Jack opened his laptop but couldn't help feeling regret. He had enjoyed their interaction. From then on, they didn't engage in any more talk, other than an occasional fleeting glance.

4

The train finally lumbered into the Lahore station at midnight – two hours late from their scheduled arrival. Stepping onto the deserted platform as if in a daze, she stumbled into the muggy air. It felt good to be warm again after sitting in the freezing cold compartment all day and night. Her luggage was waiting for her at the side of the train and she tugged at her suitcase.

"Miss Martins. Where are you staying?" Jack was right behind her, a duffel bag slung over one shoulder, his computer bag on the other.

She closed her eyes for a second, trying to remember the name of the hotel. It took some effort for her befuddled brain to remember. Never a fan of sleep deprivation, the toll of traveling and changing time zones was finally catching up with her. She named one of the downtown hotels.

"That's where I'm staying. Why don't we share a cab?" Jack suggested.

He didn't wait for her to say anything but waved down the first taxi waiting at the curb. She should be thankful. Somehow traveling through this city at night by herself was looking less and less attractive. Suddenly the darkness seemed more threatening than before, making her imagination go wild. Someone sneaking up behind and knocking her unconscious came to mind.

You've been reading too many spy novels.

Jack gave the driver the address and they shot through the streets. The city was quieter at this time of night, but there was still a lot of nightlife activity. Traffic was still chaotic at best. Cars squeezed into spaces barely large enough. Once in a while, as they came within inches from the bumper of the vehicle in front of them, Emily flinched and grabbed the handle of her duffel bag tighter.

They made it to their hotel in one piece, but with plenty of honking and squealing of tires. Emily stumbled out of the cab and followed Jack into the pleasantly cool lobby, the bellhop carrying her bags. After checking in, she turned back to her traveling companion and held out her hand.

"It was a pleasure to meet you, Mr. Russel. Happy travels."

He took it and held it, noting the softness and surprising strength. Jack nodded, reluctant to let her go without one more word of warning.

"And you. Enjoy your stay in Pakistan. And remember. It's not suburbia."

"Got it," she said.

She retrieved her room key and followed the bellhop to the elevator. Her room was elegant, decorated with plenty of local artifacts and furnishings. The bed was comfortable enough. As soon as her head hit the pillow, she fell fast asleep.

Emily woke up the next morning, her muscles tense and tired after sitting on a train for eighteen hours. After a long, hot shower, which helped to untangle some of the knots in her neck and back, she picked up the phone on the nightstand.

While she waited for room service to bring a traditional breakfast she stepped toward the window and gazed out at the view of the old fortification.

Perhaps I have some time to visit it after breakfast.

What if...

After consuming a delicious spread of fruits and nuts, with a cup of coffee, she quickly dressed in jeans and T-shirt and discovered Jack Russel's sweater still among her things. The easiest way to return it to him would be to drop it off at the front desk.

Emily closed her eyes in prayer.

Lord, I'm here! Where are You? I know I'm running. The thought of facing life by myself... to be a lonely old spinster, makes me sad. Why can't I have the dream? What's wrong with wanting the house with the picket fence, a loving husband, a happy, successful family? I thought You were in the business of granting dreams? I just don't understand why I'm still single. What's wrong with me? It's not like I'm getting any younger!

One eye popped open, not at all satisfied with her prayer. When had she succumbed to whining? She used to be able to pray so fervently, so powerfully and full of trust. Sighing, she tried to read her scripture verse of the day and found it impossible to focus.

She flipped through her Bible in a distracted way and came to the Psalms. Her heart stilled a moment when she flipped to Psalm 23. It was one of her favorite scriptures. The Lord *was* her Shepherd.

Was He?

It seemed lately that He had abandoned this sheep.

Emily swallowed hard. Wasn't *she* the one who was running from God?

But He was supposed to come looking for her, the sheep. Along the way she had lost her path and now she was disappointed and pouting that she wasn't getting what she wanted.

I shall not want!

Oh! Right, there was that!

How was it possible not to want? It was not like she was dead! She still had desires, needs.

W*ants are not needs.*

Okay, she needed the whole package, the whole house, husband, kids, and van! Emily bit her lip violently, the metallic taste of blood spreading over her tongue.

I don't want to give up on this.

Tears blurred her vision because she knew that her dream had to die, had to end up on the chopping block. It was just too painful to go through with it.

She dropped the sweater off at the front desk, inquiring about private transport to the small town where the orphanage was located. The clerk at the desk told her that he would arrange everything for her. He promised to have a car waiting for her when she was ready to leave.

She walked the city streets. Within minutes her face was slick with sweat. She followed the flow of foot traffic. Lahore, the second largest city in Pakistan, was a beautiful city.

Welcome to Lahore, the capital of the Punjab region. We pride ourselves on our ancient architecture, our universities, and beautiful gardens, she read in the brochure she had snagged on her way out of the hotel.

Emily made her way through the gate into the inner part of the city. It was as though all the traffic squeezed into the small space. The honking was driving her nuts!

Enjoy this exotic part of the old city, which dates back to the Moghal period in Pakistani history. The heart of this ancient part is still surrounded by an age-old wall with its original gates. Only six of the thirteen original gates survived British rule.

What if...

Emily was so involved in reading the pamphlet, trying to remember every word, that she jumped when a motorbike sped past her on the sidewalk.

You're in a foreign city. Becoming roadkill isn't an option!

Emily forced herself to pay attention to where she was going. She walked past the fort, taking out her phone to take pictures of the huge structure. Her family would be speechless when she posted it on her social media site when she had a moment.

The heat was finally getting to her and she purchased a bottle of water from a roadside stand. For the next hour, Emily explored the outdoor market with its exotic sights and sounds. She also bought a Sari – a deep hunter green blouse with long, fluted sleeves, gray cotton pants, and shawl. Her top was embroidered with an intricate design.

On her way back to the hotel, she spotted her traveling companion from the previous day. Jack was sitting at a table in an outdoor restaurant, deep in an energetic discussion with a brunette. Emily got the impression that neither was enjoying it.

Tempted to investigate, she thought better of it. He may get the wrong notion that she was following him, and it would mean crossing to the other side of the road. She wasn't ready to throw her life away just to quench her curiosity.

Besides, it was time to return to the hotel and travel to her final destination.

On her way back she lost count of how many outdoor vendors were displaying their food in the hot sun with flies and other insects having a literal picnic.

The health inspector would have a field day!

How different everything was from her serene home. A slow ache began to form in her belly. Suddenly she longed for her family, her apartment, her sensible sedan. She even missed her boring life.

Note to self: Don't make a life-changing decision right after a breakup.

The sweat dripping down her back dried as soon as she stepped into the air-conditioned lobby of her hotel. She was about to pack her overnight clothes into her luggage when she realized how much grime she had accumulated on her walk.

All of a sudden she wasn't sure of the facilities at the orphanage, so Emily decided that a quick shower might just be in order. Clean and refreshed, she dressed in the Sari. It was surprisingly comfortable and soft.

When in Rome, she thought and snapped a selfie with the view of the old city behind her.

As soon as she was done checking out of the hotel, her driver pulled up in front of the door. A huge smile spread over his face and he waved to her excitedly.

"Good morning, miss," he said and opened the door for her.

Surprised by the chipper greeting, Emily settled into the back of the sedan. Her driver, who introduced himself as Rashid, turned to her as soon as he settled behind the wheel. The smile faded and he wiggled his head from side to side.

"I am so sorry, miss, but the air conditioning stopped working on the drive over here. It is a good thing it's not too hot today." He spoke with a quaint, melodic accent and she nearly missed the meaning of what he was saying.

It sunk in quick enough, though. *Not too hot?* The sweat was beginning to accumulate on her face, the loose shirt she wore was starting to cling to her. And that was after only a few minutes! How was she going to survive the next couple of hours?

"Good day, Miss Martins."

Jack Russel ducked his head into the open door.

"Mr. Russel, what a surprise to see you." Why did she have this feeling of weightlessness whenever he looked her way? Emily steeled herself.

You're acting like a teenager! Snap out of it already.

Apparently, he was used to the temperature outside because he seemed completely at ease in this crushing heat. His pale blue dress shirt was free from any sweat stains, whereas she could wring the moisture out of hers. It looked like he was just out for a stroll in the park on a beautiful spring day.

"I see you've taken my advice? That was smart." Jack nodded approvingly at the car.

"That remains to be seen," she mumbled almost more to herself. "Apparently the air conditioning is not working. It must not be my thing, air conditioning. It's either too cold or, as in this case, non-existent."

Jack chuckled and spoke with the driver in soft tones.

"He says that he could get another car if you're willing to wait an hour or so."

Emily swallowed a groan at the thought of delaying the final leg of her journey. She was travel-weary and anxious to find out what she had gotten herself into. The worry was making her slightly on edge and tense, which only added to her fatigue. The thought of waiting for another car was unappealing. But so was traveling in the heat.

"Would you?" she asked her driver, whose eyes bounced nervously from her to Jack and back again.

The man nodded his head enthusiastically. "Oh, yes madam. Right away, madam."

He helped her unload her luggage from the trunk and even carried it inside the lobby. Then he hurried out to the car and promised to return quickly.

"I was about to have some lunch. Care to join me?" Jack asked.

"Do you usually eat lunch twice a day?"

Oh, wait! She shouldn't have said that because now his gaze fastened onto her and she could feel the heat travel to her cheeks.

"I don't understand."

Hiding her hands behind her back, she twisted her fingers together. It was a trick she had learned during her residency. "I... spotted you at a restaurant on my stroll through the city. I wasn't... I didn't follow you, or anything like that."

Jack seemed to enjoy her embarrassment and laughed. "I see. I met an associate for a cup of coffee. I wouldn't be caught dead eating at a street restaurant. Never know if the food was meowing in the alley the night before."

Emily had a feeling he was playing with her. She'd been through plenty of newbie pranks.

"Ha-ha. That's too funny," she said keeping her tone even.

Jack grinned. "Sorry. I couldn't help it. I'm still starving and you have a long way to travel. Why don't you get a bite to eat before you head out?"

"I'm not sure if I should eat with a virtual stranger."

Jack laughed. "Touché. I guess I deserved that."

She lifted her chin and looked down her nose at him. "Yes, you did!"

Once they sat down at the linen-covered table in the swanky restaurant, it seemed that he was dead set on continuing his interrogation of her from the previous night.

"Are you excited to get to the orphanage?" he asked.

What's with this guy? "Do you always take an extended lunch-break in the middle of the day?" she demanded in the same tone of voice.

Grinning, he put his fork next to his plate and rested his elbows on either side. "You'll find that everything stops at noon. Business starts again at two or three in the afternoon. The work goes late into the evening. Everyone works at a slower pace because it can get hot here."

CAN get hot?! "Oh!"

The slower pace would take some time to get acclimated to since she was used to working without breaks, going at a fast, mind-numbing rate.

The waitress clad in a fancy Sari took their order.

"No meat?" she asked in surprise.

"I'm a vegetarian," he replied slightly smugly. "I prefer my food growing on a stem."

Before she could say anything, Jack's phone rang and he quickly excused himself to answer it. When he returned, the smile had disappeared.

"Looks like I have to get back to work earlier. It's been a pleasure meeting you, Miss Martins. I hope you find what you're looking for at the orphanage."

He nodded his head and walked away. Emily didn't linger on feeling slightly disappointed.

Emily sat in a plush chair, nibbling on her thumbnail, glancing at the time now and then, and reading every pamphlet she could find. She had nearly given up on him when the driver sauntered through the door as if he was right on time – three hours later!

What is it with people in this country? Don't they have watches?

Emily suppressed the urge to yell at the man. After all, she was a guest here. Watching him silently load up the car she began to wonder how long this leg of the trip would take. However long it was, she was already bone weary.

At this point, she had been traveling for close to a week and it was getting tedious. She got into the backseat of the small sedan. As they squeezed into heavy traffic, she tried not to react whenever they came close to another car. The sedan became hot and sweat once again made her clothes stick to her.

They finally reached the limit of the city in one piece.

"How much longer?" she asked, feeling like a child.

"Oh. Only three more hours."

Emily suppressed the urge to scream, taking a swig of her now tepid water. It only made her more thirsty.

"Can you turn up the AC?" she asked as they pulled onto the four-lane highway. Traffic slowed down again for a moment, but soon they were on their way.

"Right away." He turned a nob and stared. With a forlorn look in the rear-view mirror, he murmured apologetically, "I'm sorry, miss. This AC is also broken, too."

He opened his window. A blast of hot air hit her and took her breath away. Irritation rose in her. She had waited three hours for a car whose AC was broken too! She stared moodily out the window and wasn't interested in the beauty around her. She saw nothing beyond her annoyance.

I shall not want.

Yes, yes, yes.

Why was that verse coming back to her, following her?

I'm doing the most selfless thing anyone could. I'm a doctor, giving six months to an orphanage! And You keep accusing me of wanting?!

Hadn't her church leaders praised her for giving up her career for six months and choosing to take care of these children? Emily's pastor had even done a sermon about her selfless act.

Her selfless act!

She snorted softly.

She knew the truth. Emily Martins, the selfless, charitable young woman, who put the children before her own comforts and desires! In reality, she had them all fooled. Even her parents had looked so proud when the church had commissioned her to go.

The only one who wasn't fooled was God. He was the only one who knew exactly what she was doing. She shook her head. It wasn't working.

She wasn't able to run from Him!

Because despite all her efforts to distance herself from Him, He was here with her. He was giving her tiny, irritating reminders of where her heart truly was.

She shook her head. She wasn't doing this!

She was taking care of the orphans. Jesus had directed them to do that!

At least give me credit for that, God!

The heat blasted her face as though God was laughing at her.

If you want to hear God laugh, tell Him your plan. She could hear her mother's voice now.

Well, she had a plan and it was a good one! She would follow it through and make the most of her six months here, in this hot, arid country. She just prayed that they had running water. That was all she needed.

That and a bed!

5

Emily wrenched her eyes open as the car rolled to a stop at the side of the road. Now what?! She looked about, her vision blurry from sleep. The sun was about to go down and the surrounding area was painted in its hues of reds and golds. Green grass spread throughout the valley, with majestic mountains rising darkly in the distance.

It was worth another look.

The driver mumbled something she absolutely had no way of understanding, popped the hood, and hovered over the engine.

Seriously? What else can go wrong?

Emily groaned and exited the vehicle to stretch her legs. The evening was pleasant, not too hot. She walked to where the driver was muttering under his breath, kicking the tire.

"What's the problem?" she asked and peeked over his shoulder.

"Oh, there is a problem, yes." He waggled his head. "I don't know what it is," he continued dejectedly.

"Ah," she said and glanced at the car as if she could figure out what was wrong.

A few vehicles passed them on the road. They rushed by without stopping, some even honking at them.

Thank you!

"How far are we from reaching the orphanage?"

The man studied his surroundings. He shielded his eyes against the sinking sun, while he glared into the distance.

"Well," he said hesitantly, wiggling his head again. "We are about two hours away."

"Wait," Emily said, her throat closing up against the heat. "The whole trip was supposed to take three hours."

"More or less three hours, miss."

Emily groaned and kicked the tire herself. "So what are we supposed to do now?"

The driver shut the hood and rested against it.

"We wait until someone picks us up."

Emily ran her hand over her face. Sweat trickled down the back of her spine.

You've got to be kidding me!

She stomped off to the side of the road, kicking a few rocks here and there. The distant foothills of the enormous Himalaya mountains seemed to Emily to be so near and yet unreachable. She was so close, yet so far away.

"Miss, if all else fails, the regular bus service will stop for us. They should be coming by within a half an hour to an hour... Maybe," the driver called to her. "Unless, of course, they aren't running the route today. But that is highly unlikely. I hope." He seemed totally, irritatingly unconcerned.

With another kick at a rock, Emily decided that she was entitled to a good, long pout and rant. After all, she was hot, she was tired, and she had been traveling for a long time – first by planes, then by train, and now in this confounded car with a broken AC and broken whatever else.

She was in a country where people were radically different from her. They spoke in a language she couldn't understand and had strange customs, which made her even more uncomfortable. And they didn't appear to care if the car was sitting on the side of the road!

What if...

Emily suppressed the urge to scream as her frustration built inside her.

I shall not want.

Not now, Lord!

Why did He have to pick the most inopportune time to remind her of her shortcomings?

The external heat gauge was rising and so was the one inside her. Whenever she found herself succumbing to her own ranting and ravings, her stomach reacted and Emily felt the sharp twinge of hunger. Even though she had eaten a scrumptious meal several hours ago, she craved something sweet and chocolaty to chase the blues away.

After rummaging around in the trunk for her bag, all the while getting blasted by hot air and sand from a passing truck, she found her melted stash of chocolate. Tears began to prick her eyes when she picked up the gooey mess.

Why can't anything go right today?

Emily leaned against the grime covered lid of the trunk and allowed herself a moment to fall apart. Tears streamed down her dusty face, leaving streaks down her cheeks.

Coming here had been a mistake!

She was tired, hot and desperate.

Did she expect too much of her life? Other people in her family had someone to lean on. All she had was – a God who constantly reminded her that she didn't measure up, that she wanted too much.

She thought about her parents. They had each other. Her sister had her husband and daughter. She had... herself.

Having a family of her own was too much? Coming home to a loving husband after a tiring shift at the hospital, children who shared their excitement from a day at school when they sat around the dinner table at night, vacations at the Cape...

Those dreams were too much?

Thank You, God! I guess I'll have to lower my expectations.

To what?

He maketh me lie down in green pastures: He leadeth me beside the still waters.

Green pastures!

In her ranting and ravings, she had forgotten that she was in this exotic place, which nobody in *her* family had visited. The landscape was dotted with green fields, splattered with colorful flowers in full bloom.

Green surrounded her!

“I am sorry, miss. But not to worry. The bus will pick us up.”

Emily startled at the sound of her driver's voice. He was leaning comfortably against the bumper of the car, smoking a stinky cigarette, and had the look of a person completely at ease with himself and his surroundings.

Trying to get herself out of her mental funk that would soon lead to depression, Emily came to stand next to him, keeping herself up-wind from his smoke.

“So, this happens to you often?”

“Oh, most definitely,” he said, earnestly nodding his head.

Emily gagged as she suppressed a laugh. Something was seriously wrong with this picture!

The sound of a loud air horn blasting at her made her jump to the side of the road, ripping the sleeve of her blouse on the fender of the car.

“I told you.” The driver pointed triumphantly, and slightly relieved, at the large bus pulling over in front of them. “And it appears that

Providence is laughing at us. The bus is going in your direction. So you don't even have to switch in Rawalpindi."

He said it as if she should be dancing for joy. As it was, Emily eyed the new mode of transportation suspiciously. Jack Russel had warned her about traveling this way. He had expressed his opinion that a Western woman traveling alone using public transportation could be in danger.

The bus parked a few hundred yards beyond her broken down car didn't look too scary. Nobody was hanging off the sides. It seemed to be working fine, which was more than could be said for her rental car that came with a driver.

Relieved, she followed him as he rolled her suitcase toward the waiting vehicle. Emily looked back at the car, resting on the side of the road.

"What about the car?" she asked.

Her driver looked over his shoulder and scowled. "Nobody can take it right now. It doesn't work. I will call the company when we get to Rawalpindi. They will send someone to pick it up."

What kind of a crazy country was this?

Weariness wrapped itself around her like a lead-lined blanket, when she wondered how many more hours had been added to her travel.

"Great!" she grumbled to herself and followed the bus driver who was chattering excitedly to her driver.

As soon as she climbed the stairs into the coach, cool air blasted her and dried off the sweat in her face. To her great surprise, most of the seats were unoccupied. In one of the occupied seats, she spotted a familiar face.

"What are you doing here?" she asked and slid into the empty seat across from Jack Russel.

He was resting his head against the backrest and flinched when she addressed him. Recognition dawned on his tired face and, Emily couldn't be sure, concern. It had been there for a fleeting moment and then it was replaced with a pleasant smile.

"Why, Miss Martins. This is a surprise. I didn't expect to see you again. What happened?"

"That private car you advised me to hire?"

Jack nodded and waited expectantly.

"It didn't work out so well. First, the AC went and then the whole thing just stopped working. So we were stranded on the side of the road for an hour." Emily's tone was pleasant, with none of the frustration she felt earlier evident. Only her face could attest to the tears, sweat, and dust she had accumulated during her latest adventure.

"Ow, I'm sorry I suggested it, Miss Martins." He crinkled his nose up comically.

"I think it's time we drop the formalities. I'm Emily. It looks like we're going to be traveling companions once again." Now, that wasn't all that bad – if she was honest with herself.

"All right," he grinned. "Jack."

Emily nodded and wondered if getting to know him was such a good idea. Certainly not! It was in all likelihood an even worse idea than coming here! But Emily was a magnet when it came to poor decisions.

"My question to you, Jack, is why *you* are on the bus yourself. Aren't you working in Lahore?"

Jack chortled. "Something came up and I had to make a quick change of plans. Considering your experience with the private car, it was most definitely the right thing to do."

Emily grinned. "I suppose you're right. But honestly, why aren't you taking the quicker way? Flying would be faster for you."

"Where I'm going, there is no airport," he said, leaning forward just a tad. "I'm a sucker for the slow and steady transportation in this country. I see so much more than if I'm flying. And I get to meet the folks that can't afford to fly."

Emily shot him a glance. "For a computer guy, you are not *computery*. If you know what I mean."

Jack laughed. "I guess. I like traveling. I only work with computers. It doesn't mean that I want to surround myself with them all the time."

Emily nodded and found herself beginning to like his laugh. That made her want to jump off of the bus and walk to the orphanage. Was she ever going to learn?

"So exactly what do you do, when you aren't traipsing through a foreign country?" Jack's dark blue eyes searched her carefully and thoroughly.

Emily pulled up her knees to rest them against the seat in front of her.

"I work in the healthcare industry."

He cocked his head. "Thank you. That tells me a lot!"

"Okay. I'm a doctor, a pediatrician."

Jack coughed as he took a swig of his bottled water. She stood ready to assist if he showed any signs of distress. His face became a deep red as he tried to catch his breath.

"I didn't see that at all. I had you pegged all wrong. That doesn't happen to me often." He sneezed. "You certainly aren't easy to read."

"What, you're trying to read me?" *Oh, come on. Keep your head to yourself and your heart locked!*

Jack turned his head away from her to mask his surprise. "No. Well, I guess." He turned back to her, a disarming smile playing on his lips. "It's always good for me to know who I'm dealing with."

Emily swallowed as she felt herself return back to the old ways, the ones that always ended in disaster. Why couldn't she smarten up when it came to her personal life?

For the next hour or so, they chatted. The bus stopped at several stations along the way with some people getting off, others getting on. In Rawalpindi, the largest town since she got on, most of the passengers left. Emily was surprised that Jack wasn't among them. Her driver waved to her cheerfully as he departed, telling her not to worry about the car on the side of the road.

Jack turned toward her.

"Shouldn't you get off here too?" he asked.

Emily stared at him moodily. "No, apparently this bus is going my way. I don't have to change. At least that is a good thing."

Jack turned toward the window.

"Where are you going?" she asked.

"I have a meeting in the country," he said quietly. *No kidding!*

Jack watched her out of the corners of his eyes. She certainly was different. He had not pegged her for a doctor. She was too feminine, too sweet, for that. He would have thought of her as a teacher, maybe a kindergarten teacher. He would have to be careful not to underestimate her again.

Emily's eyes were closed at the moment. Jack could tell that she was bone weary. How long had she been traveling? To come here, alone. He didn't know if he should be impressed with her or think she was lacking some brains. In the end, he couldn't help but be impressed. Coming all this way alone had to have taken some guts and determination.

When the bus stopped at the next town, three people got off, nobody got on. They soon made their way through treacherously winding roads in the foothills. Dark had long made it impossible to pinpoint their location. The road headed to another small town where a mother and her son got off the bus. From then on, they only spotted an occasional cluster of light in the distance.

Emily opened her gritty, tired eyes. She hadn't been this beat since her residency. Her stomach growled and she felt the need to use the restroom. The one on the bus was not up to her standards so she ignored the urge. At least it would help her to stay awake since she wasn't exactly sure where she was.

When they passed a sign it was in English and Arabic, but it might as well tell her they were on the moon. She had no idea where they were and how much further she had to go until she'd finally reach her destination. It seemed that her travels would never be over.

She stared out past Jack into the night. The darkness was so complete she saw nothing but an occasional flicker of light high above them.

"How are you doing?" he asked kindly. "You look beat."

Emily tried not to read anything into the way his voice seemed almost tender and caring.

"I am. I don't even know what day it is," she replied softly. "I left New York on a Tuesday."

Jack uncrossed his legs and rested his knees against the seat in front of him, just as Emily was doing. He looked slightly uncomfortable. He took out his phone, swiped the screen to examine it, then pointed it at her.

"Says here that it's Sunday today. No wonder you're exhausted."

He looked around, appearing relaxed and totally at ease. On the inside, it was a different picture. If he had been hooked up to a heart monitor, all sorts of bells and whistles would be going off. They had almost reached the spot he was waiting for. His muscles were coiled tightly, ready for action.

He prayed for protection and for wisdom.

"So, which town are you going to?" he asked, his eyes still half closed.

"Murray, or no. Myrray. No, that's not right either." Emily screwed her eyes up in concentration. She blinked a couple of times. "I remember. It's Murree."

"I thought so," Jack mumbled. "I think we are about an hour away."

He took this bit of information poorly. But only internally. On the outside, he was as cool and smooth as a scoop of ice cream. This job already made him more on edge than he ever had been. He gritted his teeth, not liking the options that were being presented.

Emily groaned.

She pinched the bridge of her nose and shook her head. If she had known...

If she had known, would she have come? The way things stood right now, no! She would *not* have traveled halfway across the world only to miss her home, her family and her job. She longed for her car. She even missed her co-workers. Emily chided herself for feeling so absolutely gloomy.

Suddenly the bus lurched to a stop! She lost her balance, her knees pushing painfully into the empty seat in front of her. As she peered outside, all she could see were headlights of a car, blasting into the windshield of the bus. A group of people was silhouetted against the light and they were all screaming at the driver, aiming guns at him! A volley of shots shattered the windshield. The driver slumped in his seat.

A scream came out of her mouth before she could stop it. Jack flung himself across the aisle into her seat and clamped his hand over her mouth.

"Quiet!" he hissed. "Get down!"

6

"Have you lost your mind?" Emily asked, her voice muffled by the strong grasp he had on her mouth.

Instead of answering, he focused his attention on the front of the bus, where the group was about to force the door open.

Jack pushed her onto the dusty floor, shielding her with his own body as well as he could in the cramped space between the seats. Emily trembled from head to toe and came to a very serious conclusion.

She had made a huge mistake coming on this trip!

A pair of dusty boots crunched on the dirty floor of the bus – coming steadily toward them. It was only a matter of time before they found them, cowering between their seats.

Her mouth had gone dry.

Okay, Lord. This is it. I'm sorry for wanting things my way. Please watch after my family.

The boots stopped at their row. Screwing up her face so she could see, she peered into dark, angry eyes. Satisfaction rippled across the man's face and he sneered. He pointed his semi-automatic rifle at them. Jack's hands went up into the air immediately.

"We're Americans," he shouted, his voice quivering in terror. "Don't shoot!"

"Up!" the man screamed at them.

Jack flinched.

He helped her to her feet. The man in front of her grinned, satisfied, and shoved both of them roughly to the front of the bus. Jack stumbled and almost went down. He caught himself on the seat and continued walking. Emily glanced at the driver, hoping the man was still alive. Nausea rose to the back of her throat. She didn't have to be a doctor to know the man was dead.

Emily lost her footing on the steep stairs, and Jack steadied her at the last moment. Loud whoops and yells greeted them making her knees tremble like tree branches in a hurricane.

"*Y'Allah!*" The leader shoved the business end of his gun into Jack's back.

Arms grabbed at them. Emily was maneuvered roughly into the middle of the road and toward the blazing headlights. A hand wrapped tightly around her wrist, twisting it harshly and cutting off the circulation. Something inside her snapped. If they thought she was going to go with them willingly, without a hint of a fight, they didn't know her.

She shoved back!

Her captor awarded her with twisting her arm harder, more cruelly. She bit off a groan. Behind her, Jack stumbled and fell flat on his face.

"Up!" The man in charge yelled at him. He pointed the gun at his head, ready to fire.

"No!" Emily shouted and wrestled against her gaunt assailant. He didn't seem to care at all, and only grunted when she stepped on his toes with the heel of her sneaker.

I'm too young to die! There was so much she hadn't experienced.

The man holding her twisted her arm up so that the tendons stretched beyond their natural limits.

I don't want to die in this strange country!

Tears sprung to her eyes as she forced herself to comply with her aggressor's rough treatment.

What about my parents?

What would happen if they killed Jack right here, in front of her?

He leadeth me beside still waters.

The tender whisperings reached far into her heart. Emily stilled and closed her eyes, picturing herself by a steady bubbling brook, surrounded by towering mountains. It worked to calm her churning stomach and soothed her shattered nerves. Until...

"Up!" the leader yelled, shoving the semi-automatic into Jack's cheek, pressing the cold steel into his skin.

Oh, God! This isn't happening!

Her happy place was gone instantly.

Jack held up his trembling hands, rose and dusted off his pants, an act that resulted with the butt of the rifle being jammed into his kidneys.

"Okay, okay. No need to be rude about it," he groaned while he collapsed onto the road again.

The man behind him grabbed him by the hair and pulled him up, almost ripping his scalp off his head. He grabbed the hand that held his hair. A fist connected with his chin, sending him back down onto the ground.

"Up!"

He had to admit, the yelling was trying his nerves! Jack stumbled to his feet, feeling slightly dizzy and light headed. He tasted blood from a cut on his lip and swiped the back of his hand over it.

"Go!" The man shoved his rifle toward the beat-up truck, whose headlights were blinding him. "*Y'allah*!"

Trembling with fear, Emily was forced toward the vehicle. Her breathing became labored as she fought the urge to fight. How, she had no idea.

I'm not going in there!

One thing was certain. If she entered the vehicle she was as good as dead. Her offender felt her tense and, with a slight grunt, he hoisted her over his shoulder.

"Let me go!" she shouted. That just resulted in more raucous laughter and guns being fired into the night sky.

She was tossed into the back of the canvas-covered bed like a useless sack of trash. As soon as the terrorist let go of her, Emily struggled to get up and out of the deathtrap. She didn't make it very far because another member of the group twisted both arms behind her back, securing her hands together quickly and efficiently. A filthy rag was stuffed into her mouth, making her gag. Before she could dislodge it, someone had secured it with tape.

As her stomach heaved, she struggled to jump back out of the bed.

I have to get away!

She didn't get very far. Someone slapped her hard across the face, sending her flying backward. The back of her head collided with something sharp and unforgiving. Her cry came out muffled, unnoticed. Defeated, and slightly dazed, Emily surrendered herself to her fate. Her vision was obscured when a sack was slipped on top of her head. Her stomach convulsed in response to the stench that slammed her.

The Lord is my shepherd!

There was no time to let that thought sink in because something – no someone heavy – was tossed on top of her and whatever air she had in her lungs came whooshing out under the weight. Thankfully, whoever it was rolled off her right away.

The tires squealed on the loose gravel of the road and Emily struggled against the force tossing her about like a limp rag doll. It was difficult to steady her ragged breathing. Her lungs burned with the need for oxygen, which only added to the need to breathe heavier. Pretty soon she'd pass out.

Oh, Lord! Oh, Lord! What have I gotten myself into?

Jack touched the space around him and his fingers graced against something soft. The ripped fabric of Emily's tunic. It had made the golden specks in her brown eyes stand out.

Focus! he chided himself.

She jerked away from his initial prodding, a muffled cry escaping from under her hood, then relaxed as his fingers came around her bound hands and squeezed. Her breathing was loud and raspy. Scooting closer after he had been tossed so carelessly on top of her, he kept a steady pressure on her hand.

As they bounced around in the back of the beat-up truck, he did his best not to squash her or pin her underneath his own weight. He also never let go of her hand. It seemed a lifeline not just to her but to him as well. Soon her breathing became less labored.

Good girl.

He wasn't able to remove the burlap sack over his head. As they sped down the winding roads, Jack tried to formulate a plan. He couldn't. There in the back of the truck, bouncing on rough roads across the foothills of the Himalaya mountains, he asked for help, for peace, and for angels to surround him and Emily.

His previously carefully wrought plan had been turned upside down because of one thing: Emily's presence.

If only she hadn't been on the bus.

If only he hadn't gotten to know her.

If only he could get them out before all hell on earth broke loose.

You have to succeed, Russel, if it's the last thing you do. You can't let them hurt her!

Keeping that in mind, he prayed even harder for God to do a miracle because he was plain out of ideas.

They bounced along on rough roads, winding around sharp turns for what seemed like hours to her. Her hand was clasped tightly in what she hoped was Jack's hand, giving her reassurance. Emily concentrated on the touch, not thinking of what awaited them once the truck had reached its destination. Obviously, they would not kill them right away.

Hadn't she heard of people being kidnapped? Her parents couldn't pay a ransom! They didn't have money growing on trees!

She didn't even want to imagine what they had planned for her. Her stomach started heaving. She tried to take a steady breath but the stench from the sack and the tape over her mouth made breathing a chore. She felt the bile rise violently up her throat. She managed to swallow it before it came back up again. She tensed as she repeated this over and over again. Soon she wouldn't be able to keep going. She would drown in her own vomit.

Yea, though I walk through the valley of the shadow of death I shall fear no evil: for thou art with me.

Her stomach settled down, thankfully. Her erratic breathing slowed as she allowed the words a few seconds to sink in. Her peace didn't last very long because the truck took a sudden, sharp turn at high speed. Her head banged roughly into something hard and sharp. Pain shot through her temple and she grunted. Jack's body slammed into hers, pinning her against the hard, cold wall of the truck.

Okay, that hurt! Groaning, Emily turned onto her back.

She tried to push herself into a sitting position. It wasn't as easy as she had thought, with her hands tied behind her back and the bouncing of the truck. She managed it just in time to be thrown about again. Her head banged something again. This time she didn't bother to get up. Her eyes stung with tears, waiting to be shed.

At least she was still alive. That was more than could be said for the poor driver of their bus. Emily prayed that he didn't have a family, a wife, and children.

7

The truck stopped abruptly, tires squealing, tossing them about easily. Jack was pulled out of the truck and the stinky, smelly hood was yanked off his head. Cold, clear, pure air blasted him in the face. He stared, slightly disoriented, into the face of his captors, seeing nothing but anger, hate, and greed. A leer, menacing and cruel, spread across the face of the man in front of him.

He so wanted to wipe that sneer off his face!

Emily shivered as a blast of mountain air tugged at her, her sweaty blouse clinging to her back. A moment later, fear rippled through her as the hood was ripped off, snagging some of her loose hair, making her grunt in pain. The tape came off next, another highly unpleasant experience.

She stumbled across rocks as rough hands shoved her up a steep path. With her hands tied behind her back, it was difficult to keep her balance, and she slammed into the man in front of her. He shoved her back onto her feet, not without groping her in ways that deepened her regret of making the trip. A nasty smile spread over his dark, bearded face, causing more goosebumps to rise on her skin.

They hiked over hills for what seemed an eternity. Emily's leg muscles trembled, and she was filled with utter, dark dread.

I'm going to die tonight, she thought and stumbled forward.

This time, nobody was there to catch her and she lay on the ground, panting, a sharp pain spreading over her knees and her face. Something slick and wet spread into the fabric of her pants and began to run down her cheek. She had no time to concern herself with this.

Everything seemed so unreal.

"Are you okay?" a soft voice, tender and encouraging at the same time, whispered. Jack hovered over her, his eyes filled with a fire that threatened to consume her whole.

She began to shake her head, to wish they were somewhere far away from here, when calloused hands once again lifted her to her feet.

"*Y'allah,*" the dark face growled in her ear and forced her onward.

Emily caught the shudder that went through her and focused on the pitch black path they were forcing her to hike up. They finally came to a small, dark house, constructed of large rocks. The leader of the group knocked three times on the dark wooden door, and it opened. Light from an oil lamp shone into her face, causing her to look away from the sudden, searing brightness.

Mercilessly, hands shoved her toward the blaze.

"No!"

If she entered, she'd never come out again in one piece.

Fighting with whatever strength she had did her no good since now the man beside her found pleasure in taking a chunk of her messy, dirt and sweat soaked hair and dragging her behind him into the dingy abode. Ignoring the pain that stabbed across her scalp, she turned the opposite direction – back toward the darkness.

Other hands, just as ruthless and strong, touched her – pressed her forward into a place she didn't want to go. Finally, as if she were just a rag doll, someone picked her up and slung her over his shoulder. His comrades seemed to enjoy that immensely because they jeered and laughed loudly. When she lifted her head to look behind her, Jack was forced into the room, stepping inside as if he had prepared all his life for this moment.

His eyes sought hers, filling her immediately with courage.

He had been handled just as roughly as she, bleeding from his lip and a cut on his forehead, but that look on his face...

She clung to his gaze for as long as she could, willing it to fill her with fire and determination.

At least ten men entered the room around her, filling it with loud, rough laughter and talk in a language she couldn't understand. But she didn't have to. She knew what they were discussing and it filled her with a bottomless, hopeless dread.

Smoke from a fire in a rusty old potbelly stove filled the hut. The room was devoid of furniture. A pile of filthy pillows had been tossed into one corner. The room was a basic fifteen by twenty rectangle. Shutters on the two narrow windows on the side of the house opposite the door blocked out the night. The floor was dirt, with small holes in several places. The walls were rocks, an abundant building material in this area.

A lone grimy oil lamp sat on the floor, illuminating the room just enough to make her shudder involuntarily. Another door made of roughly-cut timber led to the only other room in the house, a gaping black hole without any light. A few rusted pots were stacked unwashed on the floor next to the wood stove which was also used for cooking.

Her stomach clenching into a tight ball, sweat beginning to bead underneath her nose, Emily imagined spending a night in this place. Tears burned in her eyes, obscuring her vision temporarily until she blinked them away.

I hate camping! Where's the bathroom?

The question was ludicrous. This was the basic habitation for people who didn't want to be found, who lived so far off the grid that they only had the very basic of needs.

What in the world was she doing in the mountains of Pakistan?

This whole trip has been a bad idea!

Emily examined the men around the room, her lids lowered in an attempt to hide her gaze. They were as rough as the house they were standing in. Their dark faces, obscured by dirt as well as thick, unkempt beards, were as if carved of the same rocks as the hut in which they were standing. They looked nothing like the people she had encountered on her travels so far. Their eyes, hard and dark, roamed over her, making her wish she could melt into the ground to disappear from their leering scrutiny.

They wore the same kind of outfit as she. Only hers had been clean and pretty this morning. Now her sleeve was ripped at the seam, dirt clung in clumps to the blouse, which had ripped across her stomach. The fabric across her knees was stained with the blood from her falls and stuck to her skin.

The men's tunics were ruddy looking, covered with dark mysterious stains. Swallowing the sick feeling creeping up her throat over and over again, she imagined that they were covered with another poor victim's blood.

As a doctor, she didn't have a problem with body fluids. She just had a problem with seeing it on the tunics of these men!

The whole room began to take on a smell. Emily was reminded of the first time she had to examine a cadaver. If only she could suck on a menthol cough drop, to mask the stench of unwashed bodies that settled around her. It was a trick a fellow student had shared with her. The room began to spin. She blinked her eyes quickly, sucking in the thick air through slightly parted lips.

Oh, how she wished that God was with her!

Had He left her when they entered this room? She couldn't really blame Him. It was not a pleasant place, and He certainly wasn't welcome here!

What if...

Jack kept his eyes averted as he took stock of the situation. He had found himself in some hairy ones before but this... He usually avoided being kidnapped. A dastardly smirk tugged at the corners of his mouth and he quickly turned his head to avoid detection.

This could be fun...

The men standing around in a circle, gesticulating and posturing, had no idea whom they had just snatched. He just had to be careful because Emily also had no clue of the game he was playing.

With that one thought, it ceased to be a caper.

Getting out would be difficult with only one possible door to the outside and windows he would never fit through. The hair on the back of his neck stood in attention when he thought of having to amend his almost perfect plan from before. He didn't have the luxury of time because the moment that hood had been slapped over his head, things had been put into motion that were out of his control.

Time was of the essence.

There was no room for error.

The shouts of the men were almost primal.

Emily shivered as another scream of triumph cut through the air, making her want to cower in the corner, to hide from all of this. The front door opened again, and an old, wizened man entered. In comparison to the men around the room, his clothes and his appearance was almost kingly.

His tunic was clean, devoid of dark stains. The wrinkles in his face and the long, almost white beard, bespoke of leadership as did the respectful hush that fell over the place as he strode toward her and Jack. His eyes were like those of his men – dark, angry, and dangerous. Only his eyes gleamed with greed. Abounding greed! It frightened her more than the shouts of the men around her.

He stared at her, a finger curling around her chin to lift it up, forcing her to meet his gaze. A smile, devoid of humor, formed at the corners of his lips, greed oozing out of every pore. When he turned to study Jack, he didn't seem pleased at all. Out of the blue, he started yelling at his men.

It made her heart pound harder in her chest, fear curling around it with icy fingers.

He's going to kill him now!

Something about Jack caused the man to tense, to gesticulate angrily as he addressed his men.

Jack hid his exhilaration.

This is too easy, guys. Come on! Can't you at least try to make it harder for me?

But how were these poor men to know that he was fluent in several languages – including the one they were conversing in now? They were oblivious that he had majored in foreign languages, Arabic being his main language, and had graduated in the top five percent of his class.

It would have been much too hilarious if he had told them that he could understand every word they were saying. And yes, the leader was right to worry. He had just let a snake into his den.

A big, fat Texas rattlesnake!

"You bring this into our midst? This man has military written all over him! What is wrong with you? Didn't you see that?" the leader shouted, spittle spraying those nearest him. His eyes darted back and forth between his men and Jack. "Get rid of him! Now!" He pointed a crooked finger at him.

Okay, that was not so good! This situation may unravel quicker than he had anticipated.

"No wait!" the leader shouted.

The man's hand shot up and he glared at Jack. He strode up to him, sizing him up again and again.

"You!" the man yelled in accented English.

Spittle hit Jack's face. There were a few things that turned his stomach, and this was one of them. He swallowed the bile that crept its way up his throat. His brain went into hyper-drive, thinking of ways to get out of this precarious situation. Jack choked back a grin when he found a solution to his problem.

Time to work your magic, Russel.

"You are military! You are in my country! Why?"

More spittle hit his cheek.

Jack worked up the partially digested food and drink still remaining in his stomach. Projectile vomiting was always something he had prided himself on. Especially on command. His sister had always envied him his ability, which had gotten him out of a lot of trouble as a kid. Or into trouble, depending on whether his father was around or not.

Now he would call upon his ability to save his life again. Like that time he hadn't studied for his chemistry exam! A lifesaver right in front of the teacher!

Oh yeah, it worked like a charm.

His vomit splattered the leader square in the face! It ran down his beard. Partially digested chunks of bread and fruit stuck to the man's pride and joy. Jack knew how much the beard meant to these men.

Stunned silence and a soft moan coming from Emily was all that could be heard. And this was why Jack loved his job and got paid the big bucks!

Because he could throw up on command!

He wiped his mouth on his shoulder, because with his hands still tied he knew he would look totally pathetic.

"I'm so sorry," he groaned. *You have come to the master, my friend! Your game is about to be called.*

Fists pounded him hard in the face and in the gut. He collapsed into a ball on the dirt floor to protect himself from most of the blows that rained down on him. The leader stomped out of the room.

"Take care of him! Make him regret the day he was born!"

Emily watched the proceedings in horror. They were beating Jack to a pulp. Already she could see that he was bleeding from several cuts on his face. He cried in pain as they kicked him hard in the sides and gut. Just watching him receive pummeling caused her to hurt everywhere. She struggled in vain to free herself from her captors.

What if...

They thought he was military? He was a computer geek! Didn't they see that?

Oh, Lord! Help me! Don't let them kill him!

8

When it seemed like Jack could take no more they stopped and dragged him through the door on the far side of the room – into the dark hole. Emily was dragged after him and tossed into the room like a sack of old, moldy potatoes. Her back hit the hard dirt floor and her head connected with the stone wall, making her cry out in pain. Before the door was slammed shut, cutting off all the light, she tried to get her bearings on where Jack's unconscious body lay slumped.

"Jack," she whispered, her voice sounding unnatural, quivering with the panic she felt deep in her heart.

His groan came from right next to her and she scooted closer.

"Jack! Where are you hurt?"

Her voice was once again strong and almost professional. She was used to receiving an answer. Her patients usually told her exactly where they were hurt.

"Try, where am I *not* hurt!" he breathed and groaned, rolling onto his back. She just about laughed at his reply – it was so unexpected. "Emily, listen to me..."

He couldn't finish his sentence.

The door was wrenched open again, light spilling into the dark room. For a fleeting moment, Emily saw a rusted old bed frame and mattress, with stuffing coming out of it. A chair, also looking as if it could never support anyone's weight and a table on three legs, leaning against the rock wall. No sink.

And definitely no bathroom!

Rough hands yanked them out of the room, back into the larger room. The leader was sitting on the cushions in the corner as if he was holding court. He had changed his tunic. His beard was wet but clean.

Jack bit back a devious grin. He was too good to show his hand before the last hoorah. He forced his face to convey sheer panic and terror at the sight of the man.

He could win an academy award for his performance.

Emily, on the other hand, wasn't faking her terror. Her bruised face was pale, nearly ghost-like. Blood and grime darkened her hair. An unexplained anger rushed through him at the sight of her ripped clothing. It was at that moment Jack knew that he would protect her with his last breath. Her large, fear-filled eyes held his, searching for something to give her courage.

And there hadn't been time to tell her the truth!

Not that he would tell her the whole thing, but he wanted somehow to reassure her that he was all right. Her mocha eyes widened in panic as the man crooked a finger toward them. Jack noted that she fought the hands that forced her forward.

The girl had some spunk!

She may make it through this after all.

They're going to beat him again, Emily thought in horror as the leader, the man on whom Jack had emptied his stomach, pointed to them.

She had to stop him! But how?

She was a woman!

She was weak.

She was terrified!

Jack's almost cocky reply to her question of where he was hurt came back to her. Maybe he wasn't all that weak after all. But she could see he was hurting badly. He was holding his side painfully, horror on his face as he stood in front of the old man. How terrified he must have been to throw up all over him!

This whole situation was a dreadful nightmare!

"You!" The man indicated to Jack.

His head henchman forced Jack onto his knees, and Jack almost chuckled when he thought of the man as such. The man pointed his gun at Jack's head, and irritation ran through him.

He didn't like to be on the receiving side of the bullet!

"You are military! Why are you here?" The man said in terribly accented English.

Jack lifted his head in feigned horror. "I'm not military!" He made his voice quake. "I work with computers... sir." He threw that *sir* in just for good measure. He would like to show this guy how much he respected him!

"You are lying," the old man shouted, spittle raining down on Jack again.

He pointed toward his associate and the man's face took on a look of pleasure. A balled fist rammed into Jack's face nearly driving his head into the ground, had he not been held by someone behind him.

Yeah, that hurt!

Groaning in real pain, he swayed and fell forward, rolling over onto his back.

Emily screamed.

Someone slapped her hard, making her stumble backward. The sound of the hand connecting with her soft skin just added to the fury burning in Jack's gut and beginning to spread through his body.

They had no idea what was coming their way!

“What are you doing here?” the leader hissed at Jack. His stale breath with a hint of tooth decay and garlic nearly made him throw up for real this time.

“I work for Najeed Inc. They hired me to work on their website,” he groaned as hands pulled him back into the kneeling position.

“Every time you lie to me, my friend here will beat you.” He pointed to a wisp of a man with hard, empty eyes, who took the butt of the rifle and jammed it into the back of his head.

Ohh, look... Stars...

He went crashing down onto the dirt floor, his teeth rattling at the impact. He tasted blood and spat it out.

“Stop!” Emily yelled and sobbed.

They were going to beat him within an inch of his life! Just because they thought he was military! What kind of people were they?

You idiot. They're terrorists!

Of course, she had stumbled into a cell on her way to a missionary orphanage! Why wouldn't she?

As the men crowded around Jack who lay in a tight ball on the floor, striking him wherever they could, she knew she had to do something.

Her inner nature to save people, to restore them to health, kicked in full force. She made her living rescuing people from death. She couldn't just stand by while they beat him within an inch of his life. Another thought hit her harder than the brutal slap she had just received.

What was his spiritual situation?

Was he a Christian?

Did he know the gospel message?

Her heart leaped into her throat and she almost collapsed in anguish. How could she stand by and do nothing while he was slowly being killed?

She had to do something!

She wouldn't just watch him die.

Jack, groaning in pain, turned onto his back and shot her a look that tried to convey her to be quiet. Watching her have to go through this was almost worse than being on the receiving end of the blows. He had been trained long and hard to withstand the pain and pressure that came from being captured and held for interrogation.

But not her!

Her face was red and swollen from the rough treatment she had met. Thick tears streaked down her dirt and sweat-stained cheeks. With every part of him, he wanted her to know that he would be okay, that she could trust him.

But how?

Hands grabbed at him again and pulled him onto his feet, where he stood swaying. He wanted to congratulate himself on the convincing performance he was giving them. Grudgingly, he admitted that the room did spin slightly and seeing those stars hadn't been pleasant, but really!

He was still in complete control. For now.

"You are lying!" the old man screamed, a bony finger poking into his chest.

Jack forced himself to cower. Once this was over, there would be no more groveling.

"I tell you the truth." His voice squeaked for effect, "I work with computers! I design websites! Please, no more!" He even turned his cheek for good measure.

The old man nodded at his cohort next to him, and his balled fist went right into his side. This time, he wasn't able to suppress a real grunt as he felt his ribs break.

He may have to rethink things if he was to see everything through.

"Stop!" Emily wrenched herself out of the hands of her surprised handlers. She flung herself in front of him, shielding him with her body. "He's not what you are accusing him of! I should know! He's my husband!"

The air exploded out of his lungs. Actually, someone had gone and vacuumed the air out of the whole house! She had just tossed a major wrench into the whole thing.

"Shut up!" he hissed.

Pain from his side shot like fire through his body.

"Please," Emily whimpered. "He is just a computer guy. He's done nothing wrong! Leave him alone!"

The room began to fade.

This was bad! This was really, really bad!

The leader turned toward her, satisfaction and greed now so evident on his face it was oozing with it.

"No," Jack panted painfully while hunched over in pain. "She's lying. I just met her yesterday!" He glared at her as menacingly as he could.

"Then why would she lie for you like that?" The old man's words were laced with satisfaction, with pleasure. They had him now.

Jack gritted his teeth.

Didn't she understand she had just put herself into a terrible, horrible, really not-so-good situation? Didn't she understand that he would not be able to stop what would be coming down the pike?

"*Khalas,*" the leader grunted, that nasty grin spreading over his face again, and spread his arms.

His henchman pulled Jack up from the floor. The room was definitely spinning like a top. As Emily and Jack were tossed back into the room, the tape that bound their hands was cut.

Emily cried when her hands came free. Blood seeped through her arms, making her moan as the pins and needles effect happened. As soon as the door was slammed shut and darkness enveloped them, Jack collapsed onto the dirt floor next to her. He pulled her face to his so he could whisper into her ear. Her matted hair tickled his nose and he pushed it out of his way.

"What did you do that for?" he breathed.

"Let me take care of you," she whispered back, her voice filled with extreme compassion.

An arm around Emily's shoulder, she practically dragged him through the absolute dark to the smelly mattress. He collapsed, gritting his teeth against the pain in his side. His side throbbed with every breath he took, every beat of his heart. His injured head, he could deal with.

The fact that Emily had just stepped in to save his hide bothered him immensely.

She had just put her life on the line for his.

"Emily," he grunted.

"Stop talking," she breathed back. He could hear the ripping of clothing. "You're hurt. I'm a doctor, remember?"

Something soft touched his face, wiped the blood from his eyes.

She gently and examined him as well as she could. Oh, yeah. He had cracked a few ribs. That couldn't be pleasant. He grunted in pain as she touched his pulsing side.

"I'm sorry," she breathed. "You're going to need to rest. They cracked a few ribs."

"Really?" he panted. "Tell me something I don't know." Sarcasm laced his voice. "What did you do that for?"

"Well." She ripped more of her filthy garment and gently secured it around his rib cage, hoping it would keep the bones from rubbing against each other and puncturing a lung. "I'm a doctor and it's my job to take care of people."

"No," he whispered, barely audible. "You just put yourself into the hot seat. Emily, they're going to torture you!"

"But, Jack," she replied right into his ear. "Why would they?"

He grabbed the back of her neck and positioned her head so he could speak softly into her ear. "Because that's what they do, Emily. How can you think otherwise? Are you strong enough to deal with what they are going to do to you – or me?"

Emily shot up, making the metal rungs under the mattress creak. Her whole world seemed to have shrunk down to one thing. This room and this whispered conversation was all that remained of it.

"But you're not a threat to them! They can't get anything out of you. And all I could do is give them a prescription for penicillin."

Emily had acted, once again, without thinking!

Stupid, stupid, stupid!

Jack painfully pushed himself into a sitting position. She had done an expert job with his ribs. He was trained to live with the pain!

Training, training!

It was that important. That and hiding the truth.

He flipped his legs over the side of the bed and felt for her hand. She gripped it, hard.

It was ice cold!

He pulled her head toward him again and found her ear.

"Listen to me. Whatever I do, trust me! Don't react when they come to beat me. Are you listening?"

"No," she whimpered softly. "If they beat you any more, you'll die!"

"Well," he snickered softly in the darkness. "I have you to doctor me up, remember? Just trust me!"

"What do you mean?" She turned her head to where she thought his face was. In this darkness, it was hard to tell. She could be speaking to the back of his head for all she knew.

"They have leverage to force me to comply with them. You. By telling them that you're my wife you played right into their hands." His breath tickled her cheek and caused her skin to pucker up with goosebumps.

But not in a pleasant, cozy manner.

What would they do to her?

Tremors rushed through her.

"What was I thinking, coming here?" she whispered and covered her face with her hands.

The tears came.

She sobbed so hard her shoulders shook. Jack put an arm around her shoulders and drew her to him. He wasn't usually so easily influenced by tears, but she was... different.

His ribs throbbed painfully but he ignored it. It wasn't the first time he had broken a rib. Nor would it be the last.

"Okay, we have to get out of here," he finally hissed into the darkness. "That will prove to be somewhat challenging. There are only two doors and the windows are of no help. You're going to have to be strong, Emily. You need sleep. I'll work on a plan to get us out."

The mattress shifted underneath her as he quietly walked away. Suddenly, she was more afraid than she had ever been in her life. She couldn't see him, but she could hear him stumble around the room.

"Jack," she breathed.

"What?" he whispered back.

"I-I'm afraid."

She heard him shuffle back toward her, bump into the chair on the way, and sit down next to her. She shivered. It was chilly in the room, but not enough to cause her to tremble as much as she was.

"Hey," he said softly. "It'll work out."

His arm came around her shoulders again. She was infused with warmth immediately and stopped quaking. Her eyelids were heavy and sleep pulled on her with all its might.

"When peace like a river attendeth my way, when sorrows like seabillows roll, whatever my lot, thou hast taught me to say, it is well," Jack started to sing softly and slightly off-key. "With my soul."

Emily startled awake. "Are you a believer?" she whispered.

He chuckled. "Been one for twenty years. After my father died Christ became my refuge, my shelter. He became more than a religion that year."

He soothed the dirt, tear and sweat crusted hair out of her face.

"Look. We're going to be just fine. The Lord is with us, okay? He is watching over us."

The truth of it spoken out loud settled into her heart. She closed her eyes, finally giving in to sleep.

9

It seemed that no less had her eyes closed than the door was wrenched back open and she was pulled onto her feet. Her hands were once again roughly tied behind her back. Emily's fingers turned numb instantly. She squinted as her eyes adjusted to the dim light coming from the other room. Jack, who had fallen asleep next to her, startled awake and was forced to stand up, too.

He looked terrible.

His battered bloody face turned ashen. Swaying on the spot, he looked like he was about to pass out any minute. Sweat beaded on his upper lip and forehead.

And they thought he was a spy!

Her captors gave her a shove, forcing Emily to stumble into the main room of the hut. The windows were still shut tightly but, oh glorious God, light escaped through the cracks in the wooden shutters, passing on a heavenly message.

The sun couldn't stay away, not even after the darkest night.

She let that settle into her heart, along with the fact that Jack was a believer. For a fleeting instant, everything seemed to be so much less terrifying.

They would be okay. Eventually.

She watched as the group of men forced Jack onto his knees again. This time, he didn't comply right away. The man behind him kicked the back of his knees hard. Jack fell face forward onto the ground. He lay there panting, his face scrunched up in terrible pain.

Emily almost sprang to his rescue but was restrained by strong hands.

"Up!" the man, who had forced him into that position, screamed into his ear.

Jack wanted to ram his fist into his captor's face. He swallowed down his anger and stumbled onto his knees. Raucous laughter filled the room. A group of men was lounging on the cushions in the corner, seemingly enjoying the show. In front of them was spread a cloth with various foods and drinks for them to enjoy.

His stomach growled. When was the last time he and Emily had eaten?

The leader sat, as if on a throne, in the middle of them. His cushions allowed him to tower over them slightly. He let his gaze travel over them, a look of hunger spreading over his wrinkled face.

Her stomach clenched unpleasantly as the scent of food tickled her nose. Bile rose, perspiration slicked her forehead when his gaze raked over her in a slow, greedy manner.

I have to get away! I can't stay here another minute!

Emily's skin crawled and she struggled against the hands that held her captive. They just tightened their grip around her, making her feel trapped like a helpless mouse whose meaningless life was about to expire.

"Please let us go. My family doesn't have any money to pay you," Jack pleaded in a weak and unsteady voice.

Rowdy, hugely satisfied laughter followed his pathetic appeal.

"Are you just pretending to be stupid, or are you really that ignorant? We don't want money from your family. The American government will pay for your release. Until then, you are ours to do with whatever we wish."

Her stomach dropped as if in free-fall.

No! I can't be here! I have to get out!

Whoops and hollers followed their leader's statement. One man raised his rifle over his head and quickly lowered it again when the leader glared at him.

"Now, it is time to stop playing the fool."

Is that a touch of Oxford British I hear? It would make sense that some of these men have gone to university in England and studied-

Jack gritted his teeth, forcing himself to remember that it wasn't only his life on the line. He couldn't have moments of weakness of mind if he hoped to get them both out alive.

Dark, cold eyes rammed into his. Jack felt his soul crying out to God. Evil and hatred slammed into him with relentless force. That had never happened before!

He trembled for a moment, and this time it was not an act. His heart was being attacked in an utterly painful manner.

Lord, please protect us from the evil that is before us.

Then, he was reminded that he was not fighting a battle against flesh and blood, but that this was a spiritual war and that Christ had already conquered. He had overcome death! That thought gave him such a huge amount of assurance he almost laughed at the man sitting on his throne in the dim, smoky light of the oil lamp.

Jack trained his face and forced himself to look the man in the eyes. For a split second, the old man flinched. For a fraction of an instant, so fast that even he didn't think he had done it, Jack's lips twitched into the semblance of a smile. Then he trained his face to convey fear and terror.

Again, it was an award-worthy performance.

Emily trembled from head to toe. She watched the exchange between the two men, saw the hateful look that passed to Jack and saw him flinch, replacing that almost cocky look with absolute terror.

She bit down on a whimper. If he was that afraid, there was no hope for them! They wouldn't get out! No way, no how. That realization made Emily's knees give out.

You're stuck! You are going to die. You see, there are consequences for not following God. Sin eventually leads to death.

Her vision was obscured by tears and she blinked them away, but not before one or two managed to sneak out. They made a slow trail down her dirt crusted cheeks and splashed on the floor in front of her. When she forced her gaze to the leader, she knew that whatever was about to happen, it wasn't going to be pleasant for either her or Jack.

"You're not in suburbia, Miss Martins."

He had warned her! Not once, but several times. She should have known what was coming.

"We are done playing around, American filth! I know you are not a computer programmer." The leader's face turned to disgust as he allowed his gaze to slip to Jack. "I can see it in your eyes. They are filled with fire! They remind me of myself." The accent was thick, and his voice came out lazily. It was as though he was talking to a friend.

Jack's head snapped up at him. "I'm nothing like you!" he said, his voice quiet, dangerous even.

Emily flinched.

"Tell me what I want to know, spy. Why are you here? What are you looking for?"

Jack shook his head. Strength from an unknown source surged through him. It would serve him well.

"I'm not a spy. I'm a private contractor, hired to develop an extensive website for a company in Lahore. They sent me out here to help in one of their offices."

What?! Emily's head nearly popped around. That's not what he had told her. He was going to meet a friend, he had said. She bit down on her bottom lip.

What was he doing?

The outside door opened and light flooded into the room. Real, soft light that warmed the very center of her heart. She glanced over her shoulder and all the fuzzy feelings evaporated into terror.

They were dragging in a large collapsible table, like one of those massage tables. Three men set it up in the middle of the room. Some more brought in some extensive wire contraption hooked to several rusty batteries. She feared her heart would stop. Buckets of water were placed next to the table.

A scream made its way up her throat and she clamped her lips into a tight line. Jack's gaze rammed into hers. She couldn't read what exactly lay behind them, but she saw determination.

"Tell me again, what you are here to do?" the leader yelled.

He had settled back down into his cushions, after yelling instructions to his men. Jack steeled himself for what he knew was about to happen. Hopefully, they would start with him because he wasn't sure how he could stand by to watch them torture his traveling companion. But he saw it in the leader's eyes, in the way they kept bouncing in Emily's direction.

She was about to get a lesson she would never forget.

Jack clamped down his lips into a thin line. "How many times do I have to tell you? I work with computers! That's all I do." He turned to the leader, hoping to keep his attention. "I'm a boring kind of guy and a bit of a health nut, really. I go to the gym every day. I'm a vegetarian. I don't eat sweets. I swim three times a week in the ocean. I run five miles a day. I don't smoke or drink and I only date occasionally. That's it." His tone was conversational like he was discussing the weather.

Emily almost smiled at the flippant way he said it. She would have if their situation wasn't so hopeless and scary.

The butt of the rifle connected with his forehead and Jack blinked hard.

Wow, that hurt!

His vision blurred momentarily as blood from a fresh cut trickled into his eyes and he wiped it with his shoulder. The leader's face tightened with anger.

"You think this is funny?" he yelled at him, staying well away from him.

Jack would have loved to have had a repeat of last night. But unfortunately, his stomach was completely empty. Even he wasn't that good, to produce projectile vomiting on an empty stomach.

"*Y'Allah*!" the leader shouted again and pointed to Emily.

"No, wait!" Panic rose in Jack's voice. "What is it that I'm supposed to be doing here? What do you want to hear?"

"I want to hear the truth. That you are a spy. I want to know what you have come here to do!" the man screamed and pointed at the table with a wave of his hand.

"No!" Emily screamed, terror making her tremble so hard, her teeth chattered.

With every ounce of strength left inside her, Emily fought the hands that roughed her up as they shoved her toward the table. She glanced at Jack, whose face was set, eyes avoiding her. His Adam's apple bobbed up and down as they thrust her toward the table. His battered face shone with perspiration.

He's going to need stitches for that last blow. It's going to leave a-

She was about to be tortured and she thought about stitching up his forehead. Emily shook her head mentally. *She* was about to be in need of medical attention – if she made it through. Gritting her teeth and drawing on courage she didn't have, she made a decision.

I'm not going to make this easy. They'll have to knock me out first.

Emily ducked out of the grasp of her captor and attempted to make a run for it. She rammed into his side and sent him stumbling backward, to both of their surprise. Her stomach fluttered nervously when she dove at the door.

I made-

Her world went fuzzy when she took a blow to the head. In her semi-conscious state, she was lifted and carried back to the center of the room and flung onto the hard surface. The back of her head slammed into the unforgiving table and she gave a soft grunt.

"Okay, okay!" Jack yelled, straining against his own bounds. *I can't watch this! God, please...* "I'm a spy. I'm a spy." The men stopped tying Emily to the table and leaned closer – greedy expressions on their faces. "I-I came here to destroy your organization... and to take you all back to the States for trial against the American people... by myself." He swallowed hard. What was the point? Even if he told them the truth, they weren't going to stop.

Through the fog of coming out of her semi-dazed state, Emily heard amused chuckles from around the men in the room.

"That's very funny," the man behind Jack laughed. "Tell us more, spy."

They went back to securing Emily.

The leader slowly rose from his seat and walked toward her. His eyes roamed over her, making her stomach heave. If only she could do what Jack had done the night before. It would have given her such satisfaction to vomit all over him. He glared down at her and his eyes came to rest at her neck.

Her breath hitched. *He's going to slit my throat!* Panic, fear, horror all rushed through her body violently.

The old man grabbed her necklace. She had forgotten that she even wore it. It was a silver fish. Her mother had given it to her when she had graduated from medical school and it had never, ever left Emily's person. It was meant to be a reminder of how much God wanted to be a part of her life.

How had she let that slip her mind?

The man's eyes met hers and his lips turned into a snarl.

"You are a Christian?" The words were hurled at her and hit her in the gut, making her feel violated and dirty.

Emily met his eyes, undaunted. Her courage was in the cross of Christ. Her hope was in Him. She may lose her life in the next ten minutes or so. She may meet her Lord in a relatively short time. Much to her disbelief, she wasn't afraid anymore. She had made her peace with Him.

"Yes, I'm a Christian," she said and her voice was steady, sure.

The man snarled and yanked the silver chain off her neck. He threw it onto the dirt floor and stomped on it, grinding it into the ground.

"Oh, come on!" Jack shouted and struggled against the man holding him. "Was that totally necessary? Can't you leave her be? Take me instead!"

The leader motioned to his men and sank back down onto his cushion, as though he was ready to enjoy a show.

"No. Torture is so much more effective when it's done to someone you care about." A gruesome smile spread over his lined face. "Like your wife."

Jack let out a shuddering breath. How true! He wouldn't walk away from this job without the nightmares haunting him for a long time.

"Okay, okay." He lowered his face. "I have come to be part of your group and destroy you from within. I'm here to join you."

Again roaring laughter.

"You are very funny, *spy*. Very funny. It is almost like we have a court jester among us. Maybe you will be more entertaining than torture! You westerners with your wrong sense of honor." He laughed loudly and then stilled immediately. The sneer came back into his eyes. "No, perhaps torture is very effective in this case."

He nodded to his men, who stuffed a stained, vile smelling burlap sack over her head.

Jack was not going to watch this. He knew what was coming.

"Emily, don't fight. Don't panic!" he yelled before a fist connected with his chin, spinning him around from the blow.

The burlap sack was secured around her neck, smelling of stale vomit, causing her stomach to roll. She gagged and struggled against the ropes that held her. Water soaked through the pores of the sack, choking her as it filled her mouth. It just kept on coming and coming...

I'm going to drown!

She wasn't even in the water. She fought, panic setting in. Her lungs burned with lack of oxygen.

Please God, make it stop!

As soon as the thought came to her, the assault was over! She gasped at the air, stale and stinky, but at least she was breathing. She almost thanked Him when they started again.

She didn't know how much longer she could hold on.

Jack clenched his fists into tight balls. If only he could just...

Having to stand there and watch them almost drown Emily was the worst torture he had yet to endure. He prayed and prayed that they would stop. It seemed that they had no intention of doing so.

"Well, spy? What do you say?"

The leader rose in an agitated manner and stomped over to him. Jack would have loved to tell him exactly what he had to say for himself. With the business end of a rifle, like the one his guys were holding on him.

Jack lowered his eyelids. "I came to destroy your cell. I came to kill you and your men!" he growled softly.

A bit of truth. A lot of truth!

They laughed out loud. In fact, they threw they heads back in roaring laughter.

Oh, well. He tried.

If they didn't want to believe the truth, it was their mistake. Jack looked at Emily. She had stopped struggling and lay deathly still.

Please don't be dead, don't be dead!

"Tell me, spy, what I want to know!"

Jack ground his teeth.

"I pray to God that He would rid the world of murdering scum like you!"

A fist rammed into his side, right into his already broken ribs. Fire surged through him. He groaned in pain, real pain, and doubled over. They ripped the hood off Emily's head, pouring water all over the dirt floor which turned into a mud puddle. Her face was chalky white and still! There was no evidence of life and Jack gritted his teeth so hard he feared they'd shatter.

This one was on him.

It seemed like ages until her body convulsed and sent a jet of water spewing out of her mouth. Coughing, she weakly turned her face to the side to allow water mixed with bile to run out of her mouth and nose. Jack took in as deep a breath as he could without collapsing in pain. She made it through that.

She's stronger than I expected her to be. Thank you, Lord!

Emily focused on breathing in and out. It was something she would never take for granted again. As she lay panting, she allowed a thought to sink in. She had made it through torture! She almost cried out loud in relief but clamped her lips tightly together.

A look at Jack told her he was still with her. Even though his face was set and filled with worry, his eyes conveyed something else.

Was it pride?

Her wet hair clung to her face, threatening to suffocate her. Her shirt was soaked and clinging to her in a most immodest manner. The need to hide from the eyes of those around her added to her discomfort, but now was not the time for modesty.

She had made it through their torture. A very slow and tentative smile began to play on her lips. Maybe this wasn't so bad after all. The men pulled up the wire contraption and plugged it into the battery.

You've got to be kidding me!

She fought back a scream again as her eyes opened in panic. This time they gave her no warning once they connected parts of the batteries to her wet person. Heat and electricity sizzled through her, her body twisting and convulsing with the force of it.

A long, loud scream escaped from her lips.

“Enough!” Jack roared. The smell of burned flesh almost turned him into a madman as he fought against those who held him. “Take me! What kind of cowards are you? Take your hate out on me!”

Watching Emily convulse from the electricity that ripped through her, made him want to tear out everyone's throat. He spun around and rammed his elbow into the face of the man who was holding him, momentarily distracted by Emily's screams.

He was forced to the floor, a rifle pointed at his temple. A black hole filled his heart, hatred engulfed him. He was going to make sure that these men got what they deserved if it took him the rest of his life. The butt of the rifle connected with his temple and the world went dark.

They finally pulled her off the table and dumped her unconscious body back into the dark room. Then it was his turn to be tossed like garbage next to her. Fierce anger, hot as lava from a spewing volcano, flowed through him as he crawled over to her. Checking for a pulse, he exhaled hard when he found one. Then he gathered her carefully into his arms, aware of her injuries.

A deep, soul-shattering groan came from her lips.

“Hey, Emily,” he whispered into her ear. “You did really good.”

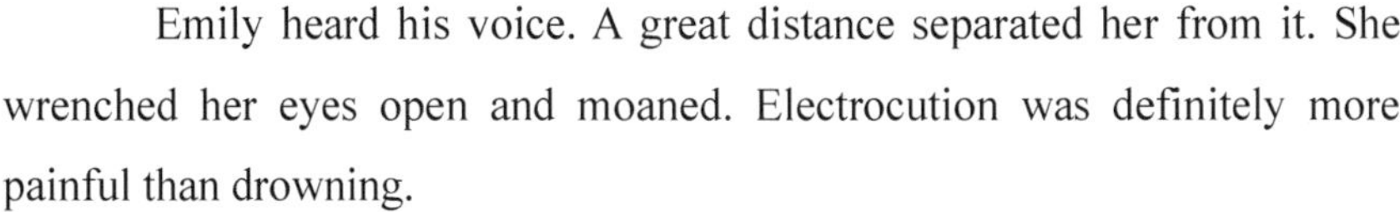

Emily heard his voice. A great distance separated her from it. She wrenched her eyes open and moaned. Electrocution was definitely more painful than drowning.

“Emily, listen to me,” he whispered. “The Lord is my shepherd.” He waited for a moment. “Come on, say it with me!”

Was he serious? Her head rolled back as darkness threatened to swallow her.

"No, come on. Emily. The Lord is my shepherd! Say it! Say it!" he hissed.

"The L... is.... shepherd," she managed to whisper. It took all her strength.

He softly smoothed back her sopping wet hair.

"I shall not want."

"I... not want."

It hurt to talk. It hurt to move. It even hurt to think.

"Good girl," he said softly. "He maketh me to lie down in green pastures: he leadeth me beside the still waters."

She groaned softly. This was way too hard. She couldn't go on. She gulped in a few shuddering breaths.

"Emily, say it!"

"He... me to lie... in green... leadeth me... still waters."

"He restoreth my soul."

Emily's eyes teared up. She shook her head. She was having trouble believing that one right now.

"Yes, He does, Emily. He is with you right now," Jack whispered softly as he gently touched her face. "Say it!"

"... restoreth my soul," she breathed.

Repeating the verse did give her strength and infused her with courage. She nodded slowly.

"He leadeth me in the paths of righteousness for his name's sake."

Her voice was stronger now, barely. "He leadeth me... paths of righteousness... his name's sake."

She nodded to herself. Yes, she felt it! He was leading her.

"Yea, though I walk through the valley of the shadow of death, I will fear no evil: for thou art with me. It's only a shadow, Emily. Only a shadow!"

She took a deep breath. "Yea, though I walk through … shadow of death, I will fear no evil. For thou are with me!"

"Thy rod and thy staff they comfort me." Jack reached down and took her hands. "Repeat it, Emily!"

"Thy rod and thy staff they comfort me."

Jack untied the ropes around her wrists. Her eyes opened wide in surprise.

"Thou preparest a table before me in the presence of mine enemies."

In the dark, she began to see Jack's face. It was as if he was someone completely different. She could discern his features as if the room had been lit by a thousand light bulbs.

He looked at the door, his face twisted into a snarl. Gone was the computer programmer she met a few days ago. There was something dangerous about him. He no longer looked terrified. And she had a feeling he was about to unleash the fury she saw written all over him.

Emily trembled and sat up painfully, ignoring the agonizing fire licking throughout her body.

"Thou anointest my head with oil, my cup runneth over. Repeat it, Emily."

She could almost feel that oil, soothing the burns all over her body.

"Thou anointest my head with oil, my cup runneth over!"

Jack sat back on his heels and inspected her in the darkness.

He lifted her chin, peering into her soul. "Surely goodness and mercy shall follow me all the days of my life: and I shall dwell in the house of the Lord forever!" He nodded.

She nodded back. "Surely goodness and mercy shall follow me all the days of my life: and I shall dwell in the house of the Lord forever! I got it!"

This man in front of her was no computer programmer.

What have I gotten myself into?

"Good," he whispered into her ear. "Are you ready to get out of here?"

Her breath hitched in her throat. She was about to say something but his hand covered her mouth gently.

"Can you walk?"

She rose unsteadily to her feet. Her legs were like rubber, her knees were shaking badly once she stood up. But she was standing!

"Then let's blow this popsicle stand!"

9

This was it! He was about to bring down death and destruction on these men because there was no way he was going to sit around while they tortured her again. She had made it through once. They were just going to keep going, and even escalate things. His respect for her had surged when she repeated the Psalm, her voice growing stronger and stronger. He didn't want her to have to go through any more pain.

"Follow my lead!" he hissed into her ear.

He banged at the door with his fists. "Help! I need help! My wife! She's... Help!"

They heard scuffling on the outside of the door. It was wrenched open and Jack grabbed the muzzle of the rifle that pointed into the room. He pulled it toward him, catching the man completely off guard. He struck him with his palm and rammed the flat of his hand into the guy's throat, crushing his windpipe.

He went down in a heap.

Jack grabbed Emily by the hand and hefted her weight, not exactly easy with a few broken ribs. Forcing himself to ignore the fire shooting through his torso, he pointed the end of the muzzle out. Nobody was in the larger room. He sprinted toward the outside, keeping his back toward the wall. Emily's body quaked, but she nodded when he glanced at her.

Three of the terrorists sat on a stone bench, right outside, smoking and laughing softly. They were discussing the torture they had just enjoyed. Disgust rising, he aimed the rifle and fired one bullet into each. They collapsed before they ever knew what hit them. Jack pulled Emily out the door, sprinting into the light. On the way out, he collected the ammunition off the dead guy's bodies. He would need it if they wanted to get out alive.

The path disappeared downhill steeply. Emily tripped over her own feet but Jack shifted to get a firmer grip on her. He wasn't leaving her behind now. He held his rifle ready as they ran and dove behind a rock outcropping just in time. Bullets sprayed small pebbles into his face. He returned fire. The men down the path hid behind small boulders to protect themselves. Emily pressed hard into the rock, her eyes wide and full of fear.

“It's okay, Emily. We'll get out of here.”

Bullets sprayed all around them again. He returned fire and ducked.

“Can you run?”

She nodded her head. She would die trying anyway.

“I want you to make it to those rocks over there.”

He pointed to another outcropping approximately one hundred feet to the right further down the path. She gathered her strength and gritted her teeth, flaring her nostrils in determination.

“You ready?”

She nodded. Emily wasn't going to waste the breath she didn't have to answer him.

“Go!”

She took off running. Bullets whizzed past her but she just kept on going. Her body screamed at her that it could not possibly take any more. She ignored it. She dove behind the rocks, covering her head. Rocks and small pebbles had embedded themselves into her skin all over her body. Her clothes were now completely tattered and torn.

Jack appeared next to her quickly, panting hard and rough. He growled as he looked at the men stacking up. It was time to call in the help. It was time to let someone else have some fun. He sprayed some bullets in the direction of the terrorists. Satisfaction seeped through him when one of them yelled out in pain. He touched his watch. A tinny voice commanded him to identify himself.

"This is Rattlesnake. I need assistance. Do you have my coordinates?"

Emily stared at him and snorted softly, shaking her head in disbelief. She was tempted to look around for the hidden camera of the reality TV show producers.

"*Affirmative, Rattlesnake. We have your position. You are a thousand yards from target. Do you want us to light it up?*" the detached female voice asked.

"Better do that pretty quick," he grunted as more rocks peppered his face.

"*Help is on its way. Will you be ready to be extracted in twenty minutes at the coordinates we are going to send you?*"

Jack noticed someone trying to sneak up on him. He pointed the gun and pulled the trigger. The man fell backward as the bullet hit him in the chest. Jack wiped the sweat mixed with blood from his own brow.

"Will try," he panted. "Send the coordinates now and be ready to transport plus one."

"*Roger. Incoming in five, Rattlesnake. Good to hear your voice.*"

Transmission cut off and Emily stared at him, again.

"You *are* a spy!" Her voice was filled with a mixture of awe and condemnation.

Jack grinned sheepishly and leaned against the rock.

"I would love to chat some more, but right now it would be in our best interest if we found a better shelter further away from here. We have a bomb coming our way in a couple of minutes."

"Of course," she mumbled, pressing the ball of her palm against her throbbing forehead. "Why not?"

He pulled her out from behind the rock outcroppings and ran, as fast as he possibly could down the hill, putting some distance between themselves and those pursuing them. The bullets didn't follow them. He took shelter behind another large bolder, hoping and praying that it was far enough away from what was about to fall out of the sky. He looked at his watch. In about thirty seconds he would know.

Emily tried to catch her breath. How had she managed to get entangled in this? It stood to reason that God was punishing her for her insatiable wanting. But this?!

The guy was a spy!

She pulled herself into a tiny ball behind the rock outcropping. A bomb was on its way to destroy the hut they had been held captive in! This was one *bombastic* nightmare! She heard a soft screeching noise above her and Jack dove on top of her.

Booom!

Heat and air swirled around them a few seconds later. The earth shifted underneath her and threw her several feet uphill from the boulder they had hidden behind. Her head was ringing from the noise and air percussion. Dirt, rocks and other debris rained down on her and she covered her head and face with her arms, curled into a tiny ball. Jack lay a few feet away and crawled over to cover her. A large rock crashed down where his head had just been.

Blood trickled out of his nose and he wiped his forearm at it. His shirt had been shredded. Emily lay on the ground, her mouth opening and closing, like a fish out of water. A thin layer of dirt covered her from head to toe.

"Are you okay?" he asked. His voice was thick and gravelly from the dirt and dust.

Her gaze locked onto his lips in an attempt to read what he was saying. The ringing and screeching in her ears almost tore her head in two.

"Emily! Are you all right?"

Slowly, he helped her into a sitting position. The world had turned into a giant roller coaster. Leaning over to the side, she heaved up bile. Jack held back her knotted hair and rubbed her back gently. Then she slumped back on the ground and lay still.

Finally, a soft wail came out of her mouth and tears sprang to her eyes and ran down her cheeks. Pulling a sharp rock out of her hair, she gingerly inspected her head and winced at several tender spots, where her head had met some rough treatment – and not just diving to the ground and having a bomb explode near her.

"Emily, are you hurt?"

Her eyes snapped to his. Concern stared back at her.

"Define hurt!" she groaned. "I just survived an air raid attack."

Jack grinned sheepishly. "Technically that was not an air raid. It was just a bomb. And I think it was a relatively tiny bomb. An air raid would have been a few more bombs, don't you agree?"

Emily opened her mouth, then closed it again. She had nothing!

Jack flopped back onto the ground and rolled onto his back. He rubbed his sore head, panted, and held his side. Pain seared through his torso, no doubt a result of their hasty and violent retreat.

"That was about as close as I ever want to get to one of those," he mused and grinned again. He turned his head to stare at Emily. That was one tough chick!

"Hey!" He touched her arm. Emily flinched. "You did really great back there. I'm impressed!"

Emily smiled for a split second, then it was as though someone had wiped that smile off real quick. She looked like something from a horror movie. Rocks and dirt stuck out of her hair. Tears had left clear lines down an extremely dirty face.

Her mocha eyes turned stormy as she brushed off the dirt from what was left of her tattered trousers.

"Well, thank you so much. That makes me feel so much better, *Jack*. I want to impress you, after all! And is Jack even your real name? What is it? Bob, Dave? Do you even know what it is?" She spewed the words out at him.

He scrambled onto his hands and knees, feeling the rocks dig into his skin. Poking his head around the smaller boulder they were hiding behind, he noticed that the men who had been pursuing them were nowhere to be seen. Not bad for a day's work. He gave her a sheepish grin and offered his hand.

"You got me there." He shrugged his shoulders, not at all sorry. "My name is Connor Williams. And yes, I do work with computers in my spare time and live in Texas."

She pursed her lips and put her hands on her hips. As her gaze traveled over him, she exhaled slowly. "That's a good thing, then. You're not a Jack. And Russel..." Her lips flattened. "It didn't fit you. Is there anything else you want to tell me? Confess, so to say?"

Connor laughed and glanced around nervously. “I'd love to tell you all about it, but we really have to scram. In a few minutes, these hills are going to be crawling with very ticked-off terrorists. And I may be a good shot, but I don't want to measure my ability against the numbers.”

Mumbling to herself as she continued to dust herself off, she swayed slightly. Connor was about to reach out to her when she slapped his hand away.

“No, thank you. I'm fine.” Her chin lifted defiantly. “Now, if you can direct me to where I might find transportation to the orphanage, I would be most obliged.”

Connor laughed softly and brushed a hand carefully over his face.

“I'm afraid you're going to have to deal with me for some time more. I insist that you come with me to catch the helicopter ride out of here to be debriefed.”

He glanced at his watch, suddenly doubting they would make it to the rendezvous in enough time.

Emily made a face, her eyes narrowing and filling with fire.

“I'd rather not. I was expected at the mission days ago! There's always a bus that stops to pick up straggling travelers, right? I'll just make my way to the road if I can find it.” Her attempt at looking dignified failed as she took a step away, tripped on a rock and stumbled, catching herself before she fell.

“Listen, Emily. I'm really sorry you were part of this. Why do you think I suggested a private car? I didn't want you anywhere near this. I knew what I was walking into. You didn't.” His voice was soft and gentle, kind.

That tone was her undoing. Tears sprang to her eyes again and her knees gave out. As she sank into the dirt, she covered her face with her hands.

"Why did this have to happen to me?" she whispered.

10

Connor didn't have time to give her a moment. They had a lot of distance to cover and as he turned his head, the sound of irate voices bounced off the rocks surrounding them.

"I'd love to contemplate your problem, Emily, but we need to get hiking. We have an army of people coming toward us and I don't think they are in a more hospitable mood than before. I don't want another bomb dropped on my head, do you?" He had meant it as an encouragement, but Emily just moaned and rolled into a tight ball. "Up you go."

He reached down and hoisted her to her feet, gritting his teeth against the pain in his chest. She stumbled after him, mutely, her vision a complete blur. Her hand was tightly clasped in Connors which prevented her from falling flat on her face several times as she struggled with accepting the disaster she found herself in.

This isn't real! I'm having one of those dreams again, like when I fall asleep after reading an intense book. Come to think of it, I was reading one on my way here.

That was entirely more plausible than her being entangled in a real scenario that had her walking next to a real life-

"And to answer your unspoken question, no," Connor interrupted her thoughts, his eyes crinkling in the corners. "I'm not a spy. The name I go by nowadays is operative, agent. A spy is too...." He pulled a disgusted face. "I am a Christian."

"You're not real," Emily whispered, keeping her eyes peeled on the ground in front of her. "You're a figment of my overactive imagination."

Connor laughed and ducked behind another outcropping of rocks. A group of rough looking men was coming up the trail.

Oh, man!

A shot of adrenaline rushed through him when he recognized the man yelling at everyone else. How had he missed him?

His mission parameter had changed the moment Emily stepped onto the bus. The terrorist coming their way, screaming at everyone in sight, was his ultimate objective. He was the reason he had come to Pakistan. He was on the agency's watch list and Connor was charged with his removal.

But Emily-

She looked like she could barely stand up on her own. She wasn't in any better shape then he was. Even if they started hiking now, without finishing the objective, they were likely to miss the chopper.

He opted for finishing what was set before him.

"Emily," he whispered, his blood beginning to boil as the group of men followed their irate leader – coming ever closer to them. "Stay here. I need to check this out. Don't go anywhere!"

She turned to him, her eyes widening in fear before she caught herself.

"You have to be kidding me!" she hissed.

"Just don't move," he shot back hurriedly and scurried from one rock outcropping to the next.

Her breath stuck in her throat when she saw Connor crouch down and run closer. Pressing her lips into a flat line, she sprinted after him.

"You can't leave me here!" she humphed ever so softly and Connor would have laughed if they hadn't been so close to the enemy.

"Shhh!"

The group was standing around the smoking pile of rubble that used to be the hut. The men shouted angrily and pointed to the sky. The leader pointed to the men and motioned for them to take action. They started to heave at the debris. Shouts sounded when they found the bodies of the men caught in the bomb blast.

Apparently, the lead terrorist was more than put off. He yelled at the remaining men to scatter, to find him and Emily. Instantly, he knew that it was time to scamper.

They couldn't be caught or this would be the end of them.

Live and fight another day.

He tugged on her arm and pointed away from the camp – uphill. The path was rocky and rough going. But there were enough places to hide them from view. Urgency drove him to run faster but he slowed when he heard Emily stumble and cry out softly.

Emily staggered numbly and silently along next to him. She still hoped that any moment now she'd wake up. Not that she didn't enjoy the company. But that was not how she was thinking anymore.

Father God. She hadn't addressed Him in such intimate fashion for a *long* time. She huffed out a breath before she continued, *Thank You for being with us, giving me something to focus on to get me past my terror. If this is real, and I'm beginning to think that it is, I'm glad You never left me. I'm sorry for trying to hide and run from You. I guess I should have known I never could outrun You. I suppose it's time to...*

Her thoughts slammed to a halt as her breath caught.

This next part was going to hurt!

And I know You have plans and dreams for me. I suppose I can let go of my own desires.

She felt better immediately, except for the tightness in her gut that informed her that perhaps letting go of her dreams would require some work of obedience on her part. And that was what Emily was afraid of.

She planted her feet on the ground, refusing to move another inch. She may have given God her dreams, but that didn't mean she wanted to wander aimlessly around Pakistan for the rest of her life with a guy who wasn't who he claimed to be.

"How do you know we're going the right direction?" she asked, her ire up because she was sore and tired and wanted a long, hot bath. She looked him over, challenging him to answer.

He gave her a thin, pained smile. "I know where I'm going."

She shook her head and leaned over her knees to catch her breath.

Connor poked her shoulder before looking behind him and urging, "We've gotta keep going, Emily."

They walked silently for what seemed like hours. Emily was blind to the wild beauty around her, only focusing on taking one step at a time. When her foot snagged on the uneven ground, she just rolled to absorb the shock of her fall and came to rest on her back. She lay gaping, staring at the brilliantly purple and red sky above the towering mountain range.

"Okay, let's take a break," Connor panted and groaned when he sat down beside her, his knees tucked carefully to his chest. His face was pale and bruised, covered with dirt and mud, and he held his arm stiffly against his side.

He stared at the sky when a soft *bing* sounded from his watch. Surprised, he glanced at it. Then his face cracked into a mischievous grin, and he nudged Emily softly.

"Look at this, I've walked my ten thousand steps today."

She gave him the most expressionless look she could muster, but couldn't help the corners of her lips twitching into a smile. Wordlessly, she closed her eyes and bit back the soft giggle that threatened to escape.

After catching her breath and regaining some of her strength, she lifted her head and struggled to sit up.

"Let me take another look at that." She pointed to his side.

Connor cocked his head. She had just gone through a terrible, terrifying ordeal and she wanted to look at his injury when she was probably hurting just as bad as he was. He swallowed his pride and painfully lifted his shirt.

Emily hissed when she saw his bruised battered ribcage.

"If you were my patient, and you are in a sense, I'd send you off to bed for a few days," she tsked. "How are you even functioning?" she asked and gently adjusted the makeshift bandage.

The world began to spin around him and Connor held his breath, trying to focus on anything other than the pain. Her fingers, for instance. Her touch was soft, and yet fire raced through his torso at her gentle administration.

Drawing in a few steadying breaths as she finished, he took stock of where they were. This area was familiar to him and he was coming to the conclusion that they were walking too slowly. Exhaustion and pain drained his strength before he could stop it.

Emily had rolled onto her side, her head resting on her arms, her eyes closed.

"We aren't going to make it to the chopper," he mumbled. "Let's see if we can't get them to come to us."

He touched his watch again and quickly brought the detached voice up to speed.

"Copy that. That is a negative on finding another ex-fill point near you. The mountains around you make it difficult and you are too far in country."

Connor stared at the darkening sky. That meant the cavalry was not coming to get him. He let out his breath slowly, careful not to jostle his aching ribs.

"Why, thank you so much. I feel the love," he said flippantly.

"Command out," the voice said tersely and the transmission cut out.

"They aren't coming to help you?" Emily asked, eyes filling with tears again.

"Nope," he drawled. "We're on our own."

Emily swallowed the groan. What else could go wrong? The cavalry was not coming. They were lost in the foothills of the Himalaya mountains...

She shuddered. People died out here!

There were wild animals in the mountains that would love to feast on them! And then there was the cold in the night. They didn't even have food or water! How were they going to make it back to civilization?

Connor touched her shoulder gently.

"It's going to be okay. Can you believe that?"

She sniffed and lifted her face to his. His gaze was sincere. And yet-

"You lied about what you do for a living, gave me an alias for a name, dropped a bomb on my head, and you're asking me to believe that we'll be okay. I need a bit more to go on."

Connor swallowed a yawn. "You can trust me."

If she wasn't so exhausted she would have laughed and told him what he could do with his trust.

But opening her mouth and forming the words seemed beyond the strength she had. As the sky turned purple and red with the sun disappearing behind the towering mountains, which were now bathed in dark shadows, and the air became crisp, Emily shivered and closed her eyes.

We're going to freeze tonight.

Her mind snagged on the pictures of the climbers on Mt. Everest, who didn't make it back down after one disaster after another. Sleep tugged hard at her and she succumbed to it gladly.

Is that how they felt? They didn't care if they lived or died.

Connor snapped awake at the sound of something approaching through the twilight.

Fool! he cursed himself and snatched up the pilfered rifle, aiming it in the direction of the sound. A hare, lean and skittish, dashed into the encroaching darkness, and he slowly, painfully, exhaled.

Beside him, Emily shot up, her eyes unfocused and wild. He reached out to assure her.

"It was just a rabbit, Emily," he said soothingly.

She exhaled and the crazy, lost look disappeared.

"How do you know? Do you have a GPS in your belt?" Her voice sounded gravelly and yet he didn't miss the challenge.

He laughed. She still hadn't lost her mettle.

"A GPS? In my belt? No, I don't happen to have a GPS in my belt. But that would be pretty cool. I do have a GPS on the watch," he grinned.

"Now I've seen everything."

"This is actually old technology," Connor laughed. "We've just tweaked it to fit our purposes. If you want a watch, I can put in a good word."

"Ya know," she said wearily and leaned against the rock. "I'm good. I'll keep the phone I got."

"I don't need a GPS. I know where we are."

Emily's eyebrows shot up. "Really? Good for you. How far to Murree?"

Connor squinted at the surroundings and nibbled on his bottom lip before he managed to say, "About a day's hike. But we aren't going there."

He pushed himself up. He looked at his tattered clothes.

"Come on. I know a place we can find food and shelter." He took a sniff of himself. "And a bath. This one is free of terrorists, I hope," he added quietly.

"Are we there yet?"

Connor glared at her as she repeated her question for the fifth time.

In the small beam of light coming from his watch, Emily stumbled over a piece of rubble on the ground, catching herself just before she landed flat on her face. They had walked silently for what seemed like days. Jack... Connor had set a brisk pace, draining all her strength out of her legs.

And yet, she was still walking, scrambling to keep up with him.

"We're almost there," he murmured for the tenth time and Emily gave him a disgusted look.

The way he walked, the way he held himself so stiffly, Emily knew he was hurting even more than she. It was amazing that she was unable to feel any of the physical effects of her torture at this moment.

Once they rested... Emily knew that the pain would be excruciating and she was dreading it.

Connor took in a painful breath and let it out slowly as the dark landscape became more and more familiar. It had been fifteen years since he had set foot in these parts and yet, he still recognized it as if he had run through the hills yesterday.

Fifteen years!

They paused at a crossroads and he turned to his silent companion. His respect for her had gone up every hour she stumbled next to him.

The path he was about to take was steep and it went uphill. As Emily's gaze followed his, a tiny whimper escaped. A village, with dark silent homes on either side of the dirt road, spread out in the mountain above them.

"Maybe you should stay here," he said.

Emily's face did something he couldn't quite determine. She shook her head and lifted her chin, defiantly.

"Are you kidding me? I've tagged along all evening. Now you're telling me to stay? I don't think so."

She swatted a snarled piece of hair out of her face, the move meant to show her determination not to be left behind.

Connor gritted his teeth. "Okay. Let's go. Just-" He turned to her and let out a sharp huff.

Emily stared at him and planted her feet.

"Just what?" Her eyes widened, suddenly frightened. "Are there more terrorists here?"

"No, just..." He sighed again. He never mixed work with his personal life. "Just let me do the talking, okay?"

The hike up the hill was more difficult than he had anticipated. But then again, the last time he had done this, he didn't have a few broken ribs and hadn't spent the day escaping terrorists. His feet slipped on gravel making him twist to catch his balance. A soft grunt of pain escaped.

Emily's hand touched his arm.

"Can we... just stop... here?"

She pointed at one of the many dark structures that lined both sides of the path. Each home was surrounded by a wall, approximately chin high. No light came from the houses.

Did anyone even live here? Had they stumbled onto a ghost-town? Emily shivered when she thought of what might be going on behind the walls.

Connor shook his head. "No," he replied sharply.

The house he was looking for, the one he knew so well, was at the top of the hill, overlooking the valley below. His step faltered. Was he making a mistake, showing up all battered and wounded on the front step?

"Come on."

He wrapped an arm tightly around her waist and almost hoisted her weight. Emily stiffened and slapped his shoulder.

"Just put me down! You can barely stand up yourself. If you can make it, so can I!" Determination snaked past the dirt and grime on her face.

Connor nodded, almost thankful. He really didn't have it in him to carry her up the hill. But he would have given it a really good try.

"We're almost there. See that house up there?"

The building he pointed at was indistinguishable from those around it.

"What is that house? Is it a safe house of some sort for you spy-guys?" Emily panted as she struggled to keep pace with him.

"It is for this spy," he grimaced.

Leaning wearily against the foreboding-looking wall, he took a moment to catch his breath.

"How do I look?" he asked, suddenly somewhat anxiously.

Emily did a double take, then laughed. "Well, you have a bit of dirt right here."

She took the sleeve of her tunic, which was just as dirty and torn as his own, and licked it. Then she gently wiped it across his cheek. The one place where he was not tender.

Spunk galore and a sense of humor!

11

Clearing his throat carefully, he opened the ornate gate and walked through a dark yard to the front door. The doors in these parts were the most decorative part of the normally stark, bleak houses. Connor drew in another shuddering breath and knocked. It seemed like forever until the heavy wooden door creaked open.

An old man with a long gray beard peered at him, his eyes opening in fear and worry. Connor smiled at the smaller man in front of him. A memory of a long time ago, when he was a child running wild in these mountains, came rushing over him.

"*Aasalam-o-Alaikum, Nana.*"

The man's jaw dropped and he stared at him.

"*Wa'alaikum... Salaam,*" he said, taking a cautious step back as he continued to examine Connor.

He's going to slam the door in my face! Perhaps I shouldn't have called him grandfather yet. Let him warm up to the idea of seeing me like this.

The old man's face became more wrinkled and worry spread throughout until he gave him another long stare. His face lit up and he laughed.

"Connor? *Nawasa?*"

Connor let out the pent-up breath he had been holding and nodded. The old man opened his arms to him and he stepped toward him, like a child in need of comfort. Strong wiry hands touched his shoulders, prodded his sore, battered face.

Dark eyes searched him. “You have been in a fight again, no? When will you ever learn?” he asked in Pakistani.

His grandfather's matter-of-fact tone made him smile. Sweat, dirt and dried blood cracked on his face, and all the man could assume that he had been in a fight.

“You got a little older since the last time I saw you.”

“And you have shrunk, Nana,” Connor smirked.

The old man snorted.

“Who is that?” he pointed at Emily.

Connor lowered his head. He pondered about how to best answer his grandfather. “She's a friend, Nana.”

“Ah.” The tired eyes sparkled in mischief. “A friend!” He chuckled to himself and shuffled into the interior of the house. When they didn't follow him, he turned and waved a hand.

“Well, don't just stand there all night. Come in,” he said in perfect English. “Before you fall down.”

Emily stared at the back of the man in front of her. He obviously knew Connor well! She would have to be blind to miss the resemblance that gave her the greatest hint that they were family.

What else does he have up his sleeve?

Even though she felt the twinge of irritation squirrel through her, she couldn't help but admire Connor.

More surprise hit her when she entered the main house. She had expected shabby old furniture, a lot like the shack they had just been holed up in. She didn't expect to find this house, with its indistinguishable exterior, to be furnished so extensively and so beautifully.

A large TV sat on a recessed oak shelf. Was she just seeing things? Expensive Berber carpets covered the beautiful hardwood floor.

The floor was not dirt!

An off-white leather couch sat in the sprawling living room. Large windows faced a courtyard, that was now bathed in darkness.

The place was gorgeous.

Recessed lights illuminated the room softly. The pale adobe walls were decorated with pictures of family and exotic places around the world. A long, rectangular glass coffee table sat in the middle of the floor surrounded by the couch and matching leather chairs.

This was not what Emily had expected.

A woman, dressed in a beautiful violet sari appeared in the door. She stared at them for a moment, then her eyes lit up. She gathered Connor into a soft, loving embrace.

"Connor!" The woman's eyes misted over for a second, then she blinked and sniffed. "You look terrible, Nawasa," she said, her English accented but very precise.

"Nani," Connor said softly and touched her gray hair. "You look beautiful, as always. You haven't aged a day."

The woman laughed softly. "Ah, you were always a charmer and such a good liar. Am I right, Inderpal?" She turned her head to her husband, who shuffled toward the living room couch. The man nodded and stared at the two of them.

"And you, dear grandson, look like you have had a very terrible day." She touched his forehead gently. "Did you pick a fight again?"

He laughed, wincing painfully as he became aware of the aches and pains everywhere.

I'm getting too old for this.

He ground his molars to bite back a groan.

"Never, Nani. The fight always picks me. You know that!" His eyes twinkled and the woman shook her head, muttering to herself.

Grandson! Of course.

Swallowing a laugh, Emily gave Connor a quick once-over. There was that resemblance between him and his grandfather. The cut of the face, the deep-set eyes. Connor's hair was thick and black.

"I hope you don't mind if we stay here for the night? We were in the area," he said, a charming smile spreading on his face.

Standing still with nobody chasing them or dropping bombs on their heads, Emily began to feel all the aches of the past days. She felt as though she had practically drowned, been electrocuted, and then almost blown up.

Oh, right. I have been through all that.

The heroine in her spy novels never complained that they hurt, so she was not about to mention it.

Both his grandparent's looked at each other and shook their head.

"You were in the area?" his grandmother said and her voice picked up a notch. Her eyebrows rose and fell. "Were you going to stop by and visit with your family?"

"I had the intention," he said slyly, looking like a little boy with his hand caught in a cookie jar. "I just ran into some problems."

They grunted at him.

"And who is this lovely, yet filthy young woman?" his grandmother asked and nodded kindly toward Emily.

It made her feel warm and welcome.

"This is Emily Martins. She's a doctor." Connor frowned at her when he noticed that she was swaying slightly. "Who is in some serious need of food and drink. Just like your poor battered grandson."

He flashed his most charming smile at his grandmother, which used to work wonders. It would have done so today if his face hadn't looked so grotesquely beaten up.

"You poor dear," his grandmother purred and put her arm protectively around Emily. "A bath for you first and then some much-needed food. I think I have an outfit that will fit you, you poor thing."

She led her down a narrow hall to a door. "And don't you sit on that couch, Connor Williams. Inderpal, get the boy something to sit on!" she shouted over her shoulder. "Before he falls down!"

The water felt wonderful. It soothed some of the aches in her muscles, although the pain from her burns was another story. Now that she was resting, it felt as though her body was on fire. It took a great amount of willpower not to break down in tears at the anguish she was experiencing. It was as if someone had put a torch to her skin and lit it.

Once out of the tub, Emily gripped the side of the porcelain sink so hard she was afraid she'd break it. Taking inventory of her injuries was frightening. Her face was covered in one massive bruise, with cuts on her cheeks and chin. Burn marks covered her body. Groaning, she gingerly dried herself.

What if...

Had she really survived being kidnapped? Had all that torture and pain been real? Had a bomb really exploded within a mile of her, taking out everything in its path?

Oh, yes!

This was real and not the product of her over-imaginative mind.

All she used to be, a spoiled brat living in a spoiled society, was gone.

Was she happy?

How could she be after all she had just endured?

It could have been worse! She could have been maimed, raped, or beaten to death. God had protected, provided, and was guiding her. She just hoped that she was not so stubborn in the future and that more trials could be avoided.

As if!

Life was one big trial, always either drawing her nearer or pulling her farther from God. She decided that she wanted to be drawn near.

She was done running!

As she lifted the loosely fitting blouse and pants Connor's grandmother had given her, everything hurt.

Now *there* was an interesting turn of events! Who'd have thought that he was half Pakistani, had relatives here in the mountain, and... She looked into the mirror again, studying herself hard.

And...

There was always that. What were the chances that she, an ordinary doctor from Connecticut, would run into an agent?

Slim to none. It did sound like one of her novels.

At least you're alive, Emily. If it hadn't been for him, you might not be here.

There was no doubt in her mind that God had provided for her protection and the more she thought about it, the more she felt like singing.

Let's just keep that inside, shall we? If I start to sing, I may just wake the neighbors and Connor will run as far away as possible.

That thought, the one with Connor running away, didn't sit well with her and she ignored it.

"How's it going in there, dear. Are you okay?"

The soft knock and tender voice drew her out of her musing and she opened the door to find Connor's grandmother standing on the other side. The older woman gave a soft hiss and her eyes welled up with tears, which she quickly blinked away.

"Come, I've prepared some food for you."

As they approached the living room, voices drifted toward them. It sounded so safe that Emily was tempted to just lean against the wall and listen. It was then that her stomach made it known to her that it hadn't had digested food in quite some time.

When the men turned their heads, an expression rushed through Connor's face before he was able to check it. Her breath hitched at the intense gaze of the blue eyes.

Connor's grandmother extended a hand toward the table. "Come and eat. It looks like my grandson has left you some food. He ate like he hasn't eaten in days."

"That's because I haven't," Connor whined tiredly and stuffed another piece of fruit into his mouth. He dipped his bread into hummus, a contented look on his dirty, battered face.

"It's your turn to rinse off the mountain." His grandmother pointed toward the bathroom, her nose crinkling in disgust.

Emily sank into the couch, swallowing a pain-filled groan.

"I'll be back," Connor winked. "Grandfather, do you have some clothes I can borrow?" He pointed at his clothing, hanging in shreds.

His grandmother pursed her lips, considering her much taller grandson.

"I'll ring your cousin. He's about your height."

"I'm sure they've already retired for the night," her husband dared to point out. His wife graced him with a glance, and he obediently walked down the hall to where the phone was located.

While they decided how to resolve the clothes issue, Connor tried to rise out of the soft sofa. As he attempted it, his body reminded him of what he had gone through. A burning sensation exploded in his chest.

I'm getting too old to be dodging bullets and punching bad guys.

A smirk twitched the corners of his mouth.

Maybe the punching isn't that bad, but receiving the punch is becoming too painful.

At another attempt to rise, his legs refused to support his weight. Drawing in a ragged breath, he remained where he was. His eyes wandered to where Emily was sitting, enjoying the feast his grandmother had spread out before them.

She cleaned up real good! Too good, in fact.

Connor shook his head mentally, realizing that he was in terrible need of sleep. And after that, he needed to take care of the problem he had left behind. Allowing the terrorists to live had been a terrible mistake, one he would have to remedy as soon as he was able to. And after he had taken care of that, he'd get back to reality and forget all about this mission – and Emily.

When he finally managed to find the strength to make it to the bathroom, a flooding of good memories overwhelmed him and he leaned wearily against the door.

In his mind, he saw his former child-self and his father laughing as they sanded and stained the wood to build this door. The inside of the room hadn't changed. The claw-foot tub was still the same. The walls had been decorated with extensive stencil designs, courtesy of his mother and sister. He touched one of the faded flowers, remembering the laughter that rang through these walls.

Good times.

Soaking in the tub helped but he found it almost impossible to get out.

I could just stay in here, he thought as exhaustion gripped him.

When he finally gathered his strength to rise, he found that every touch hurt. Flinching as he examined himself in the mirror, Connor realized that he had received more than his fair share of blows. His face was black and blue and his chest could be considered one massive bruise

He painfully dressed in the loose tunic and pants his grandfather had procured from his cousin, thanking God once again for preserving his life. He did this after every mission whether it was successful or not.

He was alive and so was Emily. It could have gone very differently.

Combing his hair, hoping to look more presentable for his grandparents, his mind was already calculating what it would take to get rid of the evil that lurked in these mountains – that had spread like a disease through these good, honest people.

To accomplish that, he would need firepower. Feeling uncharacteristically naked without his personal firearm, Connor contemplated asking his cousin for help.

Smirking, he recalled all the trouble he and Rabeel had gotten into as kids. Since then, Rabeel had served in the Pakistani army, gaining the rank of colonel. Perhaps tomorrow they could begin making plans.

After all, his cousin lived in the area. He was an asset. Besides, it would be like old times.

But tonight, I won't be able to do anything except maybe make it back to the living room, he decided as he stiffly walked toward the living room.

"That's so much better," his grandmother smiled approvingly as he stepped, painfully, into the soft light.

He felt like he had come home!

Settling onto the couch next to his grandfather, who offered him a cup of tea, Connor nodded.

"*Shukriya*," he said.

"It's good to hear that you haven't forgotten your mother's tongue," the old man said.

"Never, Nana. It's just as much a part of me as my blood."

Emily's head weighed about as much as a train wagon and her eyelids drooped, but when Connor sat down she could sense his pain.

She cleared her throat. "Excuse me, but before my brain shuts down completely from all this wonderful food and warmth, I need to tend to Ja... er... Connor's injuries. Do you have bandages I could use? We'll need some pain medicine as well if you have them." Secretly, she hoped they would because she wasn't going to be able to sleep tonight with the fire ripping through her.

"I don't need any *tending,*" he bristled indignantly. "I'm fine."

"Uh-huh," she said and looked at him sharply. "Who's the doctor? When we were out there with terrorists kidnapping us, did I tell you how to do your job? Did I get in the way?"

Connor stared at her.

"Uh..." *Yeah!* "You're not serious, right?"

Emily ignored him, turning her full attention to his grandmother.

Both his grandparents snorted softly, then his grandmother got up swiftly and mumbled something about finding the first aid kit. His grandfather grabbed the plates and leftover dinner and shot out of the room as though the couch had burst into flames.

"Well?" Emily stared at him, her hands propped on her hips.

"Well, what?" he huffed, turning his face to hide his smile. "And actually you did get in the way. Big time!"

Emily stared at him, her mouth gaping open. "Exactly how did I do that?" Her face, the part that wasn't covered in a bruise, turned red as she recalled her blunder. "Don't answer that. That doesn't negate the fact that I am a doctor. So... Where would you like me to do this?"

"I have a choice?" he growled. "Are you always this pushy with your patients?"

Her eyes narrowed dangerously. "They usually get a lollipop if they behave, but you won't get one from me."

12

He trailed her back to the bathroom, every step agony. He would have preferred to stay on the couch and just fall asleep where he was, but Emily had a very persistent, borderline nagging way of keeping after him.

After his grandmother had come back with the first aid kit, Emily had pointed silently down the hall toward the bathroom. He heaved himself off the couch, ignoring the multiple aches and stabbing pain.

"I know, this hurts you a lot more than it hurts me!" she said, her voice kind and gentle; professional. "Just suck it up, Mr. Spyman!"

He breathed a laugh and regretted it. "Are you accusing me of being a sissy?"

She shook her head, giving him an appraising once-over. "No, those are your words! I know you aren't. Anyone who can do what you just did and walk away from it alive is not a pansy. But now you're being a baby."

Fine! She wasn't going to hear another grunt or moan out of him!

When they had somehow reached the bathroom, exhaustion crept into every pore of his body. He wasn't sure if he could even stand, let alone weather the painful examination.

"All right, let me see the damage."

She gently pulled up on his shirt.

Connor put his hand over hers, stopping her. He shook his head.

"Nope, I got it. I wrapped it up again after my bath. You can tend to the cuts on my face." There was no way he was going to bear his chest, so to speak, in this almost claustrophobic space.

Emily propped her hands on her hips and took on a menacing stance. "Are you still arguing with me? Did I tell you how to do your spy stuff? Now are you going to take the shirt off or am I?" Her eyes conveyed that she wasn't joking.

Connor painfully ground his teeth again and reluctantly pulled off his borrowed tunic.

Now it was Emily's turn to draw in a sharp breath. She covered her mouth with her hands quickly. The bruise spread out from underneath the bandage.

"I'm so sorry. That must be painful."

"Just get on with it," he growled through gritted teeth.

Expertly, with nimble, tender fingers, she applied a clean bandage, and he was able to breathe easier again.

"You know, you should probably have some X-rays done on that chest," she said softly as he slowly replaced his tunic.

"Why?"

"Just in case you punctured a lung. I don't hear a rattle, but it would put my mind at ease," she replied. She turned to wash her hands and hid her face, gathering her thoughts.

How had he managed to hike all this way without passing out? She recalled that he had even shouldered her exhausted self a few times along the way.

Connor's eyes darkened, focusing on her. "Don't mention this to anyone. And if my lung is punctured, hey. You're the doctor." His eyes twinkled mischievously.

Suddenly it was as if the room had shrunk to the size of a pea. Feeling as if the air had been sucked out of her lungs, she backed away from him only to bump into the linen cabinet.

"What's the matter?" Connor asked, almost tauntingly.

Quivers rippled through Emily as she tried not to focus on his keen gaze on her.

She yawned big, fearing that her jaw would dislocate in the act.

"I'm... just really, really tired. And I need to get to the orphanage. Is there any way you can get me there tomorrow?"

"Of course. What kind of a *spy* would I be if I let the damsel in distress walk all over creation to get to her destination?" he taunted and earned himself a glare.

"I'm not a damsel in distress."

"Whatever you say," he snickered with a bow. "Let's see where my grandmother can put us up."

"Of course, I have a room for both of you. Connor, your old room will do. Although the bed may just be a bit too short. You were a lot smaller when you were twelve. And Emily, you may stay in Connor's parents' old room," she said when Connor asked about sleeping arrangements. "I assume that is acceptable to you?" Her eyes searched her grandson's face.

"More than acceptable, Nani. Thank you. *Shabb bakhair,*" he said and kissed her wrinkled cheek.

She swatted his shoulder gently and he bit back a groan. Even a love tap was too much for his aching body.

"Good night to you too, Connor. I'm so happy to see you, in person and not just on the computer. Emily, sweet dreams."

Where are they keeping their computer?!?!

Emily almost giggled at that thought.

She followed Connor to the last room at the end of the hallway. Connor hesitated before he opened the door, making it look like it weighed a thousand pounds. He let her precede him into the room and stood on the threshold – as if he dreaded to enter.

The walls were painted in an eggshell purple. A four-poster bed, made of maple, sat in the middle with two nightstands on either side. Pictures of a large family stood on one and an old-fashioned alarm clock on the other. A sizable maple dresser and a vanity stood along one inner wall. The chair to the vanity was antique, as was the vanity itself. On it were delicate bottles of perfume, brushes, and combs, as well as an assortment of makeup. An intricately carved hope chest stood at the foot of the bed. A sliding glass door led to a courtyard, now dark and mysterious.

It seemed that all his strength had finally been sucked out of him. Connor just couldn't enter the room, in which nothing much had changed. He could almost feel his parents, hear their laughter. His father's deep voice seemed to resonate off the walls. He shook his head to dislodge the ghostly images.

Focus! Get through this night somehow, talk to Rabeel and finish this mission.

When Emily moved, he forced a smile onto his face.

"So, you'll be comfortable here. This bed is the bomb! Well, pardon me," he grinned.

She laughed softly. "I hope not! I don't want to *sleep* on a bomb. Too many flying around my head in the last couple of days."

Connor turned around and paused. "Hey, listen. You did great out there. I don't know many people who would have been so courageous and strong. You managed to impress the dickens out of this spook. If the doctor gig doesn't work out for you, give me a shout. We could use you."

Somehow it felt as if he had placed a crown on her head and named her queen. A slight giggle escaped and she forced her lips into a tight line.

"Since we're talking about it, thank you for what you said back there at that place. You reminded me that God was with me. I needed that. I was not going to make it, you know."

"Yeah, well. Don't underestimate your strength," Connor said softly and tapped the door frame. It was time to go. "We both needed it at that time! *Shabb bakhair*, Emily. Sleep tight."

"Connor," Emily called just before the door closed.

When he turned around, she was illuminated by the soft lighting of the lamp on one of the nightstands, making her look nearly angelic.

"Yeah?"

"Thanks for bringing me here. This is really, really nice."

Connor grunted and closed the door, leaning against it to steady himself. He got the impression that this mission would leave him changed and somehow it scared him more than the thought of hunting down the leader of the cell.

13

A blood-curdling scream woke him out of his sporadic slumber. He shot up in bed, forcing his vision to focus on the pitch black around him. When his hand automatically groped for his handgun under his pillow, his breath caught in alarm when his fingers weren't able to touch the cold steel because it wasn't there. Then he remembered.

He wasn't anywhere near home!

He was in the mountains, with his grandparents. And Emily was screaming! He shot out of bed and almost fell headlong as he tripped in an attempt to stuff his legs into his pants.

He heard footsteps outside his door and ripped it open. His grandparents, eyes wide in fright, stood in the beam of their flashlight. The power usually shut off around ten, and the solar cells his father had installed were old now, leaving the house pitch black.

"Get back," he hissed and shot past them.

He quietly tiptoed up to the bedroom door when another scream rippled through the silence.

Lord, protect her!

How in the world had they found them? He had let them get past him as he slept? Connor would never forgive himself if-

His heart raced as he forced the door open. Emily, illuminated in the beam of the flashlight, was thrashing about in the bed, the sheets thrown onto the floor. The room was completely empty otherwise. Breathing more easily, he made his way to the side of the bed.

Sweat coated her face, glistening in the beam of the flashlight.

Nightmares!

As his eyes trailed her body, he gasped when he saw the burn marks. She was riddled with them and they had to be hurting her.

"Nani, do you have a salve to soothe the burns?" he asked his grandmother standing in the doorway. She turned wordlessly.

Just then Emily flailed about, moaning in pain.

"No! Leave me alone!" she mumbled.

"Emily," he said softly, trying to wake her up as gently as he could. "Emily!"

He grabbed her wrist as she was about to slam her fist into his face. With a start she sat up, eyes wide in terror! Her mouth opened as she was about to let out another scream. Gently, but determinedly, he covered her mouth with his hand.

"Emily! It's me, Connor. You're at my grandparent's house in the mountains of northern Punjab. You're safe. I'm going to take my hand off now. You're okay, Em."

He took his hand off and Emily leaned against him, shaking.

"I'm so sorry," she whispered hoarsely.

He put his arm around her. "It's okay, you're safe," he whispered.

Emily felt anything but safe. She had just gone through the water torture again and they were about to electrocute her. Tremors surged through her.

"Here you are," Connor's grandmother said softly and came into the room with a large candle. "This will give you some light. Keep it burning all night, if you must. And here," she placed a pitcher of water on the nightstand next to the bed and handed her a bottle of painkillers and a tube of ointment. "This will help with the pain. You should have said something."

"I'm so sorry for waking you," Emily whispered and immediately took the pills, downing a handful with water. She eyed the ointment suspiciously.

Connor's grandmother cupped her face in her hands. "Don't be, sweetheart. It was nothing."

She nodded to her grandson and walked back to where her husband stood, a bat the size of a small tree branch in his hand. He glanced at his grandson, then walked out with a soft grunt.

Connor slipped onto the edge of the bed. He wasn't going anywhere right now. He owed her that much.

"You okay?" he murmured.

"I've never been so afraid in my life," she said, her voice shaky and weak.

Her fingers trembled when she unscrewed the cap of the tube and, after taking a sniff, spread the ointment over the sores on her arms and legs, exhaling slowly as the pain became bearable.

Once she was finished, Connor handed her the sheets and she arranged them around her, feeling very conscious that it was late and they were alone in her bedroom.

"I'm okay now. You can go back to bed." She pulled the sheets up to her chin. Connor averted his eyes.

"Yeah, I'm awake now, thanks. I don't sleep much anyway. Not going to happen."

"Well, you can't just sit there, staring at me all night long!" she said, irritation lacing her voice.

Boy, she was something! Connor raised his eyebrows.

"Tell me about your family back home," he said, leaning against the footboard, his gaze on her.

He remembered sitting here in the evenings, listening to his mother read stories. She had captured his imagination with the tales of Rudyard Kipling and other classic writers. His craving for adventure had been kindled here in this very room.

She sniffed softly, her eyes heavy with sleep. "My family?"

Connor nodded. "I assume you have one?" he teased, lightening the mood in the room.

She glared at him. "Of course, I have one! My mother gave me my necklace." She reached for the chain that usually hung around her neck. Her breath caught when she realized that it was no longer there. Her eyes filled with tears. She blinked them away quickly and lowered her hand.

"I... miss her meddling ways right now. She would have told those guys where to go. My father is an amazing man. He... ." Emily looked past Connor to the door. "He's my protector, you could say. Always there when I need him."

"You're close to them?"

He envied her. His family had been close for a time when they lived right here.

"You could say that! I live above their garage." Emily laughed softly.

Talking about her family was soothing. Her nightmares were no longer nipping at her, threatening to overtake her.

"I have a sister. She's a shrink. And according to her, I'm in need of some major professional help. Instead, I took off to Pakistan." Emily shook her head. "What a good idea!"

"Well, you could have done worse. Drinking, drugs, fast cars, gambling." He grinned at her. "People always flock to those when they try to get away from their trouble."

Emily wrinkled her nose, looking adorable. “No, thanks! Getting kidnapped is a lot more exciting.”

He shook his head. “I don't think I have met anyone like you before.”

Emily grimaced. “That doesn't sound comforting.”

“It's good. I guess I keep underestimating you. I'm usually a good judge of character. You're always throwing me a curve ball.”

“I want to know something.” Emily pushed up on her elbow, looking right at him. She rested her head in her hand. The light of the candle caught the highlights of her blonde hair just right, making her look like an angel. “How did you manage to throw up on the leader like that? It was amazing.”

Connor laughed and bowed his head. “Thank you. You liked that? Yes, I'm the envy of a lot of my colleagues. And my sister.”

“That was on purpose?” she said, awe in her voice. Connor nodded, grinning.

Emily laughed. “I'm impressed. So you weren't petrified?”

He waved a dismissive hand. “I had it all under control. Except for you.” Connor rubbed his chin, feeling the cuts. “As I said. You were a total curve ball. I don't like surprises when I'm working. And then...” Connor swallowed. “You just kind of jumped into my way! I'm sorry, Emily.”

“You're good at pretending you're a computer engineer.”

“But I am. When I'm not traveling around.”

Emily raised her eyebrows. “Tell me, you lived here for a while. How come?” she said, redirecting their conversation.

Connor hesitated slightly. This was getting much too personal for his taste. A huge part of him wanted to, the other – much smaller part –

warned him to keep his distance, that she was only part of the mission, his job.

He never mixed the two because it could become complicated.

"Okay," he finally said. "My father was employed at the American Embassy in Islamabad. Political attaché, if you get my meaning."

Emily's gaze lifted to his. "Your father was a sp – uh – an agent too?"

"That's correct. This is a family business, I guess." Connor rubbed the top of his head and yawned. "Growing up. we didn't know exactly what he did. We had our suspicions, which proved to be correct. He taught my sister and I how to defend ourselves. When I was fifteen, I knew I wanted to be an agent. A year later, he was gone."

"Wow," Emily whispered. "Go on. Tell me about your time here."

Shadows danced in the corners, bringing back a flood of memories. Good times!

"We moved here when I was seven. My dad helped my grandfather straighten this place out. He put in indoor plumbing, the newest rage in these mountains. That and the solar panels, which are now outdated. He installed a wood floor and updated the kitchen – including running water. He loved working with his hands, fixing things and tinkering."

Emily smiled. Connor seemed to relax as he recalled his time here. The bruises and cuts on his face only added to the enigma of who he was and what he did. She reminded herself not to get too close to him. After all, God was directing her path now and getting involved with a mysterious guy was not appropriate. If she allowed herself, she could easily fall for him.

Except, he probably had a girl in every country he operated in.

"My sister, mom and I stayed with my grandparents during the week, while my dad was in Islamabad. We have a lot of family here, and I always got into trouble with my cousin, Rabeel," he grinned. "We're closest in age. But I was usually the one who got us into trouble. A lot of trouble. My grandmother's gray hair? All my doing," he exclaimed proudly. "At first it was hard to be accepted here. I had to prove myself to everyone. But after a couple of months, both my sister and I were part of the local gang of kids running around. My mom homeschooled us. We used to sit on this very bed while she read to us."

"Sounds really great. How long did you live here?" Emily yawned, her eyelids heavy. She could fall asleep listening to his rich voice, reminding her of her mother's thick chocolate pudding.

"We left when I was thirteen. At first, going back to the States was incredibly hard. I missed my family and running around in the mountains, shooting up rabbits and other small rodents. I couldn't get used to having everything at our fingertips. Here, we'd wait breathlessly for the spring thaw, hoping it would not wash out the road. I had everything I wanted in America. There was no adventure in living in our gated community. It took a year to acclimate, during which my aptitude for languages became clear. My father started training me, pushing me to excel in languages as well as in the classroom. When I was fifteen he asked me what I wanted to be. I told him, I wanted to work for the Agency. I was hooked on the adventure!"

He looked down at Emily. Her eyes were closed and her breathing was soft and rhythmical. She looked so peaceful, beautiful. His fingers twitched to touch her cheek, to brush an errant strand of hair out of her forehead and he forced his hands to his side.

"Thanks, Connor," she murmured sleepily.

He quietly got up off the bed, making as little noise as possible.

"Sleep tight, Emily," he whispered. "See you in the morning."

The cozy feeling rumbling through him made him aware that it was high time to get back to his own room.

14

Emily woke with a frightful headache. Her body felt like it had been bashed about, fallen off the cliff and smashed into rocks. She moaned softly when she sat up, disoriented and slightly dizzy.

In a rush, all the events from the last couple of days came to her.

Last night she had woken up the entire household with her screams!

How was she going to face everyone?

She extracted herself from the tangled bed sheets. After Connor left, she had slept fitfully at best, her dreams haunting her and waking her in a state of fright – without the screams.

She opened the door and stole quietly into the bathroom to rinse off the sweat and the memories. The sweat came off easily. The rest remained.

She applied more of the soothing cream over her skin and took more painkillers. Finding a pair of shorts and a T-shirt placed on the hope chest, she dressed in the clothes provided by Connor's grandmother, and headed toward the sound of the voices coming from outside. She opened the sliding door and stopped in her tracks.

It was as though she had stepped into one of those yards displayed in the home and garden magazines. Color exploded everywhere from flowers she had never seen before. Trees shaded the stone patio and vegetables grew in raised beds. A man-made pond trickled in the corner, surrounded by more flowers and vibrant colors.

"Good morning, Emily," Connor's grandmother was the first to greet her. "We didn't wake you, I hope?" Her face was bathed in concern.

Emily quickly shook her head, her stomach growling at the sight of the food on the patio table. “No, I'm sorry I slept so long.”

“Hush! Don't you even think about that. Now come and eat, child.”

Connor greeted her with a nod when she sat down next to him. On the other side of him sat a tall, hefty man. There was no mistaking that they were related. Both had the same shaped mouth and both had a grimness to them that frightened Emily.

She had seen Connor in action and he was impressive, but she also hoped never to get him mad at her.

“Emily, this is my cousin Rabeel. We've been talking about how to get you to the orphanage. He is willing to lend me his car so I can take you.”

Emily shook her head, her mouth full of a deliciously sweet mango, its juices running down her chin. She picked up a napkin to mop up the liquid.

“It's okay. I can take the bus. I don't want to impose on you any longer than I have to.”

Rabeel covered his mouth with his hand quickly, but she saw a smirk in his eyes. They crinkled just like his cousin's.

“I don't think Connor minds, Dr. Martins. I think he would insist.”

His voice, clipped and precise, was nonetheless accented.

Connor stretched his long arms, making his joints crack, and slapped Rabeel's shoulder with a loud thud. When he looked at Emily, his face lost its mischief and his eyes darkened.

“Exactly. I know these roads better than the roads in my neighborhood in Texas. You'll be safe with me.”

She cocked her head slightly. “That is not comforting. Not at all.”

Rabeel coughed discretely.

Connor shot a glance at him that should have struck him dead. The two had obviously been close, and their relationship had not suffered from the years of separation.

Connor handed her the keys he was playing with. “By all means, Emily. You drive. I am too beat anyway.”

She glared at him and grabbed the keys. “Before I go, let me look at your injuries again.”

Connor shook his head and held up his hands in protest. “No way. It's just fine. Feels good as new!” He resisted the urge to pound his chest.

He wasn't going to tell her that he had not slept a wink after leaving her side last night. It wasn't just pain that kept him awake. He could have dealt with that.

His thoughts centered mostly around *her*.

And that was unacceptable.

He still had a mission to complete, which was why Rabeel was present. His cousin had promised to help him restock his weapon cache and give a look-see to investigate. There were no secrets between them since they were as close as brothers. Rabeel wasn't a man of many words. His eyes, however, told Connor he would be on hand to help in any way he could.

And he was letting him borrow his car! That was a major thing around here. His grandparents had a battered old thing, but Rabeel... He had a sweet ride!

“Abbu!”

Their heads swiveled toward the door in the tall wall surrounding the garden.

“Abbu!”

A young girl, about six or seven, shot through the door, her hands covered in blood.

"Nur!" Rabeel shot out of his seat and grabbed his daughter. Rapid Pakistani followed and Emily could sense the tension in everyone.

"What's going on?" she asked Connor, whose face was grave with concern.

"Nur's mother cut herself badly."

Emily's breath hitched and she rolled her eyes. "What are you waiting for? Take me to her, silly. I'm a doctor, remember?"

Connor blinked rapidly as if wrapping his brain around that information once again. He shouted something to his family and took off running, pulling Emily behind him, the aches and pains they both experienced forgotten momentarily.

They raced up the hill to another terrace, where several houses stood close together. He burst through a bright green door into the kitchen, where a young woman leaned against the cabinet, clutching a hand over a gushing wound. Connor explained quickly and quietly who Emily was, trying to assure his cousin's wife, who peered at them frightened and surprised by their presence.

Emily quickly managed to staunch the bleeding. Using a sterilized needle and thin thread, she stitched up the cut, quickly and expertly. The woman looked at her.

"*Shukriya*! *Boht boht shukriya*!"

"She thanks you very, very much," Connor whispered into her ear.

"I think I got that," Emily whispered back leaning into him slightly.

Connor flashed her a grin. He would definitely miss her!

That afternoon they jumped into the large souped-up SUV. Connor started the engine, grinning in anticipation of the drive.

"Rabeel!" He winked at his cousin, who shot him a huge grin.

"Connor, if you hurt my baby, I will have to hurt you."

"I will treat her with kid gloves!" Connor revved the engine with a sly wink.

"Hey," Rabeel shouted above the din, a hand resting protectively on the hood. "Go easy on her!" There was panic in his voice.

"Maybe this wasn't such a good idea after all," Emily squealed as they careened down the steep dirt road, sending dust, goats, and chickens flying.

"This is a really, really good idea!" Connor grunted as they skidded onto the paved road.

They reached the orphanage in one hour and in one piece, although Connor had seemingly tried his best to make it a memorable trip. Connor asked for the orphanage and quickly got directions to the outskirts of the town, which stretched along a riverbed. They approached the somewhat dilapidated building cautiously.

Connor rubbed his bearded chin since the scabs from his cuts were beginning to itch like crazy. He wasn't willing to leave her in a place like this. Instinctively, he wanted to put his arm around her and take her back to his grandparent's.

But she belonged here.

Emily swallowed hard. She was not ready for this!

She wanted to go home!

God, remind me why I'm here again.

"Are you sure you want to stay?" Connor whispered as they walked to the rusty gate.

"I-" Emily's throat tightened, cutting off the reply.

Peering into the courtyard, they stilled. It was not a mess, as they would have expected. Flower beds grew here and there, a huge vegetable garden grew in a corner with a few older children and some adults tending it. Goats wandered freely, eating the grass. There was a small playground, with several swings and a slide in the shade of a large tree. Children played and sang, while adults grouped around them, talking.

Emily took a deep breath and turned to him.

Oh, those eyes! She once again found herself under their scrutiny and it caused her more distress than it should. She found herself wanting to fall into whatever was behind their depth.

With a shake of her head, she came to her senses.

It was high time to leave Agent Connor Williams/Jack Russel behind. Briskly, Emily held out her hand.

"I can't say it's been fun. But it's been a rare experience, Connor. I wish you the best, and please try to stay alive! Don't let them drop another bomb on your head." Her stomach did a funny twist, which she completely ignored – or at least she tried to.

Somehow, thinking of him leaving, hurt.

Connor accepted her hand and held it. "It's been something, I'll give you that. I'll not underestimate you again, Dr. Martins. Thank you for trying to save me. And thank you for what you did today."

"Make sure you get those ribs checked out."

"As soon as I'm done here, I'll see a doctor," he promised. "And Emily. You be careful, okay? Remember, this is not suburbia."

She gave a muffled laugh. "You're absolutely right. I think I got that!"

A man, roughly in his fifties, emerged from the building. He wore a worn, but neat tunic and pants. His eyes and hair color made it impossible for anybody to confuse him for anything else other than American. He scowled and looked at them. His eyes widened when he saw Connor's battered face.

"We're full," he explained in Punjabi.

"I'm just delivering your doctor," Connor replied in English, a disarming smile spreading over his face.

"Dr. Martins?!" The man opened the gate. "We expected you several days ago! We've been trying to contact you. We spoke with your mother, and she assured us that you had made the trip."

Emily groaned and pressed the heel of her hand against her throbbing forehead. "You spoke with my mother?"

"Yes, doctor. We assumed something happened on your side."

"Well, yes. I was-" she paused and looked at Connor. "I was delayed! Is there a phone I can use to call my mother to assure her I made it?"

"Of course, doctor. In the office!"

Emily turned to Connor again. "Bye, Mr. Williams."

Connor gave her a crooked grin and mock salute. "Dr. Martins. I can't say it was a pleasure, but it was an adventure."

Emily bit her lip and scooted through the fence. She resisted looking back and heard the engine of the high powered vehicle roar to life. It was high time she start her job here.

Lord, please help me to put him out of my mind.

Thinking about Connor Williams would be detrimental to her new resolve.

15

"Mom, everything is perfectly fine. I just hit a snag with the transportation." Technically that wasn't a lie. A thin layer of sweat covered Emily's forehead and she decided that it must be the oppressive heat.

"Emily, we've been so worried that we put you on our emergency prayer list. We didn't know if you had been abducted, killed or worse!"

"I'm really sorry, Mom. My travel arrangements were all messed up. But I'm here now. Safe and sound."

Safe anyway, but sound?

She wasn't so sure she was of sound mind. Whenever she closed her eyes, she was back in that hut, electricity blistering her skin, threatening to tear her body in half.

No – she was nowhere near a sound mind.

"Perhaps you can come home sooner. I'm not sure it's safe for you."

Emily just about fell out of her seat. She knew it wasn't!

"Don't worry. I'm exactly where God wants me to be."

"Oh, Emily," her mother whispered and a sob could be heard through the line.

"I love you, Mom. And tell Dad that it's pretty hot here."

They hung up, and Emily sat in the creaking old chair, resting her pounding head in her hands. How had she ever decided to come on this trip? She missed her mother terribly, a deep ache starting in her heart.

"Is everything okay?" Mr. Holland entered the room and sat down across from her. "You look like you could use some rest."

Emily winced. "Yes, it's been several extraordinary days. I wouldn't want to relive them under any circumstances."

The director's eyes became moist and he looked away. "Dr. Martins, are you sure you're up for the job? I wouldn't think any less of you if you went home. After what you've experienced... I don't blame you."

Emily glanced through the dusty window at the children playing in the yard. This was why she had come. The kids, who had been discarded by their parents, needed her.

"I'm staying," she said, her voice cracking slightly.

"Good. We certainly need you."

She explained that all her clothes, her money, and her passport were gone.

"We can find clothes for you among the donations we receive. At least you'll have something clean to wear until your bank can transfer some money here. As far as your passport is concerned, you'll have to apply for a new one when we go to Islamabad. The American Embassy is there and they will be able to assist you."

"Thank you," Emily said. Connor's father had worked for the embassy. She shook her head to dislodge the thought. *This isn't helping.*

Tom Holland continued, somewhat more subdued, "We're advising our staff to be careful when they go into town and not to go alone. This mission used to be well accepted by the people. But in the last few months, there has been a change. Trouble is on the horizon."

A shiver of fear squirreled into her heart. But God was was still in charge. She was ready to live with a higher purpose than finding the perfect mate, having the perfect house and family. It was time to look after those who had less than she ever had.

The fear evaporated and energy rushed through her.

"Show me my patients," she said, noting a satisfied look on the director's face.

"Follow me."

They walked along a hall decorated with pictures and childish scribbles to another shorter one. At the end was a large room with several mattresses and several pale children.

"Meet your patients. My wife will assist you. She's a nurse."

An elderly woman with kind dark eyes looked up as they entered and smiled. Her salt and pepper hair was arranged neatly into a bun.

"Doctor. I'm so pleased that you're here. You have no idea what a blessing the Lord has given us with your arrival."

Emily moved down the four occupied mattresses, her hands clasped tightly behind her back.

Just like home, Emily thought as she prepared for the rapid-fire briefing that was sure to follow.

"This is Aysha. She came to us last week, malnourished and plagued with internal parasites."

Emily's heart tightened painfully at the sight of the tiny baby, sleeping fitfully on the clean sheets.

"Because we are at the mercy of our sister churches in the western countries – mostly America – we have a limited amount of conventional medicines. We make do with substituting them for herbs when we run low.

"There is a local hospital. But the doctors there have become increasingly hostile to our orphans. It used to be that one doctor would come out here, once a month, but they refuse to set foot inside our gates. That was why we asked for a doctor. And we are so blessed to have you, Dr. Martins."

Little Aysha stirred and was given a bottle. Emily guessed her to be no more than four months old. Her body was riddled with open sores and wounds.

"Aysha is seven months old and she's been with us for a week. Her mother left and her father couldn't keep her because he had three other mouths to feed."

The baby whimpered softly when Emily touched her.

"That's horrible," she whispered, swallowing a frog that had jumped down her throat at that inopportune time.

Mrs. Holland gave her arm a squeeze. "At least this father was kind enough to bring the baby to an orphanage. Many children don't fare so well."

Connor frowned as he looked through the binoculars at the scene before him. He was hiding among the dry grass, watching the leader of the cell. The man had surrounded himself with a few new recruits, who were busy building a new hut.

I could use some help.

His fingers hovered over his watch to call in with the new information. He knew better than to request backup. They had sent him here to do a job for a reason. He was the guy that got it done.

Except for this time.

A thin face with soft mocha eyes, framed by dark blonde hair appeared in his mind.

Whoa, rein it in there, Spyman! He snorted silently.

Spyman!

That woman had some gall calling him that.

The truth was that he missed her like he had no business doing.

After dropping her off at the orphanage a week and a half ago, she had generally invaded his mind at the most inappropriate times – like when he was on a stakeout or trying to sleep or eat, or when he was talking to his family. Basically, wherever he was and whatever he was doing, she was there with him.

But she wasn't.

It had taken an enormous amount of determination not to borrow Rabeel's baby again to drive to the orphanage just to check on her.

Mixing business with personal never worked and he had been very determined to keep the two separate. Except for this job, he had never felt the urge to become involved with any of the people he worked with. There was something different about Emily that made keeping his mind on the task difficult while he pondered if she had settled in and hoped she was safe.

His attention bounced back to the half-constructed hut, where the leader was yelling for his men to move faster. He himself hadn't picked up as much as a rock.

Anger sliced through his gut and worked its way throughout his body.

He couldn't wait to cut off the head of the snake. Things had changed recently with the local people becoming easily influenced and scared into submission by bullies coming into the region. If things didn't change, the whole area would be overrun by terrorists pouring in.

His grandfather still held the reins of control over their little town. When he went to his heavenly rest, his cousin Rabeel would take over. The little village would be safe for another generation. But he had to ensure that they wouldn't be overwhelmed by outside forces.

That was why he had agreed to take this job when his handler had placed the particulars into his lap. He loved the people of this country for their generous and fun nature.

He would do anything to protect them.

Leaning against the rock, he shifted his weight for a more comfortable position. The grass and rocks camouflaged him well enough. He focused his attention back to activity on the hillside, where the workers were still busy building and their leader was still yelling.

He about to pack up and leave. The safety of his Pakistani family was in jeopardy.

The hairs on the back of his neck suddenly stood in attention, and he knew someone was watching him. Snapping around, his weapon in hand, he discovered the perpetrator. His cousin, crouching a hundred yards from him, stared back at him.

“You're a hard man to find, brother.”

Connor secured his weapon with a scowl. “And yet, *Bhaanja*, you found me. I can't be that hard to find.”

“You forget, I know you.” Rabeel scooted up next to him. “What do you see?”

Wordlessly, Connor handed him the long range binoculars. Rabeel grimaced, tugging at his thick beard.

“I know that man, the one yelling. He and a few of his 'friends' have been coming to the town council meetings. He is not a good man.”

Connor grunted in reply. “Yeah, no kidding. He's the one I'm after. He's the one who ordered others to play with my face.” Connor's bruises were almost gone, but his ribs were still smarting now and then. “And with my ribs. I also have a score to settle for Emily.”

Connor could feel his cousin intense eyes on him. "Would you be needing some help?"

Connor turned to him. "Are you offering?"

Rabeel let out a breathy laugh and turned his attention back to the scene in the distance. "To get rid of that man? I can feel evil oozing out of him. His eyes are on my wife when I have the men over after meetings. He frightens her. She doesn't even come out anymore when they are here. Yes, cousin. I will help. But in an unofficial capacity, you understand."

"I'm not really here, of course," Connor said, snickering. "So, yeah, I understand. I don't want a tribal war, Rabeel. You know that."

"Neither do I. I like my peace and quiet now that I'm semi-retired."

"Mm, a little too much, by the looks of you." Connor slapped the back of his hand into his cousin's slightly pouchy gut.

Rabeel rubbed the area almost affectionately. "Hey, my wife is a good cook. Speaking of which. What about you? Do you have someone in *Amrika*?"

Connor huffed. "Sure. I got me a wife in every state."

His cousin chuckled. "Isn't that against scripture?"

Connor waved dismissively. "Eh, depends on the interpretation. I mean, Solomon had how many wives? And think of King David."

"Yes, but the poor man had many family issues." Rabeel's face cracked into a wide smile. "It's good to have you here. It became entirely too dull when you left."

"Sure." Connor inspected the area. "Is that why you joined the army?"

"Of course!"

"Oh, man! Take a look at that!"

What if...

The leader smashed his fist into the face of one of his workers, screaming at him. The others cowered in fear and returned to work.

"You know," Rabeel mused. "I know those men. They are good people. What if we were to try to persuade them to stay home, we may have results."

Connor looked at his cousin. "And just how are you going to achieve that?"

Rabeel slapped him hard across the shoulders, sending shock waves up his ribcage and causing him to wince in pain.

"I got it!"

Connor steadied himself. "What are you going to do?"

His cousin grinned. "Sweet-talk them."

"You're going to let me do all the talking, then?"

Connor looked back through the binoculars and heard his cousin snort softly in reply.

16

Under the cover of night, the two stole through the small village to a certain dark house, where Rabeel knocked quietly on the door. A slit of light escaped through the slightly cracked-open door. Rabeel quickly gained them entrance, talking in hushed tones. The room was filled with frightened men, whispering and pointing at them discretely. Women rushed around to serve them tea.

Once the tension eased slightly, Connor and Rabeel began to explain what would happen to the men if they refused to cooperate. Stunned silence met them.

"We need money." The tallest and toughest guy shouted angrily. "Will you pay us to go away?"

Rabeel regarded his cousin, whose beard hid his expression. Leaning casually against the wall, his body seemingly at ease, Connor blended right in. He always would be one of them, and that was why Rabeel was out there tonight. That, and he really didn't like the leader of this group looking at his wife the way he did.

Rabeel glowered at the man who had spoken. "There will not be any payment. You know what you are doing is wrong. And you also know what happened to the guys who tried kidnapping an American couple. They are no more! Are you willing to leave your families for a few dollars? Who will support them when you are gone?"

The group murmured.

"Think of it this way. Would you want your wives, your children kidnapped?" Connor, who had been watching the whole scenario wordlessly, asked quietly.

"Of course not!" the tall man answered.

Connor cocked his head. "Well then, why are you willing to help this man do that to someone else's wife and child?"

The group murmured, beginning to look ill at ease.

"He threatened our families and they're only foreigners," the short man, the one who had been beaten earlier, said timidly.

"And why are you letting him order you around? Are you Punjabi or not? The Punjabi people I know and love would never let anyone threaten their families!"

Murmured consent rose around the room.

"How can we defend ourselves?"

Now, Connor grinned devilishly and pushed away from the wall. "Don't go to work tomorrow. We'll take care of it!"

"Tomorrow we are supposed to go and get rid of the infidels in the orphanage near Murree."

Connor's blood froze and his face became a mask. He swallowed slowly and exchanged a quick glance with his cousin.

"When, my friend?" Rabeel asked, his voice betraying no emotion.

"Early in the morning."

"Well, then," Connor said darkly. "I suggest you feign some sudden affinity against rising early. Perhaps an outbreak of the plague would be helpful. Because if you go, you won't come back. You have my word on that!"

He walked toward the door, not even indicating to Rabeel that it was time to go. His cousin was right on his tail. It was good to work with someone you knew so well. Wordless, they drove through the dark mountains and arrived at their grandparent's house before midnight. Once inside, they sat on the couch, staring into space.

"I need to call the orphanage. They should be prepared."

"Hold on, Connor. It's late and they won't even answer. You only have the word of those men on what is going to happen, and they might not have been telling the truth."

Connor gave him a blank stare, then he narrowed his eyes.

"We need to be there, first thing in the morning. I can't call in my cavalry, because really, I don't exist. I'm not supposed to even be here. The State Department doesn't want more bad publicity. I need to get to that orphanage and make sure those Americans and the children are safe."

Rabeel sucked on an orange slice.

"You mean to make sure the doctor is safe."

Connor put down his cup of tea and glowered at his cousin, only slightly taller, slightly bigger than he. He could still take him down. And a comment like that certainly warranted a pummeling! Connor bunched his hands into fists.

Rabeel noticed.

"Whoa there, cowboy," he teased and held out his hands. "I didn't mean anything by it. Just an observation."

"Keep your observations to yourself from now on!" That came out much more forceful than Connor had expected.

Rabeel's grin faded. "Aha," he said triumphantly.

"There's no a-ha!" Connor grumbled menacingly. "You're not allowed to say *aha*!"

Soon they were rolling on the floor like boys. Both laughed and panted hard. Connor's sides hurt from the playful punches he had received.

His grandfather stood in the hallway, hands on his hips, glaring at his grandsons.

"What's going on here?" he asked in a thunderous voice. "It's one in the morning and the two of you are behaving like children? Rabeel, go home to your wife! Connor, go and find a wife!"

"Nana!" both whined.

Their grandfather shuffled back to his room, muttering to himself.

Connor cuffed his cousin on the arm one last time. "Go, Nana is right. Go home Rabeel. We're not children anymore. I'll see you at first light. I'll be on my way to Murree, with or without you."

"I'll be there, count on it!"

He ignored his cousin's soft, teasing laughter as he walked toward his room.

Emily woke again to the whimpering of the baby girl. She had been sleeping next to Aysha on a cot since she got here.

Was it really almost two weeks ago that she had been kidnapped?

She leaned against the pillow, watching the child breathe. She wasn't doing well, struggling against an infection and unable to keep down the food and medicine, losing weight instead of gaining it.

Aysha woke and cried softly until Emily picked her up. Stilling immediately, a look of trust burned in the baby's eyes causing Emily's heart to shudder.

If only I could have my own bab...

Shaking her head, Emily reminded herself that she was on a new path, one that caused her to trust her heavenly Father like Aysha relied on her.

Why was trust such a hard thing?

So, she missed that certain dangerous yet handsome spy – excuse me, operative. Placing herself in God's care was difficult and sometimes her old desires would surface. Although it was only a dull ache in her heart that was immediately replaced with something much stronger.

"Shh, baby-girl," she whispered, putting a new bottle to Aysha's lips and expecting her to throw it all up. While the baby was drinking, she quickly changed the bandages.

The little one watched her, knowing that she would take care of her. How much horror had someone this age witnessed and yet she snuggled into Emily's shoulder when she was done feeding.

Aysha would be scarred for life, making it very difficult for her to find a husband later on. Hers would be a hard life.

They settled back on the cot, while Emily took her temperature, noting that it had decreased. Maybe there was hope yet!

There was always hope!

How quickly she forgot!

She started humming the song by Horatio Spawford Connor had sung to her the night she was tortured. She softly sang it to the baby and watched in pleasure as her eyelids drooped closed.

It is indeed well with my soul, she realized and allowed sleep to overcome her.

The early light of morning woke her and she stretched. She looked at the baby, who watched her without making a sound.

"Good morning, Aysha," Emily whispered.

The baby touched her nose with her chubby fingers and played with her lips, making Emily laugh.

Quickly, Emily took care of her feeding and bandaging, discovering that for the first time she was without a temperature.

Thank You, Lord.

Once all the other patients had been taken care of, the breakfast bell sounded. Everyone lined up in two neat lines according to size, one for boys the other for girls, underneath the open structure that doubled as a dining facility and later as a schoolroom. The children's laughter turned into soft chuckles here and there as she walked past them.

"*Sub bakhair,*" she greeted.

"*Sub bakhair,* Dr. Martins," the chorus of happy voices answered.

The children had taken to painstakingly teaching her a few necessary phrases.

A young girl coughed and Emily's head snapped around immediately. When she examined her, she discovered swollen lymph nodes and a slight fever.

Emily knelt beside her.

"How are you feeling?" she asked gently.

Dark eyes glistened with tears and she tried hard not to cough.

Emily slipped her arm comfortingly around her shoulders. "Come with me. I'll take care of you."

How, she wasn't sure. Their supply of medicine was running dangerously low and funds were stretched beyond limits. They had plenty of herbal medicine but Emily scoffed at using them.

When she discovered that her patient indeed had a fever that needed tending, she took note of the cures they had in stock. Her hackles went up when she discovered herbal remedies like "feverfew" and "Belladonna".

Do they expect me to cure these children or ward off evil spirits and werewolves?

Indignation ran through her. She was an MD and this was medieval!

Her fingers hovered over the offensive herbs when she heard a repeated *crack* from the direction of the courtyard, followed by the screams of children as they ran through the yard. The adults herded them quickly into the dorm, looking fearfully over their shoulder.

"What's going on?" Emily asked Mrs. Holland, who had rushed into the hospital room.

"That *man* is threatening to kill us all if we don't swear allegiance to him and pay him an astronomical fee," she replied, her voice trembling in anger. "I've about had it with him! He's threatened us every other week. But now he's brought artillery."

As if to emphasize, shots were being fired and bullets embedded themselves in the adobe walls. Instinctively Emily covered the baby with her body and dove for cover beside her cot, thinking that a lot of good it would do her. The other young girls in the ward screamed in terror and Mrs. Holland hushed them tenderly.

Someone had to protect them!

"Mrs. Holland," she hissed and handed Aysha to her.

The older woman gaped at her. "What... are you going to do?"

Emily growled, the muscles in her jaws tensing. "I've been bullied, beaten and tortured by that man. I'm not going to stand by while he does it to the children under my care!"

Not really having anything to defend herself with, she quietly groped around among the surgical instruments and came away with a scalpel.

Better than nothing.

A surge of determination and courage urged her forward. The children needed her! This time, she was not going down without a fight.

The spray of bullets stopped momentarily.

"Get the children into the back room," Emily whispered.

Mrs. Holland glanced at the weapon in her hand and shook her head.

"You can't seriously defend us with that. We need professional help."

"There's no police to come to our aid," Emily hissed. "Go. I'll distract him."

Mrs. Holland shook her head violently but ushered the children into a more secure room. She peeked her head around the door frame and urged Emily to follow. Emily shook her head.

She ducked and rushed to the door. Just then, pebbles and plaster hit her face as bullets again embedded themselves in the walls. She stayed low and crawled to the corner.

It was here that her courage evaporated into the morning air.

In front of her was the man who had contributed to her nightmares. He strode purposefully toward the building, a nasty looking machine gun in his hands. This whole scene looked like something out of a really bad movie as the spent shells flew everywhere!

She trembled terribly.

The scalpel in her quaking hand was not going to stop him! If only she could get to him and... And what? She was a doctor – not an operative! She knew someone who was, but he was far from here.

What was she supposed to do?

No help was coming, as far as she knew. They were in a foreign country and people didn't really want them here.

She took a deep breath. She had to protect the kids and she had to be smart about it.

I know how to cut him just right!

After all, she knew where the major arteries were.

If she rushed out into the open like GI Jane, she was sure to be dead within seconds. A lot of good that would do for the children.

The bullets stopped hitting the wall. The terrorist growled at the gun in his hands and shook it. Taking his distraction as a sign from God, she threw herself into his path. The man's head snapped around to her, even before she reached him. He grabbed her with lightning speed and twisted the wrist that held the pathetic scalpel. With a satisfied sneer, he snapped her arm.

A loud scream cut through the air.

Emily fought to stay conscious as the world around her became fuzzy.

How do I always end up in these situations?

"I'm ready," Connor grunted. He lay on top of the flat roof of a crumbling house, sniper rifle in hand.

Rabeel was crouched next to him, binoculars pointing at the orphanage.

"Its six five two meters," his cousin grunted as he took the measurements.

Connor adjusted and focused his scope. "Roger, what's the wind?"

"Wind is four knots."

Connor adjusted and drew in a breath. "Okay, taking the sho... Whoa!" It took him a fraction of a second to release the trigger. "Do you see that?"

"You have to be kidding me!" Rabeel grunted. "What is she doing?"

Connor readjusted the scope on the rifle, a deep scowl forming.

"I don't know but she continually gets in my way! Change of plans."

Connor jumped from the roof onto the top of their vehicle and grabbed his gun from the holster on his belt under his shirt.

"Back me up, Rabeel! Fire away! Just don't hit me."

Could he feel his cousin's grin on his back?

Rabeel's gunshots peppered the compound. The objective, the same man that held him and Emily captive, and a very small contingency of followers, turned around. One by one, they dropped as Rabeel's bullets found their mark. The man quickly shed his semi-automatic and held a handgun, now pressed against Emily's side, using her effectively as a shield.

Too effectively!

Connor slid over the hood of a rusted old sedan and sprinted toward the gate, his gun trained at the intruder.

"Drop your weapon!" he shouted in perfect Arabic. "Now! Drop it!"

"You cannot stop me! Will you shoot her?"

Connor connected with Emily's eyes. He could just about throttle her! That woman had too much spunk for her own good.

"Emily, what are you doing?" he asked conversationally.

The man grabbed Emily around the neck with one hand, pinning her left arm under his. Her right arm hung loose. He had seen him break it. Just for that, he wanted to kill him! Emily's face was a chalky white.

"Don't do it, spy. I will shoot her first."

"Well, you see that is not an option. Drop your gun!" He trained his eyes on where the man's head poked out from behind Emily for a split second. He took the shot. It missed. Not a problem. He was just testing.

There was no way she was getting out of this alive. So, she might as well give it everything she had. They had one shot to save everyone in the orphanage. She shook off the pain numbing her brain.

It was well with her soul.

"Hey, Connor," she whispered. "The Lord is my shepherd."

Connor squinted and he focused on her. What did she mean? What kind of crazy stunt was she going to do now?

"Emily!" he said, his voice carrying a warning.

"Just take the shot, Connor." Her voice was weak and soft.

What did she mean? Shoot through her? He would kill her!

Emily picked up her foot as the man behind her dragged her toward the corner of the grounds. With all the might that she still had in her, she kicked – hard – and felt her heel connect with something because she heard a slight crack.

The sound of a shot ricocheted off the building, and painful heat seared through her side. Her knees buckled and she slid into the dirt instantly. Another shot fired and the bullet whizzed right past her ear as she went down. The man behind her grunted and let go of her. The gun in his hand clattered to the ground.

She lay in the dirt, the world becoming much more focused on one thing. The light. The light in the sky, burning its way through her insides.

She had never felt more pain in her life!

"Emily!" Connor skidded to a halt next to her, covering her with a cloud of dust.

Her blood soaked into the thirsty dirt as he stripped his shirt off and used it to try to staunch it as much as possible. Instinctively, he fought the feeling that it was in vain. She was bleeding out right in front of him and there was nothing they could do to stop it.

"You always get in my way! What in tarnation were you doing getting into my shot again? And don't you dare die on me now! I demand a word with you!" he grunted through tightly gritted teeth.

He felt his cousin next to him. "I got it, you call your cavalry. Or call someone, because she is quickly losing way too much blood!"

He touched his watch. "This is Rattlesnake! I need a med-evac immediately. Do you have my coordinates?" He wanted to shout, to tell them to answer and send someone, now! Instead, he kept his voice even, measured.

"Roger, Rattlesnake. We can have someone there in ten. Affirmative on your coordinates."

"I have a civilian down, repeat an American civilian is down. I need immediate medical attention!"

That ought to do it!

"Roger that. Ten minutes out!" the voice answered calmly.

Ten minutes? It might as well be ten hours. Emily didn't look like she had even two minutes.

"Hey, crazy woman!" He shook her gently. Her head bobbed from side to side. "Emily. You're not checking out on me. It's not an option, you hear?"

The courtyard filled with kids and adults all watching, eyes wide in fear. A hand pushed him away.

"I'm a nurse. I can help!" Mrs. Holland went right to work, checking for a pulse and respiration, keeping a tight hold on the wound on the side. Carefully, she turned Emily and winced.

"You! Hold your hand here!"

"Come on, Em," Connor whispered as he covered the gushing wound.

He sensed his cousin next to him and could feel that he was gravely concerned. His cousin had seen this kind of stuff before, as had he.

Emily wasn't going to make it!

Lord, You got this! I know we constantly call for help from You, but You are the one who guides our feet! We need Your intervention.

He looked at the distraught faces of the staff and children. "You might want to start praying!"

"Of course," the director murmured and sank down on his knees. Everyone around him followed suit and soon everyone was praying. It wasn't chaotic, it was peaceful.

Emily's blood was running through his fingers, and as he listened to the prayers, he didn't feel sad. God was with them and He was with her. No matter what the outcome, He surrounded them.

Rabeel knelt next to him, his eyes closed and his lips moving, praying just as hard as everyone else.

It seemed like ages until the sound of chopper blades interrupted the peace. The courtyard was filled with dust and debris from the swirling rotors and Connor covered Emily with his body.

"Sir, we are your extraction team." A marine saluted him and he looked down at Emily, who was already being attended by a medic. Her face was pale, splatters of blood in her hair.

"Sir!" The man put a hand on his shoulder. "Do you want a ride or not."

"Go, Connor! *Kuday hafez*, cousin." Rabeel hugged him quickly and shoved him toward the hovering chopper. "And don't be such a stranger! You can call once in a while!" he shouted as Connor hurried behind the marines, whose guns were trained out.

The stretcher was hoisted up into the chopper and he scurried up. He just kept on praying!

Part II

Unto thee, O Lord, do I lift up my soul. O my God, I trust in thee: let me not be ashamed, let not mine enemies triumph over me. Yea, let none that wait on thee be ashamed: let them be ashamed which transgress without cause. Shew me thy ways, O Lord; teach me thy paths. Lead me in thy truth, and teach me: for thou art the God of my salvation; on thee do I wait all the day.

Psalm 25:1-5

17

Eight weeks later, Hartford Connecticut

Mom! I've got this!" Irritated at her mother's constant fussing, Emily worked her T-shirt over her arm. A sharp, intense twinge made her catch her breath.

"Emily, please humor your mother!"

"I'm a grown woman!" She bit her lip at the way those words came out, obviously hurting her mother – who excused herself.

With a sigh, she sank down onto the bed. Even dressing was exhausting, leaving her completely spent and more cranky than she had meant to be.

Frowning, she looked around the room that had been her home for the last three weeks. After what seemed like a never-ending process of surgeries and recuperation, she had been sent to a private recovery facility near her home. It had been a long and arduous ordeal back to health and so much had happened that Emily didn't feel like she was the same woman who had left home the first time.

It was amazing how her perspective had changed. Emily usually found herself on the other side of the coin, ordering treatment for her patients. Being on the receiving side had been... challenging. It was so much easier to be the one who was in charge, asking where it hurt.

Then again – she had learned the hard way that she was NOT in control.

Swallowing a groan and gritting her teeth so hard she feared they would shatter, she finished dressing. Sweat coated her face by the time she was done.

"Em, honey. Are you sure you're ready for this?" Her mother stood by the door, her hands on her hips, watching her like a hawk.

"Of course, Mom. Just give me a second," Emily smiled a fake, yet surprisingly convincing, smile.

Slowly and painfully, she walked out of her room, feeling like she was a hundred years old. It was hard to be cheerful when everything hurt. Except, there was so much to celebrate. She was alive!

How?

This was the question she had asked over and over again.

How was it that she was alive, walking around? She remembered the pain, the heat from the shot. She recalled the whistle from Connor's bullet whipping past her head. She recollected the grunt of surprise from the man behind her.

Then, there was nothing!

She had woken up for the first time in Germany at the military hospital, where she was rushed about to receive emergency surgery and several blood transfusions since much of her blood had soaked into the dirt in the courtyard at the orphanage. The second time she woke her mother was by her bedside at the same hospital, weeping.

When she was stabilized enough, she was transferred stateside to a hospital in Hartford Connecticut, the same one she worked at. Seeing both her parents stand by her bed, their faces lined deeply with fear, had been sobering.

The look in their eyes would forever be burned into her memory.

She was *making* herself be thankful. It was more than a feeling. There was a deep knowledge of Christ in her heart. For that, she was beyond glad!

It had been there when she had woken up and never left her through the grueling period of pain and rehabilitation that followed.

Every morning she woke up thanking God for her life. She prayed for Connor and his family so often that it had become a habit. Every morning she hoped that he would step through the door of her bleak room and sweep her off her feet.

The longing to see Connor again and the possibility of what could happen between them, didn't fill her with deep desperation. Her time in Pakistan had matured her. It had taught her so much of God, of herself, and her plans.

She no longer put her hope in the family, the house and the minivan. She would wait on the Lord, all the way. It wasn't that the dream was dead. It just didn't mean as much to her anymore! Her deepest desire was in living for Christ and knowing that He had bigger aspirations for her life than she could even imagine.

After all, He was God.

Jesus would lead her and He had that plan, that perfect dream; whatever it was.

She expected to have the courage to pick up her life with that in mind. Most of all, she longed to feel normal again, without pain.

Because deep down inside, Emily was different. The jokes that her dad told were old and forced. Her mother's smile was fake.

She slowly walked to the elevator, passing the nurses station. They greeted her with smiles and cheers.

“We're so glad you're going home, Emily.”

She grimaced and brushed an errant strand of hair out of her way.

"I was a terrible patient, wasn't I?"

Her nurse, a woman about her age, touched her arm lightly. "I've had worse."

Emily laughed. "You're too kind. Thank you for your help. I may have been a terrible patient, but I appreciate all your hard work."

"Doctors make the worst patients," the head nurse mumbled and winked at her.

Her mother was waiting anxiously by the elevator, wringing her hands.

Emily, you are walking out of the hospital instead of laying in a pine box six feet under.

When the doors opened, a team of doctors got off, but none of them even took notice of her as she and her mother entered the elevator.

Had she really been like that before she went on her trip? Had she been so callous that she never noticed anything around her, when she was on duty?

God didn't want her to be unfeeling, too busy that she didn't notice the people. She prayed that she would pay attention more from now on.

The August heat shimmered off the asphalt as they stepped onto the curb, yet it felt so good to be on the other side of the walls of the rehab facility.

"Em, your dad is bringing the car around," her mother said, nervously watching for the vehicle while keeping an eye on her daughter.

"Mom." Emily put her arm around her mother's shoulder and held her. "Thank you. You and Dad have been wonderful. I don't know what I would have done without your support and love. You got me through the hard stuff."

"Oh, honey!" Her mother's eyes filled with tears. She shook her head. "I told myself I wouldn't do that! And here I am, just a-blubbering away."

Emily kissed her cheek. "It's all right. I feel the same way sometimes." She smiled wearily.

Before her mother could answer, the honking of a familiar horn drew them apart and they stepped into the car.

"That heat, huh. It's something. I don't think we've had a hotter August in a long time. They're calling for a water ban. Nobody can water their lawns. And you look around, and you know that guy next to you is still watering his lawn. Why? Because it sure is a lot greener than your own yellow grass!"

Only half listening to his usual rant, Emily rested her head against the window. Her mind wandered back to Pakistan, riding the train on a trip that never ended! She swallowed the frog that had jumped down her throat.

Would she ever really come home again?

Her mother turned around, eyes full of concern.

"How are you feeling, honey? Are you up to being on your own? We were thinking of moving you into the house. What about it?"

Emily shook her head vehemently. "Nope! I need my space, Mom. I'm fine!"

"Debbie, she's thirty-three years old. She isn't a child anymore. Please, let's just not baby her, okay?"

She shot her dad a thankful smile when he glanced at her in the mirror. She could always count on him to be her protector!

Her mother exhaled softly. "Fine, your freezer is stuffed with meals for this week. And I shopped for you so you won't have to until you go back to work in a month or so."

Emily opened her mouth, then snapped it shut. The thought of sitting around for a month with nothing but her thoughts was unpleasant. She had planned on being back to work in a week or so.

As they drove on the highway, Emily once again prayed for Connor, who was always in harm's way. Had he gotten out of Pakistan? Was he back at his home in Texas? Did he ever think of her?

None of that, Emily Martins!

Recalling the low timbre of his voice gave her goosebumps. She could almost see him now, the last time they had come face to face. He'd looked so dangerous, so intense – she shuddered involuntarily.

Watching the scenery pass by and yet not even seeing it, she imagined what it would be like if she called the agency and asked for Connor's information. It all played out in her mind, bringing a smile to her face.

"You would like to have the home address of agent Connor Williams who also goes by the alias of Jack Russel? Ma'am there is no agent by those names listed here. And no one by the call name of Rattlesnake. You must have been hallucinating."

She knew for a fact that she had not made this whole thing up. After all, she was the one who had nearly bled out, who had a bullet almost lodge in her spine. It was a miracle that doctors in Germany had been able to remove it without any permanent damage.

Emily had a lot to be thankful for.

Her studio apartment above the garage was small, but it was her own space. She groaned in pleasure when she let herself inside. Nothing had changed here. How long had it been since she had last been here?

It felt like a lifetime ago.

She walked around and inspected her belongings. Her diploma sat proudly on the oak entertainment center right next to her Christian movies. She didn't even bother to turn on her flatscreen, finding that nowadays she preferred the quiet. Everything had its exact place, almost standing in attention. Checking out the fridge, she found that her mother had indeed stocked it well.

Even her freezer was full. Emily pushed past the containers of meatballs and lasagna and found what she was looking for. A pint of Moose Tracks ice cream. With a sigh, she settled on her baby blue couch and dug into the creamy, cold treat.

Emily closed her eyes, finding herself immediately back in Pakistan, carrying Aysha in her arms and humming softly to her. A second later, pain radiated through her arm as she was being dragged behind the terrorist.

And then the shot and...

She wrenched her eyes open.

Everything had changed eight weeks ago!

Even as she swallowed the spoonful of ice cream, she could taste it. It was different. A bitter taste lingered in her mouth and followed the food into her stomach.

Perhaps once she went back to work, she'd feel normal again.

What if...

Connor closed the trunk of his car, unlocked the front door and threw his keys onto the granite counter top. He tossed his duffel next to the steps to his loft bedroom. For the first time since he had moved in, he realized that his condo smelled stale, unused!

"Welcome home, stranger!"

Connor spun toward the voice and whipped out his handgun from its holster. Immediately, he clicked the safety back into place and lowered it, letting out a sigh when he stared at his sister's face.

"What are you doing here, Alicia? You scared me half to death and almost got yourself killed!"

"Touchy, touchy! I thought I'd have to duck and cover," his sister teased. She offered her cheek which he pecked dutifully. "You look tired, brother. Job getting to you?"

There's another barb against my occupation. I can't wait to see what she'll do when she finds out...

Connor walked toward the fridge and checked the status of it. He had been gone for three months, so it should be empty with nothing crawling around in it. He poured himself a glass of water and guzzled it down, giving himself time to think.

"No. The job's great. I'm just tired, you know. Traveling does that to you."

And thinking constantly of a young woman with blood seeping out of her body wasn't helping him get much sleep either.

He knew Emily was alive and that she had been released out of the hospital and had been sent to a rehab facility. Connor also knew that he needed to see her again. It was something that kept him awake at night when he was tossing and turning.

"What are you doing here?" he asked, keeping his back to his sister.

“Just drove by and saw your car.”

“Mm.”

He sauntered up to his sister and stood in front of her, looking down at her. “Hey, Alicia. I'm moving.”

His sister's already dark eyes became darker and she took an involuntary step back as if she had been struck. “Say what?”

He roughed his hands over his face as if trying to rub away the exhaustion he felt. “Yeah, I'm gonna relocate to Connecticut. Check out what it's like up there. The company is moving me next week.”

“Right!” his sister huffed and spun away from him, clearly peeved.

Connor got into her path and dipped his head to be level with her.

“I'm serious!”

She gave a disbelieving laugh. “Connor! Why are you doin' this? Doesn't family mean anything to you? We hardly get together as it is and if you're moving east, we'll never see you! What about Mom? And me? Do you even care? Gimme a break!” His sister stomped past him and gathered her keys. “Have a nice life, Connor.”

He grabbed the back of her shirt and hauled her back.

“Oh no, you don't! I'm still your older brother!”

Darts shot out of his sister's dark eyes. She twisted her thick black hair into a bun and let if fall down again. “Are you sure? You haven't been my older brother for a very long time. Ever since you took off and became like Dad you haven't been around! I...” She spun away from him as tears stung her eyes.

Connor let out his frustration in a puff of breath and let her go. Turning to his luggage, he pulled out a carefully wrapped package. “Here, brat.” He thrust a small package her way. Her face split into a smile for a second, then faded to be replaced by a scowl.

"That's what you think this is about? Me wanting something out of you?"

"Of course, it is. What else is new?" he laughed.

Alicia threw the package back at him. He caught it expertly mid-air. Maybe he had gone a little too far this time.

"What I want is my brother!" she yelled.

"Wow," he breathed to himself as the front door slammed shut.

As long as he lived he would never understand the opposite sex. Leaning against the fridge, he counted the seconds that stretched between now and...

The front door opened and slammed shut again as Alicia stormed back in, tears streaming down her face.

"Come here, kiddo," he said softly and pulled her into his arms.

She stood sobbing for a moment and then gathered herself together.

"I know. It's what we do. No tears. Dad used to tell me all the time. *No tears when I leave. You can cry when I'm gone.*" She blinked. "He's gone and the tears won't come! And now you take off, too. When will I ever see you? I need my brother around."

"Alicia," he sighed and tucked her head against his chest. "I have to do this."

"It's okay, Connor. You have a life, I have a life, Mom has a life. It just doesn't include each other. I got it." Alicia sniffed and straightened up.

"I can't help it. The computer company is moving." Indeed, it was. Because he was.

"Baloney. That's just a front for your agency job. What if you don't go?"

"You know how it works, squirt. They say jump, I ask how high," he said with a slight slump in his shoulders.

"Okay, Connor." Her eyes were still glistening with tears. "See ya. Have a nice life." She held her hand out for the present. "Do you want me to tell Mom? That way you don't have to talk to her."

His face contorted as if she had just punched him in his gut. "Ouch. I feel the love, sis. You don't have to do it because I've already told her."

"How did that go?"

He cocked his head and thought about the tearful tantrum that had followed his declaration. "Let's just say, you're handling it much better than her." He winked and placed the package back into her hand.

Alicia looked down at it for a second. Tears once again spilled out of her eyes. "It's so sad that the men in my life, you and Dad, always think that you can buy me. I don't want this. I want my brother."

Connor shook his head and opened his arms. "I'm right here!"

"See ya later, Connor." Alicia walked out of the door, closing it quietly.

That had gone just about as well as expected.

18

Emily was amazed by how beat she was after only working half a shift. She pulled her car into the carport and walked up the stairs to her place, feeling achy and a hundred years old. Her back hurt so bad, she hadn't been sure she could climb the stairs to the front door. But it was good to be back to work because it gave her something to do other than think about questions she couldn't answer.

Today she had taken her time with her patients, even though her boss would not be too happy about it. One of the little girls reminded her of Aysha, with her soft, shy smile and big brown eyes that looked at her so trustingly.

At the top of the stairs, Emily paused to catch her breath and took a look around. Street lights lit the neighborhood up and down the road, and all she saw were lights, lights, and more lights. The stars were barely visible, not twinkling as brightly as in Pakistan, where the illumination from a few homes couldn't drown them out. Her parents were still awake, watching the late night news.

Wearily, she opened her door and automatically hung her keys on the hook. She leaned her head against the glass as she closed the door.

I have to snap out of it. I'm alive, so why can't I feel it?

Fingering for the light switch, goosebumps rose up and down her arm and spine. With a sense that someone was in her apartment, she swallowed hard and lowered to the ground to crawl into the kitchenette. Maybe there was a knife to at least defend herself with.

That had worked out so well for you last time.

She was half-way there when the lamp on her side table by the couch was clicked on, illuminating a dark-clad intruder. Emily's heart stopped beating as her breath caught in her throat. She clasped both hands over her mouth and suppressed a scream!

"*Shabb bakhair*, Emily."

Her heart decided that it needed to make up the time it had taken to stop and began to beat in double time, threatening to pop right out of her chest. Slowly, Emily stood up.

Sitting on her couch, grinning like there was no tomorrow, sat one smug-looking spy – well, operative, agent; whatever! He still looked as good as he had the first time she had seen him on the train.

Strike that thought.

He looked better because now she knew him and that made Connor more attractive than ever. Emily wrapped her arms tightly around herself for fear that she would rush to his side and throw herself at him.

That wouldn't do at all.

So instead, she stood her ground, staring at him from across the room with a deepening scowl on her face.

He greeted you in Pakistani.

Her heart started to do a tap dance inside her chest when she found herself caught in his gaze.

This is not the time to fall for him! You made a promise to God.

But oh, she had missed him!

"You broke into my apartment?" she finally managed to whisper when her heart slowed down to a more normal beat, one that didn't take her breath away.

Connor looked rather pleased with himself as he lazily inspected her door.

"I did. It was a piece of cake. You really need to get some sort of security system. A deadbolt and a lock? Really, Emily?" A low pleasant rumble trickled out of Connor's mouth as he tried not to focus on how great she looked.

And how his comment had riled her.

Her hands went to her hips and her lips pressed into a tight line. Her pale, tired-looking face contorted and she looked like she was about to unleash a slew of fury on him.

Man, he had missed her!

He picked up a rectangular package from the seat next to him.

"Got this for you."

Connor almost regretted the way it sounded so lame. He had imagined their meeting going slightly different than this. In his imagination, Emily had let out a squeal of delight and had thrown herself into his arms.

He hadn't expected her to be so guarded.

But perhaps breaking into her apartment hadn't been the brightest idea he could come up with.

Emily stared.

Connor was not ten feet away from her, right here in her apartment. Why was her heart once again acting like she was going into cardiac arrest? She no longer desired the attention of a man. She had accepted that God's plan for her didn't necessarily include a mate. And the first guy who walks into her life after accepting it was Spyman!

"What's in it?" she asked, looking suspiciously at the rectangular package in his hand, not daring to let go of the counter she was leaning against for fear of her knees giving out.

Connor rose and slowly closed the distance between them, feeling like he was taking a step into the great unknown. Adrenaline surged through him as though he was on a job. He stopped right in front of her, the toes of his sneakers almost touching hers.

"When my father was still alive he would come home with presents. My sister thinks that he was trying to bribe us or make himself feel better about leaving us. But it wasn't. As he traveled he thought of us. So, as I was traveling I thought of you."

"You thought of me? How did you know I was still alive?" Why did her voice have to sound so breathless and squeaky at the same time?

It wasn't like she was overwhelmed by his closeness! Emily stared at the string of his black hoody. Then slowly her eyes traveled up until they met his and a fog began to settle on her brain.

Connor winked at her. "Come on. Did you really think that I wouldn't be able to find out what happened to you? I thought you knew me better than that."

She did. Oh, yes she did!

Her fingers trembled as she attempted to open up her present. A soft gasp escaped her lips and then a smile spread over her face. Finally, she giggled.

"You bought me chocolate? German chocolate?"

Connor nodded, a woozy sort of feeling going through him. He hooked his thumbs through the belt-loops of his black jeans and took a step away from her, just to give himself some breathing room. The apartment was more stuffy than he had expected.

"I went through Germany and thought of you."

When he noticed her mocha eyes glistening in the light, he was tempted to reach out to caress her pale cheek. Instead, he tightened his grip on his belt-loops.

"How are you?" he asked softly.

"Wait!" Emily held up a trembling finger and placed the bar of chocolate onto the counter behind her. "I need to regroup... for a second. I'm still shaken from this whole break in-thing, okay? I'm not quite ready to be part of a suspense thriller again."

Connor laughed and scooted next to her, while still giving her space. They stood silently, listening to the clock tick away the seconds. Finally, he nudged her gently with his elbow.

"I'm serious. How are you? I..." He roughed his hands through his hair. "I was concerned."

It was still as dark as she remembered, with that slight wave to it so like his grandmother. And those eyes! How could she ever forget about them and move on with her life? He had shaved his thick, black beard to reveal a strong, not surprisingly stubborn chin.

She pulled herself back to the present. "You were *concerned*?" she laughed.

"Hey! Yeah, I was worried about you. I had to scrub for a week to get all your bloo..." Just being so close to her was doing a job on his brain. He needed to change the course of this conversation. "And by the way, ya did it again! You got right into my perfect shot, thus foiling my beautiful plan to rescue you."

"Excuse me? Rescue me?" Indignation and fire shot through her. He had the gall of accusing her of messing things up for him? "Who almost died? Who got shot, other than the bad guys? May I remind you that it was my blood that got dumped all over the ground?"

The intensity in Connor's eyes flickered and went out. It was replaced by a soft glow.

"No, you don't have to remind me of that," he grunted. His face took on a pained look as he leaned back against the counter. "You tend to do that!"

"What?" she asked, her voice suddenly thick.

"Get in the way of my plan, then end up hurt."

Emily drew in a shallow breath.

"Connor!" she whispered. Her stomach flipped nervously. She turned to face him and put her hand against his chest, feeling his heart beating steadily against her palm. "What are you doing here?"

Her touch sent electricity through him.

"What?" he croaked as a lump had formed in his throat.

"What are you doing here?" she repeated, her words even softer.

Connor moved away and cleared his throat.

"I needed to know for sure, Em. I needed to see that you are alright, that you haven't lost your spunk. I needed to know that you can still put me in my place with a few words."

Her whole face turned bright red. "I don't... I mean... I wouldn't!" Again she desperately was in need of taking a breath. "What do you want?"

He couldn't help it and touched her chin. "Are you okay?" he asked, his voice husky, rough.

The roughness of his voice, his touch, caused her to tremble, and she almost wrapped her arms around his neck. But then she recalled that it wasn't appropriate and they were alone in her apartment.

"I'm home, I'm alive, I'm thankful. And now that I know that you're not dead, all is well again with the world." *Oops.*

A smug smile appeared on his face and she braced herself against it.

"So you came all the way from Texas just to break into my apartment and to ask if I was okay?"

He laughed softly.

Emily motioned to the couch. “Can we sit down? I've been on my feet for too long today and my back hurts.”

“Of course!” He felt like a heel. She looked pale and tired. He hadn't even given a thought about how else she might feel.

19

They sat down next to each other. Emily pulled her legs under her and leaned against the pillow, wishing she could do something about the fluttering in her stomach.

Connor grinned triumphantly because this part was going according to his carefully-constructed design.

Every mission will be a success if you have a plan.

He had spent a lot of time and effort setting this meeting up, just about more time than he would have if she had been an international arms-dealer. He had learned her routine and followed her wherever she went. It felt wrong to do, but he had enjoyed knowing that he'd surprise her one night.

Connor took his gaze off her and tried to remember what she had asked. "Where were we?" he asked sheepishly.

"I asked if you came all the way from Texas just to break into my apartment and to ask if I was okay?" she repeated with a slight scowl.

"No," he laughed, although he wasn't about to tell her that she had been the main reason to leave Texas. "My company moved to Connecticut." True, since he was the owner of the company. "So I looked you up. It turns out that we are practically neighbors."

She pulled the pillow out from behind her and hugged it tightly, wishing she wouldn't feel so out of control when it came to him.

Just rein it in! This is your chance to prove to God that you've changed your mind. Anyway, nothing can ever come out of this. He's a spy!

She cleared her throat. “You moved to Connecticut? But don't you have family in Texas? What about your mother and sister?”

“Let's just say I'm *persona-non-grata* – not welcome right now with my sister. But she'll get over it. It might take her a decade or two.”

Eventually, Alicia would stop pouting and let him into her life again.

“Where are you living?”

“Well,” he drawled in his Texas best. “There was a charmin' li''le white house, just down the street. I saw it, it was for sale. I convinced the owner to rent it to me for a year.”

Her heart slammed into her ribs.

The *charmin' li''le white house* at the end of the street, with the beautiful front garden and the picket fence, had been for sale since just before she went to Pakistan. Her dream house! She had even played with the idea of buying it but the thought of adding to her school loans hadn't been attractive.

“Can I get you a drink?” she asked, her throat as parched as if she had walked through the desert for a week.

Connor leaned into the couch and stretched. “Sure, water would be great!”

As soon as she handed him his glass, he downed it. She did the same, hoping he hadn't spotted the quaking water. But he was observant and that annoying smugness returned to his face. She wasn't going to allow it to stay there!

“You're right. You're just about my neighbor. Welcome to the neighborhood. Was moving next door unintentional or on purpose?”

Connor grinned roguishly. "On purpose and totally intentional, once I found the house was available and close to you!" He was nothing if not honest – usually.

Emily rose and put the empty glasses on the counter. Her heart was pounding, her nerves were tingling.

This is not happening! Wait a minute! Her eyes narrowed dangerously.

"Excuse me!" Her gut began churning and heat traveled to her face. "You... knew... where I live? How long have you known that?"

Connor looked like he had just been caught holding the cat by the tail and lifted his hands in defense.

"Mm. I... can't tell you or... or I'd have to kill you." He gave her a disarming smile.

She gasped and was about to go off on a tirade about the agency having no right to target private citizens, when he reached out and touched her arm.

"I was wondering since it's the weekend... and I don't work... and neither do you... How about we have dinner at my house? Tomorrow night? I'll cook. We can catch up."

The outrage she had worked herself into evaporated into thin air and left her feeling vulnerable.

"Eh," She gnawed her bottom lip. "Connor."

Her heart had not beat that quickly in – forever! Was he really that close to her? She could feel his breath on her cheek and that made keeping her mind on God even more difficult.

"I... can't," she breathed.

"You can't, or you won't?" he asked softly.

She lowered her head. Connor gently lifted her chin up.

"Don't! You, of all people, have earned my deepest respect." Then he smiled again, cockier this time. "It's okay, you know. I can take it. I'm a big boy."

She didn't know just how to respond. Her face tingled where his thumb had touched her chin.

Emily! What are you doing?

A sharp rap on the door was followed by it opening immediately and forcefully, causing both their heads to turn.

"Emi! I saw your lights were on and figured you are sti-" Her mother's voice faded as she stared at the two of them and she closed the door slowly, leaning her back against it. Her gray eyes became wide, then surveyed the situation with increasing interest. "I didn't know you had company. I'm so sorry."

The blood left her body and accumulated in her left big toe, making her fear that she was going to faint dead away.

"Mom!" she breathed. "Apparently my apartment is just too easily accessible and locks don't matter anymore."

The only other sound in the room came from the refrigerator.

Finally, her mom cleared her throat. "Hi, I'm Emily's mom, Debbie," her mother said and stepped into the room, holding out her hand.

Connor shook it as if they had were at a backyard BBQ.

Wow, could this be any more mortifying?

Emily cringed. She grabbed at what courage she had left. Her stomach twisted into a tiny ball – kind of like it had when she stood before the review board to get her medical license – only worse.

"This is Connor. He was with me in Pakistan."

Her mother's interest doubled – if that was possible. "Oh, you were at the orphanage? Did you see what happened to Emily?"

Connor gave her a very kind smile, one that would have had Emily scrambling for control, and said gently, “I did. I saw the whole thing. Your daughter was very brave.”

“Can you tell us what happened? She's being very closed lipped about it.”

Connor glanced at Emily, who was busy gnawing her bottom lip off again.

“It wouldn't be my place, ma'am, to tell you. That has to come from Emily herself – when she is ready.”

Debbie's face fell. “I would like it to be sooner rather than later.”

She gave him a very curious once over, then turned to Emily as if it wasn't in the middle of the night and she hadn't just barged into her apartment, practically disturbing what could have been a very tender moment between her daughter and Connor.

But her mother didn't know that, or at least she didn't have any proof. Moreover, Emily wasn't about to supply any evidence.

“I wanted to remind you, Emily, that your sister is finally on her way. They'll be here in the morning. They're driving through the night so the baby can sleep. Remember how we discussed having a girls day out? I thought I'd catch you before you went to bed.”

“Great! That sounds great, Mom.” Did her voice really just squeak?

Her mom leaned over and kissed her cheek. “Okay, good night. Nice to meet you, Connor. I'm going now!” Her mother backed up to the door, grinning from ear to ear. “As you were.”

Emily released her breath very slowly, feeling the tension leaving her muscles, and hid her face with her hands. Once the heat had gone out of her cheeks, she turned back toward Connor.

“You see... My sister,” was all she managed to squeeze out.

"Yes!" Connor's eyes shone with merriment. "I heard. Girls day out. Sounds like fun. But that was not your reasoning for not having dinner with me. Because we can do it on Sunday, too."

"Sit with me," she said shakily and walked into her living room.

"Yeah, sure," he said, his voice becoming like a gentle spring rain.

Concern replaced the teasing look on his face. As soon as they sat, Emily pulled her feet under her and shielded herself with the pillow.

"I... have to be honest with you, Connor. Since my time in Pakistan I've changed, a lot. My life before was all about finding the perfect guy and hope that it worked out." She reached to the back of her head and tightened the ponytail. "I have to admit that I have a dismal track record. The guys I dated were all Christians, but they all found me lacking. Not pretty enough, not girly enough, I don't wear enough make-up for them, I'm not curvy enough. I've heard it all. After the kidnapping and... you know... it didn't seem to matter anymore because my perspective has changed.

"I want what God has for me, not the perfect family and the perfect house, or the perfect husband." Emily rubbed the back of her neck, feeling her muscles tense.

Connor let that marinate for a moment. Would there ever be a time when she didn't surprise him?

"Em, I think you've been looking for the wrong guy!" he said softly.

The way he said her name... Emily had to stop imagining the *what if* with this guy.

Connor continued to say, "I respect that you're running to God! I think that there is nothing more honorable than that. But, that said," he shot her a sly smile. "I'm patient. I can wait. That's one thing my job has taught me. Patience and when the target moves, you follow it."

Emily's whole face heated up, becoming bright red – even under the roots of her hair. She opened her mouth and closed it, repeating several times without a sound coming from her lips.

Did he just do what I think he did?

A shot of something hot went through her gut and spiraled around her whole body. She pursed her lips and narrowed her eyes dangerously.

"Excuse me! Am I to understand that you consider me nothing less than something to aim at and take a shot?" The indignation she experienced was better than feeling something soft and gooey for him. "Is that how you see me?"

The laugh that was about to pop out of Connor's mouth died before it left his lips. The look on her face indicated that he'd better withdraw to fight another day.

"N-o... no, you totally misunderstood."

"Oh, did I, now?"

Heat now traveled up the back of his neck as he rose and backed toward the door. "You are more than just a mark, Em. Although, if you were... I could have taken a shot already." He couldn't help himself.

Emily's eyebrows scooted up into a perfect arch and she struggled to maintain her breathing at a normal rate.

"And... I... would have told you that you have no business aiming at me," she ground out between tightly clenched teeth.

Connor roughed a hand over his face. This woman got under his skin with ease. How had they gone from having a normal, very pleasant conversation to him defending himself?

"I wouldn't think of it," he stammered, an unusual occurrence for him. "On that note, I'll take my leave."

He walked to the door and stopped.

"Don't worry, I'll be back," he said and heard her snort.

It was hard to keep her face even, expressionless. The truth was that she didn't want him to leave, that she was having way too much fun sparring with him.

"Good enough. I hope you know that you are going to miss the mark."

"Just to let you know, I never miss!"

20

Emily didn't sleep a wink! Every time she finally drifted off to sleep, Connor's comment came back to her and she woke herself up.

How... dare... he!

She didn't like the way it left her wondering if she was missing something. She finally resorted to praying, trusting that the Lord would know best. After all, hadn't she seen His work in her life recently?

Lord, I can't do this! I feel myself slipping into the old habits of looking for a relationship. I want You to be first in my life. I want to cling to You, instead of running to a guy, someone who isn't going to be around. I want my life to be guided by You.

The Lord understood, which filled her with love, peace and total confidence that God would lead her. It was an overwhelming feeling, one that she hoped would not fade.

At six in the morning, she finally gave up on sleep.

She was invigorated with a sudden desire to bake!

I don't bake, she thought as she swung her legs out from under her sheets. *And definitely not at six in the morning.*

This was going to be an unusual day for her, she decided, as she gathered the ingredients for muffins in her small kitchen. She stared at them, thinking to herself how ridiculous she was being. As a busy doctor, baking and cooking were not on her list of priorities.

Her first inclination was to make chocolate chip muffins, her favorite. She could almost taste the sweet gooeyness until she realized that she really didn't feel like it. When her gaze slipped onto her nightstand where she had placed the chocolate bar Connor had given her, she grimaced. She had made impressive inroads on it throughout the night. Perhaps she had already exceeded her chocolate limit for the day, not that there was one.

Lord, a little help here!

It was a new concept for her to seek advice not from a human being, but from her Lord, her Father. Leaning against her counter, watching the sun rise higher in the sky, she waited for an answer.

The air conditioning in her apartment hummed, the fridge buzzed. When no reply came, she frowned and came to the conclusion that waiting on God wasn't going to be as easy as she expected.

All her life, she had been prepared. If she wanted an answer, she did her research and found it on her own. Emily had to be self-sufficient and not rely on anyone. Not knowing the solution was never acceptable.

Yet here she was, standing in the middle of her kitchen, waiting and listening for directions on what she was going to bake – of all things!

Finally, there was a soft whisper in her heart. It was more like a comment Connor had made. He ate healthy snacks. Whoever heard of healthy muffins? She pulled out her smartphone and scanned the Internet for recipes.

What she saw made *her* mouth water!

As she prepared the treat, she realized why she was doing it. These delectable goodies weren't meant for her. As the last batch browned, it became very clear that she would be delivering them to the new neighbor.

The one who had caused her to spend a sleepless night!

Connor had made a statement last night that he thoroughly regretted now!

What were you thinking?

As his feet thumped on the pavement, he felt the question pound his heart, battering it back and forth. She had just finished telling him why she couldn't begin thinking about a relationship with him, that it had to be something God would direct.

He should have just kept his mouth shut. Bantering with Emily was not healthy for him because she had somehow planted herself into his heart.

Panting, he walked along his sidewalk, enjoying the beautiful flowers blooming on either side leading to the front door of this charming house. The home had attracted him from the get-go, with its white picket fence surrounding the well-manicured front lawn.

Once he entered through the side door in the garage, he stepped into the utility room. The laundry machine sat silently. Connor didn't do his own clothes but always dropped them off at the dry-cleaners. Perhaps he'd do his own for a change, just to be more domestic.

He had left a glass sitting around on the granite kitchen counter. He walked over and filled it with cold water, guzzling it up immediately.

Shower!

Then he would spend some time reading his bible. Running gave him a chance to pray. The rhythm of his feet on the pavement helped him keep his thoughts on God.

Today, however, he needed to talk about things that didn't come easy.

Ever since Emily had gotten shot, things didn't feel right anymore. His job had lost its allure and all that was left were the lies and the mounting body count. When had he become so unfeeling about taking someone's life? Was there ever a time he had not been hard and callous?

It was not a good place to be before God.

He rested his head against the tile in the shower as the hot spray of the water hit his shoulders, slowly untying the knots that had formed. When his father had trained him, it had been all about the adventure and the excitement.

They were supposed to work together!

That had never happened! It was during that first year after his father's death, that Jesus had become his rock.

He had been there when his father could not be.

Now, he felt a slight disconnect from Christ. He didn't like it at all and he was doing his best to figure out just what was wrong. His job was necessary! There would always be bad guys.

Was he just tired of uncovering plot after plot? Or was there more to this empty feeling inside him?

He wasn't getting any younger! At thirty-six, he still felt on top of his game. His father had been an active agent in his forties and he could do it too.

Still, he had to talk to God.

Lord, Father. You have always guided me. I just feel spent, Father. There has to be more to life than chasing down one plot after another, threatening to destroy the world. I feel that so much of my life has been spent squirreling out secrets, rounding up bad guys and putting an end to them. I know that You put me up to this, but I don't feel right about doing it anymore.

He was tired of the lies because, even though they were meant to protect his country, they hurt someone. That, *someone*, had been Emily. She had tried to protect him when he didn't need her to.

She had gotten hurt instead.

Then again, if she hadn't stood up for him, she probably would have gotten just as hurt. He shook his head. He was getting nowhere with this kind of thinking. Any deep pondering was best left on the wayside. It usually led to regret, to feeling sorry for himself because he didn't have the storybook life. His life was a solitary one.

And until recently, he had preferred it that way.

Once he had padded downstairs for something to eat, he glanced at the time. When he discovered that it was almost nine, he decided to be the annoying brother and call his sister in Texas, even though he knew that it was only seven in the morning. Truth be told, he hated fighting with her. Waiting expectantly for her to pick up the phone, he fixed himself a healthy breakfast of fruit and toast.

"Connor, you had better be dying! Because you know it's way too early on a *Saturday morning* for a phone call." Her voice was thick with sleep and irritation.

"Have you opened my present yet?" he teased.

Huffing and grunting could be heard. "Whatever! My affections can't be bought."

"You know what, brat?" he asked lightly. "Has it ever occurred to you that I like picking things up for you on my travels?"

"Right! To placate your guilty feelings!" she growled. "I'm hanging up now!"

"Come on, Alicia!"

What if...

"Call me at a more civilized time, so I can yell at you without falling asleep!"

The call ended. Connor stuck his phone back into its pouch and scowled.

Sometimes he wondered why he bothered.

The front doorbell snapped him out of his thoughts. He padded on the cool tiled floor to the door. He hadn't lived here very long but he thought that nine in the morning was a little early for a social call.

He wrenched the door open to give whoever was on his front stoop a thorough dressing down, but the words stuck in his mouth when he saw who it was.

What had she been thinking, coming here?

Wasn't bringing muffins over for him exactly what she had told herself she wouldn't do? And here she stood, practically quivering in anticipation.

"Good... morning," she stammered, feeling as if she had sprinted all the way to his house from her apartment.

Connor's sapphire blue eyes stared right into the center of her heart. She took an involuntary step backward trying to protect herself.

This was *not* happening.

Finally, the corner of his mouth twitched and he opened the door wider.

"This is a pleasant surprise. C'me in."

Emily's stomach lurched and she reached out for the door frame to steady herself. “I really shouldn't, but I really want to.” She gave him an apologetic grin. “To tell you the truth, I've always liked this house!”

“Come on in, then,” he repeated in his Texas best, ignoring the way his heart began to pound against his chest. “Don't just stand there like a bump on a log.”

Anticipation spread through him as he watched Emily take a very tentative step past him into the beautiful entry hall, his nostrils twitching at the scent of something delicious as she brushed past.

Sunlight poured in through long windows on either side of the door, giving the cream-colored tile floor just a touch of summer warmth. A winding staircase led to the second story, its banisters wrought iron. A large matching chandelier hung from a vaulted ceiling in the center. Rounded archways led to the empty dining room on the left and the living room on the right. Straight ahead was the kitchen.

“I'm... sorry. I didn't mean to stare.” Feeling self-conscious, Emily longed to step into the rest of the house to see if it was just as amazing as the entry.

She peered beyond Connor into the living room, feeling slightly let down. The only furnishings in that room was an extensive personal gym with a weight bench and other paraphernalia of strength training. Of course, there was a large flatscreen TV hanging on one wall.

“You might want to invest in some chairs,” she suggested, her tongue pushed against the inside of her cheek.

Connor followed her gaze and grinned. “Yeah... I haven't really had time to fill this house. All my furniture in Texas was rented. You wouldn't happen to know a place, would you?”

Emily took a step backward, bumping into the wall. "N-not really." *Oh, you're so pathetic.*

"You have a beautiful yard," she said and pointed out the back, alive with color from the thickly blooming flower beds and luscious green grass.

Connor threaded his fingers through his wet, uncombed hair. "I'm not much of a gardener. I'm sure I'll have to hire someone to take care of that."

Emily leaned against the arched doorway, still holding the plate covered with aluminum foil.

"That's a shame, Connor. I like digging around in the garden. My dad and I get right into it. We used to anyway. That was before I grew up and got a career!"

She looked around, suddenly at a loss for words. With more force than she had intended, Emily practically tossed the plate of muffins at him.

"I baked. Hope you like 'em. Welcome to the neighborhood and all," she murmured.

The smell spreading out from the muffins in his hand reminded him that his breakfast was sitting uneaten on the counter, and that he had just gone for a very brisk run. His stomach growled.

"You baked? Should I be worried?" he teased and took the plate from her hands. Their fingers touched a split second.

The charge that traveled through Emily was much too pleasant and she quickly withdrew her hand. Connor's face turned unreadable and he took a step backward toward the kitchen, the plate in his hand trembling for what seemed a fraction of a second before he had himself under control again.

Just because she needed to give him attitude, she cocked her head and scowled. "I can take them back home if you like. They are healthy apple-carrot muffins. In fact, I already tasted one when they came out of the oven and it was delicious."

Connor's face unfroze into a devilish grin. "Wait, these aren't your regular chocolate chip muffins?"

"I was moved to try something different this morning," she grimaced comically and brushed her fingers nervously through her loosely hanging hair. She should be on her way home, but in truth, she was enjoying this conversation way too much for her own good.

"You were *moved*?" he teased.

"Yes."

"So when did you make these exquisitely smelling muffins?"

Emily shuffled uncomfortably from foot to foot, her eyes darting nervously to the tiled floor and the coffee colored wall behind him. She finally cleared her throat in order to speak.

"First thing this morning. I had no intention of making them for you." *Right!* "I just felt like doing it, you know. And as they were sitting on the plate they called out to me that I should come down and welcome you to the neighborhood properly. This was all totally something I usually don't do, you understand." *Quit babbling already. He's staring at you like you've grown another nose.*

Connor put the plate down and pulled out two paper plates from his bare cabinet. Emily backed toward the front door, twisting her fingers together nervously.

"I need to get going."

Connor frowned and thought about blocking her retreat. "Come on," he said gently instead, deciding not to scare her off. "You look like you could use some food."

"You know, too much healthy food in one day isn't good for me," she replied, her lips twitching. "Thanks, though. I just wanted to come by to peek at the house, now that you're living in it. May I make a suggestion?"

"Any time." He winked at her, causing Emily's pulse to spike.

"Your exercise stuff. It might not be so attractive to have it in the living room. You may want to hire a decorator just for a few pointers."

Connor waved a hand dismissively at her and bit the muffin. He closed his eyes and suppressed a groan.

"These *are* really good, Emily," he said, his mouth still full.

"You sound surprised?" She put her hands on her hips, facing him. Her eyes flashed in quick anger. "You didn't think I could cook?"

He held his hand up protectively and wiped the crumbs from his mouth. There wouldn't be many muffins left after breakfast!

"I didn't know. I assumed you stayed away from the kitchen, being a busy doctor and all."

She stepped closer to him again, allowing her irritation free reign.

"I cook... I bake... I clean. I even have furniture in my house. It's more than I could say for yours!"

He grinned. "Would you care to help me find some?"

Emily took in a deep breath as she fumbled for the door handle.

"See you around, Connor." She closed the door quickly before he could change her mind.

21

After she returned from Connor's house, Emily got into a cleaning frenzy as if she needed to show him that she did indeed have a domestic streak. She scrubbed her floors, and cleaned her bathroom and kitchenette like never before. By the time she was finished, she was hot and flushed. All this kept her from having to think.

When she was done, she curled up on the couch, utterly spent.

"Knock, knock!"

Emily's eyes popped back open as her attention snapped toward the door, where her sister poked her head through the opening. Her face split into a huge smile as her fatigue was quickly forgotten. The sisters embraced and gave each other a quick inspection.

"You look amazing, as usual," Emily said, aware that her hair had turned into that puffy mess it usually did when it was hot and humid.

Her sister blushed and tucked a perfect strand of hair behind her ear. Whenever she blushed, it was a dainty thing, a slight and very becoming touch of pink coloring her already rosy cheeks.

Emily's blushes were neither dainty nor flattering, covering her whole face from the top to the bottom.

"And you..." her sister said, holding her at a distance. "Emily, you look terrible!"

Thank you so much. Just what I needed to hear this morning.

"Oh, honey, are you doing okay? I was so worried about you, Em. What a horrible thing to happen to anyone. And especially you, my tenderhearted sister." Her sister's face twisted compassionately.

"I'm fine, Lizzy. Really, I'm fine." Emily pushed herself out of her older sister's embrace.

"You're so full of it! I can tell when something's wrong, Em. Getting shot and almost dying, in a foreign country no less, is not something to sneeze about. Those barbaric people!" her sister spat out.

Emily stiffened. Even though she felt that she had met the devil, there were many nice and wonderful people she had been blessed to encounter.

"Lizzy! How could you say that? If you get a bad grape do you throw out the whole bunch? I met some wonderful people while I was over there."

"Okay already, Em. No need to get so defensive. I didn't mean any harm by it," her older sister bristled. "Did you talk to anybody about what happened?"

Emily sank down on the couch. She brushed a strand of frizzy hair out of her face. "No, thanks. I already talked to God about it."

Lizzy's scowl softened. "Of course, you did. I meant that you might want to seek a professional?"

Emily snorted. "A professional? Isn't God better than a professional?"

Her sister always insisted she talk to someone. The truth was that she couldn't unload this internal turmoil she was carrying on anyone. Talking about it would just open up the wounds that had started to scab over. She could trust God not to go blabbing to anyone else. After all, the nightmares had almost ceased to keep her awake all night long and she was able to sleep a few hours at a time.

"Liz, I don't want to talk about this right now. Let's just enjoy the afternoon. I'm so ready to be pampered."

Lizzy scrunched up her nose, an absolutely adorable gesture like everything else about her sister.

God doesn't see the outside of the person, but the heart.

Emily's heart swelled at that reminder.

"Fine, Em. But you know I can hook you up with some really good therapists."

Emily got up and grabbed two glasses of iced tea, made fresh that morning. "I know. Thanks for caring."

Lizzy shook her head, recognizing the slight touch of sarcasm in her voice and murmured, "Sure! If you say so!"

She rose and Mitch, her super-handsome husband, entered with their adorable six-month-old daughter, Carrie. The look of adoration that passed between husband and wife made Emily's heart stutter for a second or two, and her breath got caught somewhere in her throat. It took some determination to turn her thoughts back to the great and unknown plan God had for her life.

For I know the thoughts that I have toward you, saith the Lord, thoughts of peace, and not of evil, to give you an expected end.

Emily swallowed hard and fought the knot starting in her stomach.

His plan, *His* thoughts.

Mitch came to her side and hugged her gently.

"Doin' all right?"

If anyone in her family could understand what she had gone through it was Mitch. As a cop, he saw plenty of stuff. She reassured him that she was *just fine* and reached to place a great big kiss on her niece's chubby cheek. The baby squealed in delight.

How ironic. She loved children and had no prospect of having any of her own.

What if...

In God's dream for me, He had better include kids!

The somewhat rebellious thought was out before she could put a stop to it.

It was late morning when Emily, Lizzy and their mother finally got into the sweltering hot car to start their girls day out.

Emily turned to her sister, who was riding shotgun, to ask, "When was the last time you got away?"

"It's been a while," Liz confessed and rested her head against the seat. "This is going to be nice! I haven't had a massage in such a long time."

"Mmmm," Emily groaned with pleasure. "I can't wait to get there."

Her mother nodded as she drove slowly through the neighborhood. This was still one of those areas where the kids played in the streets.

"Yes, a massage. The spa I contacted is... Oh..." her mother uttered in surprise and slowed the car to a crawling pace, her head slowly swiveling to the left.

Emily turned in the same direction and that elation she had just experienced was sucked out of her with what felt like a commercial-sized vacuum cleaner.

Oh, no!

Connor was in his driveway, washing his car.

"Isn't that the fellow who was at your apartment last night, Em?" her mother asked, her voice squeaking slightly, looking at her in the rear-view mirror.

What was she going to say? *No?* Emily felt her face turn that ugly burgundy color.

"That guy was at Emily's apartment last night?" Lizzy asked. Her voice held a slight touch of awe, of admiration. "Em! What are you *not* telling me?"

"It's nothing, you two. Can we just go?" Knowing that her companions were aware of her discomfort, she focused her gaze on the clock in the front.

"Nice, Em!" her sister whispered approvingly.

A touch of irritation mixed in with dread spread through her gut and seeped into the rest of her. Before Emily could utter a word, her mother had opened the window and stopped at the curb, where Connor was busy washing his black Mustang. His sopping wet T-shirt clung to him and stretched over his trim muscles.

No, no, no! This can't be happening.

Aside from her gut being a mess, her heart did that Cha-Cha dance it did every time she thought about Connor or saw him, or... Swallowing hard, she forced her breath to steady and focused on the rip in the seat next to her.

"Connor, right?" she heard her mother call.

Don't come over! Don't come... Oh, well!

Emily was a doctor, trained in hiding her emotions. She wasn't sure why her face had turned burgundy. It was not like her to allow her embarrassment to show. She steeled her expression and prepared to face whatever came her way. In this instance, it was Connor, sopping wet, yet sauntering smugly toward the car.

"Mrs. Martins," he said, totally unconcerned of the trouble his unexpected presence was causing Emily.

She forced herself to remember what he did for a living: he was a master at pretending and misleading people, not to mention putting them six feet under if they crossed him.

He was dangerous.

"Connor, this is my eldest, Elizabeth. Lizzy, this is a friend of Emily's. He was also in Pakistan." She lowered her voice and said, "He saw the whole thing. And he is new to the neighborhood because I knew the elderly couple that owned this house."

Lizzy trained her smile into that sweet, innocent thing she always did when she met new people, especially someone like Connor. Because, even though he was not a bodybuilder, the evidence pointed out that the weight equipment set up in his living room was put to good use.

His muscles were toned, all right!

But she had already known that!

Come on, God! You're not playing fair!

"Nice to meet you," Connor nodded, glancing into the car with mild interest. "Have a wonderful afternoon. Oh, about those muffins, Emily – they're gone. I just couldn't help myself. Thanks again."

Emily suppressed a groan, nearly choked on her own saliva, and steeled her expression on Connor's brilliantly blue eyes. "Glad you liked them."

He laughed, crinkling his eyes in the corner. "Any time you feel like baking again, I'm right here!"

"I don't think that's gonna happen any time soon," she bit back under her breath, keeping her face trained and expressionless. It took a good amount of strength.

"Say, Connor," her mother said, entirely too happy and excited. "We're going out today, but are you a church-going man?"

"Yes ma'am," Connor replied. "Southern Ba'tist, born and raised."

Liz snorted uncharacteristically and focused her gaze out the passenger side window. Emily was sorely tempted to do the most childish thing she could come up with on such short notice: to smack her older sister in the back of the head.

"Excellent. We attend the little brick church at the corner of Louisiana and Main for the eleven o'clock service. Would you like to join us?"

"Uh, yes. I suppose that would be very... pleasant." Connor rubbed the back of his neck, avoiding looking Emily's way.

"Wonderful, Connor. Would you also be able to join us for dinner after? It would be our pleasure to have you, since I'm sure you have no other plans tomorrow, being Sunday and all."

Connor's lips twitched but he held on to his training of hiding his elation. God was good to him today. First the muffins and now an invitation to dinner. Unfortunately, Emily seemed to have other ideas, as she was about to pass out in the back seat.

"That is too kind of you, Mrs. Martins. Are you sure that it would not disturb your family time?"

This time Lizzy had the presence of mind to cough. Emily glared at her, shooting her barbs that Lizzy couldn't see.

"It would be our pleasure. Perhaps you could tell us more about your travels."

Emily's head popped up and her eyes narrowed. "Eh, Mom..."

Her mother lifted a finger and continued, "Emily hasn't told us much about her time in Pakistan, so it would be wonderful to hear it from someone who was there."

Connor's eyes trained on the woman's face. She was a shrewd one! He might have to watch himself with her around.

"Thank you, Mrs. Martins. I would be glad to bring something."

Emily's mother swatted his arm playfully, giving a silly laugh.

Uh, really Mom?

"Don't be ridiculous. A bachelor like you doesn't want to be in the kitchen on a day like today. We eat right after church."

"Very well, enjoy your time out, ladies," Connor said and tapped the roof of the car. He walked back to his car, humming a sprightly tune.

Emily became aware that she had been holding her breath for far too long and gulped in the life-giving air in lungfuls. Liz's quaking shoulders indicated that her sister had long since given up holding it together. Her mother put the car into drive and closed the window. Carefully, she pulled away from the curb.

"Don't!" Emily growled.

Liz broke out in roaring laughter. She turned her body to look at her younger sister and pointed at her.

"Don't!" Emily repeated somewhat breathlessly.

"Emily, honey. You baked this morning?" her mother said, her voice thick. Her face twitched uncontrollably as she concentrated on keeping the car on the road.

"Why did you have to do that, Mom?" Emily asked, her breathing still not steady.

"Invite such a nice young man into my house?" her mother replied innocently. "My dear. The situation just kind of presented itself, didn't it? What's wrong with inviting that poor Christian man into my home after church? Your father and Mitch will enjoy the company."

Emily thought she heard Lizzy mumble, “And so will we,” under her breath but she wasn't quite sure.

By now tears were rolling down Lizzy's cheeks.

“Mom, Liz.” Pressing the heel of her palm against her forehead, she felt the telltale sign of an enormous headache. “Seriously! Stop! You two really have no idea what you are doing!”

Her sister exploded into laughter again.

“Oh, I think Mom has a perfectly good idea about what she is doing,” she giggled between hiccups. “She's been around the block a lot longer than either of us. She is a professional at this. Look at how suavely she just invited that fine looking man to dinner. After you made him muffins! I thought I smelled something under all that bleach. Were you trying to hide that you had baked?” Lizzie wiped her face. “I haven't had a good laugh like that in ages. This day is definitely turning out to be quite spectacular.”

Emily wilted against the window finding it refreshingly cooler than her forehead. How could she tell her mother and sister that Connor may be a fine looking man, he certainly was, but that she had no interest in pursuing him or anyone?

If this was God's plan for her life, she wasn't very excited about it because right now she felt like she was in a free-fall.

“Please!” she whispered, tears suddenly burning in her eyes. “Please, Mom. You have no idea. There is nothing between Connor and myself.”

Lizzy snorted again. For a shrink, she certainly was not doing a good job keeping her emotions to herself today!

“Of course not, Em. You bake all the time! Right, Mom? Weren't you saying just the other day how much you have enjoyed the baked goods

Emily brought over?" her sister had the audacity to ask, her face a mask of innocence.

"Okay, so I don't bake!" A fire ignited in her heart and unfortunately spread to her face, making it once again red and hot. "I just woke up and felt like baking."

Lizzy doubled over in her seat as she exploded in laughter.

"And there is nothing between the two of you?" Liz asked when she had collected herself after receiving a sharp glance of reprimand from her mother.

Tears shot to Emily's eyes and she blinked them away as soon as she felt them. It wasn't lost on her sister, whose face fell in true compassion.

"No! Trust me, a relationship with him is out of the question."

"Why? Does he not bathe enough? Does he have a wife?"

Emily looked down at her hands, noticing for the first time that her fingers were tightly twisted together.

"No to either! Just... Please trust me on this one. I can't explain it."

"He certainly drives a nice car!" Lizzie grunted to herself.

"I'm not looking for a relationship right now with anyone! Won't you just go back there and un-invite him? Make up some excuse. You ran out of chairs. Something... Anything, please!"

"Emily," her mother said sharply. "You're acting like a spoiled brat. Of course, I can't do that! Besides, it'll be nice to get to know him."

Emily swallowed her groan, bit a hole in the side of her cheek, and stared moodily out the window. "I'll find a homeless person you can invite, Mom. Anyone, but Connor!"

Her sister stared hard at her. "Wow, Em. I didn't expect that from you. What's gotten into you? You used to get all excited when you had an opportunity to chat up a guy. And now you want nothing to do with him? I have to agree with Mom. He seems really nice and she can't go back on her word!"

"You have no idea," Emily whispered. "Maybe my perspective has changed. Maybe it's not about the guy but God." Both her mom and sister raised their eyebrows.

Her day was practically ruined!

22

So he had been smartly bamboozled into going to church! *That* was an achievement and if Emily's mother realized whom she just so suavely invited, she'd probably have a good laugh about it.

It had been a while since he had stepped foot into a building of worship since he wasn't home long enough to make a connection with the other believers.

Connor grinned as he finished tying the Windsor knot his father so painstakingly had taught him. Snapping his phone onto his belt, he prayed that he wouldn't get a call in the middle of the service or afterward at dinner since he was looking forward to both.

Watching Emily squirm with discomfort was well worth dressing up for. He tucked in his shirt and donned his jacket. This was church and he wanted nothing but the best for God, especially on Sunday.

The rest of the days He may be getting leftovers, but never Sunday, right?

Connor groaned. Since when had he felt that God wasn't front and center in his life? When had he stopped praying about everything?

Parking his car in the crowded lot, he walked into the cool building and was welcomed by a greeter with a bright smile and a firm handshake. Once he was in the crowded sanctuary, he scanned it to search for Emily and her family.

He spotted the Martins family sitting on the left side, halfway back from the front. They were all chatting with various people, who were obviously enjoying the interaction. Emily was wearing a very becoming, yet modest summer dress with a floral print.

Watching her without her knowledge always gave him pleasure. It's what he did for a living – standing back without anyone being wise to the situation. She paid full attention to whoever she was speaking to, making that person feel special. Kind of like he felt when he was around her because she was making him have all sorts of emotions.

For instance, when the guy next to her touched her shoulder tenderly, Connor felt something explode deep inside him. It was a feeling he usually only reserved for the subjects of his missions – the ones he was paid to neutralize. Shaking his head and fighting to find that relaxed place again, he moved forward to greet the family.

Are you for real, Williams? Are you letting your emotions get all knocked about by a pretty face?

She was more than a pretty face. The fact was that... he had allowed her to sneak past his defenses. This one was personal for the first time in his career, and he didn't like the way the guy was looking at her so adoringly.

His jaw set, he walked toward the group, not taking his eyes off Emily.

"Good morning," he said quietly and everyone's head turned his way.

Emily's mother greeted him with a bright smile and she clasped his hands in both of hers.

"I hoped you wouldn't forget," she said.

"No, ma'am. An invite to church and dinner doesn't come around every day."

Mrs. Martins introduced her husband, who scrutinized him hard. The man had a good handshake. When she introduced the tall man standing next to Emily as Lizzy's husband, he mentally took a step backward and felt the tension in his gut leave. As the two measured each other up, an understanding passed between them.

Emily tried to be gracious, but Connor being there was... unnerving. He had the uncanny ability to rob her of her sleep without meaning to and to make her wish for things that couldn't be.

She swallowed the nerves that caused her stomach to twist into a pretzel as she observed him through lowered lids, pretending to study her bulletin.

He looks great in that suit.

As the service started, her mind wandered and she found it impossible to pay attention. Once in a while, she got a whiff of something masculine and strong when Connor shifted in his seat.

Stop that!

She shook her head softly. She must be going out of her mind. She needed a professional, just like Liz had suggested.

Lord, please don't let me fall for this guy. Guard my heart. I can't stand it to be broken again.

"Did you like the sermon?" her father, George, asked Connor on their way out.

"I did. It's been a while since I have been able to go to church. I travel a lot," Connor said and followed the older man outside after meeting the pastor and several of the elders.

He liked him instantly.

There was a calmness about him that reminded him of his father. Or perhaps it was the way he watched and protected his family. A sharp stab of pain went through Connor's heart when he recalled how much his father had adored his mother, loved both his children and had spent as much time with them as possible. All that went away when he didn't return home from a job, leaving them all with a hole in their lives they had attempted to fill ever since.

"We'll meet you at the house," Debbie Martins said and shook his hand with a solid handshake.

"Mom!" Emily gasped when she tried to get into the backseat of the family car. "Where am I supposed to sit?"

"Oh, my dear!" her mother said and clasped her hand over her mouth in exaggerated surprise. "I forgot. Jean returned all the pots and pans they borrowed for that special dinner last month."

Emily opened her mouth and closed it. Then she glared at her mother, who wore a perfectly innocent expression.

"I'll go with Liz and Mitch," she growled, narrowing her eyes.

Her mother had something up her flowing sleeve! She would never have asked her best friend to return some old pots and pans on a Sunday!

She stared at the back seat of her sister's car, full of baby things! Her sister's expression was that of naivete when she sighed and put a hand on Emily's shoulder.

"Traveling with a child will do that. You should see the trunk. I can't believe we fit everything in there!"

"Fine!" Emily stomped off toward the street. "I'll walk!"

She made it out to the street when she heard the purring of the engine of a sports car behind her. She didn't want to turn around. It wasn't even worth it!

"Goin' somewhere?" Connor asked as he stuck his arm out the window, slowing down to match her speed. He had discarded his jacket and rolled up the sleeves of his shirt.

"I'm walking home, as you can see," she grumbled as she continued in her pursuit of putting some distance between them.

Connor pushed his dark sunglasses on top of his head to study her more closely as she continued her *angry walk* down the sidewalk.

"Emily!" he called. "I've got plenty of room."

She spun around and her eyes jammed right into his. Big mistake because now her stomach did that uncontrollable flutter-thing again.

"No, thank you! I've driven with you, remember, and I'd like to get home in one piece!"

Connor laughed softly and had the audacity to wink at her, making her feel even more out of control. "I promise I'll get you home. I'll drive like a little old man on a Sunday ride," he drawled suavely.

She turned and blushed when a picture of Connor cleaning his car entered her mind.

Like that's appropriate. Blinking several times, her mind cleared.

"I doubt very much that you could drive like a little old man in that thing," She lifted her chin in defiance to his teasing stare. "I'm not getting into that car with you!" There, she had put him in his place.

He raised an eyebrow and slipped the glasses back into place while revving the engine and grinning devilishly. Emily bit off the laugh that wanted to escape to freedom, determining not to give him any more ammunition.

"Suit yourself, Em. You should be there in about..." He scrunched up his face. "What is it, three miles from here, at least? You should be there by the time we have dessert!"

"Enjoy your dinner," she bit out, her mood now turning foul, and hoping that somebody, anybody other than Connor, would take pity on her!

As she resumed her walk, she winced upon twisting an ankle. It was going to be a long, hot, bothersome hike!

"Seriously. Are you really going to be that stubborn?" he asked. "Why?"

"I told you!" Her eyes shot daggers. "I'm not getting into that car with you! Last time we barely made it to the orphanage in one piece," she hissed and looked over her shoulder.

Connor roared a laugh. "Suit yourself!" he said and closed the window, pulling into traffic.

He went home to change. Maybe by the time he made it back, she would come to her senses and accept a ride from him. He took his time to change into shorts and a T-shirt and picked up the flowers he had bought yesterday for Emily's mother.

Ouch!

She had lost count how many times she had twisted her ankles. Her favorite summer dress stuck to her in a most unflattering and immodest way! At this point, she was avoiding the sun as much as possible, which proved to be highly difficult at one in the afternoon on the hottest and most humid day of the summer. Swatting at a sweat-soaked strand of hair, she pulled out her phone from her purse, discovering with great dread that she had forgotten to charge it the night before and therefore it was now D. E. A. D.

When a car pulled over next to the curb, she almost melted into a puddle in relief before turning.

No! No! No!

She would rather take her sandals off and burn the bottoms of her feet before she got into the cool interior with *him*.

"Hey, how's it goin'?"

Connor had gone home and dressed more casually. He wore that smug look and she longed to wipe it off his face. He pushed his sunglasses onto his forehead again and cocked his head at her with an annoyingly pleased smile.

"You look hot!" he said and snapped his lips shut. "I meant to say... it's hot out here, Emily. You look like you're in pain." He kept his face expressionless. After all, it was what he did best. Put on the face. Tauntingly, he tapped the passenger seat. "Air conditioning is working just fine in here."

Emily exhaled with a long, agonized sigh.

Okay, Lord. I'm trying my best here and You make it impossible. If this is what You want, fine!

She stomped over to him and wrenched open the passenger side door. Cool air blasted her face and she groaned as she sank down into the soft leather seat. Connor closed his window, adjusting the vents so they hit her square on.

He concentrated on getting back into traffic. "You could have avoided all that, you know."

"Yeah, sure," she growled and pulled her seat belt on, then crossed her arms tightly over her chest. "I don't like being manipulated!"

She looked a mess. Her hair stuck to her sweaty and flushed face in clumps. Her dress clung to her and sweat stains adorned its side. His mouth twitched for just a second.

Training.

Keep it under wraps.

"I'm not playing you, Emily."

She growled. "I know! But my mother and my sister are. And for once I'm not going along with them. And they don't like it."

Connor used the car blinkers and changed lanes. "Why not?"

She turned her head to look at him. "Why not? I know what you do, Connor. I can imagine what it was like for your mother to wait for your dad, mission after mission. And in the end, he didn't come home! Your poor mother." Her throat tightened as she sympathized with the woman.

Connor huffed softly. "So that's your objection? My job? If I were just a computer guy would you give me the time of day?"

Emily stared at the mahogany dashboard, admiring the interior.

"I don't know. Honestly, I told you. I need to see what God has for me. Not what my mother sets up."

"Fair enough," Connor replied. "And I told you I'd wait."

"Really?" Sarcasm laced her voice. "You told me I was a target. That you never miss!"

Connor's face twisted. "Ah... yeah. I did say that, didn't I?" He scratched his chin. "About that, well, I'm sorry. That came out all wrong."

Connor glanced at her and turned onto their street. "But I wasn't the one who brought muffins over." He couldn't help himself.

Emily burst into a laugh. "No. Might I remind you that the muffins were not from me. They were a gift from God. He suggested I bake them and bring them over to you."

Connor grinned. "God suggested that?"

Emily nodded her head seriously.

"I will have to thank Him, then." His eyes crinkled as his smile widened. Connor pulled into the driveway and parked behind Mitch's small sedan. "You still made them and brought them over."

She groaned and got out. The heat and humidity hit her like a punch in the gut. She slung her sandals over her shoulder and pointed to her apartment.

"I'll be there in a bit. I just can't... Not like this."

He didn't know what she was talking about. She looked amazing to him.

23

Dinner was pleasant and full of fun. Lizzy's adorable baby was fed first. She enjoyed some Daddy time, as he watched the ball game, explaining to his daughter the rudiments of the game.

Connor watched out of the corner of his eye, a sudden yearning tensing the muscles in his gut. Lizzy came over and placed a hand on her husband's back for a split second. In that single gesture, she conveyed how much she loved him.

Emily had cleaned up nicely but was teased by her family. She stared at them moodily, which only increased their joking.

“That was very nice of you, Connor, to go back for her,” Debbie said as she placed a platter of roast chicken in front of him.

“I would have left her to fend for herself,” Lizzy muttered under her breath and stuck a tongue out to her younger sister.

“Girls,” their father thundered, while Mitch grinned in amusement.

Oh, no! I didn't tell her that he was a vegetarian.

Avoiding his gaze, Emily trained her eyes on the spot on the tablecloth right in front of her.

He kept his lazy grin in place.

Today he would not be a vegetarian. He had done this so many times when he was undercover. This was a mission – perhaps the most important one of his life. The likelihood that Emily would change her mind about a relationship with him was slim. After all, she had a point.

His mother had paid an extremely high price for his father's job. That was why he stayed away from dating. The cost to the other person was too high. Except right now he would do anything to have Emily look at him the way her sister looked at her husband.

"So, which branch of the military are you?" Mitch asked as he handed him a cold glass of lemonade.

Emily's head snapped around to her brother-in-law. Her heart took a huge, painful lunge and she refused to look at Connor.

Connor smirked charmingly. "I'm just a computer guy, Mitch. I've never been in the service."

Mitch considered him closely and narrowed his eyes. "Could have fooled me."

Hot and cold gushed over Emily.

Tell me what I want to know! You're a spy!

The room faded into darkness and she was back in the hut in Pakistan. It seemed impossible to breathe and she began to tremble from head to toe. She blindly reached forward, spilling her glass of lemonade all over the table. Silence sliced through the room as Emily became aware of where she was, and blushed in embarrassment.

"I'm... so sorry," she gasped. "Let me clean that up."

She stumbled into the kitchen where she attempted to rip off enough paper towels with her quivering fingers. Unable to complete the task, she pressed her hand to her forehead and, closing her eyes, fought for control of her emotions.

"Are you okay, Emi?" She jumped at her sister's voice behind her.

She swallowed hard. "Of course, just feeling a little weak from this afternoon's walk." She steadied her breathing.

"Emily, you are not acting like your normal self. What's wrong?"

Emily turned to her and her face turned bright red again. "Other than my sister and mom trying to set me up with a guy I know will not work out? Nothing!" she bit out.

"You are pretty sure on that?" Liz wrapped her arm around her younger sister. "He's here, isn't he? And he went back to get you."

Emily leaned against her sister, wishing she could share what she knew. But that would put Connor in danger.

"Yes," she breathed. "It would never work."

Connor nibbled on his chicken, refusing to give into the urge to throw up. The conversation resumed after Emily stumbled into the kitchen to quickly clean up the mess she had made.

After Mitch's question, she had gone so deathly pale...

He recognized the symptoms. The sleepless nights, the waking up in a sweat because he thought he was still under cover. The flashbacks during the day were the worst, although he had been able to control them. There was no doubt in his mind that Emily had just experienced one.

He himself had been hard-pressed to keep it cool.

He forced his attention back to the sisters, who had come out of the kitchen arm in arm and had cleaned the mess together. They were very close, yet completely different.

Emily's sister was the epitome of beauty and grace. But she lacked something Emily had in spades. Inner beauty as well as outer beauty, spunk, and guts! Whereas Liz had all the right curves, Emily was slender and tall. Liz's hair fell right into place, and Emily's curled around her face, especially since she had just let it air dry. Her sister wore impeccable makeup. Emily's face was the color of a porcelain doll.

Once dinner was over, the family worked together to clear the table.

"Hey, Connor," Mitch said with a dastardly grin. "What do you say about a game of hoops outside? Before we devour that delicious and delectable dessert my mother-in-law has prepared."

"Yeah? Why not? I'm game for a little one on one." He cracked his knuckles.

"No. Em and Liz are likely to join us," Mitch grinned.

Connor nodded approvingly. "They play?"

"Did I just hear my husband mention basketball?" Liz poked her head around the corner of the kitchen door. "We'll be right there!" she stated in a sing-song kind of tone.

The afternoon sun had gone down, leaving only the humidity, when they stepped onto the court on the side of the garage. The hoop looked like it had seen a lot of usage over the years.

"Is the baby okay, babe?" Mitch asked and put an arm around his petite wife, who swatted him in the gut.

"Really, Mitch? She's with her grandparents."

"Me and Em on one team, and you and Liz on the other." Mitch jerked his thumb in Connor's direction.

"Wait, don't you want to be on your wife's team?"

Mitch shook his head. "It's better this way for all of us, especially me. Lizzy knows that I love her and how much I like to win." He kissed his wife's cheek. She glared at him.

"So you would abandon me?"

"In a heartbeat, my darling." Mitch grinned at her and clapped his hands. "Let's do this!"

Within the first five minutes, it was painfully clear what Mitch meant. Emily played with such excellence that they were soon ahead by ten points.

"What am I missing here?" Connor panted after Emily stole the ball from him yet again.

She grinned sheepishly. "My dad and I used to play all the time. In college, I was on the team. We won a few championships."

"Oh, yeah? State championships?" Connor bounced the ball around her only to lose it. She made the basket with ease. Mitch grinned from ear to ear.

"No. Nationals."

Connor drew in a surprised breath. She continued to exceed his expectations.

When they entered back into the cool of the house, he had gained more respect for Emily. Whatever God would allow to happen, he hoped that their paths would continue to cross because she was amazing.

"Sorry, man," Mitch said and slapped his back. "But since you aren't ex-military or anything like that, I felt that I was safe tonight if I let you lose."

Emily and Mitch high-fived each other triumphantly.

"They always do that," Liz said softly, a frown crinkling her brow. "It's so annoying."

"Good game, Liz." Connor shook her hand.

"You aren't too shabby, Connor." Emily laughed when she came to stand next to him.

"Yeah, I got my way through college on a basketball scholarship. But I'm nothing compared to you. I once again underestimated you," he whispered.

Emily escaped to the bathroom before she allowed herself to make more of that statement than she should.

She was impressed with him too.

Not once had he complained about dinner. He had eaten the chicken her father dished out for him like it was something he always did. He hadn't even picked at the gravy that had slathered his mashed potatoes, even though she knew he didn't like meat. But he had kept it down and even complimented her mother on the superb food.

It was seven when he reluctantly made ready to leave. He was in the process of thanking Debbie for a superb afternoon, when his phone rang.

Emily's head snapped around at the sound.

He lowered his gaze as he saw too much raw emotion in hers.

"Go ahead," he said after he quickly excused himself onto the porch.

"Code in," an unemotional voice on the other end of the phone commanded brusquely.

"Tango Sierra, nine, four, two, Bravo, zero." His voice was quiet and his eyes peeled to the door to the backyard in case someone came out to find him.

After a few beeps and static, a different voice came on.

"You have a mission, Rattlesnake. Arrive in Washington at nine tonight for a briefing."

You're kidding me! "I won't make nine," Connor grumbled.

"You have three hours!"

Connor wanted to curse, but he didn't. He had learned at a very young age that swearing was detrimental to his health. His father had seen to that. It was the only time he had ever taken a belt to him.

Grinding his molars hard together, he contemplated saying no. The day had been so perfect, why did he have to be called in now? What devastating emergency threatened the country that it had to end his time with Emily?

"Copy that," he finally managed to say.

Just then, a shadow moved on the other side of the kitchen window facing the deck. Emily looked at him through the glass and his whole world shattered at the look in her eyes.

She was saying goodbye.

Feeling as though he was wading through quicksand, he walked back into the house.

"Thank you for a delightful day," he said with a tight smile as he bid everyone good night. "I haven't had such good fun in a long time. And the food was delicious."

The smile didn't slip once.

"Our door is always open, Connor," Debbie said kindly and hugged him. "Don't be a stranger. We expect you next Sunday too."

He was an impostor, playing with the affections of everyone in this family! Suddenly, he felt like the world's biggest liar and a hot wave of shame descended upon him.

"I may not be here then. I have to go out of town."

"Oh, dear. Was that the phone call you just got?"

"Yes, ma'am. There's a problem and I'm the guy they call."

He heard Emily suck in a sharp breath.

"Good night, Mom and Dad. I'm working all day tomorrow just so you don't freak out when you don't see my car," she said lovingly and turned to him, keeping her head down. "I'll walk out with you."

On the way to his car, she kept a considerable distance between them as she fought the thickening in her throat.

"I guess I'll see you later," he said softly.

"I don' think so," she whispered. "I can't..."

Against his better judgment, he drew her into his arms and held her there, surprised that she didn't pull away. Instead, she leaned her forehead against his chest.

"Good night, Connor. Take care of yourself. Please be careful."

He smirked lopsidedly. He tucked a strand of hair over her ear as he memorized everything about her; her arms around him, the silkiness of her hair, the cool, smooth feel of her skin. It was the look in her eyes that was almost his undoing.

"Careful gets you dead, Em. I'm never careful. I plan and I pray."

"Now, there is someone else to pray for you too."

His breath stalled and he fought for control. "*Shukriya,* Emily. *Khuda hafez."*

She did something against her better judgment. She stood on her tiptoe and kissed his cheek.

"Goodbye," she responded in kind, the pricking of tears urging her into her apartment.

His heart was about to rip apart when he got into the car and drove the few houses to his rented home. It took every ounce of training not to follow her up the steps into her apartment and forget the job. Within moments, he was on his way to the airport.

Emily stared moodily at the last piece of chocolate. If she ate it, it would all be gone, just like Connor. She didn't want to admit it, but part of her had fallen for him, but in a different way. She wasn't trying desperately to get the guy's attention. She was waiting and listening to where God was leading her. Today, Connor had been part of her life again.

Tomorrow, he would not be.

"Hey, care for some company? I thought we could have a sleep-over as we're leaving in the morning."

Her sister walked in, carrying her pillow.

Ah, the dreaded heart to heart.

"What's up with Connor? He just splits like that? Mitch thinks he's not a computer guy. He just has that intensity about him." Her sister took on her best shrink stare. "I know you know. I see it in your eyes. So, who is he?"

As the room began to shrink, Emily fought for control.

You're in your apartment, in Connecticut. Nobody is going to torture you and you are relatively safe.

Once her breathing evened out again and her vision cleared, she found her sister staring at her.

Shaking the remnants of the terrors, she answered as smoothly as she could, "Just a guy, Liz. Leave it be, please. It's just too complicated. Just so you know Liz, despite your and mom's effort, there can never be more between us other than friendship. I want what God wants for me."

"But don't you think that he's the right guy for you? I watched you in the driveway. That was more than friendship, Emi."

"Then you had better start praying!" Emily leaned tiredly against the pillow.

Kissing him on the cheek had been a mistake!

The demons lurked and taunted her dreams that night.

24

Connor was sitting in the office of the man who had been his mentor, staring at him. Everything about what he had read in the brief told him to fling it right back at the guy and walk away. He could still catch the last flight back to Bradley International Airport and be at Emily's door in no time.

"I'm not doing this! You can't send me out after an ex-operative. Why me and why this guy?"

His mentor tossed a folder with *Eyes only* onto the desk in front of him. "Name was Black Horse. He was one of our best, until twenty years ago. We thought he was dead, but he showed up on the radar about the same time you were making a mess in Pakistan. Bumped into one of our Far Eastern operatives."

"So, the guy went dark for a while. Now he wants to come back in? And you need *me* to babysit him while he comes back into the family?"

"Connor," Bryan Murphy's eyes were steely gray and cold. There was no feeling in them, not even a hint of a smile. Connor could count on one hand the number of times he had seen the man laugh. "I'm doing you a favor, son. Trust me. You'll be on a flight to Hong Kong. That's where he was last seen."

"But why do I have to bring him in, sir? My time is wasted on this!"

Anger turned his cheeks red. The same cheek that still tingled from Emily's totally surprising kiss.

The man's eyes increased in intensity. "You know you can trust me, son, right?"

Connor cocked his head. The man had been his father's partner and best friend and had taken Connor under his wing when he had been part of the first mission at the tender age of nineteen.

Connor swallowed the loneliness that always followed this line of thinking, as he admitted that Bryan had done the job his father had promised to do!

Even all these years later it still stung!

"Then know that this is important. That's why I'm sending you in, to go after one of the top operatives. Bring him in alive, Rattlesnake." The man lowered himself into his chair with a sigh. "It's in your best interest."

Connor froze as he opened the folder and stared at grainy pictures of a man with a cap. His insides turned to ice as he stared at images of a man who looked an awful lot like his father.

His hand trembled for a moment before he touched the frame before he caught himself.

"This is him?" he croaked.

His superior nodded.

"Here he is twenty years ago on his last mission." A picture of his father slid over to him. Connor could feel the bile rise in him. "He was sent into Tel Aviv to retrieve an agent under deep cover. We lost him, but the agent made it out. She was important, very important!"

"Why me?" His voice was barely above a whisper. He needed all his composure to keep himself planted in his seat.

Bryan Murphy turned to him and held his gaze in his icy stare.

"He's your father, Connor. Wouldn't you want to bring him back?"

The picture in his hand trembled for a slight moment.

Connor shook his head. "I don't know this man! The man you're looking for is not my father," he finally said through tightly clenched teeth. "He would never abandon his family!"

"He wouldn't?" Cold eyes stared back at him. Was Connor that unfeeling? "The man in that picture *is* that man! And he had to have a really good reason to abandon you. As you said, he wouldn't do that. But what if something went wrong, he was compromised and his family was threatened?"

"He wouldn't!" Connor's eyes matched Bryan's in hardness.

It was as though all the good feelings he was just harboring from the afternoon had vanished. Poof, gone up in smoke! There was only anger and fury left, smoldering under the surface.

The man leaned forward onto his elbows. "He would in a heartbeat without even a thought. You were the most important mission he had. Bring him in, son, safely. If *we* can find him, so can whoever made him go under. Do you understand?"

Wordless, Connor shoved out of his chair and stomped off into the long hallway. Anger, rejection, frustration, doubt. They followed him out and caught up with him by the vending machine. A good swift kick made a candy bar and a soda drop down. He didn't even crack a smile.

He stared at the pictures again. There was no mistake. His father was alive and he had been sent to fetch him!

Connor donned his dark sunglasses and made his way through the masses of people to his hotel.

He had shed every emotion on the long flight over.

He was now empty, more empty than he had ever been.

He hadn't prayed in days, nor tried to seek the Lord. His anger, frustration, and doubt had kept him away. He hadn't done what he told Emily.

He had no plan and no prayer had left his lips.

Hong Kong was a beautiful city but really, it was crowded and not Connor's style. He longed for the mountains of northern Pakistan.

He could breathe there!

He entered the climate-controlled lobby of his hotel, no idea what day it was. His watch told him that it was Wednesday noon. He had an hour before he was to meet his contact at a local restaurant. Connor ran a hand through his travel-matted hair as he checked into his room as Alex Browning, a wealthy entrepreneur from Dallas.

A shower would be nice!

Ten minutes later, showered and changed into a light gray suit to be identified by his partner, he called a cab and set off. His stomach flipped so badly as if he was on his first job. He had no clue who was going to meet him. It may be the cabby himself!

He entered the restaurant and a young Asian woman showed him to his table, set for two. Moments later a slender woman, a couple of years older than him, breezed into the restaurant. She wore a tailored tan suit with a red rose in the lapel of her jacket.

Of course, he smiled when he recognized her. They had spent a few months training together and she was quite the actress.

Let the fun and games begin!

"Alex, my da'ling." An air-kiss landed somewhere above his ear. "I have had the most frightful experience. You have to come with me to deal with it. The man charged me twice for this watch!" His companion pointed at the gold designer watch still in its case.

"Okay, sweetheart. I guess all good men must die," he said and grinned. His smile never made it to his eyes. He had just given the code.

"Yes, indeed. The clerk will wish he was dead once you are done with him." Ah, the counter-code. "We'll sue him to high heaven. Won't we, honey?" She lifted her glass of water in a toast to him.

Ah, the sue-happy American tourists! That was how they would play it.

They made small talk during dinner. His partner playing the outraged customer, and he playing the bored husband. It worked. People around them ignored them and even scoffed at them.

When they finished their very loud vocal discussion, his partner, Sally, made it a point to complain about the food. She was masterful at playing the annoying customer.

They walked through the crowded streets to a small jewelry store, where she had bought the watch. As the proprietor was busy serving other customers, Connor looked around. He was drawn to a particular piece of jewelry, which he ended up purchasing.

So, his father had worked here. Connor clamped down on the seething anger that threatened to devour him every time he thought about him. The interrogation hadn't lasted long since the owner was more than willing to help them.

After returning to their room and scanning it for bugs, they sat down at the small table, ready to discuss their assignment.

"I get to work with the legendary Rattlesnake." Her arms were crossed lightly over her chest. "This is going to be a sweet job!"

Connor rolled his eyes and rocked his chair back. "No, not so legendary, okay? I need a time-line."

Sally sighed. "I heard you're all business and no pleasure," she gave him a wink, her face falling when he didn't react. "Our man has been working for that store for on and off ten years, as you heard. Besides that, there isn't much we know. I think he made me when I tailed him last month. He disappeared two weeks ago and hasn't shown up for work."

"Do we have an address where he lives?" Connor asked.

He was travel weary and angry. A deep sense of betrayal and bitterness had made its way into his heart.

"We do, thanks to the extensive records our store owner kept. We gonna check it out tomorrow?"

Connor yawned and nodded. He stretched wearily, feeling every muscle and joint in his body complain. He went into the bathroom and showered, feeling filthy from the dirt of the city. When he came out, Sally was sprawled on the bed, a cat-like smile on her face.

"I got the couch," he murmured and snatched a pillow and blanket.

"Aww," she purred. "What a waste."

He didn't even move his head. "You want the couch, instead?"

It was as though all humanity was getting drained out of him with every breath he took. He felt nothing, and he wanted to continue that way.

It seemed that Emily's day would never be over. Children came in all day long, sick and in need. It was a never-ending barrage of heartache and pain on the parent's side.

Caring too much was draining.

Of course, there was also the lack of actual sleep and the tormenting nightmares and worry she faced every night. By the end of the day, she was working on adrenaline and caffeine. Eventually, she would make a mistake and people could die.

She walked to the doctor's lounge and poured herself another cup of coffee.

"Emily."

Dr. Gray, a stocky emergency room doctor, was sitting at the table, reading through some files.

"Good to see you back."

She grimaced and swallowed the bitter brew. She sat down on the comfortable couch along the wall, staring at the cup in her hands.

I just need a few seconds to close my eyes.

When she did, she was immediately transported back to the hut. With a start, she forced herself back.

"Emily?"

She startled at the excited greeting and her face lit up.

"Sarah! Where have you been?"

The tall doctor who looked more like a fashion model, sat down on the couch next to her.

"Vacation, honey. And a glorious one it was."

Her friend did look tanned and relaxed.

"You look terrible and why aren't you in Pakistan?"

Emily sighed and leaned her head against the back of the couch. She and Sarah had gone to college together, played basketball together, and roomed together. Sarah noticed little things and of course, she would dig for the truth. She was a shrink, just like her sister.

"What are you doing here, anyway?" Emily asked, hoping to avoid the interrogation. Sarah had a very plush office and she stayed away from the hospital.

"I have some patients," her friend answered, not taking her eyes off her. "When are you done?"

Emily looked at the large clock above the door. "Another hour, if all goes well."

"Meet you here and we'll go for dinner, okay?"

Talking to Sarah would be good. She was a strong believer, a good friend.

They walked the short distance to the restaurant most doctors frequented after work. Emily ordered a large side of fries and a burger with the works. Sarah ordered a salad and pasta, making Emily smile.

"So, what's going on with you?" Sarah asked without preamble and looked at her with her sparkling green eyes. Sarah, just like her sister, was stunningly beautiful. She wasn't married either! There were a lot of times when they had gone out on double dates, commiserated when the guys had let them down and cried on each other's shoulders when they got dumped.

"Where do I even begin?" Emily sighed.

"It usually helps if you start at the beginning," Sarah said and crunched on a radish chunk.

"That's just it. I don't know how to. It's... complicated."

Sarah's eyes lit up.

"Okay. Tell me anyway. I like complicated."

Emily played with her paper napkin. "I enjoyed Pakistan. I just didn't agree with bullets flying around, hitting me."

Sarah stared at her. "Come again?"

Emily haltingly told her the part about getting shot and about finding herself inside a terrorist's lair.

"Don't tell my family about this," she pleaded when she finished.

She glossed over the details of how they got out, and Connor wasn't mentioned much. She downplayed the torture, seeing Sarah's face pale.

"You need help, Emily! You can't do this on your own."

"I've been praying for help."

Sarah grinned as she daintily put a forkful of salad between her teeth. Emily was hungry. Juice from her burger and ketchup spilled out and onto her plate making Sarah laugh.

"How in the world did we become friends? We are polar opposites!"

Then her face turned back to a earnest scowl.

"I'm serious, Emily. You need help. Nobody can make it through something like that and walk away unscathed."

"Like I said, I've been praying."

Emily shoved a fry into her mouth. It tasted like a bar of soap. She forced herself to finish her food.

Sarah shook her head and laughed softly. "And look at that, Emily. I'm here! So let's just deal with the most pertinent issue. I want you to take something." She pulled out her script book and started to scribble down some prescriptions. "This should help catch you up on your sleep at least."

Emily stared at the prescription in her hand. "Sarah, I don't know. I don't like the way I feel when I take this stuff. My whole day becomes a fog."

"I don't want to hear it, Emily! Take one tonight so you at least catch up. And then, you're not working full time! You can't! I'll go to Dr. Bergen and explain that you are having a hard time and that you are not ready for the schedule."

She stared at her friend. "Don't! He's going to think me mentally unstable! That I can't handle the stress."

"Until you are getting rest at night, that's the way it goes." Sarah crossed her arms stubbornly. "And we're going to talk. There are a lot of holes in your story, Emily. What are you not telling me?"

Emily stared at her plate.

"I told you all I could, Sarah. The rest I can't really tell you."

Sarah watched her ripping her napkin to pieces. "I want to see you tomorrow afternoon in my office, chickie! We have a lot to talk about."

"I can't tell you more than I did, Sarah, okay? And we are talking about it right now. I don't really need to have an appointment." Emily gritted her teeth.

Sarah was getting into her personal space, something she had never done before.

"Get over it! You are coming! No argument from the patient. We need a quiet place to talk."

When they parted, Emily felt a glimmer of hope that her nightly torture may be over.

25

Connor stood in a spartan apartment. They had been here for ten minutes and he knew that there was nothing personal left. He could find no clue as to where his father might be hiding.

His father!

Connor gritted his teeth, the black wave of anger threatening to crush him yet again. He had never felt more betrayed by his father's leaving them than he did right now, standing in a place where the man had lived for the past ten years.

And still no sign of him.

Focus on the mission and then... Then get out!

A slight twinge of hope started in his heart and he crushed it. Better to feel nothing than to hope.

"So we have a dead end," he grumbled. What was he looking for? A neon sign, pointing to a hiding spot saying, *Connor, look here to find me*?

Better not to hope for anything.

Sally just ignored him as she glanced through the bare cabinets, looking for a hiding place. The apartment was located in a poorer section of town and his father hadn't invested in fixing up the place.

"Shut up and look," his partner snapped in return.

Temper, temper! Just because he was in a mood...

He walked over the uneven floor, feeling it give in one spot. His heart did a slight flip as he bent down to examine the worn floorboard.

Could it be that easy?

Pulling out his knife and working to pry it up, he fought hard to swallow that flicker of hope. Leaning back onto his heels, he roughed a hand over his face.

Of course not.

The hole was empty.

So much for hope.

He was about to rise when he spotted something that caught his attention. He pried the sides of the hole, finding that they came lose with some elbow grease. So there was something here for him.

A hiding place under the hiding place.

Most people would have given up when they found the first one empty. But he had found a virtual treasure trove. With a cold grin spreading over his face, he pulled a small stack of yellowed papers out of the little cubby under the floor. They looked like old newspapers. He read the first one, a chill passing through him.

It was an article from their hometown newspaper, listing the graduates and which colleges they were going to attend. It was written the year he graduated. There was a star by his name. He swallowed and rifled through the other articles. They were all on him, his sister and even his mother, who had opened a business after his death and turned it into a successful enterprise.

Wearily, he leaned against the wall. His father had kept up with them. The latest was a list of graduates from the grad school where his sister had received her doctorate in history. He shook his head. All these years and they didn't know he was alive.

God, this hurts!

It was the first time since he got the assignment that he was able to utter the name of the Lord.

“I found something interesting,” Sally called quietly from the kitchen.

Connor followed her voice, still stinging from what he had found. Sally had done a good job searching the kitchen. Behind the fridge, she had found his mother's new address was sprawled across a torn page from a phone book.

His stomach churning, Connor pulled out his phone and waited impatiently for someone to answer. He didn't care if it was in the middle of the night. He needed to make sure his mother was safe.

His stepfather picked up, and after a very short brisk conversation, Connor hung up. His mother hadn't been available, and she didn't believe in cell phones. But Al, his stepfather, wasn't aware of anything unusual.

By the end of their search, they found a German passport for a Dieter Hansen taped underneath the bed along with an envelope. He powered up his computer and did a check on him.

It didn't take long to find information. The man had been a silversmith and antique jeweler. His last known address was in Frankfurt but he had made a name for himself in making beautifully handcrafted pieces on his website.

“Let's see what happens if I want to buy a piece of jewelry,” he mumbled to himself.

“That's pretty.” Sally looked over his shoulder at the ring he had just purchased. “Got someone who might be interested in that?”

“I'm sure it will go a long way to placating my unhappy sister,” Connor grunted. The order was accepted.

When he opened the envelope, his breath caught in the back of his throat. His father had taken pictures of them. Connor saw his life played out.

There was one of him with his buddies at the beach. He and his sister at the ice cream shop. His sister at a swim meet. His mother's wedding.

Regret! It was all over these pictures. Regret and loss! Connor had never felt more miserable than he did that moment. He swallowed and swallowed again, trying to dislodge the lump that never seemed to go away.

He stashed the pictures in his pocket.

"Hey, look at this," Sally called and handed him a crumpled piece of paper she had found in one of the drawers full of useless trash.

It was an address in Sydney, Australia.

"That's something."

When they exited the apartment, he again felt that shred of hope and once again, he worked hard to extinguish it. All he had was a bunch of old pictures, old articles, and an address.

"I guess we should chase the only lead we have," he said back in their room after another sweep for bugs.

Regret and bitterness nipped at his heart. That night, as he stretched out on the couch that was a couple of inches too small for him, he wondered what he would be like, had his father chosen to stay.

I don't know how to come to You, Lord. I'm running on empty. There is nothing I can bring to the table. I've been feeling like this for a while now. I'm dealing with finding out that my father is alive after all these years, that he was close enough to take pictures and yet, so far away that we never knew he was there. That is a bitter pill to swallow! I don't know what to do with it!

The next day he was on his way to Sydney. The address turned out to be another apartment. This time Connor found nothing, no pictures, no papers – nothing. As he paced in his hotel room, weary of playing games, he had to force himself to work the problem in front of him. His father had completely vanished again, leaving only one traceable link to his website.

This mission was making him nuts. Feeling like a caged animal, he thumbed through the pictures again. His father had been close, and yet they had still been left with their pain, never letting them know he was alive.

It stung!

Did they mean so little to their father? Just as he thought it, he knew it was wrong. He stared at the picture of him and his mother at her wedding, taken five years ago. They were dancing and the tears were running down his mother's cheeks.

How had he taken that picture? How much pain had his father been in that day? Connor ground his molars together, refusing to allow the thought to stir up a sliver of compassion.

No!

His father had deceived them for twenty years. He had walked away from them! Connor's fingers bunched into a fist and punched the wall, leaving a hole. That didn't help.

Follow the breadcrumbs. He's left you enough.

Dieter Hansen!

His father used that alias. If he followed whatever he could gather about that man, he may find out more.

An hour later he boarded a plane to Frankfurt.

What if...

"Emily, what are you not telling me?" Sarah sighed as she sat across from her best friend. They had been talking for half an hour.

"I can't tell you more. A girl's gotta have her secrets," Emily grimaced, trying to get her friend off her back.

Her efforts were rewarded with a deep scowl.

They sat in Sarah's plush office. Sarah was very good at what she did and had begun to dig around in Emily's personal space, leaving her exhausted and unable to protect herself.

"You didn't take those pills did you?" Sarah asked.

Sheepishly, as if caught sneaking a peek under the tree before Christmas, Emily shook her head.

"Doctors make the worst patients!" her friend growled. "Take the pills, even if it's just for a few days. Or try this." Her friend steepled her slim fingers and pursed her lips. "Try praying when the nightmares come."

"Huh?"

Sarah nodded.

"I had a patient once who refused to take sleeping pills. She was afraid they would make her addicted. So, she prayed every time she had a nightmare. Within a week, they were gone. Tell me, what else keeps you up at night? It's amazing what the brain does when we try to shut things off."

Didn't Emily know it!

"I just worry, that's all. And it seems that at night the worry gets to me and I can't sleep."

"What are you worried about?" Sarah's voice was soft, so full of compassion.

"People," Emily said narrowly. "I worry that people get hurt."

"Like you? You worry that people get caught by terrorists and hurt?"

"Yes," Emily lied.

"You can always pray for God's protection. He is good at that."

"I do. I just can't fully believe that He will protect them. Sometimes He says no, Sarah."

"There's a lot more to this story. Am I right?" Sarah asked.

Emily cocked her head.

"Leave it be, Sarah. There are lives at stake here."

Her friend's eyes narrowed. "Whoa, Emily! What in the world did you do in Pakistan? Except for getting shot and tortured."

"That about sums it up, Sarah."

When she walked into her apartment she pondered Sarah's suggestion to pray when she awoke from a nightmare, and decided to give it a try. Her mother dropped by as soon as she entered her apartment.

"Emily? Would you like to come to the house for dinner?"

"No. Mom, I'm really tired. I haven't been sleeping too well."

"You're still dealing with the aftermath of getting shot. I can't even imagine what you are going through, honey."

Her mother wandered over to her and sat down on the bed next to her. Emily held a bottle of pills in her hand. She stared at them.

"I didn't know you were that bad, Emi. You should see someone about this, sweetheart. You can't work and not sleep."

"I'm seeing Sarah, who suggested taking these for a few days. And I'm no longer working full time. But I'm still having nightmares. Sarah suggested I pray when I have trouble sleeping. Maybe my prayers aren't working, you know?" It scared her to think that way.

Her mother pulled her into an embrace. "Emily, there isn't a prayer that God doesn't hear. It doesn't matter how quietly we utter it. It's not the words you say. You know that."

She brushed a strand of blonde hair out of Emily's face.

"I do know that. Maybe I'm just really tired. Maybe this whole thing is just getting to me."

"What whole thing?" her mother asked, her eyes soft and searching.

Emily shook her head. "Never mind, Mom. I'm going to try to sleep tonight. Would you just pray for me?"

Debbie squeezed her shoulders tenderly and kissed her forehead in that motherly fashion. "Of course, dearest. I will make my request known to God. *And the peace of God, which passeth all understanding, shall keep your hearts and minds through Christ Jesus."* She winked.

"Thanks, Mom!"

When she closed her eyes for the night, she prayed for Connor's safety and his heart. That night she dreamed that a roaring monster was about to devour Connor and her, and she awoke covered in sweat, her heart racing. Even though her mind was fuzzy, she turned to the Lord.

The Lord is my shepherd, I shall not want. He maketh me to lie down in green pastures: He leadeth me beside the still waters. He restoreth my soul.

For the first time in a long time, Emily slept.

Connor watched his mother play tennis with her best friend, both laughing and chatting as they batted the ball leisurely back and forth. She was still a beautiful woman, even though her eyes held a deep sadness that started the day his father 'died'.

He ran his hands through his dark hair. As he scanned the area, he was satisfied that his father was nowhere in the crowd.

After chasing the alias for a week, Connor had come up empty and returned stateside, feeling like a failure. The only lead he still had was the ring, which had been shipped to his place in Connecticut.

His father didn't want to be found.

He had been gone for twenty years and, even though he had left a smidgen of a trace, Connor couldn't track him down.

When his mother was done playing, she glanced his way and a bright smile slipped onto her face.

“Connor, what a surprise. When did you get in? Are you staying a while?”

He kissed her offered cheek and shook his head. “Just traveling through, Mom. I wanted to see if you were alright.”

Hurt clouded her beautiful brown eyes for a split second.

“Of course. You're busy! How is Connecticut?”

“It's definitely growing on me,” he said, keeping his voice light.

His mother searched his face. Not able to penetrate his facade, she gave a resigned sigh and slipped her arm around him.

“You have time for a bite to eat with your mother, right?” They walked into the restaurant and were seated quickly under a large Hawaiian-style umbrella.

“You look tired, son,” she said softly after placing her order. His mother was also a vegetarian, as was his sister.

“I've been on the road for a while,” he replied and sipped his fruity drink.

“How long were you gone this time?”

Connor frowned. How long was he gone? It seemed like it had been ages. “I think it's been a month.”

His mother sniffed and shook her head. “Ever thought of retiring? I mean, there is more to life than what you do, even though it's important. You have worked for a long time in that business and I think it's changing you.”She narrowed her eyes and leaned closer as if trying to break through the walls he was putting up.

He said, “I can't help that,” well aware that it was the truth. “I have been thinking of doing something different. Especially lately.”

His mother's eyes widened in surprise “Oh? Is there a specific reason for your thoughts?”

He leaned his head onto his steepled hands. “A couple. But they don't have anything to do with finding the love of my life, Mom. You just let that romantic notion of yours die.”

Unless he counted the spunky blonde, for whom he had carried chocolate in his luggage all the way from Germany. Although, it had been a while since he had seen her, and she had made her opinion of him clear.

His mother grinned sheepishly. “It's a mother's prerogative to have hopes for her children, even though they don't seem to come true. Alicia just broke up with Ken. She was pretty devastated.”

Connor had known that since he had visited his sister. First, she had punched him, then she had cried. He felt helpless when she sobbed into his shoulder. He could face bombs and terrorists, but he shied away from sisters with a broken heart.

They rose from their seats after finishing their dinner. Connor hugged her tightly, suddenly feeling horrible for leaving her unprotected from – his own father.

"I'm off Mom. It was good to see you. Be careful, will you?"

His mother narrowed her eyes suspiciously. "Of course. But you too, son."

They hugged again in the parking lot and Connor made his way back to the airport, where he hopped onto a plane bound for Washington.

26

Sitting in the comfortable office with his mentor across from him hours later, he finished the verbal brief of his unsuccessful mission, feeling once again a deep sense of failure and betrayal.

"It's not going to be easy to track him." The cold eyes measured him again.

"Don't I know it," Connor grunted. "Except for the jewelry business, my father doesn't exist. I'm going home to take some time off. After this assignment I need it."

"You can't just walk away from this. We need you out there."

Connor tapped his fingers on the man's desk. "Get someone else. I need to sort some things out. I haven't taken a vacation in years. I think that you owe me, don't you?"

The man leaned back in his chair. "I suppose so. You have two weeks."

Connor laughed, humorlessly. "Try two months at least. I'll keep on working on the jewelry angle, but I'm not going back out into the field. I'm still tracking down my father. Don't send anyone else after him. I'll bring him in. I never miss, remember?"

"Fine. Take your time off. Work from your home. We'll contact you in a month."

Connor leaned against the door frame. "Don't expect me to answer!"

He walked past the vending machine, the one that had received the brunt of his anger the last time he was there. That anger was still there. It settled into his stomach like a cancer and was spreading around in his body, poisoning every cell. He had to talk to God, but he didn't feel strong enough to approach him on his knees.

As his plane touched down at Bradley he felt a sense of homecoming. It was strange. He hadn't felt it anywhere before. He had two months in which he could figure out whether he stayed in or got out. If he got out it would be for one reason, one reason only.

To settle down, finally.

He collected his car, parked in the long-term parking lot. He grinned in pleasure as he let the top down. The day was warm and pleasant. A wonderful, late summer day. His first errand was to pick up all his mail, which included a small package. Turning the box around, he almost ripped it open as he returned to his car. Drawing in a few steadying breaths through his nose, he set it onto the passenger seat.

He drove slowly, carefully, through his quiet neighborhood. His stomach growled, telling him that he hadn't eaten since sharing the pizza with his mother, which seemed days ago.

Out of habit, he glanced into the rear-view mirror and took the long way to spot a trail, even though there was no reason for it. When he opened the door to the utility room, he sensed it again.

His house was stale, nobody was there to welcome him home from a long trip. Throwing himself onto the couch in his living room, the silence pressing in on him. At least his father had always been welcomed like a conquering hero. In the end, he was not what they thought him to be.

He felt stale and empty too!

What if...

Worn out and tired.

Angry and hurt!

There! He admitted it!

"Lord, I'm furious!" he shouted into the empty living room, his voice bouncing off the empty walls. "I feel betrayed! Why did my father leave us? Why didn't You step in to protect us and to keep us together? Why?!"

He felt like someone had slammed a gavel on top of him. He was accusing the Lord of the Universe! He was putting God on trial! God hadn't done what Connor had expected from Him. Now, Connor was pouting! He was angry at God for not playing to Connor's rules and standards!

Whoa!

Had Connor just put himself into God's spot? Had he just expected God to act according to what Connor wanted?

He got up, irritated. Frustration poured out of him. Before he punched something, he'd better find a less violent outlet. He looked at his weight equipment waiting for him and punched the large bag hanging from the ceiling. The momentary shock traveled up his arm and into his shoulder.

Perfect. Jabbing and punching released the tension in his muscles.

An hour later Connor was soaked in sweat, and the fury... it was still there but manageable. He stepped into the shower and let the spray sooth his muscles.

Then they cry unto the Lord in their trouble, and He bringeth them out of their distress. He maketh the storm a calm, so that the waves thereof are still.

He stilled at the reminder.

This was not about his feelings of hurt and anger against his father. This was about his doubt that God was not God, that He was incapable of leading Connor down a path that was good for him. It was about Connor supplanting God and putting himself on the throne of his life.

Well, that just smacked him in the face!

Connor felt his heart break. He was guilty before God of idolatry!

Come to me, all ye who are burdened and I will give you rest.

That rest was something he hadn't felt in a long time. Not since he had watched Emily take a bullet. Not since he found out his father was alive.

Lord forgive me! His heart cried out, just like he imagined David had. *I have accused You of some pretty harsh things. I have stood as the judge. Help me to find my way back to the path You have set out for me, the one that I know You were leading me down. What do You have for me? I accept it, take it and live with it. Thank You, Lord.*

Emily plopped onto her couch with a plate of lasagna in her hand, realizing that she was doing so much better lately. Food was beginning to taste like food again. She managed to get a few more hours of sleep each night. When the nightmares came, she prayed until the fear went away and she was able to go back to sleep. She could pray for Connor without worry, knowing that her prayers had been heard and God knew what He was doing in her friend's life.

She still didn't know what His plan was for her, but somehow it was okay. She could live with it.

Her God was bigger than her troubles.

Her God would make a way out for her.

Her God stood waiting for her to fall and scrape her knees. He would encourage her to get up and continue on.

Talking with Sarah certainly helped. Things were looking up since they started meeting twice a week in the last two weeks, praying together and allowing Emily to voice some of her fears. The only thing she omitted was anything about Connor. She felt a glimmer of light at the end of the dark hallway she had been walking down.

Since it was early and she wasn't working the next day, Emily put in a comedy, one that always made her laugh no matter how much she watched it. Laughing so hard her side hurt, she was surprised when someone knocked on her door.

Usually, her mother didn't bother knocking, although Emily decided to talk to her about that – again.

“It's unlocked, Mom!” she shouted, too comfortable to get up.

When the door stayed shut, she was intrigued and padded over to let her in.

She froze when she did. Unexpected tears automatically welled up and began to run down her cheeks unchecked. This time, she didn't stop herself from throwing her arms around Connor's neck, crying softly.

“Hey,” he soothed gently and stood transfixed in the door. Slowly, he allowed his arms to come around her.

“It's okay. It's all good.”

He didn't want to feel too much. Then again, what good was it to keep up the walls?

They stood in the doorway to her apartment for a long time. Emily's tears finally stopped coming and she became self-conscious about where she was. She cleared her throat and stepped out of his arms.

“Wait a moment.” The gaze from his deep blue eyes lodged itself in her heart. “I kind of liked that.”

Nah. I'm not making it that easy!

Her chin shot up. “It was a gut reaction. Don't get used to it,” she said icily and narrowed her eyes.

Connor laughed softly. So much for thinking she had gone soft on him.

“May I come in?”

He leaned against the door frame, folding his arms leisurely across his chest. Before he could stop himself, he ran a thumb over her pale cheeks, noting a slight blush spread over her face.

Her breath caught and she took a step backward.

“I suppose I could make an exception and allow you inside. Just this once, since you've been gone for so long.”

Taking a deep, steadying breath, he stepped inside and felt it immediately. Her apartment was well lived-in, in contrast to his stale house. Her scent was everywhere, soaking into him like a vapor making him feel like he had come home.

The perfume of freshly cut roses sitting in a vase on the kitchen table settled into his heart. It brought back a memory that almost knocked him back a step.

“Are you all right, Connor?”

He blinked away the burning in his eyes. His first response was to tell her that he was fine but the compassion in her eyes stopped him.

“Roses,” he croaked and pointed to the bunch in the kitchen. “My mom cut the last bunch the day we got news of my father's – death. She never cut another bouquet again. I... I hadn't thought of that in years. It caught me by surprise.”

Emily sat down slowly on her couch and pointed to the other end for him to sit. She only had the one sofa. He had shared something real, from his past, with her. A shot of adrenaline went through her. Perhaps...

"You look tired. Are you still having nightmares?"

Emily tightened the hold on the pillow in her arms, her gaze darting about the room for something to draw the conversation away from her issues.

"Emily," he said softly and touched her cheek. "I know. I've been where you are."

Her breath stalled and she fought the tears that once again pricked her eyes. "I had trouble sleeping," she whispered as if ashamed. "One night it stopped when I remembered the Shepherd's Psalm. I was able to give up my worries... about you... to the Lord which helped also." There was that rush of heat into her face again!

"You were concerned about me?" he whispered hoarsely.

He wanted to tease her but somehow he couldn't. She looked so... vulnerable. Taking her hand in his, he lifted her fingers to his lips and softly kissed her knuckles.

Emily swallowed and pulled her hand out of his grasp. Her whole hand tingled, and the sensation worked its way up her arm. Her breathing became labored and she nibbled her bottom lip.

"I was," she whispered back, looking down at her fingers now somehow intertwined with his. "I... feared I'd never see you again. But don't read anything into that!"

"Fair enough," he replied, a small smile slipping onto his lips.

"What happened on this mission?" she asked.

Connor turned his head away. He wasn't at liberty to tell her anything. Yet the more he talked to her, the more the hardships of the last operation – the pain of finding out that his father was alive and yet not finding him – dripped off him like water.

"You know I can't tell you," he said softly and regretted it immediately when she removed her hand from his. Her whole body became an impenetrable wall. "I traveled through Germany again."

Emily scooted into the corner, fighting that flutter in her gut. "Are you trying to buy your way into my heart?"

"How could I possibly? You don't know me very well if you think so."

He handed her three large chocolate bars. Emily's eyes widened.

"Too much chocolate is bad for you. What are you trying to do?"

Connor's eyes twinkled with mischief and he withdrew his offer teasingly. "Is that so, doctor? Then why are you still eating it?"

She snatched the bars out of his hand and began to instruct him on the health benefits of chocolate. Something was different about him. The eyes were colder, lacking that intensity she always found so unsettling.

Instead, there was anger.

To give herself some time to think, she got up and poured two glasses of lemonade. He may have shared a childhood memory but there were many things he would never tell her.

That thought hurt.

"Thank you," she finally said, turned to him and pointed to the bars. "You really didn't have to, you know."

Connor rose from the couch and came to her, accepting the drink.

"Don't you know that whenever I see chocolate now, I think of you?"

She leaned harder against the counter, fearing her knees would buckle.

"Listen," he continued tenderly. "I took some time off from work. Do you think you and I could get to know each other better?"

Emily's throat tightened. Something had affected him so deeply that he took a break from his agency job.

"I... don't know." She tucked a stray strand of hair behind her ears. "There's part of me that wants to. And there is the other side that tells me not to be foolish. You'll never ever be able to share a large portion of your life with me. So that leaves me as only a good acquaintance." She looked out the window.

A muscle in his jaw twitched and a soft, discouraged sigh came from his lips. "I... I wish I could tell you more." A tired, sad smile made its way onto his face. For a moment, it touched his eyes, making the skin around them crinkle.

Emily tenderly brushed a thumb over the creases.

"Tell me what you can. Why are you so sad?"

Connor pulled back as if she had slapped him. He longed to tell her everything and couldn't, knowing that he'd put her life in danger. Was there a part of it that wouldn't? He returned to the couch and patted the seat next to him, feeling a rush of adrenaline. He'd tell her something, leave out most.

"Come here?" he asked softly.

Emily sat down but pulled her legs up and hugged her knees to her chest in self-protection.

Connor ran his hand through his hair, pretending not to notice.

"I was sent to find an agent, who had gone underground a long time ago and had resurfaced recently. When I found his trail, it was a dead end. I failed to bring him in safely."

"So, this was a rogue agent?" Feeling once again like she was living in one of her novels, Emily forgot to take a breath in anticipation.

Connor's eyebrows rose considerably and he breathed a laugh.

"No, Em. This man had been one of our best agents. My superior thinks that there was a threat against his life and he went under to protect his family."

Emily let out a soft hiss and tears obscured her vision.

No wonder he was so sad. This one must have hit too close to home.

Connor put a hand on her knee to draw her attention and electricity tingled pleasantly through her.

"Every agent has a family, somewhere. I came back with a lot of baggage and no answers. That's why I need to take some time off. I don't know if I want to continue with the agency."

"What?" Emily breathed, still trying not to think about her reaction to his touch.

"Mm. It seems that lately there have been questions niggling in my heart as to whether there is more out there. You know, having a life, starting a family."

"Family?" she managed to whisper.

"Yeah, you know. A wife, some kids. That sort of thing. I just couldn't put my them through what we went through with my father; when he..." He frowned. "You know. I wouldn't want to do that to my wife. I saw the toll it took on my mother."

"Wife, kids?" Emily's face turned that ugly shade of red again. She covered her face in her arms.

"Hey," he said softly and pulled her arms down. "Don't hide. You're very pretty when you blush."

Emily groaned and rolled her eyes, burying her head once again.

"I don't give a compliment undeserved." Connor's eyebrows furrowed.

She peeked at him from her hiding spot. “There, sir, I must contradict you. You told my mother that the roast chicken you had on that Sunday was the best you ever tasted.”

Connor snickered deviously. “It was the truth. I had not tasted its equal.”

A flutter of excitement and hope squirreled through her and she immediately put a stop to it. Even though he had shared, he would never be able to completely be honest with her, and she closed her heart to him.

Connor pushed himself to his feet. Being here settled his heart. Being with her made him forget the doubts that plagued his mind. It was also time to leave since she looked done in.

“I gotta go. But before I go, there is something I have to give you.”

He pulled a delicate silver chain out of his pocket. At the end of it dangled a thin silver fish. It was not the exact replica of the one that the terrorist had ripped off her. It was beyond delicate. The silver was almost transparent. The tiny engraving on the fish had caught his eye.

My beloved is mine and I am His.

The couch underneath Emily shifted. It became hard to breathe, and forget swallowing all together! She stared at the necklace hanging from Connor's finger, trembling from head to toe as the room began to fade away again and she was in the hut, her neck exposed.

“Hey,” a voice out of the fog called. “Emily! You're okay. You're safe with me in your apartment.”

She yanked her arm away from the gentle touch, then her vision cleared.

Oh, I did it again!

Connor hovered right in front of her, a concerned expression on his face.

"Does that happen often?" he said softly.

"Sometimes. When I'm reminded... You know," she panted and pointed to the necklace with a trembling finger. "You shouldn't have."

"I couldn't not have," he said just as quietly. "You're amazing. You have a strength I have yet to see in many people. I'm just returning something that was taken from you, Emily. No strings attached." His gaze was once again that mesmerizing intensity and her world tilted.

Emily closed her eyes, shutting out the desire to lean in and feel his arms around her.

What do I do, God?

My beloved is mine and I am His!

Emily swallowed hard and opened her eyes. God had given her so many things, so many promises that were true. Sometimes, she felt like she was His beloved. Some days she knew she would be able to do anything with Him at her side.

"Thank you," she whispered softly.

Connor handed it to her. Leaning forward, he tenderly kissed her cheek. When she tried to retreat behind her arms again in embarrassment, he tipped up her chin.

"Good night, fair maiden," he teased. "I'll count the hours 'till we meet again."

"You're laying it on a bit thick."

Connor chortled. "On that note, it's time for me to go!"

As he settled in his silent home, he vowed he'd try to change it and fill it with love and laughter. He only had two months to do it.

27

The emptiness of his house wasn't as depressing as it had been because now he had a workable plan, something to hold onto. Tomorrow he would do something to make this place into a home. At least for the next two months, he could pretend that he could have a life: a family, a wife.

She hadn't kicked him out of her house when he asked to spend time with her. A smile played on his face until his hackles suddenly stood at attention.

The floorboards above him creaked as if someone was up there.

Automatically, he drew his handgun and slipped out of his shoes. Almost in a crouch, he tiptoed upstairs, hoping to avoid making any noise. Alas, the last stair let out a squeak and he melted into the wall. Adrenaline pumped through him in an explosion. He paused outside the door and shoved hard as he entered. The door went crashing into the wall and he jumped inside. A dark figure stood in the center.

Connor took a shot at him.

Thwack! The bullet entered the wall behind his bed.

Connor backed up, stunned. He never missed! The first punch connected with his hard abs making him grunt in surprise. Taking advantage of his momentary distraction, the dark figure swiftly wrapped his arms tightly around Connor's neck.

"Hold still, son, or I'll put you over my knee!" the intruder, who had a death grip on him, growled into his ear.

Connor's knees buckled as his strength and breath evaporated.

"Dad?!"

Gagging, he scrambled away from his attacker and hit the light switch, illuminating the room. Connor staggered backward a few steps, massaging his throbbing neck.

"Dad!" he croaked.

"Hello, boy." The man in front of him sank down on his bed, breathing heavily. "You used to be a lot easier to pin down." He grinned sheepishly while he removed the dark woolen cap.

In a moment of weakness, Connor wanted fling his arms around his father, ask him what he had brought him from his journey. Then, anger, frustration, and betrayal came washing over him and he took another step backward.

"You-"

"Ya look good, Connor. I see you got the ring you ordered. That was a clever idea, actually. For me, it worked great. Led me right to you. For you, well... Here I am!"

The man on his bed raised both arms, waiting for a reply. He threaded his fingers through his straight salt and pepper hair.

It was more salt than pepper, Connor observed. His face looked older, fuller. His father had always been very athletic, but he had gained a few pounds, which he wore well. His eyes held a lot of pain. Connor could almost see his own regret in them.

He stumbled out of the room, down the stairs, and into the kitchen where he grabbed a glass of water and downed it in one gulp.

"Connor. We need to talk."

Connor shook his head, his back to his father. "No, I don't think I can."

His whole world had shifted. His father was standing in front of him!

Alive!

"Connor Joseph Williams! Snap out of it. Face the reality! I'm standing right in front of you!"

"No! You're not my father!" It was a ridiculous statement and the man in front of him stumbled backward a step. Connor cocked his head and narrowed his eyes. "My father would never leave us!"

The older man leaned wearily against the wall, muscles in his jaw tightening and relaxing as he worked out what to say. "By now you must have figured out that I didn't leave on purpose. I never meant to... to cause my family any pain."

Connor spun and pointed the barrel of his gun at his father's head.

"You know," he growled, his voice not quite steady. His hand was, though. "I should just do Mom a favor. She'll never know the betrayal she suffered. Alicia will think you are the hero we all thought you were. I'll just put a bullet through your head, call in the team for clean-up and be done with it." His eyes narrowed dangerously.

His father's eyes became cold, unfeeling. He didn't blink but stared at him. "Go ahead. Finish it. Will you be able to live with yourself?"

Connor gritted his teeth. He lowered his gun and secured it. He stuck it back into the waistband of his jeans and turned away from him, breathing heavily.

"Get out of my house! I'll just pretend you don't exist. You haven't lived for twenty years so it won't be anything earth-shattering."

"There is a reason for what I did." His father took a deep breath. He pushed off from the wall and stood in front of Connor. "I never thought things would happen like that, but they did. Listen to me, Connor. I was protecting you."

"Right," Connor said, his voice laced with sarcasm and anger. "Sure thing. Protecting us. Mm-hm. I know. Thanks, Dad. That was very thoughtful of you. But you weren't there when Mom swallowed a bottle of sleeping pills! You weren't there when she tried to shoot herself, with one of your guns, might I add! You missed the time when Alicia came home from the prom with her heart broken because her date had dumped her for someone who would actually sleep with him. You may have pictures and newspaper articles of our achievements, but you... weren't... there!"

His father bristled and glowered at him. "Okay, son. Let's just have it out, shall we? No, I wasn't there. I. REGRET. IT! I missed out on what I wanted the most in life. A family, a place to come home to. But I did it because I had to. I made a tough decision. Someone was threatening my family. I died instead. I chose to keep you safe."

"The agency would have supported you, you being one of their top agents."

His father gave him a blank stare.

"Why didn't you do that? Instead, your family suffered anyway. I don't get it!"

"Is that why you don't have a family? Is that why you live a stale life?"

Connor stepped up to his much shorter father.

"I work. The agency *is* my life, thanks to you! I don't have time for anything else. I'm done talking to you! Tomorrow I'm taking you in. Then I wash my hands of you. You were dead for twenty years and you still are."

"Connor!" His father's voice was sharp, filled with disappointment. "I didn't raise you like that."

"Cut it out! You quit on me!"

His father stepped in his way, a very bold move considering the mood he was in. The muscles in his arm tightened and he clenched his fists.

"I didn't just quit on you. Remember my wife? My daughter? They both paid a high price. We all did! And I'm not going in. I am not going back. If you bring me in, who knows what they will make me do." His expression twisted.

Connor was so done with this conversation. Stomping past his father like a little boy, he walked into his room and slammed the door.

Lord, this isn't right! He shows up and thinks all is honky-dory!

As he stewed in his anger, the promise that God loved him, walked with him, was guiding him up this steep path filled with rocks, saturated his heart and mind. He grabbed his Bible and opened it for the first time in a month. Of course, it flipped to Peter asking Jesus how many times he was supposed to forgive.

He was called to forgive his father no matter what. Swallowing the lump in his throat that hadn't been there before, he realized that he didn't want to. Deep down it felt good to hold on to his anger and sense of betrayal. It was easier than going to his father and telling him how much he had missed him. Placing it where it belonged, in Christ's hands, would require for him to surrender and obey.

He sat stewing for a good half hour. He couldn't do it. He pulled the sheets back and slipped into them, fully clothed.

God was asking too much of him.

Connor woke in the morning after once again sleeping only a few hours. He carried his missions on in his sleep and every decision he made haunted him. Every life he took, every lie he told came back to him when he tried to sleep. And he was too weary to rest, always listening for someone to sneak up on him.

He was not ready to face the day. Not like this!

The unresolved feelings he had for the man who had loved him so much and had chosen to walk away from them were making him even more grouchy. There was so much they had all missed out on. His heart broke for his mother, who had lost the most.

He doesn't deserve it.

But the Lord would have him forgive.

He would have him move on and not hold him captive to Connor's hurts and feelings. His father had lost just as much as his family had.

No! He made a choice to walk away.

His gut clenched when he thought honestly about it. The evidence of what it had cost him was in Connor's bag. He pulled out the articles and pictures he had found in the apartment in Hong Kong and laid them out on his bed. His father had kept track of them closely.

A knock on the door spun him around and made him reach for his gun. As if it was the most natural thing, his father entered and froze.

He exhaled softly. “You found my stash! I thought I had hidden them well.”

Connor shook his head. There was a picture of Connor in the desert with his friends. A huge bonfire lit up the dark sky. He pointed to it.

“You saw?” His voice was raw, tight. He remembered that night or at least the beginning of that night. It was during the first year when Connor had struggled most with his father's death.

"I did. I stayed until y'all passed out. Then I took you home. You threw up three times on the way. I worried for you that year, fearing that you would continue with the drinking to drown out your pain. But you made a much better choice!" His father pushed the picture out of the way and lifted his gaze, a look of pride flashing in his gray eyes.

"I didn't know how I ended up on the front porch," Connor whispered, his throat now too thick to speak. "I thought one of my buddies had taken me."

"I couldn't just leave you out there like that."

His father looked at the picture of him walking to get his diploma from college.

"That was another proud moment." There were tears in his eyes. "I know you're angry with me, son. I would have preferred to stay with y'all."

Connor threaded his fingers through his hair, wishing he could just whisk himself away. Rubbing the back of his neck, his muscles popped. There was a right way to do things and a wrong way. His father had wronged them. He also had reaped the consequences. He also lost the day he decided to step away from a family he loved.

Connor hung his head and swallowed.

With one last look at the pictures on Connor's bed, his father crossed his arms at the wrist and held them out for him.

"I guess you can take me in, Connor. Finish your mission. I can take it. I have nothing to lose anymore."

"Dad!" he groaned.

Connor turned around and paced the span of the room.

He knew what God expected and he didn't like it. Whatever he decided, there would be a cost. He would have to give up on the anger and frustration he was reveling in. He would have to make an effort to forge a new relationship with the man standing in front of him.

God had given him a second chance!

The fight went out of him and he turned toward his father, whose resigned features cut right into his heart.

"Dad," Connor repeated.

His father lifted his head and they regarded each other for a moment. Then he opened his arms and Connor stepped into them like he had done so many times as a child.

"I'm sorry, son. I really didn't intend for any of this to happen. I love you guys more than life itself. I wish I could go back in time."

He thumped him on the back and they stepped away from each other.

Connor cleared his throat. A frog had jumped into the back of his esophagus. It was very inconvenient.

"I gotta do my workout."

Connor turned to walk to the living room with his father trailing behind.

"May I suggest that you move your equipment to another room? If you have company," his father winked, "she may not like smelling your sweat."

"Is that what smells so bad in here?" Connor laughed as he wedged himself under his weights. "A little help, Dad?"

For the next hour, father and son grunted and sweated together.

Most of all, they bonded.

28

A shower helped. The anger he had felt this morning was gone. The frustration had disappeared. He was at peace. It was amazing how a little forgiveness went a long way. It was almost as though there had been chains attached to his father's abandonment, which held Connor captive.

God was right. Forgiveness was important.

Connor realized that the consequences of his father's actions were still with him. But he was able to look at them and recognize that perhaps they had shaped him into the man he was. Perhaps they had driven him to Christ!

He stepped out of his room and sniffed the air. Something his father was concocting in the kitchen smelled... bacon! He bounded down the stairs into the kitchen to find his father standing at the stove, whistling to the song on the radio.

"Dad!" Connor stared at the heaps of bacon his father was frying up. "You are *not* using my frying pan to cook a dead animal, a dead pig on top of that! Do you know how many carcinogens are in that? It ain't going into this body!"

He pointed to himself and slipped his arms through the sleeves of his navy T-shirt. His father stared at him.

"What are you on about, Connor? A piece of bacon is like heaven on earth!" he replied and went back to stirring the pieces of meat floating within its fat. "Just like a good piece of steak, barbecued to perfection."

"I'm not touching that stuff! And you better scrub that frying pan real good. I'm not having pig grease in my kitchen."

His father laughed at him. “Are you telling me you don't eat bacon?”

“I don't eat *meat*,” Connor said indignantly and poured himself a tall glass of orange juice.

“Oh! I guess I didn't know that! When did that happen? Because when I was alive, we all enjoyed bacon and eggs on Sunday mornings before heading to church.”

There it was again. The reminder of how much had been lost!

“I guess Mom decided, a year after you “died”, to go on a diet and she became a vegetarian. Alicia and I just went along and soon it stuck.”

“If I had been there...”

If he had been there...

It would always hang over them. Yes, Connor chose to forgive, but there was still that sting. The doorbell rang and he frowned. It was not even nine. It was too early for a social call. He removed his gun from the waistband of his jeans, making sure his father was ready for an assault just like he was.

Never assume!

He was alive because he didn't. His father moved out of the kitchen, where the bacon sizzled, and took a stance around the corner, ready to defend himself. He nodded to his son. Connor's heart shuttered at how good it felt to be working with him like on a mission. They would have made a good team.

He wrenched the door open and stilled. Of course, it was not some sinister stranger, ready to shoot up the house. They wouldn't have rung the doorbell.

Emily!

He quickly stuffed his gun back under his shirt and exhaled the tension mounting in his body. Her eyes registered that something was up and she took a step backward.

"This is a very nice surprise," Connor grinned, willing his heart to slow down.

Her blonde hair was put up into a ponytail, and she wore jeans and a gray T-shirt. She didn't wear a spot of makeup and she still looked great!

"Did you bring me more of those delicious muffins?" he teased.

The corners of her mouth twitched but she controlled her smile. She wasn't going to make it easy on him, was she? He opened the door wider, knowing that his father was back in the kitchen, saving the bacon from turning into charcoal.

"I just thought I would come by. I come bearing no treats. I told you. I won't do that again."

"What a shame," he murmured and pulled her inside. He knew better than to draw her into his arms, although he itched to do so.

Emily stood in the hall, her nose twitching, looking nervously around.

"Do I smell bacon?" Her voice conveyed the shock she must feel.

He growled. "I'm afraid so."

"What's this? Are you a closet meatatarian? Do you just pretend not to eat meat? Is that part of your scheme? Your *spy-persona*?" She flung her hands dramatically into the air, nailing him with a glare. "Are you going to have to kill me now because I found out?" she teased.

Connor laughed softly, once again enjoying sparring with her. He casually leaned against the wrought iron railing.

"No! I'm not going to touch the stuff. It just seems that my guest wanted some bacon this morning and I couldn't refuse."

“Oh!” Emily's face turned bright red. She should have known. “I didn't realize you had company. I better go so... I... shouldn't have come.”

She turned toward the door and opened it part way, barely able to keep the sob from exploding out from her lips. Of course, Connor had a *guest*. He was a good-looking guy! She didn't expect him to be spending his time alone, especially not when she hadn't given him any indication of her own feelings.

Connor's arm snaked around her and shut the door, his eyes hooded, unreadable. The expression on his face was guarded. It was as though she was staring at the guy in Pakistan – the man who had shot their assailants without blinking an eye. Shivering involuntarily, she pulled her arms around her, protecting herself.

“You don't hold me in high regards, do you?” he scowled. “You think I would entertain someone after our talk last night? You think I'm that kind of a cad?” He sounded disappointed, let down.

“No... I really didn't think...” She felt trapped in an invisible cage. “You can do whatever you want.”

She drew in a quick breath. Why did she still feel like someone had punched her in the gut?

Connor put his hands on her shoulders and turned her around. He wanted her to know the truth. Emily squirmed uncomfortably while he steered her toward the kitchen.

“I really don't want to meet your guest,” she whispered, biting back tears.

“Well, tough luck. You're about to,” he whispered back, his breath tickling the back of her neck.

Emily chided herself when goosebumps rose.

"Emily." He pointed to his father, who turned around, placing a plate full of bacon on the table, next to the eggs. "Meet my father, Rick."

Emily gasped. She stared at the man, who wore the same guarded expression as Connor. Then it flickered and understanding passed over his face, then a grin.

"Emily." Richard Williams wiped his hands on his shorts before extending a hand to her. "I hope you're not a vegetarian. I made an awful lot of bacon, thinking this son of mine would join me after a rigorous workout. Turns out he has something against meat. And bacon in particular! Go figure. Would you join me? I can't eat all this by myself." His voice had a delightful twang to it and Emily found herself strangely drawn to him.

"But... but... you're supposed to be dead," she whispered. "At least that's what I heard."

He sighed and lowered himself into a chair. "I know. It came as a shock to my son too. He wasn't too happy about it either. But I think we are good now, right Connor?" He slapped his back.

"Not with you stinking up my kitchen with that vile smell," Connor growled and pulled out a yogurt from the fridge along with some blueberries and strawberries.

Agent Williams senior laughed.

"Please join us, Emily," Connor pulled out a chair for her. "Unless you have to go now."

"No," she shook her head. "Yes, I... I really shouldn't stay."

A plate full of bacon and eggs was set down in front of her. "You should. It will be only us if you leave and we are likely to kill each other by the end of the day. We are both armed and dangerous."

Connor snorted and mixed his fruit and yogurt very deliberately. His father's eyes crinkled as he grinned, making Emily's knees give out and she plopped into the chair. Connor's father bowed his head and grabbed Connor's hand in one and Emily's in the other hand. Connor did the same and waited.

It had been twenty years since he had prayed with his father.

"Lord, thank You for bringing us together today. There is a reason why we are all here. Thank You for giving me another chance with my son. Thank You for keeping us safe. And thank You for forgiveness."

The frog in his throat was back!

29

Emily stared at the two men flanking her. So this was Connor's father, who had been presumed dead. Nothing was impossible with Christ, but this was spooky. And the sad part was that Connor would never be able to tell her what had happened.

It was why she had to guard her heart and give him back the necklace. She had woken up early again this morning with a deep determination that she just couldn't allow herself to have a relationship with someone who only told her half-truths, someone who made his living deceiving people.

It was not that she didn't want to.

After finding him on her doorstep last night, she knew that her heart was already starting to feel very strongly for him. Before she lost what was left of it, she needed to step away. Everything about Connor drew her. His uncanny ability to drive her crazy, the tender way he looked at her when he had given her the chocolate – her heart stirred in the way she knew so well.

But how could she, when part of her would never know if he was being honest with her? How was she to believe him, when she wasn't completely sure he didn't whisper the same things into the ear of another woman in a remote part of the world, who found him just as irresistible as she was beginning to feel?

This could not be what God had in mind for her. She could live with the death of her dream of the picket fence, family, and minivan. But she could not imagine herself waiting for him and having to deal with the heartache his mother had dealt with. Finding his father alive somehow sealed what she had come to do. There was no guarantee that this wouldn't happen to her down the road. She wasn't about to allow that to happen.

"I need to go." She looked at her watch. "I have a meeting in town. Thank you for breakfast and lunch. Possibly dinner too."

Emily stood up and turned to Connor. "May I talk to you for a second?"

Rick stood up and busied himself with the dishes. "It's really nice to meet you, Emily. I hope I will have a chance to get to know you better."

Emily walked to the door wondering how she was to do this gracefully. She unclasped the chain from her neck and held the delicate piece of jewelry out to him. Connor's eyes became hooded and dark, his strong jaw set.

"I can't take this. This doesn't belong to me."

Connor shook his head and closed her hand over the top. "It's yours, Emily. I gave it to you. There are no strings attached to accepting it, remember?"

She motioned to the kitchen where his father was whistling while he was doing dishes.

"Does your mother know?"

Connor laughed bitterly. "Are you kidding me? Nope. I'm having a hard time getting this through *my* head. I barely accepted it myself."

"That's why, Connor. What happens when you go missing in ten years?" She shook her head violently, hoping to keep from tearing up. "I don't think God is leading me on this path. I can't do this. I don't want to spend my life wondering if you are coming home or if you're dead, or hiding, or..." She swallowed the lump in her throat and brushed a strand of hair out of her face.

Connor stared in the direction of the kitchen.

"I promise you that I would never do what he did. I would never leave my family." He dipped his head lower to look her straight in the eyes.

Emily smiled softly, sadly. "I bet your father never thought he would have to make that decision either. I won't do this."

She closed his hand around the chain and walked out the door before the courage left her.

It was as though she walked through quicksand.

"Son." He spun around to face his father. "You all right?"

"Nope!" Connor yanked the door open again just in time to see the car pull out of his driveway. He snatched his keys from the hook next to the door when he felt a strong hand on his arm, stopping him. Irritated, he shook it off.

"Connor, let it go. You won't gain anything by running after her. In fact, it will be worse in the end. Let it go."

Connor ground his teeth together. "Let it go? Seriously! That's your advice? That woman was the best thing that happened to me in... maybe in forever! I can't let it go!"

"That necklace," his father pointed at the delicate pendant. "I only made three of these. I prayed for each one of them that it would go to someone special."

Connor exhaled forcibly. "You... you made it?" Go figure!

"I know she's special, even without knowing much about her. But you can't force it! Love, Connor, can't be coerced, nor forced. Jesus didn't do that to us."

Connor balled his fists. “This is not done yet. I do not accept this.”

Longing to release the tension, he started pacing, instead of punching the man in front of him.

“Doesn't matter! For now, you must. Give her space and the decency to come to an understanding with herself. This life we live isn't for everyone. It takes a special person to make it through. That's why I married your mother. She had what it took.”

Connor turned his back to his father. “She left us the day they told us you weren't coming home. She died every day, and sometimes she tried to make it happen.”

His father's hand was on his shoulder, squeezing hard. “And you want to put someone through that? Connor, think!”

Connor bunched his hands into fists again and tried to steady his breathing. “That's why I want to quit the agency. I'm done with this, Dad. I can't do this anymore.”

“You are willing to walk away from the adrenaline rush, from the intrigue? Just because a girl caught your fancy? After twenty years? Are you sure?”

Connor groaned and rubbed his forehead. He knew he couldn't!

“What do I do?” he whispered.

His father put his arm around his son and thanked God for a chance to be there for him for the first time in twenty years. He was not watching him suffer through this from afar, as he had in the past.

“Let's pray, Connor. I always say that prayer is the most effective way to handle things.”

Connor flung himself on to the couch. “Is that what you did when you walked away from us?”

His father's face twisted before he caught himself.

"No," he said darkly. "I just ran. I didn't think, I didn't pray. I didn't trust God enough to see the situation through. I don't want you to make the same mistake."

"I've been thinking about leaving for a while. But I don't know if I can walk away. They probably won't let me just slip out. They probably won't give me my retirement package, will they Dad?"

His father smiled a cold smile. "You need to be smart, Connor. Let's just seek God in this, okay?"

Father and son bowed their heads and in his heart, Connor knew it would all be well in the end. God knew his heart. He hadn't just pointed him to Emily to remove her from him.

He had restored his father to him, he could restore Emily too.

If she was willing!

Emily walked into Sarah's office twenty minutes later, not exactly knowing how she had gotten there. She was still trembling now and then, and tears were very close to spilling out of her gritty eyes. She blinked them away for the hundredth time.

"Dr. Martins, Dr. Brown is waiting for you. She just finished with her last patient." The receptionist took one glance at her and handed her a box of brand new tissues. "Just in case."

There was compassion in her eyes.

Emily didn't even knock, she just walked right in. Sarah was looking over notes and glanced up at her over her glasses. She put her pen down.

"You look awful! Nightmares again?"

Emily sniffed and opened the box of tissues. Sarah had a very perceptive receptionist. "Call it a living day-mare! How is that?"

"Oh, man! That's bad. What happened?"

Sarah sat down across from her in an overstuffed, comfortable armchair, crossing her legs daintily at the ankles.

"The sad thing is, I don't even know how much I can tell you," Emily sighed and wiped her eyes with a tissue clumped in her hand. "Have you ever given something up to God and not been able to follow through with it?" she finally asked.

Sarah snorted. "That's a silly question. Of course. I wouldn't need to be a shrink if everyone followed God exactly the first time. Sometimes our lessons are hard to learn."

Emily shook her head. "I don't think I can learn this one. I seem to be making the same mistake over and over again. Why is that?"

"Maybe because you lack the trust, belief? Maybe because you think you can handle things yourself? I really don't know, Em. Will you tell me?"

Emily kicked her shoes off and pulled her legs up under her.

"Like, even though I want to guard my heart, it has a mind of its own. I determine to follow God, but my heart seems to lead the way. Ever since Pakistan, I want to put Him first. And that means not falling for the first guy who comes my way. But what does good ole Emily do? She falls; hook, line and sinker!" She pulled on her ponytail and tendrils of hair escaped. She tucked at them in frustration, pulled her hair out of the scrunchy, and readjusted it into a braid.

"Emi. Please tell me what happened," Sarah pleaded and handed her a fresh tissue.

Emily picked at an invisible piece of fuzz on her jeans.

"Yeah. I actually walked away. I wasn't the one who stood there, with a *kick me* sign on my forehead. I walked away first."

"Ah," Sarah said softly, understanding beginning to form on her face. "And how does it feel?"

"Just like it did all the other times." Emily dabbed at a tear and sniffed. "No, this is far worse. I feel like what is left of my heart was run over by my own car."

"So, who was this one?" Sarah asked.

"Someone I care about too much." Emily took a deep breath. "And it will never work."

"I see."

"No, you don't." Emily rested her head against the back of the chair and wiped the tears. "Nobody can see. That's the problem. He's dangerous, and that is the end of that."

Sarah's eyes gleamed. "Wow, Em. Now I am intrigued. Is he, like, a criminal?"

"Nah," Emily groaned. She pulled her hair out of her braid and finger-combed it. "I can't, Sarah. So what do I do? I told God I wouldn't fall for another guy."

" Are you sure you can turn off your feelings? The hard thing is that you need to be in control of your heart. Lead it, instead of it leading you. You may feel something for a guy, but if it's not right... If God is not in it... Well, maybe it was right for you to walk away. You know, God will direct you. If you give Him the chance, He'll come through."

"I really didn't set out to want anything from this guy. Just because he... And then he shows up and I just... Ah." Emily punched the armrest of the chair with her balled fist.

Sarah had never seen her friend this agitated. They had been through a lot. They both wore their hearts on their sleeves when it came to relationships and had gotten burned so many times. Sarah was just beginning to learn that God had something better for her.

Apparently, Emily was learning the same lesson.

"But what if God did set this up? What if He wants you to trust Him to see this through? You're such a self-sufficient woman, that it's hard for you to step back and see where God may want you to grow."

Emily's head snapped to her friend's. "I have two words for you. N. O!"

Sarah laughed softly. "That's one word, Dr. Martins. I guess math was never your strong point."

Emily bit off the smile that threatened. "You're missing the point, counselor. I know that God can't possibly be involved in this. It would be absolutely ludicrous!"

Sarah laughed and handed her another tissue. "And we *all* know that God never does anything ludicrous or out of the ordinary. What if He is teaching you to trust Him, no matter what?"

Emily huffed indignantly. "Then He's going about this in a really messed up way, Sarah! I can't believe He would expect me to go through this. It's not... I don't want to. There's way too much at stake for me."

"Love is never easy. It usually requires a sacrifice. Christ was willing to pay. Are you?"

Emily glared at her friend. "When did you become so wise?" she finally teased. Sarah wiggled her eyebrows at her.

"What do I do?" Emily asked quietly. She sniffed again and wiped her eyes with yet another tissue.

"First of all, examine your heart, Emily. Are you willing to listen to God, or not? Then pray. In everything, with prayer and supplication, right? Then be thankful for where He is sending you. It may not be an easy road, you may fall and have to learn the lesson again and again, but in the end, it will be worth it."

Emily closed her eyes for a moment. "What if it is too late? What if there is a time limit?"

"There's always a time limit, Em. We all run out of time at some point."

Emily grimaced and kneaded her brow. "Can you pray for me?" she whispered.

Sarah smiled and leaned forward. "Of course, my dear friend."

30

Bouncing the ball, up and down! There was something soothing about that.

Especially, since her day had been a continuous disaster. She had to deal with one problem after the other and when she came home, she had a massive headache.

She took the shot and heard the swish of the ball going into the hoop. Emily turned at the car pulling into the drive. Her mother exited with grocery bags in both hands. Emily jumped in to assist her.

"What did you do, Mom? Clean out the whole store?" she laughed as she carried the bags into the kitchen. "There are only two of you! It looks like you are feeding an army!"

"Be prepared, dear daughter. My new motto. Always be prepared." Her mother put the carton of ice cream into the freezer, which was already stuffed full.

Emily laughed again and made her way back outside. Maybe if she could just get her nerves back in order, she would have a pleasant weekend.

Ha! Who was she kidding?

She picked up the ball and executed another lay-up. She stared moodily at the hoop. What was she not willing to learn? Why did she feel so miserable and alone in this one?

Lord, I said that You are to lead my life! And here I am, at the same exact spot I was at before. I let myself fall into the same trap I have fallen into so many times. I wish I could trust You completely. I just seem to not be able to.

The birds chirped quietly as she took another shot. She heard the familiar noise of her father's car pull into the drive.

"Nice shot, Emi." She turned around and grinned at her father. He was standing near his car, wearing his suit and tie. "I bet I can make a basket from here."

She snorted. He was at least a half court away. She threw the ball at him and he caught it, dribbled and took a shot. He missed! Emily laughed again.

"Good try, Dad."

Her father grinned and walked toward her, loosening his tie.

"What's got you out here, looking so moody?"

"Affairs of the heart, oh father," she giggled.

He shivered. "Ugh, well." He held his hand out to her, expecting to catch the ball. "I've become somewhat of an expert with you two girls around. What's the matter?"

"Daddy," she sighed. "It's complicated."

He made a basket and passed the ball to her. "It's always complicated. But God is the master over your heart, isn't He? Or at least He is supposed to be."

Emily lowered her eyelids. "Sometimes we don't want Him to be there."

"Yes, and that is usually when the trouble starts."

He made the basket and put his arm around her shoulder, kissing the top of her head. Somehow it made her feel like a child. She leaned into him, glad for his presence.

Wasn't that how God was? He wanted her to lean into Him, to depend on Him during hard times and good times. He made a path for her, yes. But she had to choose every day if she would walk the walk. It was difficult, but in the end, it was worth it.

"I'm gonna go in now. Your mother probably has dinner ready. You coming up to the house?"

Emily stared at the hoop. "I think I'll stay out here for a while longer. There are some things I have to talk to God about."

Her father released her and strode up to the side door.

Emily took the ball and bounced it, aiming it at the basket.

Lord, I know You're with me. I just don't want to follow the way You're leading me. It will be an uphill climb with rocks and boulders to walk around. I'm likely to step off the path and plummet down into the crevasse.

She sighed and retrieved the ball. She closed her eyes.

Where would You like me to step?

As the ball left her hand, it felt as though she was letting go again. She wasn't sure if the ball would hit the hoop, but God knew. She opened her eyes after the ball left her hands, and watched breathlessly as it bounced on the rim a few times before finally going through the hoop. It bounced on the blacktop. She took a deep breath and snatched the ball out of the air.

Connor felt the shock throughout his body as his feet pounded the road. It felt good! He wiped the sweat that was dripping into his face with the back of his arm but didn't let up on the pace. He wanted to finish strong! He wasn't going to go down whimpering. He had almost finished his five miles in twenty-eight minutes. That was a good pace for him.

He turned onto his street. In a few steps, he would pass Emily's house. He gritted his teeth and concentrated on the pounding pavement. No matter, Connor slowed just enough when he approached her driveway.

Lord, what do I do?

He had a few more steps to go and then he would be able to see her garage apartment.

Connor heard the ball bouncing on the blacktop before he saw it. He stopped, breathing hard. Emily was standing in the middle of the driveway, eyes closed, ball poised to be released. He held his breath and watched the ball go through the hoop. He heard her gasp in surprise and gather the ball.

She turned around and saw him. For a moment the expression on her face was blank. Then it turned to surprise. She lowered her head and let out a deep breath. It sounded like a surrender.

"Are you just going to stand there or are you up for a little one on one?"

Connor trained his face. He took a step toward her. It felt like he was taking a leap of faith.

"You sure you are up for it?" he asked, trying to keep his voice steady, void of the emotion the statement had welled up in him.

Her face lit up for a split second. "*I* am, but last time we played, if you remember, things didn't work out so well for you."

She stepped closer. He saw the effort it took. She was in the same boat as he. Emily was stepping out in faith, hoping that she wasn't going to slip down the steep slopes.

"I'm sure you caught me on a bad day. I like to win," he said softly and grabbed the ball. "Loser buys dinner."

Her face flushed red from her chin to the roots of her hair. "I'm not sure about that."

“Why?” he teased. “You afraid you're gonna have to buy me a big steak dinner?”

Her chin lifted up, a challenge lit her eyes.

“Good thing that you don't eat meat. Bring it on!”

She passed the ball to him and he took it down the half court. Emily blocked his shot expertly, going for the rebound. She got it. She ducked low and took the ball back out.

He held up his hand and bent over. “Whoa, whoa,” he panted. “Go easy on me!”

Emily grinned at him, bouncing the ball just out of his reach. “Why, you too old? Too tired? Out of shape?”

“I just ran five miles in twenty-eight minutes!” he panted breathlessly. “That's quite impressive, you know.”

Emily cocked her head and laughed. “Good for you. Now are you going to try to take this ball from me, or do I just play by myself?”

Connor straightened and met her gaze. “I'm ready!” He wiggled his fingers in her direction.

Emily laughed and pushed toward him. She managed to stay just outside the reach of his arms, but he had a few tricks up his sleeve. He stepped into her circle and snagged the ball from her. He heard her gasp in surprise and concentrated on taking the ball back out and keeping it long enough to make a shot. He whooped in pleasure when the ball bounced through the hoop.

“Don't get used to it, pretty boy,” Emily growled.

Connor snorted. “What did you call me?”

Emily concentrated on the ball in her hands. “My mistake!”

In the end, it was a close game, but Emily walked away the winner. They collapsed on the grass that grew on the side of the driveway, laughing and trying to catch their breath.

Emily threw the ball into the air and caught it. She turned on her side to look at him. Her face was flushed to a dark red. Some of her blonde hair, now stained brown from sweat, had escaped from her braid and had curled up around her face. Her mocha eyes wore the smile, not her lips. He dragged his gaze back to hers, trying to ignore those lips.

"I have to admit," she panted. "That was a good game. I wasn't so sure I could win."

"You see," he smirked. "I told you I had some tricks up my sleeve."

He reached over and tucked a curly strand of hair behind her ear. Emily bit her bottom lip and looked at the grass, trying to ignore how his touch had sent a shot of electricity through her.

Considering that she had recently withstood torture, this was just as hot – but much more pleasant.

"Dinner! Where do you want to eat? Because I'm starving!"

He kept his voice light.

"Maybe we shouldn't," she said weakly.

He turned back onto his back. "Are you getting cold feet again?" he growled.

"Yes," she said slowly, hesitantly.

Connor lifted his head. "I have to eat!" He got up and offered his hand to her and pulled her up. "You coming with me or not?"

Emily withdrew her hand from his strong, calloused hand. It was warm and...

Stop it right there! The right thing would be to thank him, get a shower and call for pizza.

“Sure. I can always eat,” she heard herself say.

Wrong!

In less than a half hour, Emily appeared at his door freshly showered and dressed in casual black jeans and navy long-sleeved blouse. Her hair was still wet and hung down her back, leaving wet marks on her shirt.

“I was just coming to get you,” he greeted her. *Keep it casual,* he kept reminding himself. *This is not a date. You lost the game, you get to buy dinner.*

“Where do you feel like going?” he asked. It was getting late but tomorrow was the weekend.

“Do you eat fish?” she asked, as she slipped into the seat next to him, recalling the last time she had been in this car. Even though she had given him a hard time he still stuck around.

“I can do fish, on occasion,” he replied, taking his eyes off the road for a split second.

“It's extremely healthy,” she said seriously, twirling the stud of her left earring.

“And you are concerned about that?”

She turned to face him, her face serious. “Of course, I am. I'm a doctor!”

He snorted and concentrated on the traffic. “Where am I going?” he asked.

She pursed her lips and screwed up her eyes. “Are you starving or can you wait for a little while longer?”

He let out a soft laugh. “I'm starving. But I can wait. It all depends on what I'm waiting for. Remember, I can do patience.”

The statement did not miss its mark and Emily turned her head quickly to face out the window again.

“Take a left at the next light. And then follow the road to the highway. Take route nine to the shore.”

He gasped. “When I said I could wait, I didn't mean that I could wait until the cows come home!”

“So your patience has a limit?” she teased.

“Touché.”

She was something!

When they finally arrived at their destination, Connor was surprised. It was a run-down shack along a long stretch of beach. The place was busy even this late at night, and they had to stand in a long line.

“This is fast food,” he murmured. “I drove forty-five minutes to get fast food?”

“Yeah,” Emily grinned, bouncing up and down like a child, and looked out to the beach. “But it's so worth it!”

Twenty minutes later he followed Emily out to the beach carrying his stash of battered fish fillet and french fries. In his other hand, he carried a can of cola.

“You know, the last time I had fast food I was still in high school.”

Emily sat down on the sand and pulled her legs up to her chest. "I don't believe you! You went to college. They are not known for their healthy food."

"Okay, so I'm exaggerating."

Connor sat down next to her. The sun was just dipping into the water, turning it crimson. The beach was nearly deserted at this time of the evening. Here and there were a few people, walking along the shore, bending down to pick up shells. Toward the road a man was walking around, carrying a metal detector. They could hear the beeping from the machine. The seagulls gave them their full attention. Connor was tempted to use them as target practice to sharpen his marksmanship.

"Shall we pray before our food gets cold?" Emily asked shyly.

A muscle on Connor's jaw twitched. "Sure." His voice was deep and thick.

They bowed their heads and thanked God for the food. Connor took a bite of his fish and suppressed a groan.

"Okay," he said after swallowing. Emily watched him with amusement. "This is really good. It was worth the trip." He nudged her with his shoulder. "It was worth losing."

Emily concentrated on her own food. "You don't like to lose?"

"Nope. I guess that makes me very egotistical, doesn't it?"

Emily pushed her hair out of her face only to have the wind blow it back. Finally disgusted with herself, she pulled out a rubber band and secured it into a ponytail.

"I did have fun winning," she teased. She threw a shell at a very persistent seagull waiting to snag a piece of her food. It flew a few paces and settled back down on the sand.

"How's your father?" Emily asked and took a sip of her drink.

"He's good. He's probably really happy that he doesn't have to cook for me tonight. We didn't kill each other. So, I would consider that a successful day."

He chewed his fish and dunked a french fry into ketchup. He must be out of his mind for indulging in such food. But the company made it totally worth it!

Emily stared out to sea, the wind picking up her ponytail and blowing it behind her back again. She absentmindedly twirled her left earring.

"You must think I am a terrible tease. I mean, I throw myself at you last night and this morning I tell you to take a hike. And now we are here, eating dinner."

Connor glared at the very persistent seagull. He tossed a piece of seaweed at it, sending it flying a little further away.

"I don't think you are a tease. I think you are just as confused as I am, Emily. I don't do this all the time, you know. I'm not in the habit of taking a beautiful woman out to fast food fish and chips. But I could get used to this."

Emily's heart sang. *He thinks I'm beautiful!* "I want to be honest with you, Connor. I'm afraid. I don't want to end up alone, like your mother. I didn't think this was a path for me, but apparently, God has other plans."

"You think so?" Connor asked. "When you left this morning, I was all about chasing after you. My dad suggested I let you go. I almost took him out!"

Emily grinned. "So, now what do we do? I like to have a plan in order. I don't like not knowing what is in front of me."

Connor leaned back on his elbows, watching the sun glide below the horizon.

"I know just what you mean. I don't do well without a system in place, either! Maybe this is what God is trying to teach both of us. We are so focused on knowing what we have to do, that God is telling us to change. And that is difficult for so many people, myself included. Not knowing what the plan is..." Connor ran his hand through his hair. "I *need* to know what I have to do. Taking this approach will not be easy for either of us."

Emily stood up and dusted the sand off her black jeans.

"It will take living with continual humility and meekness. Those are not character qualities doctors are known to possess. I learned early on in med-school that to show weakness was a kiss of death. I had to claw my way up and fight off the competition."

"The agency doesn't exactly foster a fuzzy feeling of compassion among its field agents either," Connor said. "I have had to do some pretty gnarly stuff just to stay in the game."

Emily shuttered and drew her arms around herself. "Do you regret joining? Would you rather have been a computer guy working nine to five?"

An unreadable expression crossed his face. "I don't really care that much for computers. I would rather work with languages. I think I would have enjoyed that. I like what I do, for the most part. There is that unpleasant part of it, the flying bullets, the dropping bombs."

Emily grinned. They threw their trash into the trashcan and walked down toward the water's edge. Emily discarded her flip-flops, showing off her pink toes, and Connor took his shoes off. They rolled up their pant legs and walked in the cool water.

"But there is also that part of the job that is necessary. There are a lot of bad guys out there. And if I don't stop them, who will? That part of the job is satisfying."

"Would you give it up?" The question came as a whisper.

"I would. I told you, I've been thinking about it lately. There are only so many time you can cheat death before you start to wonder."

It was pleasant to have a conversation with him like that. She didn't feel threatened, she didn't feel like she needed to impress or be someone she wasn't. They were just two friends, walking on the beach.

She almost regretted turning around to make their way back to the car.

"I have to admit that this is a very nice alternative to spending my evening with my dad, in my empty, stale house."

Connor retrieved his shoes. Emily slipped her feet into her flip-flops.

"I like the look. Jeans and flip-flops. Not many girls would dare to appear for a date wearing that."

Emily's face turned red, her eyes narrowed dangerously. "This was not a date! You lost a game and had to pay up."

"You can say tomato and I say tom*a*to. Same ole, same ole," Connor replied and unlocked his car.

"See, now you are putting pressure on me again!"

"Nah, just checking the ground around my feet. Done checking," he laughed slyly and tugged tenderly at her ponytail.

As he pulled into her driveway, he put his hand on her arm and pulled out the necklace. The muscles in her shoulders tensed immediately.

"This belongs to you, Emily. Did I tell you my father made it? He changed careers, of course, and started making jewelry. I bought this, not knowing he had made it. He told me that he only made three necklaces like this, praying for each one to belong to someone special."

Emily's heart did that weird something.

He took her hand and turned it over to place the chain onto her palm. Then he closed her fingers over it and held it closed. His fingers were strong and once again that pleasant tingle percolated through her.

"I want you to have it, no matter what. And I certainly liked spending time with you tonight. I want to do this again since I won't be going anywhere. I want to explore if there is something lasting between us. My job will be right here, boring old computer stuff," he grinned. "So, I would like to see you again, please."

"I'm sure my mother will propose Sunday dinner again," she said weakly. She looked at the necklace still sitting in the palm of her hand. "I don't know, Connor. I..." She exhaled deeply. "Okay. We will see where God leads us."

It felt good to say that. It felt good to admit that God would see her through this.

"I'll see you in church. I have a clinic that I do once a month on Saturday in the city. I won't be around until late tomorrow." Now, why did she tell him that? "I like the necklace. It is absolutely beautiful. Thank your father from me."

Connor followed her up the steps to her door and grabbed her hand.

"Wait a moment. I was the one who bought it!"

Emily turned and the look she gave him almost had him on his knees proposing his undying love for her. She quickly changed her expression, realizing what she had done. She couldn't allow her heart to lead! But it was so much fun to see him almost fall on his face.

"Uh-huh," she said and her voice sounded like silk. "You'll get your reward."

Wow, that almost knocked him down her steep staircase. He never knew what to make of her! She had him completely off-balance!

What if...

Connor let himself into his house through the utility room and heard the sound of the TV coming from the living room. It was nice! For the first time in a long time, he didn't come home to an empty place. He hung up his keys and made his way to where his father lounged on the brand new recliner. He gasped when he noticed the change in the room.

"What happened to all the weight equipment?" he asked and threw himself onto his couch.

His father's attention came off the action movie he was watching and fastened onto his son. He muted the TV.

"I moved it. Did you know you have a perfectly good extra room? It's in there."

Connor sniffed the air. "Smells better in here already," he grinned. "Do you want a drink?"

His father snorted softly. "If you are talking an alcoholic drink, I never did like the taste. I'll take a soda since you asked."

Connor groaned in an attempt to get off the couch. He returned with two glasses of flavored sparkling water, the closest he got to soda. He handed one to his father, who nodded to him. Connor enjoyed the bubbles that made their way down his throat.

"You're home late," his father said, a twinkle in his eyes. "I suppose it went well?"

Connor nodded and put the glass on his coaster. "She took the necklace back and wanted me to thank you for it."

His father laughed out loud. "I bet you took that well."

"Not so much," Connor admitted sheepishly.

That look she shot him, though.

He could live with that for the rest of his life if he had to. "She didn't shut me down like last time. We had a good time. I just have to figure out if this is a God-thing or not."

"It will happen if God is in it, Connor. It may not go exactly the way you plan it, but God will show you. Do you know how long I have waited to be sitting here with you? How long I prayed to be reunited with my family?"

"I bet there wasn't a day that you didn't pray," Connor whispered, waiting for the regret to stop tingling through him. He saw the same in his father's expression.

"Dad. I need your advice. How do I leave the agency?"

"Not the way I did, Connor. Although it may be your only option." His father took a sip of his drink. "Did you sign anything that made it impossible to leave before your time was up?"

"I don't think so." Connor twisted his fingers together. "I've put in my share of blood and sweat. I just want a clean break."

His father sighed. "Be careful. You don't want to end up like me. I'm sixty years old. I don't know what will happen to me when I go in, Connor. I know you have to finish your mission. They may lock me up, they may just dismiss me. I guess I need to trust God in this myself, don't I?"

"Yeah. I don't want to bring you in yet, Dad. I'm actually enjoying this. But I'm afraid that if I don't, someone else will."

"I don't know. They sent their best after me," Rick said proudly.

"Yeah... well," Connor concentrated on the muted game on the TV. "I wish I wasn't so good at what I do."

"There's that!" his father groaned. "How's your mother? I haven't exactly kept up on her since she got remarried. Is she happy? And Alicia? She must be done with her schooling by now?"

"Mom's okay. Her husband's alright. He treats her well enough. They have their separate lives. She's involved in her club and he goes shooting and fishing."

"Ah, not a match made in heaven, then." For a moment his dad had a smile on his face. But he wiped it off immediately.

Connor felt sorry for his dad. "Far from it. I don't care for him, but I don't think I ever gave him a chance. Alicia is opinionated as ever, broke up with her last boyfriend and hates my guts right now. She is a great kid, though. I miss her. But she still won't take my call. So, I'll let her stew until she finally does take it."

"She always was a fiery one. She used to glare at me when I came home and not talk to me for a couple of hours. But then she warmed up to me again. I can imagine you being gone all the time is hard on her."

"How long did you date mom until you were married?"

Connor could feel his neck warming up and he rubbed his hand under the collar of his shirt.

Rick nodded his head. "I took your mother out on a few dates. But in that society, dating isn't as big as it is here. I went to her father, asked for her hand in marriage and it was a done deal. It took four months."

Connor laughed. "You had your mind on the prize, eh, Dad?"

Rick nodded and grinned at his oldest. "I was determined not to let anyone get in my way!"

"Did she know what you did for a living?"

Rick looked down at the remote in his hands and shook his head.

"No. She took it pretty hard when she found out. She packed her bags and left the apartment to go back to her parents. On the way down the stairs, she tripped and twisted an ankle. I came home from work and found her weeping on the staircase. She decided to stay, you know, on account of me carrying her up six flights of stairs."

They laughed, but there was a sadness in that laughter.

"What else do you want to know, Connor?"

Connor glanced at the father he had worshiped. "Do you regret it?"

Rick wore a look on his face that almost tore Connor's heart out.

"Not a moment. It was all worth it in the long run. Here I am, sitting with my son, talking. I don't regret having you or your sister. I'm not sorry for marrying your mother. I loved being a family man when I could. Those were the moments of real life. The rest, it wasn't important."

"What are you going to do about Mom and Alicia?" Connor asked.

"The opportunity will present itself. I'm enjoying my time with you first." There was a thin film over his father's eyes and he turned his face toward the TV. "Once God gives me the opportunity, I will know. And I'll take it." He leaned over and squeezed his son's shoulder.

32

She closed the car door and walked up her stairs. It had been a hard day. Emily was ready for a quiet night. She unlocked her door and stared. Flowers covered her apartment. Grinning, she sniffed a particularly fragrant pink rose. She set it back on the counter and laughed. Her phone rang.

"Are you home yet?"

"I don't know, but the home I am standing in smells like a flower shop. Did you have anything to do with this?" she smiled into the phone, feeling ridiculous because he couldn't see her.

"I may have. If not, I'd have to do some damage to the guy who did." She heard the soft laughter in her ear. "I was hoping that you are free tonight. I thought maybe you'd like to go bowling."

Emily nibbled her bottom lip. Bowling. It was not threatening. They would be in a public place.

"Sounds good to me. What time do you want me to meet you at the bowling alley?"

"I assume you haven't eaten yet?"

She cleared her throat and glanced at the last bite of her candy bar she had consumed on her way home.

"Eh," she stammered. "I guess the answer would be no!"

"Meet at your place in half an hour. I'll drive."

"No wait...," she protested but it was too late. She was talking to a dead line.

Butterflies fluttered around in her stomach.

Emily stared at the flowers around the apartment. Her first boyfriend, the one in medical school, had brought home an occasional bouquet for her. This went above and beyond anything she had ever experienced.

She needed to tread very, very carefully, or her heart would be subject to more pain. Who was she kidding? It was hard to guard her heart and yet be open to what God had for her.

Bowling was fun, but in the end, Emily was so tired she actually dozed off on the way home. Connor walked her up to her door. For a moment, Emily wasn't sure what to do.

"I had a great time, again. See you in church tomorrow," Connor said after a few moments of awkward silence. His eyes went to the necklace she wore. Emily fingered it nervously. He leaned over and kissed her cheek.

"Right," she croaked and scooted into the safety of her apartment.

The next morning, Connor looked at his father, dressed in a suit and tie. He sported a very convincing mustache and had changed his eye color to brown, using contacts.

Connor used them a lot, too.

"You're coming with me to church?"

"Yes, I decided to give it a try."

"But Dad, what's our cover? Who exactly are you?"

Connor stood in the utility room, wearing a blue button-down shirt, no tie, and gray slacks. Agent Williams Sr. paced back and forth, his fingers tapping on his chin, his eyes gleaming in pleasure.

"Just say that I am your father's brother, Uncle Bob. That will explain the strong resemblance. We were twins, your father, and I. I'm visiting after my wife passed away from cancer six months ago. I have no children, and you are my favorite and only nephew. I have always thought of you as a son, especially after your father passed away."

They walked to the car and Connor slipped on his sunglasses, putting on his mission face because it felt like one. He could play a part.

"No problem. I just hope Emily goes along with it."

"Tell her my life depends on it."

Emily gaped at them when they walked into the sanctuary. When Connor introduced his father as Uncle Bob, she turned red and quickly looked away, hoping her mother had not seen it. Her mother spotted Emily's bright red face and shot her a questioning look. Emily smiled at her reassuringly.

"Well, Bob. Would you and Connor come for lunch? I made a wonderful oven roast that I put in the oven just before we left. We have more than enough."

Emily bit her lip. Would Connor go along with the invitation?

"We would love to, right Uncle Bob?"

Rick looked at his son, a perfectly normal expression on his face.

"Yes, by all means. But only if we can bring the desert."

It was agreed upon.

When Emily helped her mother later on in the kitchen, her mother looked at her and smiled pleasantly.

"You like him, don't you?"

"Who, Uncle Bob?"

"Emily! Don't play games with me. I know you better than that."

Emily pulled out the good plates and set them on the counter. "It's complicated, Mom. Don't ask, okay?"

"What's so complicated about this whole thing, Emi? He seems very nice. He certainly likes you. And I meant to ask you. Where did you get that necklace? It's beautiful."

"I replaced it when the one you gave me was stolen in Pakistan." Emily felt her whole body tingle. She would never be a good spy since lying to her mother was painful.

"It is very nice, sweetheart."

Connor and Rick played the part of nephew and uncle to perfection. They were a really good team. Their story fit together seamlessly. She wanted to be impressed, but then she remembered that they were lying to her parents, of all people.

Would Connor lie to her about how he felt about her?

He did it so well. She remembered how convincingly he played his part in Pakistan.

"I don't think I can do this, Connor," she whispered as they walked down the driveway afterward. It was a nice evening, the sun had set and it was twilight. The heat and humidity of the summer was all but gone.

"Do what?"

Emily looked at him. It was so easy for her to just fall. He was handsome and smart. Like her mother said, what was so complicated? Connor seemed to like her.

"Are you playing a game with me, Connor? You and Rick pretend so well. I almost believed you guys were uncle and nephew. I'm afraid of letting myself get wrapped up in something that isn't real. Are you true with me? Or do you pretend? How will I ever know?"

Connor turned and faced her. She had a good reason to ask and he had a mind to take her worries away in the only way he knew how to. Especially since they were hidden from the house by vigorously growing Mountain Laurels and she looked so deliciously adorable.

With his face close to hers, Emily had to fight with herself not to lean forward and catch his lips with hers. She inched away, a movement that didn't go unnoticed.

Connor slipped his hands deep into the pockets of his slacks, playing with the loose change.

"I'm not playing a game with you, Emily," he said, hoping she could sense his sincerity. "I don't play those kind of games. That is something I stay away from professionally and personally. You can trust me to tell you the truth. My father's story is necessary, Emily. Remember, there are people who would like to, uh, how do I put this civilly? There are people out there who don't know where he is. If they find out, there are consequences."

Connor longed to seal his words with a kiss, but he knew that she would bolt. She was already skittish as it was. He would bide his time. He would be as honest as he could with her on all things regarding his feelings for her. It would be hard for him, who always kept his heart locked to those around. He was going to take a chance, trusting in God's leading, and be as transparent as possible.

For someone who made his living pretending, it would be difficult.

Over the next month, their relationship was based just on friendship. Connor never asked for more than Emily was willing to give. There were times when he would test the ground he was on, only to be rebuffed in a very brisk manner. For Connor, getting to know Emily as a friend was a test of his commitment and humility. He continued to go before God, praying to stay within the rules Emily set. She kept her boundaries intact.

Inwardly, her heart was softening.

Emily sat across from Sarah in her usual comfy chair, no tissues needed today.

"I think we're done," her friend said and nodded. Sarah removed her glasses and rubbed the bridge of her nose. "The nightmares are gone. You are allowing God, not your heart, to lead the way. I'm well pleased with you, Emily. You have set boundaries for your relationships and you are staying within them. That is not easy, I know that."

Emily snorted softly.

"I'll keep on praying. And, excuse me, I want to meet this guy that isn't in your life. Are you keeping him away from me on purpose?!"

"Yes, I am," Emily said with a slightly sheepish grin.

Sarah frowned at her. "I see. Why?"

"I honestly don't know, Sarah."

"Well," her friend humphed, frowning. "In that case, I think our professional relationship is over. For now," she added with a twinkle in her eye. "You know where to find me."

Emily grinned. "Good. Can't say it's been fun. But it has been an enormous help."

33

She rang the doorbell and Connor practically dragged her into the hall, wearing a huge grin. Over the last couple of months, the house had changed. Gone was the austere hall. A small cast-iron bench stood along the winding staircase. A mirror hung in the corner, illuminated by a black iron lamp. The living room was welcoming, with flower pots on the large picture window and paintings on the light tan walls.

"Hey," Connor greeted her, his voice warm and husky, making her toes curl. "I was hoping you'd show up tonight. I convinced my dad to try my specialty lasagna. He's been complaining since I got home. Been telling me that he is a meat and potato kind of guy."

He hung her jacket in the hall closet, allowing his hands to linger on her shoulders for just a moment. She shifted her weight, daring to lean into his touch just a tad.

Connor removed his hands quickly, stuffing his hands behind his back and ignoring the tingle that spread from the tip of his fingers to his toes.

He couldn't help notice that she looked good tonight in her black jeans and off-white sweater. He longed for the day when he could draw her into his arms and hold her, but it hadn't come yet. It was becoming increasingly difficult to be patient, especially when she looked like she did tonight.

"Alright, Connor!" they heard Rick bellow from the kitchen. "If I have to eat this stuff, you had better let me make bacon in the morning!"

Emily smiled and lowered her eyes. "Are you going to let your father do that?" she whispered.

"I guess I have to give a little," he replied just as quietly.

She nodded. "It would probably be best. After all, he is your father."

How different his life had become. Connor was not sure if he wanted this to end. He knew that the agency had given him a lot of time, and for that, he would be forever grateful.

During dinner, Emily observed the two men joke and poke fun at each other, totally at ease. The tension between them was gone and she had to hand it to Connor. He had acted so maturely that she couldn't help but admire him for it.

When he winked at her after laughing at his father, she felt the telltale sign of a blush starting at her chin. She lowered her head only to have Connor lift up her chin gently. His gaze caused an army of spiders to crawl over her skin, leaving goosebumps. It was amazing how much she enjoyed it.

"Fine, Connor," Rick grumbled good-naturedly and picked up the plates. "You cooked, I clean. And it wasn't half bad. You can make your vegetarian stuff for me again."

Connor whooped and did a victory dance around the dining room. He high-fived her.

"I've got to go. It's been a long day for me," she said after she helped clear the dishes.

"Let me walk you to your car," Connor offered and held the door for her. She had come straight from work.

Emily hugged Rick and hurried to catch up to him. The cool, crisp October air slammed into her.

"Thanks for dinner, again," she said and leaned against the door of the car.

Connor wanted to lean close, but he kept his distance and his hands firmly at his side. He wasn't going to scare her off again. Slow and steady! Tonight he would have to broach the subject of what he knew was inevitable.

"I've had a great time," he said and saw her draw in a sharp breath. "You know that eventually, I'll have to go back to work, right? My real job. Emily, it's still there."

Emily gripped the door of her car tightly and felt a wave of weakness rush through her. Reaching for her keys, she knew that he would eventually leave again and just that thought sat like a heavy lump in the pit of her stomach.

"I know." She slid into the driver's seat. "I don't want to think about it."

"I have to think about it, Em. I want you to be ready for it when the call comes. If I know the agency, they will give me exactly two months and not a day more. My time is up this weekend."

The dread spread from her stomach to her heart. Her chest rose and fell as she dragged in a lungful of air.

"I've enjoyed being home and I would like to think it has a lot to do with you."

Lowering himself onto his haunches he leaned toward her, lifting her chin up to meet his eyes. He dipped his head slightly toward her. Her breathing caught in her throat. Before she could say anything or think, his phone chirped. He froze, the tension in his gaze telling her everything.

Without a word, he rose and walked away.

As she drove home, she tried to draw in enough air to keep from passing out. She stumbled up to her apartment and shut the door behind her. She leaned against it, drawing breath after breath.

She could do this. She just needed to keep her mind on the positive.

What was the positive?

She liked Connor. He was kind, funny and a man of God. Her parents liked him, which was a huge improvement over some of the other guys she had dated. She liked herself when she was around him. It was like she was a better person when he was in the room.

The knock on her door caught her off-guard. If she opened the door, she knew what would happen. It would mean having to say goodbye again and she was enjoying her time with him too much.

"Emily!" Connor's voice sounded muffled. "I need to talk to you. Please."

Slowly she willed herself to turn around and open the door. Connor stepped in and drew her into his arms.

"I told you it was going to happen," he whispered into her ear. "I just want to know one thing. I'm going to ask you a question. I will not need an answer right now. My father made this too." He pulled the silver ring with ornate decorations on it out of his pocket. "It led him to me. I'm wondering if you are willing to spend the rest of your life with me. I don't know how long that will be. I can't guarantee you much except that I'll do my best to love you in the time we have been given."

"Connor!" Emily's voice was weak and she tried to extricate herself from him. He held on to her fast. "You know I can't-"

"Shh." He touched his finger to her lips. "You don't have to say anything right now. Just keep this and pray about what your answer will be. When you're ready, put it on. I'll have my answer then."

"We don't know each other that well," she whispered.

This was not how she had expected someone to propose to her. She had hoped for a romantic dinner, a movie, a stroll along the beach. Then the guy dropping down on one knee to pledge his undying love for her.

Not this!

Connor was on his way out, leaving her with unresolved feelings about their relationship. He took her hand and, just as he had done with the necklace, put the ring into the palm of her hand. It felt cool and smooth.

It didn't even have a diamond!

She blinked away her tears.

"I don't need to know anything more about you to make up my mind. I have spent the past two months with you. I know that I want to spend the rest of my life with you if you chose to let me. Are you willing to trust God to lead you down this path?" he asked quietly, never taking his eyes off hers.

Her insides were being rearranged. A whole flock of butterflies exploded in her stomach. She couldn't breathe! A soft whimper escaped her lips, which were tightly pressed together. Connor palmed her cheek softly, the intensity in his eyes lessening. She pressed her face into his hand.

She wanted more!

She wanted him.

What if...

"I have to go," he mumbled, his face so close to hers that she could feel his breath on her cheeks, feel those dreaded words in the pit of her stomach.

Snap out of it! He's leaving, Emily. He just left you with a bomb and now he's gone.

The gooey, mushy feeling of needing his touch was gone in a flash and was replaced with something entirely different. Her breath exploded from her lips and she bit back the tears that clouded her vision. When they threatened to spill, Emily quickly turned away from him.

"Have a good trip," she said coldly and walked toward the kitchen to pour herself a glass of water.

The corners of Connor's mouth twitched and he leaned casually against the door.

"What? No kiss goodbye?"

Emily's eyes flashed at him in such fierceness it would send lesser men cowering. Instead, he felt a rush of adrenaline that usually made him do stupid things, so he came to stand right in front of her.

"You think too highly of yourself, spyman."

"Are you sure? Now may be your last chance!"

The words were meant as a tease, but he regretted them the moment they slipped out of his mouth.

It was as if a hot poker had skewered her heart and she bit back a moan as she fought for control.

"I didn't mean that," he whispered and gathered her to him without so much of a grumble. Feeling her crumble against him, her shoulders quaking with inaudible sobs, he wanted to make it right.

All that came out of his mouth was, "I'm sorry."

As he threaded his fingers through her silky, fragrant hair, he knew that if he allowed himself to give in now – to kiss her tears and troubles away – he wouldn't leave.

"I'll be back, Em. I'll get that kiss, you know," he whispered.

Emily shook her head and pushed him away. "Go!"

Connor bent down to her and gently kissed her cheek, lingering longer than he knew he should. "Don't forget me."

Her mouth filled with cotton, preventing her from answering. Staring at the ring in her hand, she forced her eyes closed tightly, squeezing out more tears.

How could she possibly?

It was hard to get out of bed the next morning, so she didn't. She had nowhere to go, no one to see. When she finally rose around eleven she poured herself a cup of tea, watching as thick storm clouds gathered.

That about sums it up.

She flung herself onto the couch and, covering her face with a pillow, screamed. The sound came out muffled and weak.

She knew the day would come when she would have to let him go for good. Connor was not and would never be an ordinary person and she couldn't commit to a life of constant chaos.

Her gaze fell onto the ring which she had placed into a ceramic container. His proposal, the ring – they were not even close to fulfilling her expectations. Even though both were unforgettable, she knew her answer.

Nothing was as it should be!

"Emily?" her mother's muted voice was full of concern. She opened the door before Emily could stop her. "Are you alright?"

Her father's face appeared behind her mother, looking frightened.

"I'm sorry," she whispered, her throat dry as a desert. "I'm perfectly fine."

Neither seemed to accept that since they sat down next to her.

"What's wrong?" her mother asked. Her eyes opened wider and she nodded compassionately toward Emily's pjs. "You and Connor broke up! I knew it would come to this. I'm sorry, honey. I really liked that boy, but... Maybe it was the look in his eyes. I don't know. Come here, Emily."

Her mother's open arms would feel so good right about now, but Emily didn't lean into them.

"Mom, Connor and I aren't-" She gritted her teeth hard. "We didn't break up."

Her mother gave her father a look. He sighed and moved to the door. "I guess I'll just order some pizza for everyone."

"Emily," her mother said tenderly once he was gone. "You can admit it to me. You like him a lot more than you liked any of the other guys you picked. What happened? He didn't want to commit?" She huffed and her face turned into a scowl. "I tell you... guys, these days. They don't seem to want to do any of the heavy stuff, you know the stuff that's really important. Like, raising a family." She huffed again and continued to hold out her arms, expecting her daughter to lean in.

"It's not like that at all, Mom," Emily said, finding her voice was altogether unsteady. "He wants a commitment. I'm not ready for it."

"What?" Her mother's eyes zeroed in on hers. "What is wrong with you? You've wanted this since you were a little girl. Remember, you used to play family with your dolls?"

Emily felt the heat rush to her face and turned. “There are too many things standing against it. Besides, he left on a business trip and I don't know when he'll be back.” *Or if.*

Her mother regarded her with a shrewd look. “What's going on, Emily? This is not like you.”

Emily covered her face with her hands. “I want to follow God's path, the one that leads up that steep hill. It's just really, really hard to do. I'm not ready. I don't have the courage or strength for the steep section climb followed by the sure plummet on the other side.”

Her mother frowned and she reached for her hands.

“I don't understand your metaphor, Emily. Ever since I remember, you wanted two things. To be a doctor and to get married. You achieved one. Why aren't you willing to reach out to the other? If Connor is waiting for a commitment, what are you not willing to do?”

“I can't tell you, Mom,” she whispered and leaned her forehead against her mother's shoulder. “I told you that it's complicated. I like Connor a lot. He treats me with patience, kindness and makes me feel like a better person. I'm just afraid, Mom. Fear is one of my biggest enemies.”

“Fear of what, Emily?”

Emily curled up her legs. “I don't want to grow old alone!” she breathed.

“We don't know what is in our future. What are you waiting for, child? He cares for you. What's so complicated about the whole situation? God even moved him into your dream house. Don't pretend you haven't ogled over the place for years. Open up your eyes!”

Emily groaned and rolled her eyes.

"Besides." Her mother touched the side of her face. "I need more grandchildren. Liz and Michael live too far away. I'm waiting on you to supply."

Now Emily could only gasp and stare at her mother. "*Mo-om*! You just don't understand."

Her mother shook her head violently and rose.

"Young people today. They want everything handed to them on a silver platter."

33

Connor's fancy apartment overlooked the Eiffel Tower, lit up by the lights. Paris was one of his favorite cities, but there was a problem. For the first time, he didn't want to be here, alone. He wanted to finish what he was about to start the night he left.

This job was worse than the last.

Before his briefing on this assignment, he had gotten flack for not showing results on his father. It was almost as though they didn't believe him that his efforts to locate his father had turned up with nothing. It was nearly the truth. After all, his father had found him.

He was good at stretching the truth! He was a master story-teller. How much of his life was real? Making up stories, telling lies was becoming increasingly difficult and draining.

Emily's comment about him playing a game with her came back to him. How much of himself was he able to share with her, honestly? Her comment had stung at the time, but now-

Groaning softly, Connor clutched his head in his hands. How could he expect her to give her heart to him when he was unable to share his with her? He had put her into a difficult situation and he was beginning to feel guilty.

Because here he was... Standing in a gorgeous apartment in Paris, pondering his new identity and what it would mean becoming this person on what would no doubt be a very long-term assignment.

Connor wondered if he had been given it as a slap on the wrist for not bringing his father in and taking time off because it was by far the most challenging he'd had in a long time.

His cover was that he owned a computer security company. That part was easy because he did.

This operation was much more technical than most of his assignments. It required more support than he usually liked, depending on others to do their job to perfection so he could walk away alive.

Because of the complexity of this job, it would mean that he was undercover for longer with very direct involvement with the mark. It meant that he was going to have to get personally involved, putting himself at greater risk.

He had been sent after an agent who had gone rogue.

He grinned when he thought of Emily using that term.

This agent had disappeared a few years ago with a ton of valuable information, which made his superiors in Washington mighty unhappy. He had been selling secrets to the highest bidder, trading them for weapons, which he in turn sold again. Most of them were used against the US government as well as US citizens on foreign soil. It led straight back to the job in Pakistan.

His phone chirped.

His contacts had spread the news in town that he was the man to see if anyone had computer security issues. Thanks to a few very talented hackers in Washington, the mark was experiencing a ton of problems, which hopefully would lead to Connor being hired to take care of it.

Connor swallowed his nerves.

He was never anxious about a job. But with this one, he wasn't so sure if he could manage the technical side of it all. He was, after all, just a field agent with slightly more than average computer knowledge.

"*Oui*?" he asked in perfect French.

It was languages he was good at.

"Monsieur Brandt. *Moi je suis* Pierre Renault." There was a pause as if the man on the other end of the phone expected Connor to break out into applause. "I work for a company interested in hiring your expertise in computer security. I would like to meet with you face to face to see if you are our man."

Connor's nerves disappeared. This part he could do in his sleep. They agreed to meet that night.

As he hung up, a weight slouched off his shoulders. The waiting around was done. The preliminaries had been set up. He would either complete this job or fail.

Connor pulled his favorite weapon out of his waistband and fingered it lovingly. It would not do to meet the contact packing a gun and ready for a fight. Securing it underneath the latch to a window seat, he felt strangely naked and unprotected.

Lord, he prayed as he got ready for the meeting. *You have kept me safe so far. My life is in Your hands. I guess that's a good thing!*

Half an hour later, he walked into the upscale restaurant where his contact was waiting. The man was surrounded by bodyguards, who frisked him thoroughly. Remembering that he could still inflict permanent damage with his bare hands, he approached the Frenchman who wore a pricey designer suit. His shoes must have cost as much as the budget of a small nation. This man had expensive taste buds, something that could be exploited.

"*Bonjour,* Monsieur Brandt," the man said and offered his hand.

He had the handshake of a dead fish.

Don't trust the guy!

Connor kept his smile empty and his senses alert. This mission might be over before he even got started.

"Monsieur Renault. It is good to meet you. I'm honored that you would choose a small company like mine to help a company as large as *Aeronautic Marginal.* I took the liberty of doing some research and I find myself quite impressed."

Connor took the offered seat, keeping his eyes focused on the peacock in front of him, but his senses told him where all the heavies were located. Two were flanking the man opposite him. Another set was lingering by the bar, trying to make themselves look like patrons. He could tell by the dead look in their eyes that they were not just out for an evening drink. After assuring himself that they didn't see him as a threat, he relaxed slightly.

Once he had ordered the most costly bottle of wine, the man next to him went straight to talking business.

"The same goes for your company, M. Brandt. Your name is well respected in the computer business. The president of the company, M. Lamour, is interested in meeting with you. He likes to take a hands-on approach. I told him you come highly recommended. He would like to meet you at his chalet in the mountains this weekend. I assume you ski, Monsieur?"

"Of course, I ski. I was born in the mountains," Connor replied, pushing his fake glasses back onto his nose.

M. Renault seemed well satisfied with his answer. "I will pick you up tomorrow morning. Tonight let us enjoy ourselves."

He waved over the waiter and ordered oysters, shrimp, and lobster tails. Connor kept his smile in place as the man started to talk to him.

"You are going to like M. Lamour. He is a very reasonable man to work for. If you do your job well, who knows what will come of it," the man laughed while the waiter poured some wine into a glass. "Your company is relatively new. A patron like M. Lamour can only increase your net worth."

M. Renault swirled the golden liquid around and took a sip. He nodded and held his glass out for the waiter to fill. By the end of the evening, he had consumed a very considerable amount of alcohol.

"I think, M. Brandt," his host slurred, "you will enjoy working with us."

"I'm sure I will, M. Renault. Till tomorrow then," Connor said and shook the man's hand.

This operation couldn't be over quick enough for him.

Emily looked at the impressive pile of leaves in the middle of Connor's yard. It didn't help that Connor's property was surrounded by oak, maple, and beech trees. Rick smiled at her as he raked the last of the leaves into the pile on a blue tarp.

"Ready?"

They picked it up together and carried the tarp into the woods just across the street, like everyone else in the neighborhood. Rick wiped a gloved hand over his brow and gathered the empty tarp.

"Thanks for your help, Emily. I'm sure you had other things to do today," he said as they walked into the garage.

What if...

Connor's sports car was conspicuously absent, reminding Emily that he had been gone for three weeks already. Not that she kept track.

"You really didn't need to do this." Rick walked into the utility room and closed the washing machine door.

"I wanted to help you, Rick. It must be lonely in this house." She pulled on her ponytail hidden under a checkered bandanna. "And I needed some exercise."

She followed Rick into the kitchen, where he poured them a cup of coffee. They sat down companionably across from each other at the kitchen table.

Emily laughed softly as she thought about what Connor might think of his father cooking all sorts of meat dishes in his kitchen.

Connor again!

He was never far from her thoughts. Their almost kiss lingered in her mind. She swallowed the bitter brew and forced her attention to her host.

"Have you heard from him?" she whispered.

She knew better. He couldn't call, couldn't contact them. He didn't exist right now. He was someone else.

Her breath hitched. Was he *with* someone else? Did his missions include that sort of thing? In the books and movies that happened all the time.

She would be heartbroken if he was.

"Child," Rick said tenderly and squeezed her arm. "He can't. He won't." He shook his head.

"Then how do we know he's not..." Her face twisted at the agony behind the meaning of the words.

"We won't know. If he doesn't come back..." He swallowed hard.

She leaned back in the chair. His statement stung and she blinked back the tears.

"How long were you usually away from home?" She twisted the cup in her hand to distract herself.

Rick considered her for a moment. Then he sighed and set his drink down.

"The longest I was away was four months. That one almost broke me. After a while, things weren't so cut and dry anymore. The line of right and wrong became awfully vague. I struggled a lot with God when I returned. But He saw it was good to gently restore me."

"How did your wife manage? I mean, it must have been horrible for her." She hid behind the cup, hoping that he couldn't notice how her face had become that annoying red again.

"It was hard on her. My first mission away I came home to a sobbing wife. We were still in Pakistan, just married ten months. But once we had the kids I think me being away became easier for her. When they were old enough she had their schedule to keep her busy, you know. And she filled the home with love and laughter, keeping everyone's mind off the fact that I may not be coming back one day."

"I don't know if I can do it," she whispered, more to herself than him.

Rick leaned forward and rested his elbows on the table. He threaded his fingers together.

"We don't know how much we can handle. God never gives us too much."

She exhaled slowly. "That's such a convenient answer, Rick. Do you really believe it? Can you honestly say that God didn't give you too much when you had to disappear? You had to leave the family you loved best."

Rick blinked quickly. "That is a hard one, Emily. I don't know what the meaning of all that was. But God is efficient. He had a reason for that too. Maybe I was becoming too self-sufficient, too arrogant. Maybe He wanted to draw my children to Him. They both committed their lives to Christ, one after the other. Alicia was first, then Connor. I really wish I could have been there for them. But the past is over. I don't regret having my wife for eighteen glorious years." He had a faraway look on his face.

The question that stirred in her mind would be difficult to ask and difficult to answer. She wasn't sure if they were close enough to warrant such intimacy. Emily had grown to almost love the man across from her.

But...

She decided she couldn't stand it anymore. She swallowed hard and put her cup down.

"Rick. Did you ever have to do things on the missions that compromised your marriage vows to your wife?"

Rick's face turned dark.

"I was wondering when you were going to ask that question. I want to give you the assurance that I never had to compromise. I can't. I had a reputation, you know, of keeping business and pleasure separate. Except for one mission, the very long one, that was different."

Emily swallowed hard, suddenly feeling sick. It was hard to draw in a breath. She felt the seat underneath her shift. She couldn't do this!

"Emily, look at me." Rick's face swam in front of hers. "Connor loves you. I see it in his face, in his eyes. You're the one for him if you want to be. Whatever happens out there, you can trust him. The thing is that Connor has a weapon the enemy does not."

"What's that?"

Rick pointed up. “He has God, Emily. That is very important when the reality starts to fade.”

Emily covered her face with her hands. “I can't do this,” she panted.

Rick touched her shoulder and she jumped. “Connor has a reputation just as I had, Emily. He doesn't sleep around. Anyway, this isn't the movies, you know. The chances of him having to compromise are slim to nonexistent. Most people out there are professionals.”

“It happened to you,” she breathed.

“Emily, I compromised a lot that time. Everything got to me and I let go of my values. It almost cost me my marriage. Connor's different. He would exhaust all the other options first. Believe me, he saw the strain in my relationship with his mother after that one. At fifteen he was pretty perceptive, you know! I didn't go out again for six months. It left a real bad taste in my mouth.”

“Thanks, Rick,” she whispered and got up to put her cup into the sink.

“Emily,” Rick said briskly. “You can do this. Give yourself some credit. You're stronger than you think.”

Emily barely made it to her apartment that night. Her emotions were all over the place. She picked up the ring, still sitting in the container she had put it in.

When Connor came back she would...

She would what? She would give him the ring back?

She paced to her door and looked out into the windswept late October night. She knew that in her heart she would never be able to walk away now.

Suddenly weak, she dropped to her knees.

Lord, I accept Your will for my life again and again, with humility and meekness. I know I still have a lot to learn in those areas, but if You picked Connor for me, then I accept that too. I pray, oh Lord, that You would keep him safe, that he would not get into a situation he can't handle. Help me to continue to accept Your will for my life.

Somehow she felt much more settled, more at peace. It was amazing that every time she went to Him, she was given strength to deal with whatever lay before her.

35

Skiing in the French Alps in late October was not as exciting as they made it sound. Only the top part of the mountain was open, which still proved to be exciting as he followed the very athletic M. Lamour. The man was a cad, to say the least, and Connor chomped at the bit to get the job done.

A while later they walked into the living room of the chalet. The room was decorated by professionals. The man's wife lounged by tall windows. Connor guessed she was ten years his junior. M. Lamour was approximately his father's age, give or take a few years. His jet black hair was artificial, and his skin was way too tight.

His wife also screamed fake. Her smile was forced, her blonde hair was colored, her body was trim and proportioned to call attention to all the right parts, which were undoubtedly, manufactured.

She made Connor want to run for cover the first time he met her.

Her smile widened to include him as she rose cat-like from the chaise she had been lounging on. He kept his face tight, letting the smile barely slip to his lips. She greeted her husband with a passionate kiss, her eyes never leaving Connor.

He felt his skin crawl. He dropped his gaze and cleared his throat.

Lord, I need help here. Keep my thoughts on what needs to be done.

M. Lamour pulled out of his wife's entangling arms, clearly enjoying her attention. Connor wasn't so sure that attention was directed only to her husband.

"My wife enjoys it when I come home."

No- Connor swallowed that last part.

Lamour winked at him and Connor ran his hands through his hair, dyed dark blonde.

"It's nice to have someone to come home to," Connor said, his voice tight.

M. Lamour wandered to the bar and poured himself a large drink.

"You have someone to come home to, M. Brandt?"

M. Renault joined them at the bar. He had opted out of skiing today, instead, he lounged at the chalet.

Connor thought of Emily and their last conversation. Wouldn't it be nice to come home to her?

"No, sir. I have not found a suitable partner."

M. Lamour burst into an unpleasant laugh causing his skin to crawl with what seemed like fire ants. The sooner he was done here, the better. Lately, he had been filled with doubt that he had what it took to get out alive, and that was never good.

"As M. Renault probably told you, I'm looking for someone to prevent hackers getting into the company's network. We seem to have had a string of really persistent break-ins. I want to make sure that it won't happen again. Can you do that for us?"

He couldn't look too eager, or the whole game was over before it started. Connor leaned casually against the bar stool, pursing his lips as if considering the offer.

"It all depends on what you want me to do. I can do my best but there are excellent hackers out there. No network is ever totally secure but I can make it pretty much impossible for them to get in with this firewall I've developed for larger companies. It will require me to be on site and to have complete access to your system."

"Of course, M. Brandt. I would welcome your efforts. You come highly recommended. For someone so young as yourself, it speaks highly of your motivation. I was a go-getter myself, Monsieur."

They talked some more about computers, and Connor slipped into his part seamlessly.

"Gentlemen," Mme. Lamour pouted. She had that expression down pat. "I'm growing bored with all this talk about computers. Can't we switch to a more interesting subject?"

"Of course, *ma cherie*." Lamour kissed his wife's offered cheek. He lit a cigar, which he offered to both his companions. Connor declined, while M. Renault accepted, a greedy grin on his face.

"How is it, Herr Brandt, that a young boy from a small town in Austria had the chance to study at one of the most prestigious schools in the United States?" M. Lamour said in accented German.

Was he trying to see if Connor was legit? Languages he could definitely do.

"I had a very wealthy uncle, who doted on me. When I came to the age to go to college, he offered to pay for my education and my parents were so overjoyed that they accepted," he answered in perfectly good Austrian German.

"I have to say, you are almost too good to be true," the man's eyes narrowed suspiciously.

Connor laughed, forcing himself to relax. He accepted the drink his host offered without a flinch. "I can tell you without a doubt, that some of my employers would disagree strongly. The last one found me too cold and calculating. I have been called arrogant more than once. Others chose to use stronger words to describe me."

The man on the other couch grinned in amusement. M. Renault stared at him for a moment, then a lazy smile slipped onto his lips.

"Maybe you will fit after all." Lamour switched to English, effortlessly.

"Since we are talking personal stuff, where are you from, M. Lamour?" Connor asked. " I did an extensive search on your company but it didn't really reveal much about you. I was more than a little intrigued if you don't mind me saying so."

"I grew up in the Midwestern part of the States. I found Europe much better for business. Speaking of which, will you be able to start next week?"

Why not tonight? Connor was dying to ask. *I want to get back to my life.*

"Of course, I'll have to see to a few other projects, but I should manage to give you my full attention by Tuesday." Not wanting to seem too eager, it killed him to say it.

That seemed to be acceptable to his host, who nodded. "When we get back to Paris, we will set you up with an office and full access to the computers. I'm very excited about having you work for us. I think this is the beginning of a very lucrative business relationship for all."

As everyone toasted, Connor had to suppress the urge to hurl. He was banking on his acting skills and those of the invisible support people to get this job done. Once again, his stomach clenched into a tight ball.

Was he over his head with this one?

The first snowflakes dusted the ground. Cold November wind and snow made everything so dreary.

Connor has been gone since the beginning of October.

Emily leaned her forehead against the window panes trying not to dwell on him once again.

She needed to get a life, to get out and be with her friends. It just didn't seem right. Sarah had asked four times already if she wanted to come with her to one of the clubs. In another lifetime, she wouldn't have thought twice to accept.

Now, she was content to visit her parents for the evening or hang out at Rick's who always seemed so very appreciative when she showed up.

She considered going over tonight, just in case... But if Connor was home, wouldn't he come here?

She put a movie into the player, then took it out, changing her mind. With a heavy sigh, she grabbed her keys and walked down the steps, already covered with a slight layer of snow. A short time later, she stood in front of the now so familiar door and rang.

It didn't take long for Rick to answer and he grinned when he saw her.

"I was wondering if my dinner partner was going to show up tonight. I've got hamburgers out on the grill. Thick, juicy burgers! What do you say?"

Emily hung her jacket in the closet and kissed his cheek. "You had me at hamburgers," she said and meandered past him into the kitchen.

"Why so glum, my partner-in-crime?" he asked and pulled out two plates. "Don't you think Connor would die if he knew that I put meat on his precious plates? I can just see it now. *You will not get me to eat a dead animal. I work hard to stay healthy and to keep this body looking as good as it does!*"

His imitation of his son was funny and absolutely outrageous. It also caused a strange sensation in her belly. She pushed her hand hard against the flat of her stomach, trying to staunch it.

She hadn't seen Connor in six weeks and still, thinking of him did something to her. The doorbell rang again and he motioned with his head for her to go and check.

"Are you expecting a party?" she teased as she walked through the hall and opened the front door, catching her breath.

Two dark-haired women stood outside the door staring back at her. It took Emily only a split second to realize that they were Connor's mother and sister, Rick's wife and daughter. The younger woman stared at her with steely gray eyes that pierced right through her.

She has the same intensity as Connor.

The thought made her cling to the door a little tighter.

"Is this Connor Williams' house?" the younger one asked, her voice as cold as ice.

"Yes," she managed to say and cleared her voice. "He's... he's away at the moment."

"Emily, my partner-in-crime, have you gotten cold feet? Really, Connor will never know, and those hamb-"

Rick appeared at the opening to the kitchen and went completely still. He paled and his face fell.

A soft gasp escaped the younger woman as the older one just stared at her husband, presumed dead for twenty years. Then her eyes rolled back into her head and she collapsed into the snow.

"Miriam!" Rick sprang into action, racing past Emily and lifting the unconscious woman into his arms. He carried her through the door and glared at Emily. "Now would be a good time to show me that you're a doctor!"

Emily shot a look at the younger woman and pulled her into the warm house. Her face was as pale as the snow on the ground and Emily feared she'd pass out too if she didn't distract her. Extending a hand to her, Emily smiled.

"I'm Emily. Connor is a... He is a good friend."

Alicia wore a glazed-over look. Emily could well imagine what was going through her mind as she knelt down next to the woman on the couch and elevated her legs above her head. No doubt she was in shock! Alicia stood in the hall, watching Emily and Rick revive her mother. Emily took in that her breathing was thready but okay. Her pulse was slightly fast but that was understandable.

Medically there was nothing wrong with her other than she had just seen her husband for the first time after twenty years believing him dead!

Slowly and steadily she came to.

Her eyes flickered and zeroed right in on Rick, who was rubbing her wrist, eyes closed, praying. Emily turned toward Alicia who was trembling from head to toe.

"Why don't you sit down?"

Emily put a protective arm around her middle and led her to the recliner. Then she rushed to the kitchen fetch two cups of black coffee.

Alicia accepted hers with trembling hands and took a sip. She handed the other to Rick, who was in the process of helping his wife sit up.

"Rick?" the woman whispered breathlessly. "Is that really you?"

Plump tears rolled down her cheek.

"Last time I checked in the mirror it was," he smirked and held a hand out to his daughter, who stared, her eyes wide. "Hey, kitten."

Alicia burst into tears and covered her face with her hands. Emily felt like an intruder and inched her way to the door. Rick saw her and guessed her intentions. He shook his head.

"Where are you going, partner-in-crime?"

"Rick," she whispered and looked at the two women. "I don't belong here."

"Wrong! You do belong here."

"Is that your daughter?" Miriam asked, her voice shaky and weak.

Rick frowned as he looked at his wife. He shook his head. "No, but I hope she'll be my daughter-in-law in the near future."

Oh, no – you didn't! Emily narrowed her eyes and shot him what she hoped was a deadly gaze, which failed to impress.

Connor's mother stared at the man in front of her. "Rick!" Her voice was getting stronger.

Color was coming back into her cheeks. Anger, outrage, fear, and... betrayal flashed in her eyes as she sat up as if electrocuted. Her face was now flushed and her breathing was rapid.

"What are you doing here? What are you doing alive?" The last statement was forced out between gritted teeth.

"I'm sorry," he whispered and tears streaked down his own face. He wiped roughly at them with the back of his hand.

Rick stood up and crossed the room to cradle his daughter in his arms. She crumbled in his embrace and for a moment she clung to him. Then she sniffed and pushed him away harshly.

"How dare you!" Her eyes flashed in anger and she stood up to help her mother off of the couch.

Connor's mother was a beautiful woman with an air of tragic sadness about her. She was slim and well toned. Her hair was still jet black though her roots were turning white. She now stood in front of her husband, her hands shaking as she touched his cheek.

He groaned softly and closed his eyes.

Thwack!

Rick's head snapped back at the force of the hand that had just connected with his cheek.

Miriam's eyes flashed in anger. She raised her hand again and he caught her wrist in midair and held it. She wrenched it out of his grasp. Alicia looked back and forth between her parents.

"Stop it!" she shouted, her cheeks wet.

Emily retreated into the kitchen, praying hard for them.

36

Eyes tired, Connor stared at the screen. He had been at this for days and had found nothing to implicate his employer or the company in anything illegal. Two weeks had gone by, and still nothing.

His gut clenched tightly when he thought about returning home empty-handed. Running his fingers through his hair for the umpteenth time, he leaned wearily against the back of his chair. At least the security of the network was almost in place, nearing the end of his legit job here.

While he was setting up the security network, which was quite involved, he was also working on a backdoor system with which the analysts at Langley could read everything in the network.

He was setting up his network security to interact with a normal-looking server, which really dumped its information into the system specifically set up at the home office through the guise of an anti-virus program. It was a simple concept, too simple for anyone to even realize that the information was being passed on.

Brilliant minds had thought it up. All he needed to do was to enter in the coding.

He heard the door open, and quickly changed screens. His employer, who also put in long hours, sauntered in. It was nearing nine o'clock. Connor preferred to work late, of course. Less likelihood that he would be disturbed.

He leaned back into his chair, an expectant look on his face.

"Herr Brandt. You've been working hard ever since we employed you. We appreciate your work and it looks like you are doing a great job. It speaks well for you, young man. Come and join me for dinner at the house tonight." Connor rose to say something but was waved back down. "I don't want to hear any excuses, as my wife suggested that I invite you. My daughters just arrived home and I would like you to meet them. They could spice up your social life. I can see that you need help in that direction!"

Connor rubbed the back of his neck feeling the thin hairs rising. "I can't. There is a lot to do here."

M. Lamour glared at him. "You're coming! End of discussion."

Connor suppressed a sigh. He was not in the mood to schmooze anyone, let alone the man's family. The less he got personally involved, the better. Then again... He could get a glimpse at the man's home.

Lamour had to have a personal computer, a place where he possibly stored the information Connor needed to find the connections and contacts. The sooner he could get hold of that, the sooner he would be able to end this charade.

"Fine," he finally relented. "Let me just finish this test of the system."

It took him another ten minutes to check if the information was being related to the experts. Then he was ready and grabbed his jacket to meet Lamour.

"Good, let's go."

The chauffeur drove them to the very upscale neighborhood near the Seine River. He could hear the splashing of the water against the walls when he got out and wrinkled his nose at the peculiar scent.

Following his boss to the front door, he stood gawking in the exquisitely arranged hall. Mirrors adorned the walls. He peered at the vaulted ceiling which was painted like the Sistine Chapel. Along both walls hung paintings of famous French Impressionist painters, like Monet and

Manet, along with a few paintings by Degas. Benches were placed at appropriate intervals along the walls for the guests to be able to sit and admire the exquisite artwork.

His shoes squeaked over the black and white marble tiles. A servant, dressed in a starched uniform, opened the tall oak doors to the living room. The chaise lounges scattered around the room were taken up by three exquisitely dressed women, scrutinizing him as soon as they entered.

Their bored look disappeared immediately.

"Renè, you brought home a visitor. How wonderful of you." Mme Lamour smiled her pleasure like a hungry cougar. "It's good to see you again, M. Brandt."

"*Merci beaucoup, Madame Lamour.* I look forward to dinner."

He shook three soft hands, cordially, keeping his attention on their eyes or a spot right between their penciled in eyebrows.

His mind slipped to Emily, to her fear that he would compromise his values. As he imagined her soft mocha eyes along with the smile that always made him pay attention, his dislike for his job increased ten-fold.

"Herr Brandt is in charge of installing the new network security at the company," M. Lamour told his daughters.

They measured him up with lazy confidence, causing his gut to clench unpleasantly. In what was becoming a nervous habit, he pushed his glasses back onto his nose.

"Sit with me," Sabine, the older daughter, purred and slipped her hand through his arm. "I love talking computers. They are so interesting."

He suppressed a groan and trained his features.

"I'm studying history right now. I use computers all the time. Now, next year I may switch and pursue acting. What do you think? Do I have a chance for a leading role?" She pouted and struck a pose.

Swallowing the lump that appeared in his throat, he averted his gaze.

"A director would be blind not to notice you," he said and the young woman giggled.

"You see," she said somewhat condescendingly to her younger sister, who rolled her eyes.

Where Sabine was fair and curvy, the other sister was dark and slim. The only thing they seemed to have in common was their attitude. Both were spoiled and bored.

He was about to be their entertainment.

"He thinks I have what it takes."

Apparently, filet mignon was on the menu.

Wasn't he a vegetarian?

Here was another part of him that was fading away.

"Excuse me," he said after dinner. "Where is your facility?" He leaned close to his host, who motioned for a servant to take Connor.

On the way to the downstairs restroom, Connor had plenty of opportunity to check for the security in the residence. The lack thereof caught him by surprise and started all sorts of alarm bells going off in his head.

He could see no cameras, and the alarm system for the front door was easily accessible. Cracking it would take him only seconds.

It was as though Lamour tried to portray that he had nothing to hide.

On his way back to the dining room, he passed several closed doors, doors that he longed to unlock. The whole place was worth another look.

Later, when everyone was in bed, he would sneak back in.

As the evening progressed, M. Lamour seemed to enjoy the attention his women lavished on Connor. Sabine made him her special project. It was as though she had permanently attached herself to him.

"I would love to see what you do with the computer," she said, her voice velvety soft. She giggled.

Connor took a sip of his water cursing the day he accepted this assignment.

"Papa," she pouted. "I want to go to the art exhibition tomorrow. The Louvre is having an amazing collection from China. I want Helmut to accompany me! Everyone who is anyone in Paris will be there."

Connor stiffened.

The lines of who he was were becoming convoluted. He was becoming more and more the person he was playing. Soon there would be nothing left of himself. The real world was about to become fantasy, and the fantasy world was becoming real.

Who was he, again?

"That is a wonderful idea. Helmut, you will take Sabine tomorrow. She will enjoy your company. You work entirely too much."

Connor looked down on his china plate. It was so easy to just forget who he was and embrace what he was becoming. He was turning into Helmut Brandt. He should guard his heart, but how when he couldn't quite remember his former self?

"I don't... You're right, there's a lot of work to do. I would rather get the job done, then take some time off," he said in a feeble attempt to bow out.

"All work and no play makes Jack a dull boy," Lamour's wife purred.

Connor suppressed another groan.

37

When he finally got home that night, he leaned against his door. He was weary and tired. This job was taking too much out of him. He could feel it. After almost two months in the field, it happened.

He paced up and down his living room.

Lord Jesus! I need You! I feel like this job is stripping me of who I am. I don't know how much more I can hold out against the pressures there are around me. He swallowed hard and threaded his fingers through his hair. *Will You please help me to stand on what is right!*

He knew his request had been heard and gathered up his strength and courage to get the job done and go home.

Taking out the secure phone from the hiding spot under the window seat, he called in.

"I still have nothing," he groused. "Tonight I'll scope out Lamour's private computer. Before I go in there, I need some information on what type of security he has. How soon can you get it to me?"

"We'll have it to you as soon as we can."

He signed off. While he waited for the information, he donned dark clothing and gathered the equipment necessary to break into the Lamour residence.

That part would be easy.

What worried him was the lack of obvious security cameras. That meant that possibly they were hidden. His phone chirped and he glanced at the information. Apparently, the security in the house was lax. It just didn't make sense, unless there was nothing to hide. Then Connor would have to dig more, take more time.

He drove himself to the general neighborhood and waited until all the lights in the house went out.

He quietly closed the door of his car as he approached the house.

It took just over thirty seconds for him to open the front door.

Getting slow in your old age!

He quickly moved toward the alarm and disarmed it. Just like he thought, it was a piece of cake. He slipped on his goggles to search for the infrared detectors and took a steadying breath.

There were no beams bouncing around the hallway, which made his heart pound harder against his chest.

He quietly made his way toward the first door of the hall, finding it locked.

No problem, he thought.

It took him no time to open this door.

He found himself in an art studio. Someone had some serious talent, he decided as he quickly scanned the room, finding no computer. Quietly, he closed the door again.

After opening the next door, he breathed in a sigh of relief. He had found the office with a desktop, ripe to be hacked into. He checked for infrared sensors, so often used in home security, along the walls. Here too, there was no evidence of transmitters or sensors.

Feeling another unpleasant rush of nerves squirrel through him, he drew in a sharp breath at the sight of a camera, pointing right at the computer! As he checked closely, he found that it was not on.

What is Lamour playing at? Why is the camera not working?

Without a sound, Connor ghosted over the thick carpet to the computer, turning it on. He had to find Lamour's password and he set to work. After fifteen minutes he pushed his hair out of his face, breathing heavily.

Nothing!

If he didn't find it soon, he would have to admit defeat and retreat, to try again another day. He rolled his tense shoulders. After a couple more tries, it was time to cut his losses and leave.

Perhaps there was a way to get the password later.

His head snapped around to the sound of almost inaudible footsteps outside the door. Dashing behind the door, he drew out his gun. The doorknob turned, admitting a dark shadowy figure into the room.

His blood turning to ice, he grabbed the person in a choke-hold. The figure first started to fight him, then froze in his grip.

“Let me go!” A female voice came out strangled. “I won't fight you.”

Connor froze.

A woman? This assignment is getting better and better by the minute!

He wasn't aware of any other operatives the agency had on this. Reluctantly, he loosened his hold and found himself facing Monique Lamour, the younger daughter. He let her go as if she was a hot potato, still keeping his weapon trained on her.

“Don't move,” he hissed sharply in English.

To his surprise, he came up empty when he searched her for a weapon and pushed her mercilessly into the chair behind the desk, securing her hands and feet with zip-ties.

Her breath hitched and she gritted her teeth.

What if...

"What are you doing in my house?" she asked, her eyes flashing in anger. "If you've come to rob us, the jewelry is in the safe. I can give you the combination and you can leave right now."

She glanced at the computer and back at the grandfather clock, ticking noisily in the corner. She licked her lips nervously and began to struggle against her bonds.

"Let me go!"

"No! What are *you* doing here, *Mademoiselle* Lamour? Since I am the one holding a gun to your head, I suggest you answer."

The woman must have ice in her veins because she didn't flinch one bit.

"I had to use the restroom." Again the eyes flickered to the clock.

He shook his head and chuckled softly. "I think not!" He lifted the mask that hid his face.

Her eyes widened and she allowed a smile to play on her lips. "M. Brandt? I didn't expect you to try to break into our house to steal from us."

Connor gritted his teeth. Time to end this. "I'm not interested in stealing your jewelry. Tell me what you are doing here, Mademoiselle!"

She flashed a quick smile and sat up straighter. Her eyes became calculating and hard as she examined him. Lifting up her chin, she met his gaze with a challenge of her own.

"I suspect I'm doing the same thing as you are," she hissed. "Perhaps you should start to tell me what you are doing in *my* house. Who are you working for?"

Connor gave a cold laugh. "Mm. I don't think so. You're still tied to the chair and I still have the gun. We're going to take a walk, you and I. And then you can tell me, why you're dressed in black, trying to break into your own father's computer."

A soft laughter filled the room. "That might be fun," she purred. "But if you try to leave, you'll find it a whole lot more difficult than you think. The camera pointing at you is about to come back on in..." She glanced at her watch. "five minutes."

Connor settled a hip on the corner of the desk, his gun still pointed at the unexpected intruder. He was right to be suspicious of how easy it was to get inside. So getting out would be more difficult. Maybe it was a good thing she caught him before he tried to leave. He would have found himself in a lot of trouble if she told the truth.

"Do you have the password for this computer?"

He didn't have time for chit-chat! Time was running short.

Monique shook her head, glowering at him. "No!"

Her chin tipped up, issuing a challenge.

That would have been too easy.

Irritated at the sidetrack he was about to take, Connor stared at her.

"I see."

Monique gave a resigned sigh. "I wasn't kidding about the camera, M. Brandt. It's about to come on again."

"Then you had better explain why you're dressed in black, tied to a chair in your father's office. I'll take my chances with the security."

Connor turned to leave.

"Wait," she whispered, staring at the camera. "Untie me and I'll tell you who I work for.

He laughed, unpleasantly. "Try again."

She struggled against the ties, a thin layer of sweat appearing on her forehead. "Fine, fine. I work for Interpol."

Now, isn't that interesting. "Why?"

"I have my own reasons. I can assure you, we want the same things. Untie me, now!" Her face paled.

Connor drew out his knife and cut her free.

"I assume you're here for the computer. Is that correct? Have you found what you were looking for?" she asked hurriedly, rubbing her wrists.

He shook his head.

Monique gave a resigned sigh. "Monsieur, we're out of time. That camera is going to come active in about one minute."

Connor glared at her, then stuffed the gun back into its holster. He quickly powered down the computer. Then he turned back to the dark-clad figure who had suddenly become his ally.

"So, Mademoiselle. No funny business. And may I remind you that I still have a gun."

Monique, who wore a satisfied grin, cocked her head and studied her manicured fingernails.

"I know how to get back to my room. In about one minute this whole house is going to come active with security cameras and motion detectors. I suggest we stop chit-chatting and get you out of here."

His heart did a hard thump and increased its tempo as he held his breath. He was trapped *inside* the house.

He was about to take a step into the hall when Monique pulled him back and motioned to the front door, where a beep could be heard. When he slipped on his goggles, the whole foyer was lit up with bright green beams from passive infrared sensors, hidden cleverly among the art.

Oh, yeah! Getting out was going to be a challenge.

"Quickly!" she hissed and pulled him upstairs with her. She darted into her room and slammed the door.

"Why didn't we set off the alarms?" Connor asked, keeping his eye on the door.

"We did. He had it installed two years ago by a friend. It's linked to his security force, right next door. In about thirty seconds, my father's bodyguards will be storming in through that door," she hissed.

She started taking off her dark clothing, throwing it into her closet. She jumped under the covers and looked at him with a warning.

"Do you want to explain to my father what you are doing here? I suggest we play the happy couple right now. Hurry!"

"Nah. I don't think so." Connor turned to the window and was about to open it when Monique appeared by his side and wrapped her hand around his arm like a vice.

"No! If you open that, we're both going to be in trouble!"

Fear etched the shadow in her face.

Muttering under his breath, Connor turned in a tight circle, feeling like an animal in a cage. He could hear the doors downstairs slamming. Heavy footsteps could be heard pounding around downstairs in search of an intruder.

This should have been an easy job tonight. Get in, get out! And here he was.

Everything inside him recoiled from what he was about to do. His jaw set, he started to tug on his dark shirt.

This isn't the way!

Connor exhaled softly. The still small voice, the one he ought to heed, was still with him.

"Monsieur. They are outside my door!" Monique's voice was just a breath.

Connor took a giant step toward the large walk-in closet and put his finger to his lips. He hid his gun among one of the many pairs of shoes. If they found him, like they were sure to do, it was better that he was unarmed.

Fear and annoyance streaked over her face for a fraction of a second.

The door was opened and it banged into the wall. Light flooded the room. Three bodyguards rushed inside, their weapons ready.

"Mademoiselle Monique! The alarm went off." The bodyguards secured their weapons.

Monique looked at them with wide eyes.

"There is nothing to look at. It was my mistake." Her voice trembled slightly. "I found that I was thirsty and needed a drink. I forgot about the alarms."

"We need to check. In case."

The men looked around the room and Connor tried to blend into the various gowns and shirts hanging in the closet. This was just as bad as if he had hidden under the bed.

One of the men must have noticed movement. He dove at him and yanked him out.

"No, no, leave him be!" Monique jumped out from under the covers and stood in front of him. "He's... he's my guest." She tried to look as shamefaced as possible.

Connor's heart raced and he tried to work through every possible scenario to get himself out of this. He would have to play along.

"What is the meaning of this?" Lamour, wearing a silk robe, his hair tousled from sleep, rushed into the room. He stopped in his tracks and looked around, confused.

"Why are you in here?" He turned to his bodyguards.

"Pardon, Monsieur. The sensors went off in the entrance hall. We assumed there was a break-in. We came to investigate."

Lamour grinned for a split second and pointed to Connor, who, by now, was back in character and managed to tremble with fear. "I don't think there is a threat here. Monique, you should have been more careful."

"Yessir. We'll leave you. Sorry to have disturbed you, Mademoiselle, Monsieur."

The guards left the room just as quickly as they had entered. Lamour nodded and followed them.

"Have a good night," he said just as he closed the door.

As soon as they were gone, Connor shot to the window to peer out for a possible exit.

"Wait," Monique hissed and slipped back under the covers. "He'll be right back."

"What?" he hissed back.

"He always does this. He doesn't quite trust me. Go figure, right?"

She watched the door. Sure enough, within seconds it opened again and Lamour pushed his head into the room.

"Breakfast will be at seven, Helmut."

The door closed softly. Connor held himself still, not daring to breathe.

"I'm leaving!" he growled and tucked his shirt back in.

"You can't," Monique hissed. "Give it ten minutes. Then you can leave. In the meantime, we need to talk."

Retrieving his gun, Connor sat down on the floor as far away from her as possible, his head on his knees. This was about the worst mission he had ever been on! Tension seeped into his whole body. Connor rubbed his face.

"Talk, I'll listen."

Monique laughed softly. "That's not the way it goes. I give a little and so do you."

"I don't play nice!" He stood up and faced the window. If only he could get out that way.

"You're still alive," she said and blew out a deep breath. "If I hadn't helped you out... I've seen what he does to men that cross him." Her eyes glistened and she blinked quickly. "He... he killed my real father," Monique said, her voice oddly cold.

"Oh. I'm sorry. Is that why you're working with Interpol?"

Monique's chin rose again and at that moment she reminded him of Emily. It was like a punch to the gut and leaned further away.

"Basically. After I watched what he did to my father I hated and feared him at the same time. He's a smart, ruthless man. I would have preferred to stay at boarding school in Switzerland, but he wants to have a semblance of a family. He is *not* a family man! When they approached me, I was glad to help out."

"Okay." Connor kneaded his temple. "What have you found?"

"Sorry, you aren't paying my wages," she said.

"Fine, I'm here because your *father* left with some information that has caused my government to be concerned. They know he's sold it to some unsavory people. So, I'm here to find who he's sold it to."

"I see. And what have you found out?"

"You aren't paying *my* wages," Connor managed to smile.

"Can't you share what you found?" she purred, looking at him through lowered eyelids.

Connor exhaled sharply and nodded. “I bet all the information is on the computer downstairs. The computers at work have nothing. I wish I could have cracked the password. I'll just have to come back.”

“We could work together. I'm new at this. It looks to me like you're not.” She inched closer.

“I don't have the authorization to work with you, Mademoiselle.”

“Mademoiselle? After all we've been through tonight? I'm Monique to you, Helmut. I think tonight warrants that we call each other by first name.”

“No! This isn't a game.”

They arrived at a stalemate, and ten minutes had never seemed so long. When Monique finally gave him the all-clear, he almost ran out of the house as though he was on fire. He let himself into his car and drove back to his apartment.

With a throbbing head, he sat outside his apartment for a long time, staring into the night. Then he pulled out his phone and called in.

“I'm out!” he said, when Bryan Murphy answered.

The man's laughter was cold and unfeeling. “I think not! What do you have?”

“I tried to get into the computer tonight. I couldn't crack his password. I want out.”

“Rattlesnake, you are not quitting on me. Finish this, or someone will pick up your father at your house tomorrow morning to escort him to Leavenworth or somewhere worse.”

Connor's head throbbed even more. “You have no idea where my father is,” he growled.

“This evening he was entertaining. He made hamburgers for your pretty friend who showed up just in time to enjoy them. You know, the doctor friend you have become so fond of? And then he had an unexpected visit from your sister and mother. I tell you, the family reunion was touching. So you tell me what I don't know!"

Connor gritted his teeth and punched the steering wheel. Pain spread up his arm and into his shoulder.

"Look, you really have nothing on my father. He didn't do anything wrong. All he did was disappear."

Connor heard a growl on the other end of the line.

"I don't care. You work for me, you finish this mission. Or I'll make sure that both you *and* your dad will find yourselves in deep trouble. You will never see that pretty doctor friend of yours again. After all, I've toppled a few governments. What are a few agents, who've gone off the reservation? Trust me, you'll regret walking away from this!"

Connor concentrated on breathing, which seemed slightly difficult at that moment. A cold hand clamped around his gut and squeezed, hard.

"Fine. After this, I'm done!" he hissed.

"We'll talk about it when you have finished this, successfully this time."

The phone went dead.

Connor wanted to throw it out the window and drive away. He could disappear. He could warn his father and they could both vanish. Except, he would be looking over his shoulder for the rest of his life. And now his mother and sister knew that his father was alive. He pinched the bridge of his nose.

And Emily!

Emily!

He needed to see her. He needed to talk to her. He needed to touch her! He walked to his apartment through the cold pre-dawn. The arctic air felt good, even loosening the tension in his gut and shoulders.

Bryan would never get away with threatening the people he loved! Connor knew that there had to be a way to get out of the man's clutches, to pay him back for the grief he was experiencing right now.

After all, it was just a job.

His feet crunched on the cobble-stoned pavement and he shot a furtive glance down a dark alley. Fingertips itching, Connor reached for the handle of his handgun. With the moon casting sinister shadows on the old buildings around, and the threat of the conversation still clear in his mind, everything looked dangerous. Connor took a moment to draw in a breath of cold air, watching it puff out like a ghost in front of him. Then he remembered that he was as safe as possible for the moment.

His gut clenched at the sound of something crashing to the ground. He spun around and drew out his weapon at the noise to his left.

Only a cat!

Breathing heavily through his nose, Connor continued his stealthy walk to his apartment.

It was amazing how lonely he felt in the city of love. From where he stood he couldn't see the lights of the Eiffel Tower. And it really didn't feel like the city of love. It felt just like any other city he had done a job in. A job he seriously considered giving up after tonight.

In the distance, the bells of Nôtre Dame chimed three times.

That made it nine at night on the East Coast. As he climbed the six flights of stairs to his apartment, a plan formed in his mind. He leaned against the door as he closed it. Inside him arose a desperate needed to hear her voice, to firm up the lines that were his life.

His real life!

Knowing that he was breaking protocol – like he cared at this point – he thumbed-in the familiar numbers.

38

Emily opened the door to her apartment and beckoned her guests inside. They both stepped through the door with wooden, stiff motions. Both were too polite to forget to thank her. She hung up her keys and gestured around the room.

"This is it," she sighed. "There isn't much to it, but it serves me, for now. The bathroom is right there. Help yourself to anything you want out of the fridge. I'm not a vegetarian, but I have a salad made up."

She went to the linen closet and pulled out two towels, which she hung in the bathroom.

"I'll sleep on the couch, you two can take the bed."

"Oh, no. That is too much of an imposition," Connor's mom said, her voice sounding like silk.

"I insist." Emily poured some water into the coffee machine. "This should be ready in a few minutes. Help yourself to a cup of whatever you like."

She pointed to the different flavored coffees, hot chocolates, and teas next to the machine.

"May I?" Alicia pointed toward the bathroom.

"Oh, of course!" Emily put a hand on her shoulder.

Alicia stumbled toward the bathroom and the door closed.

"This is nice," Connor's mom said. "Your parents built this for you?"

"My dad built it for my sister, but she got married right after grad-school, so it was available when I moved back here. It's cheaper than any place I could find, and I have a lot of loans to pay back."

Miriam nodded and sank down on the couch with a deep, agonizing groan that caused Emily's heart to break.

"May I get you anything?" she asked kindly.

Miriam let out another sigh. "I would like to turn back time to about twenty years ago. Can you do that?"

Emily leaned against the counter, her face twisting in compassion.

"I'm so sorry. It must be such a shock to see him alive. I don't know how you can accept it. It took Connor a while. But I know he enjoyed having his father back."

"How do you know Connor?"

It seemed that any topic other than the one staring them in the face was safer.

"We met in Pakistan. He was on a job and I kind of got in the way," she laughed ruefully. "I was going to help at an orphanage. Things didn't go as planned."

"*You're* the reason for his move."

"I beg your pardon?" Emily turned to pour a cup of coffee, this time with lots of milk and sugar.

"You're the reason he moved to Connecticut. He didn't have to. He could have stayed in Texas." Miriam smiled softly, her eyes shimmering. "I see now."

Emily set her cup down on the table and sat down on the carpet, Indian style.

"I don't know," she murmured. "He shouldn't have."

"I must say, he could have done worse." Miriam rolled her shoulders, trying to loosen up some of her tense muscles. "I commend him for actually leaving. Although both my daughter and I were very upset at the time. She still hasn't talked to him, yet. She can be very stubborn."

"I don't know," Emily repeated, almost to herself. "In light of the new development, wouldn't you change your past if you could?"

Miriam looked at her and shook her head. "I wouldn't change one moment of my life together with Rick. We had our troubles, every marriage does. But the eighteen years we were married were mostly happy times. He made me a better person. He made me feel more like I was alive. I don't know. I can't explain it."

Emily knew exactly what she was talking about. Didn't she feet the same way when she was with Connor? His mother's statement hit her square in the gut, leaving her feeling slightly nauseous.

"But how did you manage to get through it all? The long absences, the heartache when he disappeared... I don't think..." Emily closed her mouth before she said too much.

Miriam folded her hands in her lap.

"Emily. This has been on your heart for a while, hasn't it?" Miriam asked gently.

Emily fought against answering but in the end... "Yes," she whispered.

"I know that it's a scary thought. You have to be ready to pick up and move at a moment's notice. You have to live with the possibility that he may not be coming home." She gave her a sad smile. "To answer your question, I got through it with prayer, more prayer, and thanksgiving. When he disappeared, I lost my reason to live for a long time. I tried to commit suicide several times."

Emily drew in a sharp breath.

"But after a couple of years, that prayer and giving of thanks became easier again. I wouldn't change one moment. Our life was full. I think that was what hurt the most. My life became empty after he was gone."

A thick mass congealed in the back of Emily's throat.

"But God was there. He brought my kids closer to Him. I'm thankful for that. And I love my kids. What would my life have been without them? That alone makes everything worthwhile."

"Prayer?" Emily asked, swallowing the mass.

"Prayer, humility, and thanksgiving," Miriam smiled.

Emily cleared her throat and touched the woman's knee. "I'm sorry that we met under these circumstances."

"Indeed." Miriam suppressed a yawn. "It's been a long day. I'm exhausted. Do you mind if I retire for the night?"

"If you need anything else, just let me know. I'll be up for a while."

Emily settled on the couch. Alicia came out of the bathroom and wandered around the room, daintily touching the frame showing a picture of Emily's whole family.

"Thank you for letting us stay. You didn't have to do that. We could have slept at a hotel and taken the first flight back to Texas in the morning."

"It's no problem. I enjoy having company. Gets my mind off... you know. Are you still thinking of going back tomorrow?"

"Of course." Alicia's head whipped around to her. "Why wouldn't we?"

Emily bit her bottom lip. "Maybe you can forgive your dad and appreciate that God has given you another chance. I know your brother did."

"Yeah, well," Alicia growled. "He is a saint. I have trouble forgiving. Good night, Emily. Thanks again."

Emily watched her go back to the bedroom and close the curtain that separated it from the rest of the apartment. She heard the women talk quietly while she fell into conversation with Jesus.

Lord, thank You for giving all of us another chance. And Lord, please help Connor's family to forgive Rick for leaving them when he had to. Ahh, yes. The little thing with Connor... Would it be too much to show me without a doubt? I could use a neon sign right about now. It has to be all You. Thank You, Lord.

She tried to concentrate on a movie, finding that she couldn't. Sleep wasn't an option, either. She looked at the clock and sighed. It was only nine and she was just not tired. Her phone chirped and she looked at the caller ID, frowning at the blocked number. It took her a millisecond to debate whether to answer or not.

"Hello?"

"Emily!" came the almost breathless reply.

Was she imagining things?

Her hand began to tremble so hard she feared she'd drop the phone.

"Connor!" she gasped.

"Emily!" He sounded as though just saying her name was...

She pressed the palm of her hand to her forehead.

"Okay, you know my name and I know yours. Are we just going to repeat each other's names all night or is there a point to this conversation?"

She heard him chuckle on the other end of the phone.

"That's what I wanted to hear." Emily heard him let out a deep breath. "I miss you."

She didn't know what to say. Her voice was going to crack if she said anything.

"You called me," she finally uttered and yes, her voice cracked.

"I know! I'll probably be in trouble, but I had to. I had to hear your voice. Tell me, how are you doing?"

She cleared her throat. Were they really having this conversation?

"I've been okay. Work is demanding, as usual. I haven't played basketball since you left." Should she tell him about his mother and sister? She decided against it immediately. He would just worry.

"Mm. Look, I don't have much time. It's good to hear your voice, though."

"When are you..." She stopped short. He couldn't tell her when he was coming back. "We have snow on the ground." *Yes, Emily, brilliant.*

"Drive carefully, then. It's kind of cold where I am too. But no snow yet," he replied, his voice sounding tired.

"Come home soon!" She snapped her mouth shut.

There was silence on the other end of the line and she thought he had hung up.

"I miss you," She bit her bottom lip and thought she heard a very faint groan.

"Working on coming home," he whispered. "So, you were with my dad tonight? He was cooking hamburgers? Tell him, if I find out he's been frying bacon in my pans, he's gonna have to buy me new ones."

Emily frowned. How did he know about the hamburgers?

"Connor?"

"Don't ask. Just tell that to my dad, okay? I gotta go."

She heard the phone click and knew that he'd hung up. She flung herself into the pillow, floating on a cloud of bliss.

Connor had called when he wasn't even supposed to.

"Okay, Lord. I got it!"

She closed her eyes and fell asleep. Whatever happened, it would be okay.

39

The lingering sweetness of her teasing voice stayed with him all night. She said she missed him!

Yeah!

That was music to his ears. He wished, once again, that this job was done.

He thanked God for His protection as he walked into his office, ready for the new day. He needed to find the password for Lamour's computer. Then he could go home and...

And what?

He could marry Emily, if she would have him, and start a normal life?

Who was he kidding!

He would never have an average life. He would always be traveling if he stayed with the agency. He was and would always be an operative.

He hung his winter jacket up in the small coat closet in his office, grabbed a cup of coffee, and booted up his computer. It was shortly after eight and by eight-thirty he was busy installing a virus as a test for the system.

When he was done with this job, there would be no reason to hang around. He needed an excuse to stay with the company. After last night, maybe he had one.

Playing the happy couple was never an angle he enjoyed, but he might have to grin and bear it this time.

He was in the middle of coding the last bit of virus into the computer, when M. Lamour sauntered in, cradling a steaming cup of coffee.

The man smirked unpleasantly.

"I underestimated you, Helmut. I thought you weren't interested in any of my daughters. I didn't think you'd move so fast," he chuckled as he settled into the chair opposite his desk.

Uh, I hate this assignment!

He did his best to look uncomfortable. It was easy.

"I'm not surprised that you like Monique. She's the smartest one of the whole bunch."

"It really wasn't what it looked like."

Stick to the truth. Life was less complicated.

Again Lamour laughed, not pleasantly. "Ha! But I was disappointed not to see you at breakfast this morning. I expected you to be there."

Connor managed to look even more uncomfortable.

"Keep up the good work. Don't think that we haven't noticed your dedication. We like what you do," his boss winked.

"We? Who is we?" Connor asked. His heart thudded.

"Oh, just the board members and I. They are quite impressed by your efforts, Helmut. In fact, they'd love to meet you. There is a meeting this weekend we would like you to attend. To introduce you to the members, you understand. Are you free?"

"I can rearrange anything I have on my calendar," he said, trying not to sound too eager.

"Good, it will be at my estate in southern England. It should be a relaxing time for you, Helmut. My family will be there. We will treat it as a pre-Christmas getaway," Lamour said with a wink.

"Glad to hear that." *Not!* "I need to get back to this."

Connor pointed at the screen.

Lamour walked toward the door. "Just wanted to tell you that I expect you to show up for dinner tonight, eight o'clock." He paused with his hand on the doorknob. "In light of last night's development, Sabine will need another escort to tonight's opening. If I don't make that happen I'll have World War Three at my house."

Thank You, God, for little blessings!

With a dinner invitation, he would be able to have another crack at the computer! But how would he make it through? He was sure that the longer he stayed, the less of himself there remained. If only he could prevent that.

How could he?

What if he gave God full control of his life?

Whenever he went into the field, he prayed. They were mostly prayers for protection, to make it through unscathed. He hadn't told God that he'd be fine with whatever the outcome. Was he willing, truly willing, to give his life?

He that finds his life shall lose it: and he that loses his life for my sake shall find it...

That little reminder burned into his heart, seeping into the rest of him. He hadn't given his life. He fought hard to keep it. Connor stepped to the window overlooking the Eiffel Tower, and let go.

Your way, Lord. Whatever happens.

He called me!

It was the first conscious thought Emily had in the morning, even before she opened her eyes. It was as though a huge weight had been taken off her. God had shown her in a very tangible way. Now it was up to her to accept.

The thought that God Himself had seen it important to show her filled her with peace, covering her like a snugly, soft blanket. Something deeper than happiness settled inside, filling in all the cracks of the past. It went beyond her circumstances.

God was leading her.

Preparing a simple meal for her guests, she started humming praise songs. As she set the table, Emily felt like dancing.

Soon, Alicia walked into the kitchen. She looked so much like her brother that Emily almost dropped the bread she was toasting.

"You didn't have to make breakfast. I'm sure you have other things to do," Alicia said and her voice was still sleep-laden.

Alicia thanked her for the cup of coffee, cradling it with both hands. She peered out into the dull November morning, deep in thought.

"You think I should forgive my father, don't you?" she finally murmured.

Emily glanced her way. "I can't tell you what you need to do. Only the Holy Spirit can do that."

Alicia exhaled heavily. "I couldn't sleep a wink last night."

As alarm spread over Emily's face, she quickly put a hand on Emily's arm.

"It wasn't the bed or anything you offered." She shrugged her shoulders. "You know how that *still* voice in your head is practically screaming at you?"

Emily snickered.

"Yeah..." Alicia placed the cup on the counter.

"Mm, I have found that if you just put your head in the sand, it dulls the scream," Emily grinned and took a sip. "Although breathing is a challenge."

"Thanks," Alicia laughed. "I could try that."

"Or not," Emily added quietly, blowing the steam off her cup.

Alicia shot her a pained look. At that moment, Miriam walked in. She had showered and looked crisp and very efficient. She nodded to Emily and thanked her for the food.

"That is a lot of trouble. We could have picked up something on the way out."

"It's my pleasure. Are you leaving, then?"

"It would be prudent," Miriam answered and turned to her daughter. "Unless you want to stay, Alicia."

Her daughter shook her head violently and held up her hand.

"I'm good with going home."

They ate their breakfast in silence, each of them weighed down with their own thoughts.

Emily's centered on a certain phone call and a prayer for God to help her make up her mind. She almost smiled but remembered that she had company, who would probably find it rather odd if she smiled for no reason at all.

After breakfast the women thanked her for the thousandth time and carefully made their way to their rental car, trying to avoid stepping into the snow. Emily turned to her nightstand and opened the ceramic container where she had kept the ring.

Her stomach fluttered nervously as she touched it. Connor's father must have taken a long time to make this. Before she lost her nerve, she slipped it onto the ring finger on her left hand.

It fit perfectly.

Okay, God. I want to do this. I don't care where it leads.

Immediately a verse from Psalms came to her.

You will show me the path of life: in your presence is fullness of joy; at your right hand there are pleasures for evermore.

Pulling out a journal, she jotted it down and committed it to memory for the uncertain future that faced her.

In the days leading up to the meeting in England, Connor was a guest at the house every night. Because of their *romantic* relationship, Connor now had more chances to slip into the office and try to crack the computer password. Usually, Monique was with him, covering his back. On their last night, they had a breakthrough. Together, they finally cracked the password to get in. After that, it was easy. There were some other passwords, but they managed to figure them out quickly.

They discovered some very interesting folders. Instead of taking the time to check on them and risk getting caught, he copied them onto a USB stick.

When they checked the emails, both he and Monique grinned as if Christmas had come early. In a sense, it had for him.

Bin-go!

He copied emails from Alain Laurant, a well-known arms dealer in Tunisia, one that Connor had come across before. There were other emails from names he recognized. There was a Russian arms dealer, who made some very interesting queries.

He didn't have time to hook this computer to the mainframe in the States, but tomorrow was another night.

"Well done, Monique," Connor said after they returned to her room and he was waiting to leave.

"Let's celebrate, Helmut," she purred and slipped her arms around his neck. He pushed her away gently, but firmly.

"No! This," he pointed between the two of them. "This is not going to go anywhere. It stays strictly business. Do you understand?"

"I don't." She looked up at Connor. "What's wrong with pretending to be a happy couple and to act on it? I would like to know your real name."

Her voice was smooth as silk, causing an adverse reaction in Connor.

"Nope. That is not going to happen, and you know it. And I can pretend to be your boyfriend, but that is all it's going to be. Nothing more. When that door closes and we are alone, we are not a couple."

"How boring! I thought this spying gig would turn out to be more exciting. Why not just pretend all the way? I like you."

"Cut it out, Monique!"

"Mm. Are you married?" she asked teasingly.

"Like I'd tell you?" he replied, sarcasm thick in his voice. "No, there is more to this."

"Okay." Monique brushed her hair off her shoulders, trying her best to look appealing. "Tell me! Why won't you sleep with me? You don't like me?"

Connor took a mental step backward.

"This is a job and that's all. Besides, I answer to God, who doesn't look kindly upon intimacy outside of marriage."

Monique's perfectly penciled-in eyebrows raised up. "So what? I think you're letting a perfectly good opportunity slip out of your hands. It's not like we aren't adults. We know what we're doing. And I have been told that I am quite the catch." She grinned and pointed to herself.

Despite himself, Connor laughed softly.

"I'm sure you are. But it's not how I do business. Take it or leave it."

She pursed her lips for a second. "I'll comply with your rules. I don't get the whole reason why you aren't willing to have some fun, but that's okay. I've had more results working with you than I have alone. You have a deal." She held her hand out to him and they shook.

Another thought hit him. "The information we gathered tonight belongs to the United States government."

Monique gave him a sweet smile. "I'm open for a long discussion on that subject. Why don't we share it like good little children."

"I don't share."

She just continued to smile, making him feel like a mouse about to be a tasty snack. It was time to leave.

Patting the inner pouch where he had stashed the USB stick, he left the house, quiet as a ghost. As he drove to his apartment, he felt more at ease than he had for a long time.

Ever since he had placed his life squarely into the Lord's hands, the lines between reality and make-believe were firming up again.

40

On his way back to his apartment, he texted a certain number belonging to his local contact, whoever he was.

I need to do a drop.

He didn't have to wait very long for the reply.

The bench, directly facing the American Embassy in the Jardins des Champs Élysées. Tomorrow morning.

Just as he was about to compliment himself on a job well done, and try to catch a few hours of sleep, his phone chirped.

"Hold for Director Murphy," he was instructed.

A few clicks followed and his boss was on the line.

"I hear you finally stumbled onto something? It had better be worth it," he growled.

How does he do that? I just sent the text.

Connor brushed his hand over the back of his neck, feeling the muscles tense.

"It is. I'm going to England this weekend and will have a crack at Lamour's cell phone. He never leaves it alone at work. If we can listen to his conversations, it would give us a huge edge."

"Perfect, Rattlesnake. If you do this one right, I won't come after your dad. You have my word."

Momentary relief settled over him. "Send it to me in writing, sir."

The man on the other end of the line laughed coldly.

"I don't think so, Rattlesnake. Just get this job done."

Connor ended the conversation, still feeling a high level of adrenaline zapping through him and making it impossible to fall asleep.

What he wouldn't give to be back home in his cozy house.

With sleep evading him as usual, Connor rose early and dressed in running pants and sneakers. Paris was gray and dreary, and a thin layer of ice covered the many puddles he stepped around. Circling the park three times, he was sure he had no tail and sat down on the bench facing the American Embassy. Quickly and expertly, he fastened the USB stick underneath the bench as he was pretending to tie his shoe, and continued on his run.

Two hours later the private airport came into view. A fancy plane sat on the tarmac, waiting for its passengers. Connor pulled his bag out of his trunk and pressed against the cold wind.

Emily had snow!

She missed him!

Those thoughts stayed with him as he stepped into the warm interior of the plane, where uniformed flight attendants greeted him.

“Good, you're on time. I don't like when people are late!” Lamour greeted him.

His dolled up wife shot him a coy look and he studied the plush navy carpet.

“Hi, Helmut,” Monique purred.

He nodded in her direction and took his seat opposite Lamour.

Monique frowned when he didn't sit by her.

It's going to be a long weekend!

“I'm slightly confused as to exactly why I'm here,” he said. “Not that I mind, but I'm just your computer security consultant, not a CEO.”

"Well, we'd like to change that. And for that to happen, the board needs to meet you. Enjoy, Helmut. The company will be very pleasant," he grinned and winked at Connor.

Connor set his face. He could do this.

Emily missed him!

God had his back!

The flight to England was uneventful and quick. As they disembarked the private jet, a limo waited to drive them through the small town. The quaint stores and yellow and red brick houses were nestled close to each other along the main road.

He barely prevented himself from whistling, when a large manor house came into view. Of course, the limo pulled into the gravel driveway.

I'm so in the wrong business.

Connor had been in nice places before, but this place rated up there with one of the fanciest he'd ever visited.

It was as though he had just stepped back in time. Instead of arriving in their ornate carriage, however, they had arrived in the large antique limousine complete with the gray-clad driver with cap.

The large front door of the house opened even before anyone could get out of the car, and a footman, dressed in livery, sprang forward out of nowhere to open the door for the distinguished passengers.

The house was built in the Baroque style architecture. Elaborate gardens extended around the back.

He kept his mouth from gaping when he walked into the entrance hall. The ceilings in the entry were vaulted, carved with intricate designs. The black marble floor was polished to a high shine in which he could see his reflection if he tried.

A butler approached them, bowed, and relieved them of their heavy jackets.

"Would you join me for an aperitif?"

Lamour crossed the floor to the left and opened the delicately carved doors. A cozy study with a crackling fireplace and a hunting theme welcomed them.

"The women want to freshen up and will meet us for tea in the drawing room. The members of the board will arrive after dinner. Most of them have traveled far. Tomorrow morning we are going skeet shooting."

"Skeet shooting?" Connor asked. He glared at the glass in his hand. Another night of sipping an alcoholic beverage.

"Yes, Helmut. You must have seen it on TV? Heard of it, perhaps?" Lamour asked with lazy sarcasm. "One takes a shotgun and aims it at targets that are being flung into the air at high speed. I hope you are not one of those people who won't touch a gun because they kill people."

Connor lowered his eyes for a split second. "I know what skeet shooting is, and no, I don't have a problem with guns."

Lamour grinned. "Then this should be interesting. Have you ever gone shooting?"

Connor kept his gaze steady. "With a banker for a dad and a stay-at-home mother, the opportunity never arose."

After a halting conversation and several more glasses of something that burned its way into his stomach and made him slightly woozy, he was free to go to his room. As he walked up the wide polished oak staircase, he wondered just what he had gotten himself into.

He opened the door to his room, a room that faced the front of the house, and almost walked back out. Monique had made herself quite comfortable on his couch and wore a welcoming smile that sent chills up his back.

"Mm-mm," he growled and shook his head. "Look, I've told you that this is not going to happen."

"Don't look so grumpy, Helmut," Monique teased, rising cat-like from the chaise. She hugged him, invading his personal space.

"Cameras and listening devices," she whispered into his ear.

He tensed. Of course. He had let his guard down for just a fraction and had almost stepped into a big hole. If Monique hadn't been there...

"Let's go for a walk," he said and grabbed her wrist before she could protest.

"Ouch!"

Strolling through the paths in the park-like garden, his tensed, every muscle straining. He turned to her when they were far enough from the house.

"Remember my rule. That includes a weekend away, with or without cameras in the room."

"What are we going to do? They will expect something from us," she said and wiggled her eyebrows at him.

"I think, it is time to break up," he suggested. "We both have what we need."

Monique rubbed her arms, her bare skin puckering with goosebumps. Connor handed her his jacket.

"Always the gentleman. I can't believe I'm saying this, fine. I'll just slap you on the terrace and stomp off. That should do it."

Connor grinned. "Just don't knock my head off."

Monique tossed her head and continued to walk toward the house.

His cheek stung for some time after she had slapped him with too much enthusiasm. It was worth it!

After tea time, with delicious scones with jam and fresh cream, they retired to the elegant parlor.

Monique, playing the part of slighted lover too well, wore a scowl and sat moodily on the couch, shooting him angry darts. M. Lamour reclined in a winged chair, was texting on his phone, his gaze going back and forth between the two of them.

Connor stared out the window, playing the slighted beau.

"I need a word with you, Helmut," Lamour finally said and motioned to him.

Connor followed him out the door.

"Exactly what happened this afternoon between you and my daughter?"

Connor felt the heat rise to his cheeks. Perfect!

"I'm not much of a long-term relationships kind of guy, Monsieur. Monique and I had some fun, but now it's over. I'd rather focus on work."

"You don't care if it hurts your chances if you aren't with her?

Connor drew his fingers through his hair with a long exhale. "If I have, my reputation is not as I hoped it would be. I'd rather be a professional and stand on my own merits than to depend on dating the boss' daughter."

Lamour paced, shooting him a look.

"I like your answer. Okay, I understand. But I don't think my daughter does. I hope Monique's slap rattled your brain."

Connor moved his jaw back and forth. "It sure did."

Once back in the parlor, Mme Lamour claimed her husband's attention. Connor couldn't believe that he left his phone on the table when he followed her out of the room.

Monique glanced his way as he placed his own phone in the vicinity, initiating the process to bond the phones together. Once in-sync with each other, he would be privy of all the information Lamour was sharing through the phone. A smug sense of accomplishment settled on him when he climbed the stairs to his room to dress for dinner.

He was one step closer to his goal of going home alive.

The members of the board and their impressive entourage arrived in dribbles after dinner. Soon, there was enough firepower in the house that Connor was sure that if anyone sneezed the wrong way, a shoot-out would follow. He recognized at least three well-known arms dealers, the assistant of a notoriously cruel dictator from a small African country, and a Russian organized crime boss.

The hair on the back of his neck stood in constant attention.

It was time to retire and Connor needed to know if Washington was receiving the information. Blending into the dark trees of the slumbering garden, Connor made the call.

“Are you getting what I've set up?” he asked the technician on the line.

“Absolutely,” the woman chuckled and he could almost see her rub her hands together. “You hit pay-dirt.”

Connor snickered darkly and was put through to Bryan Murphy. Did the man ever go home?

“Let's call this job finished, shall we?” he said, feeling entitled to the chip that was growing on his shoulder.

“You're not done. There is the little job of eliminating the opposition, Rattlesnake. Until we have enough information, you're staying put.”

Connor hung up his phone and stared moodily into the clouded night.

Way to pop my bubble of happiness!

41

Skeet shooting went... well. Connor almost nailed one of the valets, *accidentally, on purpose.* He was the butt of everyone's joke when they returned to the manor. With all the firepower and muscle from all the bodyguards around, it was a good thing that he had pretended to shoot his own assigned valet.

The board meeting that followed was more like an interrogation. Connor tried not to sweat when one member of the board after another fired a question at him. From the faces around the room, he could tell that they were pleased with his answers.

After finishing, he strolled back to his room. Monique cornered him before he reached his destination.

"Was that slap good for you?" she asked, her eyes glinting dangerously.

"I can still feel it," he said, working his jaw.

"Please help me," she whispered her eyes glistening with tears.

He put his hands on her shoulders and turned her away.

"Not interested," he said loudly.

That night, he took a walk to call in.

"I need an exit. There are more guns in that house than I've seen in a long time."

"Patience, Rattlesnake! What's your hurry?"

Connor thought of hanging up, throwing the phone into the first trashcan and getting on the first plane bound for New York.

"You know, I'm getting antsy. I want to get out of here!" he grunted.

"We'll give you the green light soon enough."

Trying to steady the anger swirling around in his gut, Connor tapped his phone off and returned to the manor.

Emily dried the plate and handed it to Rick. A nasty cold had grabbed her and wouldn't let go.

"He said that? He knew that we had hamburgers?"

She nodded and Rick groaned. He pulled her out to the deck and she shivered.

"I'm sorry," he said, as he handed her a wool jacket and paced the length of the deck. "It seems that they know I am here!"

Emily gasped. "How?"

Rick grimaced. "Have you heard of listening devices?"

Emily's eyes widened. Of course, she had!

"I wonder why they haven't swooped down on me yet." He kneaded his temple as he strode past her. His grimace increased the more he paced. "I have to turn myself in."

"Rick! What if they put you in prison? You can't do this to your family. They are just about to come to terms with the fact that you're alive."

"I think they're holding this over Connor's head, or else they would have come to get me already. So, I'm going to remove that bargaining chip from the table. My son is not going to get blackmailed by the government he's trying to protect. I'll see to it."

A terrible cold rushed through her, making her shiver. What did they expect Connor to do, and how was he getting it done with the threat over his head?

Rick pulled her into a hug.

"I'll set it right, Emily. Trust me on that."

Emily hugged him back. "Just be careful, Rick. I've kind of gotten used to you."

He kissed the top of her head. "Same here, kiddo. Just pray for me, okay? I know you'll have my back."

This man had become almost like a second father to her. She needed him, now that Connor was not around.

"Rick!"

"I have to do this, Emily. I need to do this for my son. For you, honey. I care a lot about you. So, would you take me to the airport?" He let a small smile play over his lips.

"Tonight?"

"The sooner, the better. I wish Connor's car was in the garage," he said and wiggled his eyebrows at her.

"We'll take mine."

Rick appeared downstairs within minutes, a bag slung over his shoulders.

Watching him walk away was more than difficult. It was heart-wrenching. Her only connection to Connor disappeared into the terminal.

A cool cloth dabbed at her forehead. In the daze of waking, she expected the deluge to follow, to choke the breath out of her. Violently, she fought against the touch. Her breath came hard and labored, struggling against what was to come.

“Emily, it's only me.”

She knew that voice! She's known it all her life. Forcing her eyes open, she squinted. Her sister sat on the side of her bed, a wet cloth in her hand and a concerned look on her face.

“Lizzy?” Sitting up, her whole world spun so she lay back against the pillow. “What are you doing here?”

Her sister's gaze softened. “It's Thanksgiving. We came down to celebrate it. Although, you won't be doing any of that.”

Her sister swabbed at her forehead again as Emily tried to get her mind around the fact that she'd been sick for over a week. Christmas was just around the corner.

Emily swallowed the momentary wave of sadness.

She sat up and reached for a glass of water. Lizzy handed it to her, her gaze wandering to the ring on her left hand. Her eyebrows formed a perfect arch.

“Is there anything I should know?” Liz asked with a widening grin.

“No!” Emily mumbled, closing her eyes against the wave of dizziness that gripped her.

Lizzy scowled and exhaled an irritated huff. “You need someone to take care of you.”

“You are,” Emily replied and rested her head against her pillow. “Thank you.”

"Perhaps the person who gave you that ring should be here, soothing your feverish brow." Lizzy gave her one of those sweet, probing smiles.

"You really aren't very subtle, are you?"

"No seriously, Em. You didn't have that ring when I last saw you."

"That's right." Emily let that statement hang there.

Lizzy sat on the edge of her bed, her gaze soft and beseeching. "I wish you'd open up to me, Emi. We've never really been close, but you can trust me. I won't say a word."

Emily laughed weakly. "It's nothing, Liz. Just drop it."

"Wearing a ring on the left hand is not nothing. It means something. Something lasting. Come on. It's not like it's a state secret that Emily has finally found a guy who wants to marry her."

Ouch!

"There's nothing to tell. Now leave it." Emily sneezed and covered her face. "I'm too sick for this."

Sick and sad. She didn't want to be reminded of the ache in her heart.

"Seriously, someone else should be doing this." Lizzy glanced at the ring on her finger and her lips twitched into a smile. "Someone tall, dark and ruggedly handsome, with amazing blue eyes that you can definitely lose yourself in."

The ache in her chest spread and Emily felt the pressure of tears building up. Closing her eyes lessened the pressure.

"So, where is Connor these days? Will we be seeing him for Thanksgiving?" Lizzy asked, her tongue pushed hard into her cheek.

"No." She didn't even look at her sister. "He's out of the country, working."

Her sister sighed. “Isn't that against the law? I mean, it's a national holiday. When will he be back?”

Emily opened one eye. “Just leave it, Lizzy. Stop fishing. I'm not going to tell you anything.”

“Okay, you rest. I'll keep my interrogation skills at bay. But when you're feeling better, you are going to tell me all about it.”

Her sister stayed with her and nursed her with a kindness she had seldom experienced.

42

"Why can't you share with me? You know we're after the same thing. We both want to see him behind bars."

Connor startled in his seat and almost spilled his hot drink over his slacks. In this busy cafe along the Champs Élysées, he listened to the conversation his phone was picking up, earphones muffling the sound around him. He glowered at her when Monique pulled out the chair opposite him.

"Are you following me?" he growled.

Monique grinned brightly and nodded her head. "Of course! You have things I need. I don't think its nice of you not to fill me in." She took a sip of her café-au-lait, giving him a look.

"You have easier access to his phone. If you really wanted to, you could be listening in on all his conversations, too. Now, scoot along!" He waved his hand at her.

"You're supposed to be nice to me," she said, pouting. "You're not."

Connor grimaced and ran his hand along the back of his neck.

"That's right. I still can't share this with you."

Did he feel bad? Nope.

Connor drew in a deep breath and tried to ignore her frown.

"Listening to the conversations, makes me like him even less."

Monique picked up her coffee and took another sip. "At least you don't have to live with him."

"Do you need me to hold your hand to access his computer?" he teased.

Monique laughed and batted her eyes. “I wish you would. I'm kidding, Helmut,” she said immediately when his face turned dark. “I guess I can respect a man for having boundaries.” Monique sucked on her lip. “But it's still a shame. What's he saying?”

“Liz is right, Emily. That is an unusual ring. I've never seen it on you. It's very pretty. Is it a purity ring?” her mother asked.

“You are just as bad as Liz,” she wheezed. “Do you want a pole and a line? Some bait too?”

This cold was not letting her out of its grips. She had missed Thanksgiving! Between her mother and her sister, they had nursed her with clear soups and plenty of drinks. She was going to miss Christmas at this rate. The antibiotics were not having the desired effect quickly enough. Dabbing at her sore, red nose, she leaned back in her bed, exhausted.

It wasn't just that she was sick, she was sad too.

It seemed that just as she was sure of what God had for her, everything came crashing down around her, confusing her. Had she imagined the whole thing about God giving her the clear steps to follow?

“Mom,” she said as her mother arranged the covers over her, tucking her in like a girl. On a normal day Emily would have objected, but today she felt – loved. “How can you tell when something is from God? I mean totally from Him, not your own dreams or wishes.”

Her mother sat down on the edge of her bed.

“Well, I have always been told that if it backs up scripture, you can be sure that it is.”

"This is a bit more on the personal level," she admitted.

Her mother gently pushed a strand of hair out of her face and hooked it over her ear.

"I mean, I thought I had a clear *yes*, and then everything fell apart. I don't know if it was a clear *yes,* or if I was just hoping." Emily absentmindedly twirled the ring on her finger.

Her mother sighed and sat there for a long time, without saying anything. "Sometimes when we get that clear answer, it is often followed by some trouble. The enemy doesn't want us to forge ahead with confidence, as the Bible tells us to. He wants to keep us in fear. So, Emi, all I can tell you is to proceed with caution and prayer. A lot of prayer." She gave her a pat on the head.

Emily cocked her head. "That's what I thought. Ever since Pakistan I've been doing a lot more praying with humility if you know what I mean. It has to be God's plan for my life. That's what I want, but it's hard."

"You've been mysterious ever since you came back, Emily. What can't you share with us?"

Emily closed her eyes. Keeping things from her family was draining.

"I want to tell you all about it... but I can't," she whispered. "But you were right that Connor gave me this ring before he left on his trip. It was made by his father."

Not that it means anything if he doesn't come back, eventually.

How long had it been since he had left? Emily's heart was squeezed tightly as she felt herself cling to the promise he had made.

Her mother took her limp hand and ran a finger over the intricate design. "That's so sweet. Does that mean you two are now official? Or is there a promise?" her mother winked.

There certainly is... Emily kept her eyes closed tightly forcing herself not to hope too much.

"We'll see what it means when he comes back, Mom."

Emily hoped that her mother would get the hint that she was done talking. After all, her eyes were closed and she was slowly drifting off into dream world. Apparently, her mother didn't get it.

"It must mean a lot for Connor to give you something of his father's. Didn't he pass away when he was younger?"

"Mom," Emily whispered as her eyes popped open. Swallowing hard, she decided that carrying this burden was too much for her. "Connor's uncle is not his uncle."

Emily's mother frowned. "What do you mean, Em?"

"He's his father. He was in hiding for years, having to pretend to be dead."

Emily's mother gasped. "And did Connor know this?"

A rueful smile appeared on Emily's lips. "Oh no, it was a surprise to find him alive and well. There were people after his father and he had to protect his family."

Her mother drew in a sharp breath. "Emily, what's going on? Are they involved in anything illegal? I mean, Connor has been gone for months. Where is he?" her mother whispered, looking about the room with wide eyes. "What are you not telling us?"

Emily fell back, entirely drained. "I..." she looked past her mom. "Nothing illegal. But don't ask me, please."

Her mother sighed and touched Emily's forehead with her cool hand. "What have you gotten yourself into this time, child? I'm afraid for you, Emily."

Emily reached out to her mother. "It's fine, Mom. It will all be fine. I know it."

"Connor does not work for a computer company, does he?" her mother whispered.

"Mom!" Emily and made a zipping motion over her lips.

Her mother groaned and shook her head.

A week later she finally felt better. Her mother had dropped the questions.

She was driving home in the late afternoon, the sun was just about to go down. More snow was in the forecast for the next week. Driving past Connor's house made her sad. It sat lonely, just like she felt right now. She caught her breath when she spotted lights in one of the upstairs bedrooms.

Her heart did a flip.

It was close to Christmas. Could it be that Connor was home?

She pulled into the drive, her feet tangling up when she jumped hastily out of the car. Her heart hammered hard against her chest as she waited for what seemed an eternity for the door to open. Her face fell, but she recovered within a split second and hugged Rick, who hugged her back tightly.

"You're a sight for sore eyes," he said and moved aside to let her in. "I guess I wasn't the one you were hoping to see."

She dipped her head hoping to recover quickly from the let-down.

"No, but I'm glad you are back. I prayed for you, a lot. I just kind of wished..." She shook her head. "Never mind."

“He's okay,” Rick told her and offered her a cup of hot chocolate. “I heard him briefly when he called in for a report. Things are winding down. He hopes to be home soon. It's been a long assignment for him.”

Emily's hand trembled but she recovered quickly. Connor had no idea how much she missed him. She turned away from Rick, in an attempt to hide her feelings.

“So you're looking at an officially retired operative. They grilled me for days. Finally, they seemed satisfied and gave me my freedom. I can't tell you how happy I am.”

Emily stared at him. “They interrogated you first? Like...” An involuntary shiver passed over her and was transported to the hut. Quickly, before she lost herself in the nightmare, she shook off her thoughts. “Why would they do that? I mean, you gave your life in defense of this country!”

Rick sipped his drink. “Uh-huh.” He watched her closely, eyes narrowed. “They needed to know if I had compromised the trust they had put in me. I didn't mind them asking me questions. That's all it was, Emily.”

She exhaled the pressure building in her head, willing the images and smells out of her mind.

The doorbell chimed and he frowned.

“The last time this happened...”

He walked to the front door and opened it. His hand fell limply from the handle as he beheld his daughter. Even though Alicia had returned, she didn't look too happy. She stood moodily in the center of the hall, glaring at her father. At the sight of Emily, she smiled.

“I didn't expect to see you again. I'm glad.” Then she turned to her father, glared and pursed her lips. “We need to talk!”

“By all means.” Rick waved her into the living room. Alicia gritted her teeth and moved past him.

What if...

Emily picked up her jacket and keys.

"I am leaving." She kissed Rick on the cheek. "I'm glad you're back," she whispered. He squeezed her hand.

When she got home, she prayed for both.

While drinking a cup of freshly brewed tea, the loneliness finally settled on her like a thick, heavy blanket and she played with the possibilities of what if.

What if he walked through the door right now?

What if he took her into his arms and never let her go?

Her feelings for Connor had deepened over the past few months even without him being around. The old adage, absence makes the heart grow fonder, had to be true. Every time she thought of him, her heart decided to do the Cha-Cha and a million butterflies exploded into flight in her stomach.

This was more than just infatuation.

She loved him!

What if... he didn't come home?

When she walked into Connor's house the next morning, the Saturday before Christmas, she found Rick and Alicia in Connor's kitchen, talking and laughing as if nothing had happened. Shaking her head, she helped herself to a cup of coffee.

"I see you two have made amends," she said, happy for them.

Alicia grinned back.

"I suppose so. I have you to thank, Emily. That little pep talk you gave me helped. You know when we got back to Texas, I just couldn't stop thinking about him." She tipped her chin in her father's direction and giggled when he toasted her. "I had a choice to make. I could continue to pout and blame him for all that was wrong with my life, that he had recruited my only brother, turning him into a replica of himself, leaving me and Mom alone. Or I could do as Christ asked of me. Forgive. Forgiveness was hard but it is so sweet."

She hooked her arm over her father's shoulder.

"Well, I am glad to hear that. How is your mother?" Emily asked. She took a sip of her coffee.

"She's sad. She can't get up and leave. She has a husband. He wouldn't be too accommodating if she flitted off to see Dad. No matter how much she wants to."

The silence in the room descended like a thick thundercloud, making the mood heavy.

All week long Lamour's phone conversations had held Connor captive, as he listened to them talk about someone called *Mademoiselle Rouge*. This person, he assumed she was a woman, had caused him a lot of grief and he was going to deal with her. Connor had no idea who he was talking about, but whoever she was – she was in trouble. Lamour plotted to get rid of her at the earliest convenient time.

What if...

The thought that someone's life was about to end in a very unpleasant manner made Connor go on the high alert. That, and the fact that the board had summoned him to attend, again!

He received the invitation to attend a board meeting on the day before Christmas, which was slightly unusual.

By now, a thin layer of snow covered the ground in dirty patches. Paris was gripped in a cold spell and the days were dreary. They were even more dismal because he knew that he wouldn't be home for Christmas.

There would be no stealing a kiss under the mistletoe for him and Emily. He wouldn't be around to watch her open her presents and squeal in delight. He would miss time with her family.

All those thoughts added to the mounting tension ever since England.

The agency wasn't making plans for an extraction. It seemed that they enjoyed having him stuck in this position, out in the field.

"M. Brandt. They are ready for you."

Exhaling hard through pursed lips, he gathered himself.

"Thank you, Suzanne," he said on his way to the elevator. "Have a Merry Christmas."

The older stout woman smiled back briskly. "And you."

As if.

The cold steel of his gun pressed against his skin, giving him a measure of comfort. Lately, he had decided to carry it with him to work. He was being... careful.

As the elevator took him up to the top executive offices for the meeting, he pondered why they had summoned him.

Everything about this day had him on edge. As he stepped off the elevator to the executive suite, his senses went into high alert when he found four teams of heavily armed security guards scrutinizing him.

Suddenly, the decision to carry his gun seemed very, very wrong.

Men like that had a sixth sense about who carried and who didn't. He felt exposed as he walked past them, shooting them a quick, furtive glance. He had been summoned and that meant he belonged. Feeling a few pairs of eyes follow him as he continued what would undoubtedly be the longest twenty feet, Connor forced himself to relax.

43

As soon as he stepped into the room, his blood turned to ice and he felt the danger. To his great surprise, Monique was among the assembled, chatting with her father.

She had better not have double-crossed me!

As soon as that thought had popped into his mind, she turned to him with a silent pleading glance in his direction. It was replaced immediately with the coy look she usually reserved for him.

Suddenly, it became crystal clear who *Mademoiselle Rouge* was. Connor worked his way toward her, hoping to have a moment to warn her when Lamour called the meeting to attention.

Everyone took their seats, leaving only Connor and Monique standing awkwardly. A cold dread filled him that this may not be an ordinary board meeting and that perhaps Monique wasn't the only one in trouble. He could feel her quiver as everyone's attention came to rest on them.

Lamour glared at them.

“I'm not a man to beat around the bush, as most of you can imagine,” he said in English and chuckles from everyone bounced off the walls. “It's come to my attention that we have traitors in our midst.”

Oy vey! This isn't going to be fun.

He scanned the surroundings for a possible route of escape.

The room went still. The only noise was from his rapidly beating heartbeat, as everyone turned their attention to him and Monique. Lamour's face scrunched up in anger and he turned toward his daughter.

“You...” He pointed a finger right at her. “You betrayed me!”

Connor heard Monique swallow loudly and she began to sway as fear gripped her. Her face became almost translucent.

"Look," he began to say and was immediately hushed up by a glance.

"I treated you like a daughter and you repay me by betraying me to Interpol?" His face turned red with rage.

Monique gave a weak squeak and looked around like a deer, searching for a get-away.

"This is what I do to traitors!" His voice shaking with rage, he spun around and pointed a gun at her head.

Before Connor could move, he heard the gun pop and her head snapped back. Like a marionette whose strings had been cut, she collapsed soundlessly onto the thick beige carpet and lay still, blood oozing from an entry wound. Connor dove behind a table and, with one smooth motion, pulled out his own gun.

He pointed it in the direction of Lamour who stood by the window, back-lit by the cold winter sunlight shining into the room through the large windows. Lamour, teeth bared in anger, aimed his gun at Connor and they pulled the trigger at the same time. His bullet hit its mark and Lamour slid to the floor with a surprised grunt. At the same time, a bullet seared through Connor's side and he bit back a groan.

He was still alive and had to get out!

At this point, everyone in the room had drawn their guns. Taking a quick aim at Alain Laurant, the arms dealer, Connor squeezed the trigger.

That makes two fewer bad guys in the world, he thought as the man slumped backward with a hole through his forehead.

As he turned to check on Monique, whose lifeless body lay surrounded by dark red blood soaking into the carpet, he knew that she was beyond help. Exhaling as a wave of weakness crashed through him, he forced himself to his feet and, firing one last time into the room and hitting the Russian mobster in the shoulder, he dove to the door.

Outside, the security guys were rushing toward the door, their weapons ready.

How had he forgotten about them? His mind worked quickly.

"What are you waiting for? They're killing each other in there! Call an ambulance!"

Connor was practically tossed out of the way as the big men dove past him into the confusion of the room. He ran to the elevator, pushing the button as soon as he got there. His hand clutched his side, pressing to staunch the flow of blood.

The first bodyguards rushed out of the conference room just as he stepped inside. They took aim at him and he pressed himself against the wall as the doors closed, and he heard the bullets pinging into the metal. Connor leaned wearily against the wall and wiped a hand over his forehead, wiping off the sweat.

Three floors down, he got out. He made his way through the busy offices. Not feeling any pain from the wound, he knew he was in trouble as blood steadily soaked his shirt. Stepping past an empty cubicle, he snagged a thick winter coat from the back of someone's chair.

"*Attention, s'ill vous plait... May I have your attention, please. This is not a drill. Please proceed to the nearest staircase to the exit, without delay. We thank you for your cooperation.*"

Threading into the murmuring crowd, Connor slipped unnoticed down the emergency staircase and past the security guards waiting for them at the bottom. He talked to the man walking next to him who looked confused, but when Connor explained that he was the new guy on the block, he was more than happy to engage him in a conversation.

"Please let us scan your identity card on the way out. Thank you for your assistance."

Connor slowed in the throng of people getting out. His security pass was sure to give him away. With the bottleneck, it gave him time to search for someone resembling him and whose pass he could snag. He zeroed in on a man standing by the elevators, talking to a group of colleagues. He had his hair color and was roughly his age. It would do for a quick scan.

"Do you know what is going on here?" Connor asked as he stood by his side. Everyone shook their heads.

"Could it be terrorists?" he asked, his voice shaking fearfully. Everyone turned to him, their eyes opening wide.

A second later, his new security pass in hand, he walked toward the exit. His insides tingled with nerves as he got closer to the security guards who scanned everyone passing through the doors.

When it came his time, he calmly slid the card through the electronic device and, after a nod from the man behind the glass, walked out into the cold, crisp air. Following the throng of people, he tossed the card in the first trash receptacle he came to.

He heard a shout behind him and knew that he had been spotted. Connor took off running, joining the many pedestrians out for last minute Christmas shopping. Drawing a sharp breath at the pain in his side as he almost crashed into another pedestrian, he felt the blood gushing through his fingers.

His heart skipped and perspiration gathered on his forehead.

Just keep going, Connor. You have to get home!

As he darted between the pedestrians, his vision beginning to fade, he was aware of the pursuit behind him and slipped into a packed toy-store. He walked through a side entrance that connected the store to a string of stores on the block. In this crowded pharmacy, Connor purchased some black hair dye.

"I thought I would try something different," he grinned at the clerk behind the counter. "Surprise the wife for Christmas."

The girl raised a pierced eyebrow and rang him up. Three bodyguards combed their way through the foot traffic, pushing against the customers. In the next store, a bakery, he managed to attach himself to a group of shoppers. Once he stepped past them and back onto the busy sidewalk, he flipped the collar up and kept his head down to avoid the bodyguards.

He rounded the corner to hail one of the many cabs that were out on this day. Not standing still, in fear that he might get caught, he moved on.

If he could just catch a ride, he could make it safely to the safe-house. His wish soon came true when one taxi stopped next to him, splashing his legs with mush from the left-over snow, and he eased himself into the warm vehicle.

"*Rue Saint-Martin, numero 113,*" he murmured and leaned wearily against the cracked leather.

The taxi threaded into the traffic and the adrenaline slowly left his body. Suddenly, he felt too much!

Blood was still seeping steadily out of the bullet wound and as he turned to examine it, a wave of searing pain almost knocked him out. His shirt was stained a deep red, and a thick, gooey path traveled down his leg. The interior of the taxi began to spin around him wildly, so he closed his eyes. A sick feeling began to rumble around in his gut, causing him more worry.

By the time he was dropped off at the curb, he wasn't sure he could even climb out of the cab on his own. But it wouldn't do to sit here all day and bleed out all over the driver's seat.

"*Merci*," he stammered and paid his driver with trembling fingers. Thankfully, he had the presence of mind to use the left hand – unstained with blood.

Stumbling almost blindly and like a drunkard, he pushed open the old, creaking door to the three-story apartment building. The hallway was poorly lit and smelled musty and old. Dogs barked and babies cried as he walked past door after door.

At the last door on the second floor, he leaned panting against the wall, forcing himself to stay awake. He gave three distinct knocks followed by two more.

The door cracked open a split, admitting light into the dingy hall.

"*Oui?*"

Drawing on strength he didn't think he'd have he stammered the password for the day, "*Joyeux Noël*," and felt himself dragged inside. Darkness enveloped him completely and he didn't even feel himself topple to the ground.

When he came to, he was laying on a brown couch. The apartment was dark and silent. Once his eyes adjusted, he shifted and flinched. Looking down, he saw that his midsection was now expertly bandaged, blood still seeping through slightly. He still felt the pain, thrumming dully through him.

"Ah, you 'ave woken up," a tall, gangly-looking man sauntered in from another room in the apartment. "'ow do you feel?"

"Like someone shot me," he croaked and nodded his thanks as the man handed him a glass of water.

The man snickered. "It 'appens way too often in our line of work, *non*? I 'ave been talking to the 'ome office and they 'ave given you the green light to return."

Connor snorted, winced, and reclined back onto the couch. "Ain't that nice!"

The man handed him five passports and several stacks of different currency. "You are to make your way 'ome as soon as possible."

Connor glanced through his travel identities. "Finally," he breathed through his nose.

"Stay until morning, then you 'ave to leave," the man, who never gave him his name, said not too unkindly and walked back out of the room.

In the morning he dyed his hair black – the strain almost causing him to pass out – dressed in the unsullied jeans and sweater provided for him, stuffed his money and passports into a duffel and hailed a cab to the airport. After renting a car, he headed for the first pharmacy and bought a supply of extra strength pain-killers as well as more bandages. Then he started the long drive to Amsterdam to return home via various countries.

Weariness clutched at him as did the image of Monique's head snapping back from the impact of the bullet.

He had been right.

He had not escaped this mission unscathed.

44

Emily's attempt at trying to enjoy the New Year's Eve celebration fell completely flat. They were all gathered at Connor's house. Alicia and Rick had come so far in the last couple of weeks, it was great to see how God had restored their relationship. The house was still decorated with Christmas cheer, which threatened to plunge her into an even deeper depression.

I'm gonna lose it any minute now.

Biting back the burning in her throat and the thickening of tears in her eyes, she turned her attention back to the game at hand.

Her sister and Alicia had ganged up on her and had interrogated her once again about her unusual ring. She had almost taken it off today. It seemed like it didn't matter anymore.

Connor was never coming home.

"Emily it's your turn. You are loosing anyway, but come on. Spin the spinner! You've almost made it to the mansion." Rick called from the cozy living room, where a fire was crackling in the hearth.

Emily turned with a resigned groan. She didn't want to spin the stupid spinner! She didn't want to play a game. Everyone was so annoyingly chipper that it was getting on her nerves.

Rick looked ridiculous with his party hat over his clown wig. But she didn't feel like laughing.

She wanted to go home to lick her wounds.

"He'll be back," Rick whispered into her ear as he came to stand next to her.

She shook her head.

“It doesn't matter, Rick,” she murmured, her voice thick.

He grunted and pushed her toward the game board. “You're doing great. Just don't forget to smile once in a while.”

She was about to spin, when her head swiveled around and she caught a figure leaning casually against the arched door of the living room.

Her mother glanced in the same direction and gasped in surprise.

“Why, Connor! You're finally home!” As if he was her long lost son, she hugged him.

“Mrs. Martins.” His voice was hoarse and he looked tired and worn. His gaze was focused intently on Emily, who felt like she was going to melt into the carpet.

“Connor.” Rick clapped his son on the back. “Glad you're home.”

Alicia let out a squeal and threw herself into her brother's arms. He grunted as pain shot through him but quickly recovered, and hugged her back.

“What are you doing here, kid? Does that mean you are talking to me again?” he asked, smirking.

“Yes, you pain. I guess I can't stay mad at you.” She tipped her head in Emily's direction.

“She's really great,” she whispered loud enough for everyone to hear.

Connor smiled tiredly and patted her arm. “It looks like we're having a great party. Mind if I join you?”

“Yes!” Everyone waved him over. Mitch thumped his back. He winced.

“You've been gone a while, so I hear. Good to see you are back.”

Connor nodded and met his gaze. There was understanding and acceptance; respect.

Emily bit her bottom lip, trying to keep it from quivering. She tried to keep the tears from spilling and found she was not successful.

"Excuse me," she breathed and hurried past her family into the hall, where she leaned against the wall, shaking. She covered her face with her hands.

"Emily."

A hand squeezed her shoulder.

"Give me a moment," she whispered.

Strong arms circled around her, propelling her into the kitchen. Before she knew what was happening, she was staring into Connor's sapphire blue eyes.

Eyes that were dark, lost and... angry.

His face was a pasty gray, strain marked lines between his eyebrows and in the corners of his lips. But it didn't matter.

She threw her arms around his neck and threaded her fingers through his hair.

"Connor," she whispered, tears streaming down her face.

He pulled her close. A muscle in his jaw clenched when she said his name. His nostrils flared for a split second. He traced a tear down her cheek. Then he took her hand, her left hand. A soft smile played on his lips, not quite crinkling his eyes. He brought her hand to his lips and brushed a soft kiss over her knuckles.

Her knees almost buckled.

"Say my name again, please," he whispered.

"Con-"

She didn't get to finish. He gently caught her lips with his. A swarm of butterflies exploded into flight in her gut. Never before had she been kissed so gently, with such passion. When they broke apart, Connor leaned his forehead against hers and took a deep breath.

"You were saying?" he whispered teasingly.

"Connor," Emily whispered, smiling back at him. She kneaded her fingers through his hair again.

He closed his eyes, and let out a long exhale. Then he lowered his head toward her again. Emily's heart exploded in her chest as he caught her lips again and she melted into him. Time stood still, reality faded as if they were the only two left on earth.

Emily pulled away from him and traced the outlines of his face, noting the thick stubble on his chin, the dead look in his gaze. It scared her terribly. She longed to fill them with light again and traced the lines between his eyebrows with her fingertips. Connor closed his eyes and tightened his hold on her before he swallowed hard.

"I told you I'd come back," he whispered.

Emily frowned and threaded her hands through his thick hair again.

"For what?" Her voice was stronger now.

"For my kiss," he laughed. "So, will you marry me?"

"I thought you'd never ask," she said softly. "I'm free next weekend."

"That's good to know," he said and his face became serious.

"Now that you're home, we can start planning. Maybe we can have a spring wedding?"

Connor touched her chin, tucked a strand of blonde hair over an ear. He shook his head.

"I'm not home," he mumbled, his voice thick as a slice of homemade bread.

Emily stiffened and pushed herself out of his embrace.

"What?" she breathed, the pleasant flight of butterflies suddenly turning into a frenzy, making her nauseous.

He smiled sadly. "I'm leaving again tonight," he whispered into her ear, cupping her cheeks with his hands.

"No," she gasped.

"I need to talk to you," he continued to mumble into her ear. "But not here."

He pulled her back into his arms, feeling her tension.

Why? Why hadn't he just walked out of the briefing room when Murphy gave him the assignment in Columbia?

Before he left, though, he needed to tell her about his retirement plan, which started the minute he was finished in South America.

"Can we go to your place?"

She was still trying to recover from their kiss and yet someone had dumped cold water all over her at the same time as pulling the rug out from under her.

"What do you mean you are leaving again?" A spiral of dread threaded its way through her.

"Shh," Connor caressed her cheek with his fingertips. "Not here."

His touch sent an electric shock into her toes. She took a long, steadying breath. She put her hands on his shoulders, his muscles hard and tight like the string of a bow.

"Connor. I-"

He didn't let her finish but caught her lips again. Instead of melting into his embrace, she became as unyielding as a wall. He eventually broke away, holding her gaze for a long time, memorizing every nuance.

"Having you... to come home to... was what kept me going. I want you to know that, no matter what."

An apparently permanent lump formed in her throat. With an exhale that released the tension she felt, she nestled her cheek against his chest, listening to the sound of his heart.

"Let's just stay like this," she whispered. "Forget the world exists."

Connor caressed her back, enjoying every second. He rested his cheek on her head, taking in the lingering smell of coconut. His anger, the tension, the pain slowly ebbed out with every kiss and every moment they spent together. The longer he stayed in her embrace, the more normal he was beginning to feel.

"Sounds good to me," he murmured into her hair.

She gave a deep satisfied sigh and snuggled closer. Time began to have no meaning, but eventually, reality caught up with them as they became aware of the noise of laughter from the other room.

"I guess we should join the others again," he said reluctantly.

Emily shook her head violently, biting back the impulse to take his hand and run. Where to? "No, I don't want to share you with anyone."

"You're not mad at me?" he asked, his voice husky.

Emily lifted her head and smiled sadly. "You came back. I'll take it, even for a few hours. If I can have that, I'm over the moon. That and those kisses. Not bad for a sp-"

She never got to finish her sentence.

When they finally joined the others, the game was over. Her mother pulled another board game out of the very extensive bag she had brought with her.

"Anyone up for another?"

"Emily and I are going to go for a walk," Connor said. "But first may I have a quick word with you, Mr. Martins?"

You could have heard a pin drop as the conversations that were going around abruptly stopped. The older man cleared his throat.

"Why... uh... of course, Connor."

They made their way to the office, which now also doubled as a workout room. Connor motioned to the chair beside the desk.

"I'm sorry but I don't have much time to do this properly. I would like your permission to marry Emily, sir."

Mr. Martins grinned and clasped his back. "Thank you. It's about time! You should have heard my wife and Liz. They were going on and on, wondering if the ring Emily has been wearing for the last month was just that or not. I take it, it is."

Connor nodded his head. "I want you to know I'll do my best to protect your daughter and to give her everything she needs."

"I'm counting on it," the older man said seriously. "She's pretty special."

Connor nodded, his throat suddenly parched. "She is that."

When they returned to the room, everyone tried to look as nonchalant as possible. Debbie Martins was chatting softly with Alicia, who had this smug look on her face. His father was gabbing with Michael as if they were sitting in the bleachers, watching a ballgame. Only Emily sat by herself, practically gnawing off her bottom lip.

Mr. Martins walked over to his younger daughter and hugged her. "Congratulations, Emi."

Emily's face became its usual unflattering red. Everyone stopped pretending not to pay attention and a round of cheers and hugs followed.

"I knew it!" Lizzy snickered and hugged her again. "Miss Tongue-tied! Couldn't fool me!"

Connor wanted to withdraw, to spend his remaining time alone with Emily. There was so much to discuss.

"Excuse us," he finally said and grabbed her hand to pull her out of the love-fest.

Once outside, the festive mood that was surging through Emily chilled with the cold winter air. She snuggled closer to Connor.

"Did you just ask my dad if you could marry me?" she whispered, her breath coming out in gray puffs.

"I did. There's so much to tell you and we only have an hour to do it in. Because I'm-"

"No, don't...don't say it."

They had arrived at her door and she was about to open it when he drew her into his arms again to whisper into her ear. "I need you to know that this will be my last assignment for the agency."

She leaned against him. Connor lifted her chin up so she could look him in the eye. He caressed her cheek with his thumb, his touch producing goosebumps all along her neck and making it difficult to concentrate on what he was saying.

"I have something for you," he said with a cocky grin and handed her a pack of German chocolates. Emily giggled despite herself.

"This is becoming quite a trend here. I don't know. Maybe I could get used to this."

Connor laughed softly, his lips pressed against her ear. "The big chocolate bar has something extra in it. When you open it, be careful. I want to ask you a question. Would you be willing to come with me if I left? When I retire, I'll need to stay out of the country, Em. I don't know how long..."

"Yes!" Emily whispered hoarsely. She threw her arm tightly around him. "A thousand yeses! I'd follow you wherever you go!"

Something deep and warm exploded throughout him, filling him with love so strong, it took his breath away.

Emily rose to the tips of her toes and kissed him tenderly.

"I've come to realize that no matter what, Connor, I want to be with you. For however long we may have here on earth, I want to wake up in the mornings with you beside me."

"Then be ready to leave anytime," he whispered. "And don't talk about this in my house. It seems to be bugged."

Emily tensed but Connor wrapped his arms around her and kissed her again.

"Let's go inside before I get sick again," she whispered breathlessly.

She stared at the chocolate bars. The largest bar was heavy. She put it down on the counter. Then she joined Connor on the couch, where he pulled her close. She traced the outline of his face again.

"You don't look like yourself, Connor."

A humorless smile played on his lips. Again it didn't touch his eyes.

"I'm not quite myself yet. But if you give me a little time, I will be again. These long missions are killers. When I called you, I needed you."

"I'd just prayed that God would show me one way or another what I should do, and then you called. Your call answered my prayer. It has been hard for me, Connor."

"Well, let me make it a little easier," he said softly and rubbed her shoulders. She closed her eyes. It felt so good. She knew that they were playing with fire, but she didn't want him to stop.

"I need to go. It shouldn't take me very long to finish this job. A week tops." These words tickled her cheek, they were uttered so softly. "And don't talk about this here or in my house."

Her breath caught in her throat. Her apartment may be bugged! She shuddered and immediately Connor's arms came around her. He kissed her again, long and tenderly.

"This is going to have to hold me over," he said, a lopsided smile on his face.

She could feel the tears prick her eyes again and tried to turn away.

"Don't!" Connor said and tipped her head up at him. "Don't hide your feelings from me. I love you, Emily."

Tears were now falling freely. "I love you too," she managed to whisper.

Connor gathered fresh clothes into his duffel bag. He looked around the room. This had been a good place. So many wonderful things, including his father's presence, had made it into a home.

The next job couldn't be over quick enough for him because, after giving his country twenty of his best years, he planned on spending the rest of his life with his future wife.

He closed his eyes.

Thank You, Lord. I finished strong. You didn't let me down. Please help me finish this last job, and start a new life, free from people shooting at me or trying to kill me. Protect me as you usually do. Lead me.

He could hear the soft voices downstairs. There had been raised eyebrows when he had returned without Emily. He had told everyone that she was tired. It was true but there was no way she was going to enjoy the remainder of the evening when he left.

She had asked to be alone.

He threw his bag into the back of his car and turned toward the living room. His dad locked eyes with him as he entered, and a resigned sigh went through him.

He knew!

"Time to go again?" he asked quietly.

"I need you to drive me, Dad," he replied just as quietly.

His father swallowed hard, then nodded his head.

"O-kay!"

The Martins gaped at him when he announced that he was leaving. He saw the confusion on Emily's mother's face. The only one who understood was Mitch. He clasped him in a brotherly hug.

"Be careful out there," he said softly. "And thank you."

He cocked his head sideways and nodded at Connor. The center of his gut twisted at the expression his future brother-in-law wore.

Nobody had ever thanked him for what he did because only a handful of people knew.

At that moment it made his pain and his sacrifices worth it.

"You're welcome."

They were quiet most of the ride, listening to an all Christmas music station. Finally, his father broke the silence.

"You aren't coming back, are you?"

Connor shook his head. "Nope. Not after what they pulled this time. The last mission was really rough. I almost didn't make it through. As it is, I lost a part of myself along the way. It'll take a while for me to get it back."

"What about Emily?"

"She knows. She has instructions."

"You're going to marry the girl?"

Connor frowned. "Of course, Dad."

They hugged longer than usual.

"I'm proud of you, son," his dad said sadly.

"You know where to find me, right?" Connor asked. His father nodded.

"Of course. I'll be seein' y'all around."

45

Emily held a fake passport in her hand, goosebumps rising up and down her arms and spine. Her stomach was twisted into a tight, hard knot. The passport belonged to a *Cynthia Brown* and had her picture and data on it. Along with this fake document was a credit card, belonging to the same person, and a stack of tens, fives, and ones – adding to a hundred dollars. A wave of weakness rushed through her as she touched the ticket from New York to Hamburg.

What was he thinking? I can't do this!

When Connor left her, everything inside her had died. Then she realized that life went on. She was counting the seconds until Connor called her. She had packed yesterday. This morning, after her night shift, she had quit her job.

A sharp thought stabbed her heart.

What if he doesn't come for me?

Her heart did a quick flip and the muscles in her shoulders tensed painfully before she realized one thing; Unless he was dead, Connor would always fulfill his promise to her.

A knock on the door made her stuff the documents into a drawer.

Her mother walked in just as she was closing it.

"How are you feeling?" she asked.

It had been four days and eighteen hours since Connor had left.

"I'm fine, Mom."

"I don't understand why he left – again," her mother said, her tone sharp and slightly huffy.

Emily turned on the TV, increasing the volume. Her mother frowned. Emily chortled as she led her into the bathroom and turned on the shower.

Just like in one of her spy novels.

"I'm just going by what I have read," Emily whispered as her mother began to protest. "My apartment may be bugged."

Her mother's face paled.

"What?"

"You were right in your suspicions. Connor is not just a computer guy, Mom. He works for the government. His branch has three letters, beginning with C and ending with A." She cocked her head meaningfully.

Her mother gasped and held on to the sink to steady herself until the weakness passed. Then, covering her mouth with one hand, she clasped the other tightly around Emily's wrist.

"He's decided to retire, but unfortunately they will not be giving him a golden handshake. I'm going with him, wherever he may be headed."

"Emily..."

"It's okay. It took me a long time to realize that I don't want to live without him. I'm ready, Mom. I gave my notice at work today, telling them that I may or may not show up tomorrow. I'm kind of on standby to leave at a moment's notice."

"Emily!" her mother wailed.

She tugged her into a hug and cried. Emily allowed herself a few tears as well.

The job in Bogota had gone well and without a hitch – for a change. Connor had installed the program and was now on his way back to the airport. He coded in and Murpy's face appeared on the screen of his phone.

"Great job, Rattlesnake. We're receiving valuable data already."

"Good." He took a deep breath, feeling a headache coming on. "I'm officially telling you that this is my last job."

The man on the screen looked like he had bitten into a sour lemon, his face twisting in disgust. His cold eyes became even icier, making Connor shiver involuntarily.

"Translation, this is me telling you that I'm quitting!" he specified when Murphy remained silent. The two men stared each other down. Finally, Murphy grunted and pinched the bridge of his nose.

"You can't do that," came the growled reply. "You have to come in to debrief. "

Seriously?! Connor laughed, dangerously low. "So you can send me right out again? No! I can, and I will. And don't come looking for me. I would prefer to retire in peace, but retire I will."

"Rattlesnake! You belong to the United States government!" his mentor snarled.

The man had some nerve!

He had sent him into danger time and time again, and now he was going to deny him whatever life he had left? What was he, a slave? Grinding his molars hard together, feeling the tension travel down his jaw and all the way through his back, Connor stared at the phone.

Taking a sharp breath, he hung up. Quickly, and smoothly, he removed the SIM chip, crushed the phone with his heel, and tossed the pieces into different trash receptors. He knew that there was a tracking device in his shoes so he took them off and replaced them with a pair of new sneakers he had purchased from a street vendor.

Once that was completed, he stood breathless on the busy sidewalk, feeling...

He was free!

His stomach churned nervously when he pulled out his disposable phone. Funny, he hadn't been this terrified when he told his boss he quit, but now he wasn't sure he could get through this phone call.

What if she decided the risk wasn't worth taking?

"Hello?" Emily answered on the first ring, breathless.

"It's time to use what was in the last chocolate bar."

He heard her take in a sharp breath.

"Okay," her voice quivered.

"Get rid of your phone. I put a burner phone under the bottom towel in your linen closet. You have about ten minutes to get out, Emily. They'll be coming for you since I've ruffled their feathers. Pack only what's necessary. It's not like we're leaving civilization. Get yourself to the airport. When you get to your destination, check into the airport hotel under the name on the passport, and wait for further instructions. Use the credit card I gave you only or the cash."

He sounded so cold, detached.

She took a shuddering breath. "Okay."

"Don't worry. I'll see you soon."

At least there was a hint of softness in his voice.

Checking his cheap, disposable watch, Connor hurried down the street. They would have his position soon, and he threaded through the crowd to enter a restaurant. Walking to the kitchen, he pretended that he was in the right place. A second later, dressed as one of the waitstaff, he exited into the back alley, where he had parked a getaway car. Threading into traffic, he drove to the airport.

You can do this!

Emily trembled from head to toe, pacing aimlessly around her apartment.

He'll be there at the end. You'll see, it'll work out.

A shot of adrenaline squirreled through her and caused the muscles in her stomach to tense and relax. Drawing a shallow breath, she stuffed the passport and tickets into her purse, found the new phone, and dragged her suitcase behind her. She was all for traveling light, but she wanted to look somewhat presentable when she met her future husband.

Although, how all that was going to come about she had no idea. Tears pricked her eyes when she closed the door.

This was it! She may never return home again!

Uncertain, she swayed and remained in place. Was she making another rash decision? Would it be another mistake?

The trip to Pakistan hadn't been a failure. She had met an incredible man who wanted to spend his life with her. God had showered her with His love, showing her that He was guiding her steps. She was able to give up her own dreams to accept His.

No – the trip had been a blessing and her new life would be also. Even if it didn't go according to her expectations.

“Emily?” Her father was taking out the trash. He saw her lug the suitcase and his eyes widened. “Are you leaving us?”

She sobbed once and pressed her lips shut. Her vision blurred as her father wrapped her tightly in his arms.

"Oh, Emi. You always had bigger dreams than any of us, huh?" He kissed her forehead and cupped her face. "You promise me to be careful. And write, if you can. I guess we won't be having a wedding come spring, will we?"

All her life she had been dreaming of her perfect day. She wouldn't be floating down the aisle in a beautiful white gown. The knot in her stomach tightened while she considered her options. She couldn't call it off.

Connor was expecting her.

The thought of never seeing him again knocked the breath out of her.

"I've made my choice, Dad, and I'm happy with it."

"Mmm." Her dad squeezed her shoulders. "How are you getting to the airport?"

"I..." She stared. Taking her car seemed a bad idea right now. "I could call Uber."

Her father gave a waffled laugh. "Hop in. This way I get to spend a few more minutes with my daughter."

At the airport, she hugged him again and walked away without looking back. An exciting future awaited her.

She sat down only a few seats from him, playing with the tip of her ponytail. He grinned as she wrapped it nervously around her fingers, her wide eyes staring at every man that walked by.

And she didn't even know she was only a few chairs from him.

This was more exciting than any mission he had ever been on, and Connor kept close tabs on her. He had spotted her the minute she had arrived at JFK and had trailed her, watchfully keeping an eye out for tails. It had taken a lot of determination not to make himself known.

Now and then she swiped a thumb underneath her eyes, wiping away a tear or two. Leaving her family must have been difficult and he wanted to let her know that he was sorry for forcing her to make the choice.

He would make it up to her for the rest of his life.

With a heavy sigh, he gathered his small computer bag and moved to the vacant seat next to her. Emily gave him a cursory look and almost turned away when she gasped, her eyes widening in surprise.

"How was your flight here, Miss Brown?" he whispered.

Oh, my gosh! I didn't even recognize him!

Her lips twitched at the corners and she focused on the colorful display of the storefront opposite from where they sat.

"I don't usually talk to strangers, sir," she said in a clipped, quiet voice.

He snorted softly. Nothing was going to keep her down for long. That was why he loved her so much.

"You doing okay?" he asked, keeping his eye on the paper he had picked up.

"What are you talking about?" she asked, her voice giving a tiny quiver. "Nothing to it. Piece of cake. I pretend to be someone I'm not all the time!"

He smirked and focused on a family of four hurrying to get to their flight.

"You were born to do this. You have more guts in one little finger than a lot of agents have in their whole body. Remember, I'm right with you. And I love you."

She gasped softly. "You have terrible timing," she whispered, her heart causing her concern again.

He grinned and rose, heading for the bathroom to check for a tail. He was glad to see that there was nobody following him. So far, so good.

She looked for Connor as she landed in Germany seven hours later. Flying first class was certainly a treat. She had forgotten her dislike of flying while she was being pampered. She took a cab to the airport hotel. Exhausted, she checked into her room. She refreshed herself in the shower and was about to crash when someone knocked on the door.

"Room service," a German-sounding voice called.

On her way to the door, she remembered that she hadn't ordered anything. Too exhausted to care, she opened the door.

"Thank you so mu-" She looked at the man in uniform, who pushed the tray into the room. She gasped. "You're really good at this disguise thing, aren't you?"

Connor tossed the cap onto the bed and grinned. He pulled her into his arms and lowered his lips to hers.

"Wait a moment," she teased. "I don't kiss just anyone."

Connor growled and tugged a strand of wet hair out of her face.

"I'm not just anyone, woman! And you will kiss me! I have been waiting all week long for this."

Her laugh caught in her throat as he claimed his prize.

“Wait, slow down,” she croaked breathlessly.

“Okay,” he sighed and pulled reluctantly away. “Are you ready to catch the next plane?”

“What do you mean? Aren't we staying here?”

“Do you speak German?”

She shook her head.

“Well, then I suggest you go back to the airport and catch a plane to London.”

“Why?” she asked and accepted her ticket and another passport. This was was in the name of Carrie Andrews.

“Because if you can't speak the language, we can't very well get married. Can we, now?”

A soft squeak escaped before she could stop it.

“Really?”

Connor just lifted one eyebrow and shook his head. “What do you expect. Of course. I didn't take you away from everything without reason. We're doing this whole thing properly, Emily Martins.”

She rested her head against his chest as he wrapped her tightly in his arms.

“I'm sorry I made you chose,” he whispered.

Emily lifted her chin and cuffed his shoulder playfully. “You should be!” Her eyes twinkled. “And you haven't even asked to marry me proper-like.”

He stared at her and a rush of blood slipped to his toes. “Uh... I... Didn't?”

Her hands on her hips, she glowered dangerously.

He didn't even have the strength to prevent himself from lowering to one knee. He took her trembling hand in his.

"Emily, will you make me the happiest guy alive, keep me on my toes for the rest of my earthly life, and spend eternity with me in heaven?"

She gave a soft moan and nodded vigorously.

Rising, he touched the side of her face. "You gave up everything for me."

Emily found her voice again. "Mm." She cocked her head. "And don't you forget it."

Connor grinned. "You're going to remind me of that, aren't you?"

Emily brushed her fingers through his hair. "I might, from time to time, when you need it."

Standing there in each other's embrace, she almost forgot the small ache in her heart.

"Thank you, Emily," he whispered and kissed her gently.

"Before we go, do you think we could pray together? It's been..." She waved a hand through the air and blew out an exasperated breath.

"You bet," he said.

He had never thought they would sit down together on her bed to pray for their future. But they did and the sweet fragrance of peace filled both of them.

"Okay, now I'm ready!" She said and stood up.

"I have a few more meals to deliver." Emily did a double take and giggled as he put his cap jauntily back on his head. "When you get to Heathrow, go to the line of cabs and wait for the first available one."

"Aren't you coming with me?" she asked, panic setting in.

Connor bent forward and kissed her again. He could definitely get used to this.

"There wouldn't be much point in getting married if I weren't coming, don't you think?"

She let out a sigh of relief.

Emily walked right past him without knowing it. With growing satisfaction, he watched her hand her boarding pass to the attendant. A second later, he did the same and followed her onto the plane, only separated by two other passengers.

He settled into his seat and glanced her way. She looked lovely in her gray, pleated skirt and hunter green blouse. Her hair was tucked over her ears, hanging thickly down her back. As the flight attendant came around to offer her a drink, Emily's face beamed back at her as she pleasantly accepted her coke.

Man, she looked amazing!

Was he really getting married? To her?

Connor's heart took a leap and he leaned into the seat.

Emily twisted her plastic cup in her fingers, staring at the seat in front of her. She wanted to take a sip, but her stomach was flipping continuously in a pleasant, yet uncomfortable manner.

As she caught her breath, she wondered – yet again – if she was leaping without looking.

But she was marrying her very own spy! Her lips twitched into a smile.

She was ready to marry Connor.

But a white dress would have been nice, she thought and swallowed the regret that flashed through her. *Nope. All you need is Connor and God. And they'll both be with me.*

The businessman in the aisle seat sneezed and the newspaper in his hands trembled. He leaned over and searched for a tissue. As he did, Emily couldn't help compare him to Connor. Not that she cared what he looked like... This guy was more flab than muscle, unlike her spyman.

Emily arrived at Heathrow and waited at the baggage claim area, her stomach now churning continually.

No sign of Connor.

Although, he was so good at disguising himself.

Once she had claimed her luggage she followed the signs to the cab area and stood in line. When one pulled up, she looked around again.

He said he'd be here! What do I do now?

The heavyset businessman from the plane lumbered over and, sweating profusely, claimed the vehicle. He cocked his head at her.

"You coming, or what?"

The butterflies in her stomach burst into flight.

"Connor Williams!" she gasped.

He winked at her and scooted over to make room for her. The backseat became quite cozy and Connor gave directions to the cabby.

He put his arm around her.

"Where are we going?"

"Wait and see."

An hour later they exited their ride at a beautiful, ancient village church. It stood surrounded by fields now covered with a thin layer of snow. The trees, bare of their splendor, bowed in the cold wind. She reached out to take Connor's gloved hand, her fingers trembling slightly.

“I need a moment,” she said shakily.

Connor looked down at her and touched her cheek. “Can we take the moment inside? I kind of want to get out of this cold.” He shivered.

Inside the church, someone had taken the time to decorate the stone sanctuary with candles and flowers. She turned to Connor, who watched her with a twinkle in his eyes.

“You arranged this?” she gasped.

He bowed his head slightly. “Guilty. I wasn't going to cheat you out of having a somewhat nice wedding. I know this isn't what you had in mind. But I want you to know how much your trust in me means to me. I want to give you the world, Emily Martins. And even though this isn't your dream wedding, I hope it will do.”

She leaned into him, which was mighty uncomfortable because he was still wearing his disguise.

“And here I was just feeling sorry for myself that I didn't get the wedding I always dreamed of. You make it better.” She tugged his face to hers.

He smirked mischievously and wiggled his finger at her. “Ah ah ah, I'm sorry, ma'am. But you are going to have to wait for that until we are married.”

"Are you going to marry me in that disguise?"

Before Connor could say something, they were interrupted.

"Excuse me!"

Their heads swiveled around to a tall man, about forty years old, striding toward them.

"I'm sorry, but we aren't open for the public today. If you wish to speak to me, I will be free later on. We have a wedding planned here."

"I can see that," Connor said, nodding. "Looks good in here, Jarred. You guys did a great job with the decorating."

"Connor!?"

"Yep, it's me."

"I didn't even recognize you," the older man laughed.

Then he looked at Emily and nodded.

"It's a pleasure to meet you, Emily. You may freshen up in there." He pointed to a door to the right of the sanctuary. "We'll be ready for you when you are."

"I'm going to turn into my charming self again, too," Connor laughed and gave her a quick hug. "I'll see you in a little while. Take your time."

He winked.

In the room, which momentarily transported her back in time to a castle in the Middle Ages with its thin windows and thick, masonry walls, she found more surprises. A lovely, designer gown was hung on the far wall with her name pinned to it.

Her breath came out in a loud whoosh.

He had done it again... God was fulfilling her dreams, just not in the way she expected. The material felt amazingly soft to the touch of her fingers and she couldn't wait to put it on.

How had Connor pulled this off?

Slipping into the dress was like slipping on a second skin. It was so comfortable and Emily felt beautiful for the first time in her life. The white symbolized more than her getting married. To her, it meant that her life was now tied not only to Connor but also to the Lord.

When it came to lacing up the back, she squirmed and tried – to no avail.

Now what? She wasn't about to walk out there half dressed.

There was a timid knock on the door. An older woman poked her head shyly through the small crack.

"Do you need help?" she asked.

"Yes, thank you so much. It's a bit difficult..." She turned and turned again to try to reach the clasps. The woman nodded and helped lace up the back.

"Thank you."

"You're so welcome, dear. May God bless you and Connor. He's a good man. And you look lovely."

More butterflies exploded in her stomach.

"I'm ready!" she said, raising her chin.

"Wait here, dear."

After a few moments, she returned, a bright smile on her face.

"We are ready for you now."

Emily walked, no she actually floated, down the aisle. Connor, dressed in a tux, looking very trim and handsome, waiting for her. Her knees felt like rubber and she wasn't sure if she would make it. But then his gaze rested on her and she once again felt his courage and love flow through to her.

After that, everything became a haze until his hand touched hers, his deep voice promising to honor and cherish her for the rest of his life. Her voice was strong and sure when she promised to do the same.

They sealed their promise with a prayer for each other and a kiss.

Epilogue
The orphanage near Murree,
Pakistan, one year later

Three tiny girls rested in their beds when Emily checked on them. All three had come here, needing a lot of care, but they were all slowly getting better. She wiped the sweat from her brow and drew another syringe full of antibiotics.

"Dr. Williams."

The excited voice of one of the boys pulled her away from her chore. What was Ali yelling about? She followed him outside and her steps faltered. Her heart went into overdrive, the way it still did whenever her husband was around. He stood next to the director, talking seriously.

Connor turned around while she was staring at him, causing her to blush deeply.

Drats!

Making his way toward her, grinning like the conquering hero, Connor carried a large, heavy box. Her stomach fluttered in reply to his gaze.

Oh, for crying out loud! She was married to the guy!

Why was she having this reaction every time he was around?

By the look on his face, the smug grin playing on his lips, he was well-satisfied with her response. He even had the audacity to wink at her, causing the butterflies in her stomach to explode.

When he came to stand in front of her, he hadn't even broken into a sweat. At least, not like her. He looked fresh as a mountain spring, whereas sweat was dripping down her forehead and back.

What if...

"I got some more supplies for you, Doc," he said softly, his breath tickling her cheek.

Emily fought back the giggle that trickled up her throat and nodded without even a hiccup.

"Thank you so much, Connor." Her voice was cool and calm, contrary to the rest of her.

Connor grinned, exhaling deeply when he shifted the box in his arms.

"Are you just going to let me stand here with this heavy box in my arms? Or are you enjoying the view too much?"

Now she giggled and snapped her lips shut.

Guilty!

"Eh..." She turned around and quickly made room for the new box on the small desk. When Connor set it down with a grunt, he had the audacity to wink at her.

Oh, dear!

She couldn't be more in love with this man than she was now.

The past year had not been easy. After spending the first weeks of their marriage tucked away in a cozy cottage in the small village in England, Emily lost count how many different countries she had been in. Of course, Connor had been by her side all the way. For someone who really didn't like flying, she forgot her dislike with him next to her. Emily enjoyed Melbourne, Australia, the most. Moscow made her feel sad. It was a dreary place in the middle of winter.

They finally settled down in the small village in the foothills of the Himalaya mountains, surrounded by his relatives, who made her feel incredibly welcome. For the first couple of months, they had lived with his grandparents, while Connor and the rest of the village built a house. Her husband, who was very handy with a hammer and drill, had worked hard to construct a small version of her dream house. She, on the other hand, had spent more time watching – eh, encouraging – him.

Emily remembered well the night they had moved in, after the long feast that included the whole village. Connor had carried her over the threshold into the house to their room, decorated with petals of locust blossoms and roses.

During the long, rough winter, Emily used her doctoring skill in the orphanage as often as the weather conditions allowed. Mr. and Mrs. Holland had been only too eager to accept.

It made her a busy woman. Twice a week, she held a clinic for the local people of the village. Their thankfulness was plentiful and as a result, they had plenty of chickens running around. Connor, in the meantime, kept busy. When the agency had caught up with him, they found out that Bryan Murphy had been dismissed for running several illegal schemes. Connor received his retirement package and an apology.

Now, he worked as consultant for various government agencies. He worked on translating different documents into various languages. He didn't travel farther than his office, set up with all the latest technology.

Best of all, they didn't have to hide anymore.

In the coming summer, there would be a lot of changes. Both sets of parents were scheduled for a visit. When Connor's stepfather found out that Rick was still alive, he had approached his wife and offered to have their marriage annulled. After much prayer and thought, his parents had remarried and were extremely happy, living near Alicia, who was now an associate professor of history at her university.

"Hey, listen." Connor's voice, soft and enticing, brought her back to the present. "I came to bring my wife home today. It's a special day, remember?"

He winked at her and touched the small of her back. As if she could forget the day she married him.

She did a pathetic attempt at a curtsy, which caused Connor to laugh.

"By all means. Whisk me away. Right after I file this medicine properly."

Connor groaned. "Uh, baby, would you let someone else do that today? I want to take my wife home!" He wrapped his arms around her tightly.

Emily snuggled against his chest and closed her eyes in pleasure.

The snow covered the ground thickly and a harsh wind slapped her in the face. The roads were passable, which was why she had come. After the hour drive home, Emily couldn't help but feel nauseous.

"Close your eyes," Connor instructed briskly as they drove up the last hill to their house.

"Uh, Connor." Emily swallowed the bile creeping up into her throat. "I don't think I should. I'm not feeling so good right now."

Connor turned to her in alarm. "Is it my driving?"

"I wouldn't make that assumption," she mumbled and tightened her lips.

"Then just don't look at the house, okay?"

"Why? What did you do to it?"

He laughed and shook his head. "Nothing you should worry about."

She tried not to look as they stopped in front of the house. When she rounded the corner of the truck, she gasped and the thoughts of sickness vanished.

"You... you..."

Before her was a beautiful white picket fence surrounding her home. She giggled and covered her mouth with her hand.

She threw her arms around her husband, who looked very pleased with himself.

"I just slapped it together quickly. I'll have to do a better job once the snow has cleared. You like?"

"I love it!" she purred.

"That's not all," he whispered. Connor took her hands and led her to the attached garage.

A minivan!

A laugh exploded from her lips. Once she had calmed down, she turned to the man next to her who was watching her intently.

"Does this model have bulletproof windows?"

Connor laughed softly and pulled her into his arms, a place where she felt safe and loved.

"'Course it does. That and automatic grenade launchers. They are now standard issues for ex-operatives."

When they walked into their cozy home, a fire crackling in the wood stove, Emily cupped his face with her hands. "You have given me all my dreams, Connor. They may look different from how I expected them, but I'm so happy right now I could burst. Tell me, Connor, what's your dream?"

He closed his eyes for a split second. "I live it every time I get to hold you in my arms."

"Come now," she teased. "There has to be something more."

"Okay." His cheeks turned ruddy. "I would like to fill that minivan with a family," he whispered into her ear.

She knew it! She kissed him softly. "Well, then be ready to start filling that van in seven months."

"With what?" he asked, a frown on his face.

"I don't know," she laughed. "With diapers, baby things, and quite possibly a baby."

Connor stared at her, his mouth agape. He pulled her so close she thought she would become part of him.

"Thank you, Em! I never expected to come away from a mission with a wife and a family. Do you regret marrying me?"

Emily touched his chin and angled her face so he would get the hint that she had no regrets! None at all. He grinned sheepishly and kissed her.

In the end, after all the insurmountable odds life threw at them, the handsome spy got his girl!

Author's note

We all see ourselves in a certain light. Mostly, we think too harshly of ourselves. I love the character of Emily because she thinks the only thing she can offer a guy is looking pretty and being what she was not designed to be. She had to give up the dream of that perfect life and allow God to show her that He had other dreams for her. I love it when I actually let God do that. A lot of times it takes the strong hand of God to help me let go of my own dreams, my own perceptions. It is usually painful. The end result is so much better than I could have imagined. During the journey of giving up and letting God shape my dreams, I usually learn a whole lot about myself.

Emily had to go through a lot of hardships to let go of her dream, which didn't look like the one she wanted. In the end, God's dream for her life was much better. The character of Connor had his own demons to get rid of. How often do we not want to face those who have hurt us? How often do we want to hold on to our anger, our hurt?

I pray that this book has helped you to look beyond your own dreams and look forward to the dreams God has for you. I hope you allow God free reign when it comes not only to dreams but also to everyday life.

May God be praised.

Acknowledgment

So much work goes into these books, that it's not a one-man (in this case, woman) job. I hope that I don't forget to mention anyone, and if I do... I'm sorry.

I could never, ever do this without the steadfast and loving support my husband gives me. He makes it possible for me to write, write, and write some more. Thank you, Tom. You know you're the best part of me, right? Can you imagine what would have happened if you hadn't frog-jumped into the room, way back in the stone age (or was it when the dinosaurs wandered on the earth)? I thank God every day for the very exciting *adventure* we are on. Just living up in Vermont these past five years has been so amazing.

Natasha... I love, love, love how you have the ability to bring all my stories to life on the cover. I just stand in awe at your increasing ability. Now that you're ready to embrace this gift God has given you fully, I pray that you'll touch many people's hearts with not only the images you produce but also with who you are. You are my cheerful, always smiling, loving, funny girl and I'm so glad you and we get to do this together. Can't wait for the next cover, my sweet daughter.

My sweet boy, Logan, who is growing up so fast! Noooooo!!!! You tower over EVERYONE in our family! I so enjoy spending time, reading my adventures to you. I know this story is your favorite. I'm so thankful for your input. After all, your suggestion that Connor would never use his real name ended up in hours of hilarious laughter, as you, Natasha, Lisa, and I came up with the ridiculous name and Emily's faltered introduction. We have too much fun, you and I. I'm so proud of you, turning into this amazing man of God. You have this way about you, sweet and innocent with a touch of mischief. I'm so excited that you're forging ahead in the way God is showing you.

Anne Perreault

Sean, my oldest son, may not have contributed directly to the book, but he's still part of this family, therefore, he's part of this process. I know that you mention me whenever you can and thus, people on the west coast have heard of me. I'm proud of you, who you are and who you're becoming. I'm so excited for what God has in store for you and your lovely wife.

Thank you, Lisa, my editor extraordinaire. Your support and total involvement in these books is so encouraging and uplifting. Jack Russel... I still get a kick out of that name. Thank you, for taking this ministry as seriously as I do and for encouraging me, standing by my side. I couldn't do this without you.

I also want to thank my new friend and beta reader, Jennifer Gainer. We haven't met in person, but I'm sure that doesn't matter. Thank you for reading this story and your feedback. Again, God provides.

Thank you, Alex DeWitt, for your computer insights. Since all I know how to turn it on and off, it's helped me greatly.

Thank you to my Wednesday night Bible study group. You girls are the best and your love for me is uplifting. To everyone who has prayed for me, given me some much needed advice... thank you. It means more to me than you'll ever know.

To my readers, I pray that my stories encourage and inspire you. I pray that you'll strive to learn more about this amazing God we serve. If you have questions, don't hesitate to ask. He'll answer them one way or another. It may not be in the form you expect.

I can't put this book out there without the continual guidance and love from my Lord, Jesus Christ. I get to do this because He plops the stories into my brain in some form or another. Thank You.

Anne

About the Author

Anne Perreault was born and raised in Germany. By the time she was 14 years old, the family moved to Dubai, UAE. After living abroad in several different countries, she met her husband and settled down in Connecticut. They recently moved to Southern Vermont, where they are building their home, something that is a huge adventure. Besides writing, she is busy homeschooling her youngest son. Anne spent most of her adult life teaching horseback riding, and has a masters degree in secondary education. Writing is something God inspired her to do. It is a gift, one that she never expected to receive.

If you enjoyed this book, perhaps you'd like others by the same author

The Royal Skater Chronicles

Skating for Grace

Learning to Trust

Broken

The Cooper Family

Love the Lord your God with all your Heart

Dangerous Relations

Rescuing the Weak

Running the Good Race

All books are available online through Amazon and Barnes and Noble. They are also obtainable on Kindle.
Check out these books and more on the website: intothelightfiction.weebly.com
Anne also has a facebook page: @intothelightfiction

Made in the USA
Columbia, SC
23 August 2018